THE SHADOW IN THE SANDS

THE SHADOW IN THE SANDS

being an account of the cruise of the yacht
Gloria in the Frisian Islands in the April of
1903, and the conclusion of the events
described by Erskine Childers in his
narrative
The Riddle of the Sands

Sam Llewellyn

HEADLINE
FEATURE

First published in Great Britain in 1998
by HEADLINE BOOK PUBLISHING

A HEADLINE FEATURE hardback

10 9 8 7 6 5 4 3 2 1

British Library Cataloguing in Publication Data

Llewellyn, Sam
 The shadow in the sands
 1.
 I. Title
 823.9'14[F]

hardback ISBN 0 7472 2191 X
softback ISBN 0 7472 7618 8

Typeset by Avon Dataset Ltd, Bidford-on-Avon, Warks

Printed and bound in Great Britain by
Mackays of Chatham PLC, Chatham, Kent

HEADLINE BOOK PUBLISHING
A division of Hodder Headline PLC
338 Euston Road
London NW1 3BH

Author's Note

I have compiled this narrative principally from papers sent me by the grandchildren of the shipping magnate Baron Webb of Dalling. Webb's obituary in *The Times* reflects the general view that during a career that took him from the inshore fisheries of the North Sea to the cross benches of the House of Lords, he was a pugnacious, sexually rapacious but on the whole scrupulous man, notoriously intolerant of pretension and injustice, with a flow of speech made musical by a Norfolk accent that he never lost.

I have checked many of the salient facts in the story that follows, and found that they square with historical accounts. Remarkably, they also square with and follow on from much – but not, as you will see, all – of the story told by Erskine Childers in that incomparable work, *The Riddle of the Sands*.

It is to Erskine Childers' memory that I dedicate this book, with respect and affection. If it is felt that I have taken liberties with his account of events, I can only say that this was not my intention. My purpose has been to publish an edition of Lord – then Captain – Webb's narrative, interspersed with other documents where germane, that will cast light on the secret history of the nerve-racking days immediately preceding the publication of the Childers narrative in the spring of 1903. I only hope that my readers will see the Webb narrative as I do – as a final vindication of the warnings of invasion made by Childers via the adventures of the immortal Davies and Carruthers in the autumn of 1902; warnings, in the view of some, as apposite metaphorically now as they were physically then.

Sam Llewellyn
Yacht *Gloria*
Delfzijl, 1996

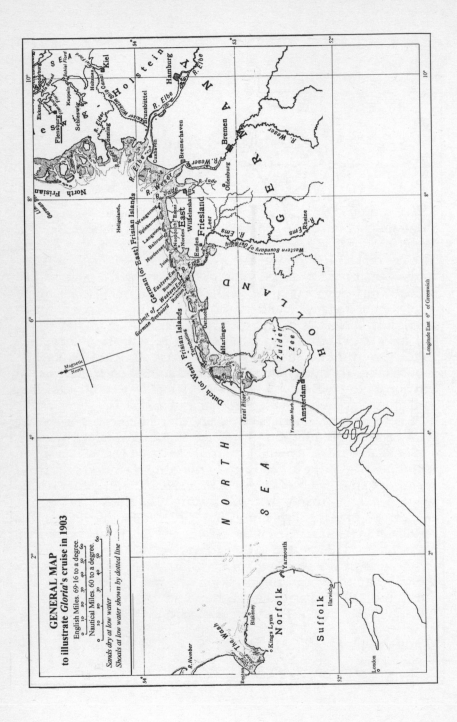

GENERAL MAP
to illustrate *Gloria*'s cruise in 1903

English Miles. 69·16 to a degree.

Nautical Miles. 60 to a degree.

Sands dry at low water ....

Shoals at low water shown by dotted line ....

Magnetic North

NORTH SEA

HOLLAND

Amsterdam

Zuider Zee

Harlingen

Dutch (or West) Frisian Islands

East Friesland

East (or East) Frisian Islands

Heligoland

North Frisian

Schleswig-Holstein

GERMANY

Hamburg

Kiel

Bremen

Bremerhaven

Cuxhaven

R. Elbe

R. Weser

R. Jade

R. Ems

R. Rhine

Western Boundary of Germany

Longitude East 6° of Greenwich

Norfolk

Suffolk

Yarmouth

Blakeney

Kings Lynn

The Wash

R. Humber

Boston

London

Harwich

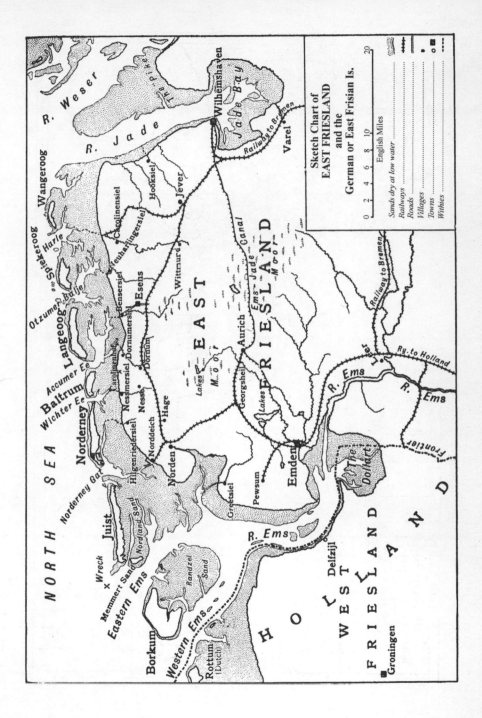

NORTH SEA

R. Weser

R. Jade

R. Jade

The Pike

Jade Bay

Wilhemshaven

Railway to Bremen

Varel

Wangeroog

Spiekeroog

Harle

Hooksiel

Jever

Carolinensiel

Otzumer Balje

Langeoog

Neuharlingersiel

Witmund

Benserslel

Esens

EAST

Jade Canal

Moor

Railway to Bremen

Accumer Ee

Baltrum

Wichter Ee

Norderney

Nessmersiel

Dornumersiel

Dornum

Carolinenhof

Nesse

Hage

Lakes

Moor

Moor

Georgshefl

Aurich

Ems

Jade

FRIESLAND

Railway to Bremen

Ry. to Holland

Frontier

R. Ems

R. Ems

Leer

Hilgenriedersiel

Norddeich

Norden

Lakes

Ems

Emden

Norderney Gat

Juist

Greetsiel

Pewsum

The Dollart

Norderland Sand

Memmert Sand

Wreck

Eastern Ems

Borkum

Western Ems

Rottum (Dutch)

Randzel Sand

R. Ems

Delfzijl

HOLLAND

WEST FRIESLAND

Groningen

Sketch Chart of
EAST FRIESLAND
and the
German or East Frisian Is.

English Miles

0 2 4 6 8 10   20

Sands dry at low water ....
Railways ....
Roads ....
Villages ....
Towns ....
Withies ....

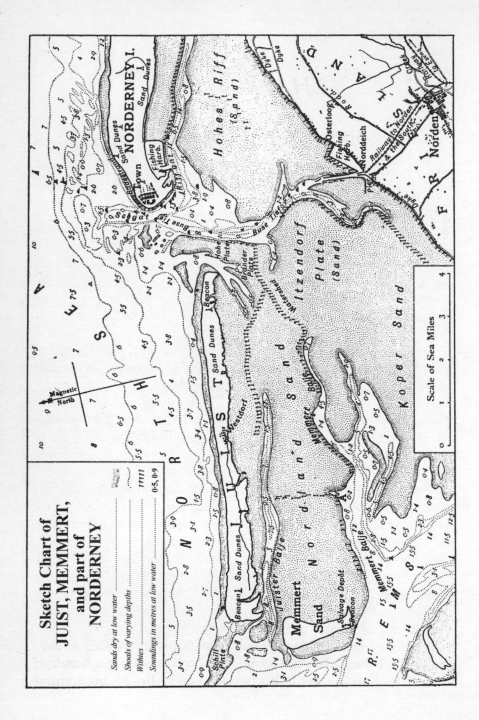

Sketch Chart of
JUIST, MEMMERT,
and part of
NORDERNEY

Sands dry at low water ....
Shoals of varying depths .... ⟋⟋⟋⟋
Withies .... ⟋⟋⟋⟋
Soundings in metres at low water ...... 0·5, 0·9

Scale of Sea Miles

0   1   2   3   4

CHAPTER ONE

Captain Webb's Match at Kiel

Imagine this here.

You are the secret weapon, eighty feet up in the armpit of a gaff sail in the armpit of the Baltic. Out there on the horizon, the thin ghosts of Fyn and Lolland mark the place where the windy sky meets the battleship-grey sea. Down the white river of the wake, the bristling masts of Kiel regatta, with the canal locks and the funnels of the *Kaiser Barbarossa* in attendance on Kaiser Wilhelm, bless his mad heart.

That was what David Davies was seeing, the secret weapon, youngest of the thirty men in my crew, perched between sea and sky. He was getting the view. I was getting the white man's burden, down on the deck with my heart in my mouth and my hip on ten feet of coachwhipped iron tiller, driving the twenty-three-metre cutter *Doria* through the Kielerfjord.

A racing cutter, *Doria*. One hundred and twenty feet of black hull with an axe stem and a gold-leaf coving line; bowsprit, mainmast and topmast carrying 11,000 square feet of Egyptian cotton sails; below, staterooms, bathroom and ladies' cabin, saloon panelled in best Honduras mahogany all complete; and in a button-leather armchair in that saloon, Sir Alonso Cummings, the owner, banker and strict Methodist, reading the Court Circular in *The Times* and breathing hard through his moustache. The *Doria* was flying across the Baltic on white wings of foam, you might say. You might say it, but not me. I was too busy trying to earn a living.

What that meant this particular forenoon was trying to beat the arse off the Kaiser of Germany, who was sailing a hundred feet across *Doria*'s nose in his famous yawl – British built, mind

– his famous yawl *Meteor*. His crew were Germany's finest, who by that second year of the century were by no means as fine as he might have hoped, but getting finer. Round *Meteor*'s tiller you could see a little clump of barons and admirals, and little Kaiser Bill himself with his gold-laced cuffs flashing in the air. And in the background, as usual, white summer top to his yachting cap, hands in his reefer pockets, jug ears flapping, belly out and bum in, that damned Duke with his Abdullah sticking out of his moustache.

As *Meteor* crossed our bow I caught his eye on me, pale blue, popped, pinkish round the edges, clammy as a dab. Not a lover of his fellow man, the Duke, unless the fellow man was a woman, or another Duke or above. I felt that eye, all right, and that annoyed me. And I think he felt mine, because he looked away pretty sudden. And the two big boats drew apart.

So I stood there on that deck and felt the run of *Doria* through the sea, 180 foot of mast up top, fifty ton of lead down below, and waited for the moment. The wind was moaning and the rigging was creaking till she sounded like a sick woman in an old house. The flat land and the grey sea was making me think of Norfolk, and thinking of Norfolk drew Hetty through my mind; more about Hetty later. Then there was a black ruffle of wind on the water out there, coming down towards us. I was thinking, that is not sense to do this. But sense or not, that was as good as done.

Me and the Kaiser had just crossed tacks. Even if you don't know what that means, remember that: crossed tacks.

The wind on the water ran down at us, and hit. *Meteor* got the puff too, and heeled hard. I waited until I had her in my sights, a pair of white ham sandwiches, one big, one little, standing on the sea a mile away. Ready to tack, I said. Helm's a-lee, walked the tiller over, and we tacked.

And eighty foot up there in the jaws of the gaff, David Davies flips the topsail up and over the peak halyard so that will draw properly, an idea of my own. Then he goes back to watching the water for wind, and we settle in on the starboard tack, the right-of-way tack, that topsail pulling like a team of horses; gaining ground . . .

* * *

But there you were on your train, or waiting for an omnibus, starting this book you have probably borrowed from the circulating library, more is the pity. And suddenly here you are dragged halfway up a mast in the Baltic in August, and a Duke is looking daggers at you, and you have just crossed tacks with the Emperor of Germany. You have got a perfect right to say, what is he on about, and pitch the book in the gash.

For I can see I have started against common sense, in the middle. Well, I am not much of a story teller, having had other things to do in life. They tell me that if you have a story to tell you should try to tell that according to common sense. So from now on I shall start at the beginning, and go on to the end.

Here goes.

My name is Charlie Webb, and until they died my dad and my old dear lived at Sea Dalling, which is a village huddled up under a sea wall on the north coast of Norfolk. Dalling is a little place with a church and some gorse bushes and a lodge in the Grecian taste in the long flint wall that keeps the riffraff out of the Hall and a couple of thousand acres of park. There is also a marsh and a seaful of sandbanks. In the sea there are fish. Fish is what people hereabouts earn their living off of, unless they work at the Hall: the herring at the October full moon, crabs from off Cromer, mussels fatted up in the beds inside the Point. If you haven't got a boat, you pick samphire out of the marsh or you rake cockles out of the big flat beach that goes out to nowhere; big blue cockles, near on the size of scallops. People love Sea Dalling cockles, have done for years. You can see them on the churches, carved on the sandstone quoins that keep in the flints.

You get low land up there in north Norfolk, salt marshes merging into beaches that go over the horizon: low land, slow folk, they say. If you grow up in north Norfolk the world looks like a great beach, and the future comes at you like the tide, fast as a galloping horse, and you have to watch yourself not to drown.

Well, we all went to the school in Dalling, under Mrs Lyte, assisted by Dora Jordan, who was fourteen and the first woman I ever loved, though far above me, me being six at the time. Mrs

3

Lyte taught us to read and write, and the parson he used to lend me shilling shockers, mother and father being of the church persuasion. In the year of the Diamond Jubilee, I left school.

As a young boy you stand out on that beach, stone cold in the wind, and you hurt your back raking cockles and picking samphire, or freeze your legs wading the creek with a butt prick, which is the spear you use for dabs. When you get older you go to sea. So I learned to set a drift net for a herring and a long line for a cod, and use a drag or a trawl for plaice and dabs. And in the evening we would sit around in the forge of Gideon Gidney the blacksmith, and natter away in the smell of red coke and singed horn.

When Joe arrived in the village, I was eleven. Him and his sister Hetty came up from Maldon, Hetty being ten. That was a bit of a mystery why they had landed in an out-of-the-way place like Sea Dalling. There were clues, though, for those with eyes to see. Hector, their dad, had a nose like a blackberry and spent most of his time in the Red Lion. Joe kept out of his way, and in so doing fell into plenty of mischief. He showed me how to put Epsom salts in Vicar's sugar bowl, and net up the sea trout in the Stiffkey river. Well of course you soon come to trust someone like that. So I took him down to Gidney's, and lo and behold he could not understand a word of what anyone was saying. (When I mentioned this to Mother, who was half-foreign her own self, she said she was not surprised. She said that herself she had been brought up to speak Fries, which they speak in the Frisian Islands just the other side of the North Sea, so she hadn't had too much trouble with Norfolk. But people from the south – anywhere south of Fakenham was the south, to my mother – hadn't a clue.)

Anyway I taught Joe how to talk proper, and later Hetty. And Joe told me a few things about the world, as he called it.

There was a huge city called Ipswich, and another called Harwich, that seemed. There was somewhere else called London, about the same size, though he had never been there. He also told me, as a secret, what had happened to his father. The father had been at the fishing, like everyone else. But in the summers he had gone out with old Bungy Hicks, to do paid-hand work on gentry yachts. Imagine going to sea for the fun of it, said Joe, and we sat there and listened to the northeast gale wailing in the eaves and he was right, that was hard to imagine. But the money was good; guinea a week, plus whatever prize money you won. Trouble was, the drink had been bit easy to come by, and the old man had got himself pie-eyed once too often. He had fallen down when he was supposed to be making up a runner in a tack, and the topmast had gone over the side, never mind what all that means, but that is an expensive way to lose a race. The long and the short of it was that the gentleman on the helm had sacked him on the spot, casual as swatting a fly, said Joe, angry, and the idea made me angry too.

Joe said his dad got downhearted after that, and took to the drink even harder. Next thing (says Joe) his dad had had a few drinks and run his smack onto Osea in a gale, and that broke up, and that was that, except that Mrs Smith's brother had a house in Dalling the Smiths could take over the tenancy of from the Duke, the Duke of Leominster, it being the Duke who owned the village, among a lot of other things. Hell, said Joe. Catch him having a drink, ever.

Hetty taught me about the world, too, only different parts of it. We seemed to find ourselves talking quite a lot, and when she saw me with other girls from the village – I never had much difficulty with girls, even early on – she would go a bit white. Not downcast exactly, but as if she was above all that slap and tickle and scurryings in the bushes on the sea side of the sea wall. Hetty was known to have Ideas, and very interesting I found them. She said everyone, dukes and beggars and women and men, were made equal. Now this was not a popular notion in those days, specially not in a village owned by a duke. I pondered that none the less, in between school and work and hijinks on the foreshore and serving at the altar Sundays. That was the thing about Hetty. She always made you think, even when she was in her contrary moods, when nothing you did was right and the world was put together upside down.

The house the Smiths lived in was half-buried in the sea wall – a cold, dark place, shaded in the morning by some scrubby willows and in the afternoon by a curve of the wall itself. Mrs

5

Smith took in washing, and Mr Smith spent what she earned in the Red Lion. The house was always wettish, what with the clay against the back wall and the splashes from the dolly tub. Hetty was a pretty girl, red cheeks, plumpish in those days, with a graceful way of moving, and as my old father used to say all correct fore and aft, above and below.

Those were the bad old days, and do not let anybody writing in magazines tell you different. The Christmas I was fourteen my dad and my old dear died of the influenza. Well, I loved my old folks, and that was no joke, but all that is no part of this story so I will pass over that, except to say that from them I inherited *primus* my person, shortish and squarish, with black hair, *secundus* a Bible, an *Admiralty Manual of Seamanship*, the complete works of Dickens bound in green cloth, and *tertius* two suits of clothes and all the fresh air I cared to breathe.

Naturally, the estate needed their house, so I was homeless. Parson tried to get me taken in by the Jordans, who were also church. But I had had enough of altars and Gods who let my old dears die one after the other, crash bang. So I thanked Parson kindly and went off to lodge with the Smiths. There was no more education, nothing like that. I could read and write and figure and, thanks to my mother, speak Fries and German like a native. I read through the Dickens pretty steady, when there was time. But mostly I worked at the fishing and ran wild.

When you are fourteen, that is hard to look into the future and see that full of cockles and herring and pulling up crab pots in the freezing North Sea, and coming back to that little flint house full of laundry steam and the whiff of wet wool. I know Joe felt that way too, because he used to moan about it, and so I must say did Hetty.

I remember that November when Hetty turned thirteen walking down the road between the ploughland and the flint wall of the Park, arguing, she saying that what was needed was a revolution, me saying that revolutions were always beat down, and what I meant to do was get to the top and then change things to suit the common man, by which I probably meant myself.

Then there was a cloud of green plovers and a clatter and a

motorcar came by with gun cases strapped to the trunk and the Duke's lion-rampant crest on the doors. In the back of the car, above a swaddle of rugs, was a pair of pop eyes. The eyes rolled at me, but the one they really settled on was Hetty. A sort of snarl came from inside the rugs, and the chauffeur said, Yes, your Grace. So we guessed that must be the Duke, our Duke, the Duke of Leominster, himself, in person.

My hand went to my cap, automatic, really, and I would have taken that off, except that I could feel Hetty steaming like a kettle at my side, so I changed what I was doing halfway, and made as if I had an itchy nose instead.

The motor stopped. The pop eyes raked up and down Hetty like a trawl. 'Who are you?' said the mouth beneath the rugs.

Of course that was when she should have bobbed curtsies, and blushed and stammered while he licked his lips under his blankets. Not Hetty. She stood up straight as a Guardsman, said, 'Harriet Smith,' as if that was a cannon-ball she was firing at his head.

'Come for a ride, Hetty,' says that damned Duke.

Hetty puts her hand on my arm most delicate, though the fingers were digging in so that hurt, and trembling too. 'I am takin' the air with Mr Webb,' says she, very curt. 'And my name is Miss Smith.'

His face did not change. He gave her his lippy smile, very sarcastic, and said, 'Pair of marsh eagles, what?' meaning I suppose that we were above ourselves.

Hetty turned her back on him and we walked away, and when we were out of sight she said, 'Dirty old devil,' and we had a giggle, or at least she did, because I was angry that someone should try to pick her up in the road like a windfall apple, and set her down for not letting herself be picked. And that, we thought at the time, was the end of that.

Some hope.

One evening soon after, Joe and I were sitting on the sea wall by his house. There was no fishing, so no money. Beyond the frozen marsh the sea was growling on the banks like a dirty animal. The cottage shivered in the shadow of the wall, reeking of washing soda. Redwings flopped in the wiry green grass, fresh in from Norway, too weak to eat. Joe stood on one, moody. He said, 'I've had a bellyfull of this here.'

We had heard this before. 'Of what?' I said.

'This here fishing. I'm off to Maldon, get work on the smacks, try for a berth on a yacht in the season. You coming?'

I had spent all that day raking cockles, wrapped up in sacks and pushing a little cart across the hard ridgy beach. To my mind that was women's work, but that was what you did in Dalling. I had seen pictures of yachts in *Titbits*. That was all white yachting caps, pretty girls and excitement on the yachts, Joe said. Hetty was half-sad but mostly waspish, saying we were spilling out our lives to become rich men's playthings. I said I would write, meaning it. Joe said he would write, not meaning it. And off to Maldon we went.

CHAPTER TWO

Death on the Gabbard

We got a job with Bungy Hicks, that Joe's dad had sailed for, who that year was on Mr Solomons' *Casuarina*. He was half-man half-devil, Bungy, but he knew his work, and I was that eager to get away from those damn cockles I would have swum to America if someone would have paid me and I had been able to swim. That wasn't much white caps and here's-a-pound-for-the-winners. That was up in the morning at five and scrub 120 foot of white pine deck. That was polish ten square yard of brass before you had your breakfast. That was knee deep in water all day, haul, damn you, haul till your black heart breaks. And every night that was take the sails off, 9,000 square feet of them on *Casuarina*, and coil down the cotton main sheet, ninety fathom of it, 180 yards to you, and kip in a wet five-foot bunk in the fo'c'sle along of twenty-odd other chaps. A hardish life.

But next to fishing, that was a feather bed.

Joe thought so too. We took lodgings with a Mrs Huggett, whose husband ran a bit of a smack. In the winter, I went fishing with old Gladstone Huggett, and Joe went with Canning Potter. The winter was when you got your practice; the smacks were similar rigged to the yachts we was sailing, and if you showed you could helm a boat, you were a sought-after man. There were prizes, too. First out to the grounds fished on the best marks, and first home was first to market and got the best price for the fish.

For a couple of years there we were doing pretty well, Joe and me at the front of the fleet, me in the *Alice*, Joe in the *Rosebud*, neck and neck. That was a sort of friendly rivalry, really, except as sixteen turned into seventeen, Joe got more desperate to win. He would get himself warmed up in his mind and he would go at a race like a bull at a gate. I took that slower, myself. I won fewer races, but I know I broke less gear. I think that what with his dad he had more to prove than I did. What money he made he spent on ties fit to blot out the sunset and girls brighter than the ties. I knew he wasn't sending any home, because I was the only one in our lodgings who had letter paper and envelopes, and he never had any off of me.

I knew things were a bit hard in Dalling, so I sent Hetty the odd pound myself. Hetty wrote back, of course, and she seemed pleased to get the money, though she did not say much about it, which I thought could be explained by natural pride. I said nothing about this to Joe, because that would have upset him – there was nothing like getting an advantage on Joe to get you wrong of him. That was one of the reasons he was a good boy in a yacht race. And I must say people said the same of me. Except that where Joe Smith would win by force, they said, Charlie Webb would win by artfulness.

Anyway one night in the Jolly Sailor at Heybridge Joe turns up looking like the Sultan of Zanzibar, not just a new tie but the full rig, new blue serge suit, striped cravat, lavender spats and yellow shoes, and demanded I drink whisky with him. I never much liked the taste of beer, let alone whisky, so I said no, ta, and asked him why he was dressed up like a bookie after a red-hot Fakenham – that was a bad month, with no herring and no cod, and the trawlers becalmed on the banks. He told me to mind my own damn business, which was more and more his way nowadays. Then Dirty Ian off of *Rosebud* says, 'He's sold his sister,' and of course that is the kind of thing Dirty Ian says, so we all laugh, a bit nervous, but Ian had a screw loose, so you made allowances.

All except Joe.

Joe flies across the bar scattering pint pots right and left, and smacks Ian one in the face and he is halfway to choking the life out of him before we pull him off. Ian gets up, spitting out teeth and roaring death by violence, and Denis gets his bung starter and vaults the bar but Joe is already out of the pub. He comes back to Mrs Huggett's after midnight, and wakes me up. 'Nobody talks like that about Hetty,' he says, and his breath is like a distillery. So I told him to be off to his bed, and in a couple of hours we were out of there on the tide, as usual.

That was generally agreed that was a bit far to go with Dirty Ian, though that was also agreed that Ian had gone a bit far with Joe. Nobody gave that any more thought, except Joe.

If Joe had worked hard and dangerous before the dust-up, he worked double after. And of course that finished him, in the end.

We were out off the Gabbard, a few of us out from Maldon, following the usual kind of theory, drifting for herring, we were, that time; sure to be herring out there, we had persuaded ourselves, and we were right for a change. That was February, two in the morning, and as the net came over the side the drips were freezing on the gunwale until the stars shone there like chips of diamond in a lady's brooch. We had oiled wool gloves, but even so you lost your hands after ten minutes. We didn't mind though. As I now said that had been a terrible winter for fish, but to-night they were flying aboard, stone after stone.

After we had been hauling for a couple of hours on the tide, there began to be a sort of a thick smell in the air, a wettish smell, and there was a bit of a heave in the deck and a dim-out of the stars. So that seemed a good ideal to put in a couple of reefs and start off home. But Joe stayed out there. Till the Dirty Ian fight, even he would never have done such a silly thing. But this was the way he had gone. He must have reckoned he was going to pull every last stone of herring out of that shoal. Then he was going to slap up full rag and come home before all of the rest of us. Last I saw of him and the *Rosebud* they were a yellow lantern and a green starboard lamp, fading against the stars.

But he had left his brains at home that day. Because that smell in the air brought what that always brings, and by seven in the morning, when that should have been getting light, there was nothing to see but the father and mother of a blizzard howling out of the nor'east. We blew into Heybridge lock on a little tiny jib. And Joe never blew in at all.

There was a sea running mountains high out there, and in all that snow you wouldn't have been able to see your hand on the end of your arm any more than you could feel it. The *Rosebud* was a terrible boat to make leeway. Her nameboard came ashore on Dengie Flats, and then we knew. A couple of boys came in after her, face down, but no Joe. As soon as that was fit, I took the *Alice* out to look.

There was snow all over the land, and the banks growling in a sea like polished steel plate. And on that sea, a line of corks. A herring net. By the way the corks were dipping, a full herring net.

Well, what that was full of was Joe, caught by his boots. He looked peaceful enough, if you left out of account that he was half ate. He must have lost hisself and got blown onto the Gunfleet, which is a sandbank, and hooked up in his net as the *Rosebud* broke up.

So we put him in his new suit and his spats, and boxed him up and nailed him down. We carried him onto the Kelling train and I climbed into the luggage van after him.

After the service there was a tea-drinking in the cottage. Hetty and I walked out onto the sea wall. That was draughty, all right. But that was dry, unlike the house. The house was wet enough at the best of times, and with her mum crying that was fit to flood you out.

I should say here that I had been noticing a change in Hetty, but that was only out in the wind that you could see how far that had gone. She had grown up, was the best way to put that. She wore a long cloth coat buttoned from neck to, ankles, no hat. Her dark red hair, that had once flown about her head like a burst sofa, was pulled back and up, so you could see the bones of her face and her fiery green eyes, cloudy now from crying—

I caught myself up. That was the day of her brother's funeral, no time for thinking how beautiful she looked. But there was no way round it. That was a long while since we had been children. That was not like brothers and sisters any more.

So as we walked along the sea wall, I think perhaps we were hoping the wind would cool that down. But I found we were holding hands, and I could feel the occasional bump of her hip, and she was looking at me sideways in a new sort of way, that thickened the breath in in my throat.

After ten minutes we came to the sluice, and walked down the coarse grass to the little wood of willow trees between the banks of the dyke. There was a pump house with no door down there, hid from the generality of the landscape. That was a place that in the life before, all those two long years ago, we had used for games and picnics. Inside that pump house we went, and looked at the cement plinth we had used as a sideboard and a card table and even a sacrificial altar, she and me, and Joe that was under the raw earth in the shadow of the churchyard wall. She started crying, and so I think did I, and we held onto each other for encouragement. Then that changed, and became something else, with her arms inside my coat and mine inside hers, and her lips and tongue cold with the icy air, locked up with mine, getting hotter by the second, the old Adam starting to rise—

She made a sort of a noise, and suddenly I was alone in that shed, and she was on the wall, running, and as she ran I could hear her crying, loud now, an awful moaning on the wind.

My soul felt like lead in my chest. We had been as good as brother and sister. And on the day of her brother's funeral I had . . . taken advantage of her, as she would see it. That was a disgrace.

I walked back to the cottage, not trying to catch her up. She did not look behind her, and when she got back she stood white and rigid in the far corner of the room, avoiding my eye, and you could not blame her for it. Well I went through the motions, and got the evening train back to Maldon. Dear, I did feel terrible.

When I got back to Mrs Huggett's I wrote her a stiff sort of letter that did not come anywhere near explaining, but did what that could. When I had posted that, I went back and Mrs Huggett was waiting in the dining-room, spilling over with sympathy like a waterbutt in a thunderstorm, steak and kidney pudding for tea. She was a good old thing, but there are gaps that even steak and kidney pudding cannot fill.

Hetty never wrote back.

Then something happened that drove her from my mind.

A month before Cowes Week the year of Joe's funeral I was

asleep in my bunk in the *Casuarina*'s fo'c'sle when they passed the word I was wanted aft. When you went aft you went in fear and trembling, I can tell you. Mr Solomons the owner was in the saloon squinting down his nose, nose like a guillemot he had, and said, 'Webb, I want a word.'

He was not a bad chap, Mr Solomons, with a sort of rich gleam, the gold tie-ring, the silk cravat, the black hair flowing past his ears like a tugboat's wake in a coaling dock. 'You're too clever for this game,' said Mr Solomons.

I thought, here come the sack.

'Lad your age,' he said. 'Bright lad. Ought to be at school.'

I shuffled my feet. He didn't know much about yachts, Mr Solomons, but he was miles up, a friend of the Prince of Wales, owned a huge great bank.

'Go to the Institute,' he said. 'I'll look after the fees.'

So at the end of the season I started to go to the Institute. They taught me navigation, real navigation, and some surveying, marine surveying, that is. I didn't like being cooped up in those brick rooms with the dirty green paint on the walls, smelling of the toilets – I was a racer, remember, young, no patience – but I put up with that, for the sake of bettering myself. They bounced us around spherical trigonometry, which came easy enough, as I imagine that would to anyone who has ever cut up an apple. They made our boots muddy wandering around at low water surveying ourselves little sketch charts. Captain Bullough who taught us, that had been with the Admiralty chart people, he blew down his yellow moustache and said had I ever thought of working for the Hydrographer of the Navy, and I said no, and I was not going to start now neither.

Then one night in early spring I went back to my lodgings, and there she was. Hetty, I mean, sitting in the parlour in front of Mrs Huggett's hummingbird fire-screen, taking tea. She stood up and dropped her cup and started towards me. I started towards her. But Mrs Huggett was in the room, so we halted after a pace each, me the colour of a red-hot brick, I should think, Hetty like marble. I swear if my own heart had not been beating so loud I should have been able to hear hers.

Mrs Huggett clattered about with a dustpan and brush, gave

us a sort of look, knowing old bird she was, and said she would leave us to it. But by that time the shadow had fallen between us again, and what would have been natural at first had gone difficult. We sort of gawped at each other. She was even more beautiful than when I had last seen her; little hat over one eye, cream dress with green ribbons and bows, and a sort of *polished* look that was new.

'How are all at home?' I said, for something to say.

'I've been travelling,' she said, and her voice was the same as ever, softest Norfolk, and all of a sudden the questions about where she had been travelling and how went from my mind, and the space between us was thicking up again. Air, I thought, or something may happen that will take us right back to the pump house after the funeral, and that will be back to no speaks again. 'Shall we go for a walk?' I sort of croaked.

She just looked back at me with those eyes, unchanged, full of green fight but now with a sort of soft look. The air was half-solid now. She took off her left glove, and looked down at her hand.

On the third finger was a plain gold band.

My heart fair to bust out of my chest. So that was the clothes, the polish. Married a rich chap. Well, what else did you expect? I started to croak about happiness and that. But she said, 'That's for us.'

'Us?'

She dropped her eyes. 'So we can . . . go somewhere,' she said.

That took no thinking about. 'Newmarket,' I croaked.

She smiled at me then, fit to frizzle the hummingbirds on the fire-screen.

On the train we held hands. We did not say much, because there was still that thickness in the air that made that hard to talk, and that was all we could do to keep our hands to ourselves. In the year 1900, you kept very quiet and discreet about such matters, on pain of someone beating you round the head with an umbrella and calling a policeman.

We took a hansom to the Bell, where Hetty pulled her gloves off and a boy carried the valise to a room, and when he asked us would there be any other article we just about tossed him down the stairs. We undressed each other slow and in detail, until there

15

was me and her on the bed, and the only thing we were wearing between us was that wedding ring on her finger.

Some time or other, I recall, we had some food. But mostly we had each other. We stayed there that night, and the next day, and the night after that. There was the feeling we were making up for lost time.

Late on the second night we were lying there, tired but happy, as you might say. We had opened out to each other after all those years – twenty and eighteen, we were, but that felt like years – and there was only one thing I wanted to clear up. 'I wanted to say sorry,' I said.

She made a sort of cat noise, that I took as meaning go on.

'The day of Joe's funeral,' I said. 'In the pump house. I'd never want to get wrong of you. I'm sorry I did that, that day and all. You were right to be angry. I thought I'd lost you that time.'

She moved her head, and I felt her lips on my neck. 'That wasn't it,' she said. 'I'm not what you think I am, you know.'

'What does that mean?' I said.

She had gone stiff in my arms. 'Can't tell,' she said.

'Tell.'

But then she stopped my mouth with hers, and there was no more talking for a bit because the tide was running again, red hot.

Later on I told her I loved her.

'You'll forget about me,' she said.

'Oh, no,' said I, and God help me I believed that. 'We've started something here—'

'That's not the first time that's happened,' she said.

Well that stopped me like a fist in the belly, proud as I was. I should have got angry, but I worked out that this was one of her contrary moods, brought on by guilt or goodness knows what, and what she needed was jollying through that, and she would be right in the end. So I clenched my teeth and let that ride, biding my time.

I went to sleep. God help me, I went to sleep.

And when I woke up in the morning and reached out for her, the room was full of dust motes, dancing in pale March sun. But that was all that was full of. Hetty was gone.

* * *

Newmarket was a racing town, with eyebrows hard to raise – that was why we had gone there in the first place. A German waiter said a lady had gone to the station in the hotel trap, and no, Sair, bill already paid. The station said a lady had got on the 7.15 for Liverpool Street, third-class compartment. I went to Liverpool Street, the first time I had been in London, and found any number of pretty women in light dresses and little hats, but none of them Hetty. So I went back to Maldon, and wrote letters, and wondered. Blast I did wonder. As the answers came in, saying nobody had seen hide nor hair of her, I wondered more, half-mad with it I was. I could smell her and see her and feel her. All I could not do was touch her. So I waited for her to write. She had put on a wedding ring and we had committed the sin of fornication for two nights and a day in the Bell at Newmarket. Of course she would write.

She did not write. I wrote to her mum, but she did not write back, so I wrote to the parson, who said she had gone into service somewhere away from home, nobody knew where. Then I got a letter from her, no return address. That was short, but long enough to say what that had to say, which was that she never wanted to see me again, she did not say why.

I wrote back care of her mum, but there was no answer. I came to feel that I had the dirty end of the stick and that she had bested me. Remember, I was a racer, and only young, and I did not take kindly to losing, and losing was what that felt like. So in a sort of cold rage I thought, all right, Hetty, if that is the way you want that, good riddance. And I put her out of my mind.

Which was less hard to do than you might think, for there was plenty of distraction for a chap as young and eager as I was. There were other women, of course, and the Institute, though after a while that stopped on account of Mr Solomons going bankrupt. Captain Bullough said he could get me a scholarship or some such, because that was not everybody who could fiddle his way through a creek the way I could, and I think he meant that as a compliment. But to tell you the truth I needed a bit more excitement that you get with a compass and a lead line. So I said, no, ta, and went back to the fishing. And one day a motor car, no less, came down Malpas Road in a storm of rain, noisy great thing called a De Dion. And the chauffeur stops, and a gentleman climbs down, soaking wet, goggles, Homburg hat, astrakhan coat.

Mrs Huggett was all a-twitter. 'That's all right,' I told her. 'That's only a rich chap.'

The man came down the gravel path, swinging his ebony stick, flicking drips out of his moustache with his finger. 'Webb,' he said. 'Recognize you. *Casuarina*, what?'

He was Sir Alonso Cummings. He took that for granted that I recognized him. Which I did, having seen him racing in the flesh, not to mention the picture papers. 'Look here,' he said. 'Built a twenty-three-metre cutter at Nicholson's. Want a man to oversee the fitting out, skipper her. Bring your lads. Sail hard. Don't let me hear about any women or drink, and you won't regret it. And you'll be nice and warm this spring instead of freezing out there on the herring grounds.'

'Yessir,' I said, blank as a plank, like they expect.

Then he named the wages. And that was that, and the boat was *Doria*.

By May she was launched and going like a train, and we were getting nice things said about us by Brooke Hextall-Smith and the yachting folk. I was even took notice of by the King. That can go to a young man's head, that stuff. There were other girls again, now, and work from dawn to midnight, and chaps from the illustrated papers waiting alongside when we dropped anchor off Cowes. So all in all and young as I was, I let that drive Hetty out of my head.

Well, just about.

CHAPTER THREE

A Passage to Kiel

In May, George the mate told me he was leaving, very sudden, and left. That was a puzzle why he had gone, and an irritation too, halfway through the workup to our racing year. That is the captain's job to find his crew, and to tell the truth I did not know where I should find a mate as good as George this late in the year short of promoting one of the hands, which none was ready for. Then one morning there shops over the rail a long brown chap with a grey moustache and a silver watch chain tarnished green, and I recognized him as Samson Gidney, a cousin of Gideon the Dalling smith. He was a Brancaster chap, good fisherman, who sailed the yachts from time to time, but a bit sharp in his ways for gentry taste. He was famous for once having been a Socialist and led a rent strike over towards Hunstanton, as a result of which he had been evicted and gone fishing. But he was a worker. So when Sir Alonso said to take him on I did not demur, and we won pretty steady – often because of Sam's artfulness, which was great, him having in the course of his life brought ashore as much Dutch gin as fish, and never once caught. Then Sir Alonso came on board as we lay off the Shrape in Cowes Roads and said we were to be off to Kiel, to sail a match with the Kaiser's yawl *Meteor* for a thousand pound. So we bent on passage canvas, upped anchor and turned *Doria*'s nose towards Spithead and the Looe Channel.

Two days later at dusk we had Helgoland light flashing on the port beam, and the Weser down to starboard. And the next morning at dawn, we were creeping up the Elbe between steep banks of blue-black mud.

That had me jumping, the Elbe. You get a bit of a tide running

19

in there, and when the wind blows across that that can stand on end something atrocious. But that day we went up there quiet as a mouse. That was a high pink dawn, and even with her heavy passage canvas *Doria* was a picture. Not that there was anyone to see it on that flat, misty sea, except a few of the blunt traders Sam said were called *muttes* – he had relatives over here, like me; a lot do, in our part of Norfolk – and a grey gunboat sliding up for Hamburg.

There was a steam tug waiting on the seaward side of the Brunsbuttel lock at the North Sea end of the Kiel Canal. Sir Alonso's agent had booked him, and that was his job to tow us across the neck of Denmark to the Baltic. As we rose up the lock wall I could see a motor car at the top. When we were up, over comes a chap from the car. He had a moustache and a bay window fit to bust his waistcoat. He hops onto the deck, into the middle of some German customs chaps in uniforms and foreign sort of beards, who had come to look us over.

'Morning,' says the chap, in the best of English. He had pinkish pop eyes, and he was wearing knickerbockers and a Norfolk jacket and brogues. His skin had a grainy look, like Morocco leather. A fat Turkish cigarette stuck out of the middle of his moustache. I knew who he was, all right, but I was too busy thinking about *Doria's* paint to think about him or the things he knew about. I looked at his brogues hard, thinking, if there's hobs in those things I don't want them on my deck.

'No nails,' he said, with that lippy sort of grin and that I-know-what-you're-thinking glare of the pop eyes. 'Captain Webb. How are you?'

'Fair to middling, thank you kindly, Your Grace,' I said to the Duke of Leominster.

I had seen him a lot, on the deck of *Britannia* and *Meteor* and the lawns of the Squadron, murmuring in the King's ear. But I had only met him once, on that walk with Hetty ten years ago. From the way he talked you would have thought he knew me up, down and sideways. You got used to that, though, sailing *Doria* for Sir Alonso. That gave satisfaction to a certain type of gentleman to pretend he was acquainted with you even when he wasn't, and as a paid hand that was best to go along with it.

I was looking over his shoulder, because the lock gates were opening now and the tug was going ahead. '*Mind* my paint!' I yelled at the tug skipper.

'You speak German?' said the Duke. 'Of course. Your grandmother was a Frisian, was she not?'

We were on the move now, and I was a sight too jumpy for chitchat. 'What can I do for your Grace?' I said, shortish.

'I have spoken to Sir Alonso,' he said, as if he was Moses fresh off the mountain. He handed me a letter in Sir Alonso's secretary's copperplate. That told me to make His Grace the Duke of Leominster welcome until he himself arrived on board at Kiel. He also said I would find him an interesting cove. Sir Alonso knew where I came from and that I did not have much time for Dukes, so that would be his little joke.

I called up Peter Bracket the steward, and Peter Bracket took the Duke from under my feet until we were clear of the lock and panting along the stripe of brown water cut through what used to be Denmark till the Germans walked in in '64. And when we were going fair and square, Pete came and told me that the Duke begged the pleasure of my company in the saloon.

He was sitting at the big table in front of a pile of newspapers. Beside the papers a decanter of Sir Alonso's sherry was glowing in the sun from the skylight. 'Glass, Captain?' he said.

In the goldish light I could see a couple of dull spots on the table. I made a mental note to tell Peter Bracket what I thought of them, later. 'Thankee, no,' I said.

'Ah, yes,' said this Duke. 'Won't have his chaps drinking or chasing skirt, will he?'

I nearly told him that I did not drink anyway, then thought, he doesn't need to know that, the nosy devil.

'You're a Dalling man,' said the Duke. 'Didn't I meet you once with Harriet Smith?'

My heart gave a bump. 'Yessir,' I said. I knew he was thinking about the time we had walked away from him on the road, all those years ago.

'Sweethearts still?' he said, with a sly sort of grin.

'No sir.' I could feel my face getting hot. To tell the truth I did not like being reminded I had been walked out on.

21

The Duke laughed, that laugh I later found out he used on everyone, that made it seem he could see inside your head. He waved away Hetty and the gross passions of the lower orders. He said, 'Ever raced against the Kaiser before?'

'Nosir.'

He squashed his cigarette and took another from a gold case. 'A great gentleman,' he said. 'A very great gentleman.' His eyelids had dropped a little, from sarcasm, I thought, or perhaps that was just the cigarette smoke. 'Loves winning.'

I said, 'Common enthusiasm, sir.'

He nodded, trickling smoke up into his moustache, smiling nice enough, but then so do crocodiles, I hear. 'Ah,' he said. 'But if the Kaiser . . . that is, if he were to be in a position where action by, ah, *you* could reverse a disadvantage of his and turn it to an advantage, be, ah, of benefit to *him* . . . In short, he is an Emperor. And Emperors need humouring.'

Now if Sir Alonso had told me this, I should have been astonished, but I should have given that serious thought, because he was my employer, and a good employer too, strict but fair. Whereas this Duke had lived near ours for years, and never paid us a blind bit of notice. So I looked at him and said very mild, 'Sorry, your Grace?'

'There may be times,' said the Duke, 'when it appears that the Kaiser or his crew are not familiar with the rules of yacht racing. At those times it would be . . . magnanimous to give him the benefit of the doubt.'

'That is your wish that we should lose, then,' I said.

'If you are given the opportunity.'

I let my mind run round the yacht, checking the sounds of her passage down the canal. All was well, except for this damned Duke, buzzing in my ear like a fly. I said, 'With respect, Sir, the Kaiser may be barmy but he's not stupid. Do we get fouled and we don't kick up, he'll smell a rat.'

The Duke said, 'Captain Webb, what I am saying is that you will appear to sail to win, but that if you see the opportunity, you will lose. And one more thing. You won't tell anyone about this little chat?'

'Sir?' I stood there and wondered if I could kick him off the boat and onto the towpath, him being a duke and all.

'Not even Sir Alonso.'

Well, that did make me stare. I said, calm as anything, 'That is his yacht, sir.'

'You really are a very stubborn man,' he said.

'Nosir,' says I. 'I work for my owner, sir.'

'And your country?'

'When my owner gives me leave.'

He tried to drill those pop eyes into my head, and all of a sudden I could smell him, if you know what I mean, as a man, not just as a Duke. A lot of chaps would have thought, well, here's a Duke who can do some damage, so let us opt for the quiet life. That did not hit me like that. Perhaps I was not being too clever, but I was thinking, who do you think you are? So I held my peace, and there was a sort of sticky silence.

At the finish he said, 'There are things more important than yacht races.'

'I'll believe that when I hear it from Sir Alonso, sir.'

So he could see that I was going to stick to my guns. 'Be so good as to give me some more sherry,' he said, as if I was the steward, and at the time I thought that was his way of giving in gracelessly. He yawned. 'Do you know, I think it is time for a little luncheon? Canal travel is certainly a splendid tonic for the liver.'

I went back on deck in a very bad humour, and gave out at Peter Bracket most unmerciful about the saloon table. There was always confusion in your mind when you were anywhere near that damned Duke. He was a big fish, that Duke, and wherever he swam he muddied the waters.

So that was why I felt annoyed out in the Kieler Fjord, with our Egyptian cotton racing sails bent on, and Sir Alonso in the saloon, and the crew lying out along the weather deck, when I looked across at the Kaiser's *Meteor* and caught that damned Duke's eye, and remembered that he had presumed to ask me to cheat my owner and my reputation, and sail to lose. Remembered that far off, like a fly, buzzing in my ear...

And here we are back at the beginning again, the real beginning. Racing in the Kielerfjord in those dirty great boats, 120 feet long, twenty feet wide, twelve feet deep; 180 tons, thundering along on that fresh and breezy day at between fourteen and sixteen knots. The cutter *Doria*, under the command of Captain Webb, on the starboard tack with right of way. Across half-a-cable of water the yawl *Meteor*, under the command of the Kaiser of Germany, on port tack and a collision course. That was the job of the Kaiser of Germany to get out of Captain Webb's way. But there was no method of being sure the Kaiser of Germany knew this. In fact, that looked very much as if Captain Webb was going to cut the Kaiser of Germany in half.

But Sir Alonso paid me to sail by the rules, and the rules said hang on. So I hung on.

Up in the jaws of the gaff, David Davies, the secret weapon, you will remember, shouted and pointed, the whole-hand point that meant a lift of breeze. I leaned on the tiller, moving up on to the wind till the luff of the topsail wanted to shiver but did not shiver, taking that up there until every last larch-on-steel inch of *Doria*, every shroud and halyard and runner, was driving light and tight through the Baltic as natural as a gannet diving—

Straight at the white-scrubbed teak planking of *Meteor*'s deck.

I could see his face, pale, with little circles, two for the eyes, a big black one for the mouth, moustaches pointing upwards. If those boats hit, that would be like 200 tons dropping fifty feet onto rock. That was the face of an Emperor playing games who all of a sudden might be going to die.

I put my hip against the tiller, tickled her onto the wind a fraction. We were going to hit, sure as eggs was eggs. 'Tell him what,' I said to Samson Gidney, and Sam grabbed the brass megaphone and gave them a hail fit to shatter the saloon skylight. And suddenly *Meteor*'s masts came in line as she moved off the wind and went to duck under our stern like she should have done in the first place. But she had left that too late, I could see that, and so could Sam, because he said, 'Coming aboard, Mr Kaiser.'

I kept *Doria* steady as a rock. I saw *Meteor*'s bowsprit swing, a hundred feet away, fifty, twenty, and whip under our stern. I saw her weather side open out, a long wall of white enamel as she steered round the back of us. I began to breathe—

Too soon.

She caught us on the counter, our extreme back end that is, with her weather side. There was a horrible crash. I could hear them shouting in German over there, all at once, the way Germans shout, getting fainter as they fell away astern.

When I looked aft I saw mahogany splinters, which did not please me. And beyond that, *Meteor*, in a terrible muddle, laid over on her side with Germans slithering down her deck like rain on a pane of glass. And over her rail, the Duke's head with the Duke's eyes: not horrified, like all the rest of them. Thinking sort of eyes. Fixed on me.

I said to Sam Gidney, 'Fly me a protest flag, if you please.' *Doria* was still thundering across the sea, stood on her ear, the water rushing and bubbling in her lee chainplates. I wondered what sweet nothings His Grace was murmuring to the Kaiser.

And I must confess that I had to smile. Emperor or fisherman, a race was a race.

CHAPTER FOUR

Enter the Gräfin

Sir Alonso had come on deck. He was leaning on the main hatch, one eyebrow raised. That was most unusual. His custom was to stay on deck for the start, then retire below with *The Times* so as not to get in anyone's way, returning after the finish, when he liked to be told who had won. 'What have we?' said Sir Alonso.

'Right of way, sir,' I said. '*Meteor* failed to give way.'

'Hrm,' said Sir Alonso. 'D'ye think the Emperor understands what he's done?'

'He's got His Grace with him. His Grace would know.'

Sir Alonso fingered his moustache. 'Question is, would he tell him?'

'Beg pardon, sir?'

'Plays his own game, that damned Duke,' said Sir Alonso, and I do not think he knew he was talking aloud. 'Well done, Webb. Showed old Hohenzollern, what?'

We waited for *Meteor* to show us her side and let out her mainsheet and turn her nose for Kiel, withdrawing. We finished the course, and then and only then we headed in ourselves. We brought *Doria* alongside the quay, and the shipwrights started on the bust bits of the taffrail. I was watching them get started when a shadow fell over me, mingled with a blast of Turkish tobacco. 'Captain Webb,' said the Duke, from up on the quay.

'Your Grace.'

The popped eyes were cold as a cod's. 'I want to talk to you.'

He did not seem to have cottoned on that I did not like being ordered about by a man who was not my employer, but you could not tell him that. So I gave the shipwrights their orders very deliberate, and told Peter Bracket to go and find a new decanter to replace the one that had gone to smithereens in the crash, and explained to him in great and needless detail what kind was required. And then and only then I went up onto the quay.

There were a lot of solid German ladies with bonnets lashed under three or four chins, and thick-waisted burghers with top hats and tight frock coats standing along the coping to gawp at the entertainments laid on below. Something kept them away from the Duke, though, as if he was a wolf and they were a lot of sheep.

'You played me false,' said the Duke, curtly.

I looked at those clammy eyes that wanted me to have behaved like an owned thing, not a human. And I thought, no more quarter will you get from me my man, not if you are the King of England himself. I said, 'I played that straight and you know it.' We were standing there in the crowd, in a little circle of quiet. 'Sir Alonso's a gentleman and a sportsman,' I said. 'As for all I know the Kaiser is too, foreign though he may be. What would they think if I told him what you told me?'

He said, 'Are you threatening me?' a bit white about the gills.

Well of course I was. But I am a racing skipper, and in racing as in cards, which I do not approve of, there is no reason to show your hand. So I looked him in the eye, and said, 'Will that be everything, Your Grace?'

And all on a sudden he laughed. He banged me on the shoulder and marched me off through the stout trippers and into a sort of a public house in a steep-gabled row of warehouses, full of fat chaps with curly pipes and beer mugs with lids. We sat down at a table, and a waiter in enough white apron to make a mainsail waddled over.

'What'll you have?' said His Grace. 'Not every day a Duke asks you what you'll have, hey?'

I said to the waiter, 'Cup of tea, please.' The Duke laughed again, as if he could see I had decided not to give him an inch. He ordered Munich beer. The tea arrived, a little ball and chain clanking in a glass of lukewarm water. 'Take my tip,' he said.

'Always drink coffee or beer. But you're not very good at taking advice, are you?' He lit one of his fat cigarettes, and his wicker chair creaked as he leaned back. 'So what do you think of the *Meteor*?'

'Good yawl,' I said, warily. 'British built, so that's to be expected.'

'And her crew?'

'Room for improvement,' I said, diplomatic as I could.

The Duke's pop eyes were on a pair of flies buzzing in the smoke by the ceiling. 'Let me ask you a question, Webb. What do you know about the German navy?'

Through the window of the public house, I could see the upperworks of the *Kaiser Barbarossa*, grey as death, bristling with guns above the wharves. I read my papers. I knew the Germans were wild to have a navy. But I could see that the Duke was about to tell me about that anyway, so I thought I would save my breath.

'I'll give you a little lecture,' he said.

'Yessir.'

'Bismarck,' he said. 'I suppose you've heard of Chancellor Bismarck?'

'Yessir.' You know how that is, the more they talk down to you the less you let on.

'Well, Bismarck put this country together. More than a country. An empire, dammit. And a lot of people this Kaiser listens to are of the view that Anglo-Saxons, that's you and me, are an octopus, and that the only way for the Germanic peoples to stop the octopus strangling their trade is to kill the octopus. Are you with me?'

'Yessir.'

'So with this in view, Admiral Tirpitz is putting a navy together. A modern navy, blast him. And do you know why the Emperor spends all that time and money sailin' *Meteor*?'

'Nosir.'

'Trainin' for his men,' said the Duke. 'He's training up a navy, much like ours as possible. And he's not doin' it for fun. He's preparing for war, you mark my words. So when a chap like you sails by the rules and blows him out of the water, you give him a hell of a shock, and you make him improve his training. If you don't believe me, I would remind you that he is an emperor, and his whim is law. You should have seen those nasty little Junkers scribblin' in their notebooks when he screamed at them this afternoon. I hoped you might give way, let him be a bit consoled. But no. You sailed as hard as you could, and look what happened.'

Well, I had to speak. 'Owner's orders, sir. Plus beg pardon but don't tell me no argument about right of way is going to help nor hinder no German navy.'

In the midst of the cheerful noises of Kiel on holiday, there was a long silence, during which I counted the veins in those pop eyes and got up to seventeen. Then the Duke said, 'Captain Webb, you are wrong. There will be a war within fifteen years. A war that will make all other wars look like schoolboy tiffs.' He fell silent, looking through me. That was nonsense, of course. There was the South African war just finished, and nobody wanted another . . .

All the same, that struck a chill. That was not just anybody talking. Like him or hate him, this was a man who knew a lot.

He got up. I got up too. We went out onto the quay into the glare and racket, forging our way through the crowd towards the masts, and near to bumped into a pearshaped gentleman with a shaved head, a peaked cap with a tassel, and a neck that bulged over his stiff white collar.

'Your Grace,' said this apparition. 'Baron von Tritt. You remember?' He had blue eyes like a clever pig and leech-shaped scars on his cheeks. 'Herr Duke. May I present . . .' He started introducing the people with him: an old chap with spectacles and a nose like a sheep called Baron Schwering, two little pink fellows with rabbit teeth in English-style pea jackets and too-high collars, and two young women, brown and fit-looking in the German style, but with dark hair. One he introduced as Clara Dollmann, and the other – well. 'The Gräfin von und zu Marsdorff,' said von Tritt, spraying spit. 'The daughter-in-law of Schwering.'

'And this is Captain Webb,' said the Duke. I stood there, cap off, awkward but determined not to show it. They could see from my clothes that I was a paid hand, so they gave me no mind.

Except for the Gräfin.

She was about my height, slim but not too slim, elegant all right, wearing a skirt of blue serge to the ground, and a white shirt with a lace collar and cuffs, and a smallish hat on top of quite a lot of dark curly hair, raked forward over dark brows heavy enough to join in the middle.

But that was the eyes that did it. The eyes were interested; very interested indeed. They were not like gentry eyes, sliding away like a cork down the side of a boat. They were deep bluey-grey, and they looked at you, not through you like the Duke's. 'Captain Webb,' she said, and the way she said the words that might have been a sugared almond in her mouth. I thought dear me, boy, here you go. 'I should like to see your boat,' she said.

Von Tritt was not as stupid as he looked. He glanced at her and then at me, and his face shone puce with fury. 'There is no time,' he barked. The Duke watched, blinking behind his veil of smoke.

'Such a pity,' said the Gräfin, holding my eye and smiling the faint trace of a smile. Her hands were folded in her lap. There was a sea-green smudge on one of them: oil paint, perhaps. Her face had that sleepy look, but her fingers looked tense.

One of the rabbit-toothed pea jackets said in a donkey's voice, 'You sail hard, Captain.'

Schwering looked down his sheep's nose and said something about gross impertinence and how I deserved to be flogged. Von Tritt laughed, a scornful sort of laugh, despising of a world soft enough not to hang chaps who would not let themselves be cheated by emperors. He said, 'The hope of prize money turns a coward into a hero. You are lucky His Highness is a sportsman, my good fellow.'

I did not ask him who he thought he was calling a coward. I did not tell him that sportsmen respect right of way rules. I was a paid hand. I said, 'I do my job, sir.'

The Gräfin gave me the trace of a wink with the eye closest to von Tritt. I realised she was doing this on purpose to annoy him. That was all very well for her, but I was a working chap and this baron was giving me looks fit to knock gulls out of the sky. She said, 'I think you do it very well.'

Blast, she was pretty. But she was using me as a weapon in some war I did not know the rules of. So I said, 'Excuse me,' deeply mortified in my pride, and left them to it.

Round the corner I found Sam, sitting on a bollard, staring out over the harbour and scratching himself under his jersey. I stood there, cooling down in the breeze. There were shoals of small German racing boats, and beyond them the grim upper-works of the *Kaiser Barbarossa*, and the ice-white mass of the *Hohenzollern*, the battleship the modern-day Kaiser used as his yacht, and that damned Duke's steam yacht *Fata Morgana*, long and black with a clipper bow and a buff funnel.

A little yawl was ploughing away from the quay. She was a clumsy thing in that press of racing boats, towing a dinghy four foot too big for her. A frayed Red Ensign whipped at her mizzen peak, and under the transom a name-board said *Dulcibella* in chipped gold leaf. There was one man in the cockpit. He finished tidying away the shore lines, went below, came up with a complicated chunk of metal that might have been part of a cabin stove, and threw that over the side. He dusted his hands, watching the bubbles rise in his wake. Then he settled to his tiller, happy as a lark on his tiny little ship.

I am not a man who goes boating for pleasure, and nor is Sam. But I stood there still breathing hard from the Duke and von Tritt, and I envied that chap. He was not troubled by no race to win, no boss to please, no horrid visions of future wars. He was off without a care in the world . . .

Or so I thought then, at any rate.

Later, when I had calmed down a bit, Sam and I took ourselves for a stroll up the quay, jostled by walkers who did not seem to know any more about the right of way rules than their Emperor. A voice behind me said, 'Captain Webb.'

I turned. That was the Gräfin, with a dark, rawboned woman who must be her maid. She smiled – not the same smile as before, but nervous. 'I'm sorry about that,' she said, and her voice was quite straightforward now, none of the sugared almond in that.

I still felt sulky. 'About what?'

'I was trying to annoy the Baron.'

31

I said, 'And there was me hoping you loved me for myself.' For her own reasons she had treated me as if I was a man, not a servant, so I thought I should treat her as a woman, not a countess, to show her what that felt like.

Oddly enough she did not seem to mind. 'My father-in-law has no manners,' she said.

'And your husband.'

'The Baron is not my husband, thank God.'

'He act like he owns you.'

'That's his affair.' She smiled. 'Sore losers,' she said. I remember those were her exact words; American sounding, I thought. 'It was your right of way. You mustn't worry. I'm not saying it just to annoy the Baron. You did a brave thing.'

Well, she did not have to say that, so I took that as handsome. 'So they keep telling me,' I said. She did not seem like the people she had been with. 'What would you have done?'

'The same,' she said, and you could see she had really thought about that. 'I hope.'

There was a sort of embarrassed silence. I would have asked her to come for a glass of something, but I got snarled up by the difference between women and countesses and by the time I had got untangled the moment had passed.

'Well,' I said, 'Things to do.'

She smiled and touched her hair with her hand. Again I noticed that sea-green paint. She was not like any other countess I had met. She said, 'It's been nice meeting you.' She shook my hand, a firm shake, and was gone.

'Berloody *hell*,' said Sam.

We sailed next morning at dawn. As the tug puffed us towards the canal, Sam said, 'Look.'

And there she was in her blue serge skirt, up there on the quay with an artist's easel and her rawboned maid. She waved a paintbrush at us, airy and natural. I waved back. She had used me to make another man jealous, then behaved like a human being. Perhaps that meant something. Certainly I hoped that did. But of course I should never see her again.

Or so I thought at the time.

* * *

Letter from Capt Eric Dacre, late — —th Lancers, to His Grace the Duke of Leominster.

Your Grace,

Yours to hand. I am deeply recognizant of the kind condescension Your Grace has shown, mixed, if I may make so bold as to aver, with a luminous understanding inexpressibly comforting to a servant of His Majesty suffering a degree of eclipse.

The facts of the events in the camp at Piemburg have been much misrepresented by the Press. As Your Grace's intuition rightly conveys, they must be seen against the background of war. You have been good enough to let me know that my clandestine actions against the Boer commandoes resulted in the deaths of many of Her late Majesty's enemies, and the capture of many of their women and young. As to the woman Alice de Blank, about whom there has been so much disagreeable fuss: she was a firebrand, perpetually inciting her companions to deeds of petty insurrection. Thanks to her neglect of the most elementary sanitary precautions, her three children perished of typhoid. In a shameless attempt to turn the passing of her bairns to political advantage, she blamed not her own lack of hygiene but the conditions in the camp — not luxurious, I grant, but if plain certified by the appropriate Authorities as wholesome — in which she and they had been concentrated.

What follows is simply the story of a soldier doing his duty, no matter how disagreeable.

After the funerals of the children, the woman de Blank became very wild and unreasonable, going so far as to plan an attack on the fence around the camp. Receiving advance warning of this from my informants, it was no more than simple prudence on my part to prevent it, which I did by eliminating the ringleader. It is easy for a Press far from the heat of war dando pondus fumo *to portray a revolver bullet in a woman's nape as murder. But the fence remained unbreached, and who knows how many lives were thereby saved?*

There has however been a cost — namely the opprobrium of those who do not, like your Grace, understand the disagreeable fact that the making of omelettes involves the breaking of eggs. This opprobrium I fear still attaches to your humble servant, unjustly, as a personage of Your Grace's perspicacious sagacity can — I am

delighted to see – appreciate. I am therefore as I say recognizant of Your Grace's kind attention, and hopeful of Your Grace's employment in the future. I shall be more honoured than I can readily express to attend on Your Grace in the New Year, as per your Your Grace's esteemed suggestion. Meanwhile I have the honour to remain
   Your Grace's most humble and obedient servant
   Eric Dacre.

CHAPTER FIVE

A Barrel of Herring

W̲e laid up *Doria* that September. Sir Alonso asked me to come back next May, and paid me a thirty-pound bonus, and left us to the herring and the cod and the hard North Sea.

One late February morning about dawn we put the *Alice* in Heybridge Basin, lifted the fish baskets onto the cart, and went to the Jolly for tea and bacon. As we were sitting over the coke fire, drinking tea and picking the cod scales off of our hands, little Jemima from behind the bar comes over.

'Charlie,' she says. 'Letter for you here.'

Mrs Huggett had sent that up because that looked important: heavy cream paper addressed in copperplate, blood-red wax seal with some crest on it. So I went and washed my hands, and broke that open.

The address at the top was in Mount Street, W1, wherever that was. *Dear Captain Webb*, it said. *Might I trouble you to send my cook a barrel of herring at this address, and to accompany it yourself, in person?* The last two words were underlined twice, in red ink. It was signed Theophilus Archer, p.p. His Grace the Duke of Leominster.

Well, I did not know why the Duke wanted my herrings, unless his cook had fell out with the fishmonger. But there was something about the man that always made you curious, plus we should get a decent price for the fish. So I told Sam, who was on the *Alice* now, to take her out that night, put on my Sunday blues, picked up a nice barrel of herring, climbed on the London train, got out at Liverpool Street and walked over to Mount Street.

That was a coolish day and just as well too, that being a bit of a walk from Liverpool Street to what they call Belgravia. But at the finish there we were, me and that barrel, standing in a street of big white houses that put me in mind of wedding cakes with black railings around them. The Duke's house was down the end of the road, so I marched up the steps and gave a good haul on the bell pull, and this chap open the door and dear me if in the year of our Lord nineteen oh three he is not wearing a powdered wig and pink plush breeches. He had eyes like a cod, so I felt at home straight away. I said, 'What ho, Jeames, boss in?'

'What neame?' he said. When I told him he shut the door in my face. I looked up and down the street, whistling. There were other folk on other doorsteps, but I was the only chap on any of them with a barrel of wet fish.

Finally, there was a shout from below and on the right. A girl in an apron was looking up from the area. She was a pretty girl, a lady's maid by the look of her, with black eyes and a red mouth and a black satin blouse under her apron. 'You're to come down 'ere,' she says.

Well, I had come to see the Duke, but you must remember I was not yet twenty-five. So down I went, into a dirty big kitchen. The scullery maid took the barrel of fish off me. 'Cup of tea?' said the maid. 'I'm Emmer.'

As I say, that had been a goodish walk, and I was parched. But I said, 'I'm to see His Grace at five.'

'Well,' she said. 'You've got five minutes, 'aven't you? Anyway, he's got someone with him. Now you're Captain Webb, I hear.' She put her face close to mine as she poured the milk-in-first. 'I seen you in the *Post*, on one of them big boats. Dint you bump into the Kaiser?'

As I told her what had happened she put her hand on mine and her eyes went round. By the second cup of tea her knee was touching mine, and I was working away at a bit of cook's Dundee cake and thinking here you go, boy, London style, and never mind what the clock say.

Then a bell rang on a board on the wall and Jeames (he was called Albert really, but to me he would always be Jeames) Jeames as I say came down the steps all plump and rosy, great calves wobbling like jellyfish in the silk stockings, and Emma she drew in her breath and jumped away from me. And Jeames he stuck his nose up high and he said, 'His Grace will see you now.' Emma gave my hand a squeeze and I followed his back up the stairs.

That was just a back in a blue tail coat, but I could see that was a huffy back. Webb arrives in London with a barrel of herrings for the Duke, and the women fall like ninepins. Because they have seen him in the *newspaper*. Oh, they'll be singing about you at the Alhambra next—

We arrived above stairs. The air stopped smelling of boiled cabbage and started smelling fresh and lively, with something that was either perfume or flowers – for some reason that made me think of Hetty. There were polished boards underfoot and red Turkey rugs on the boards, and dark old pictures on the walls, and they brought me back to the Duke quick enough. We went up another lot of stairs, huge stairs, with a mahogany banister that would have been about right for a Blue-Riband liner. Halfway up, Jeames slowed down, so I was beside him. 'Listen, sailor boy,' he said, with a sort of twist to his face. 'I'd say 'ands off my girl.'

'Say it, then.'

'No need,' says he, 'I know what's coming, because I've heard them talking.' Is Grace and the other gent.' He smirked, and tapped the side of his nose. 'Ho, yus. Not much Dundee cake where you're going.'

We had arrived outside a set of double-doors the size of a barge's hatchcover. I could smell the smoke of Abdullahs. If there was something bad going to happen, I wanted to walk into that myself, not be thrown at that by Jeames. Before he could get his hand to the knobs, I opened both doors myself and went in.

That was a big room, a library, I suppose. There were galleries round the walls, with wrought-iron railings, very nice work, better than Sam's cousin Gideon could have done. And books: books from the parquet floor to the frosted-glass skylights in the ceiling. In the middle of the room two chaps – gentlemen, I should say – were sitting at a green Morocco-topped table. One of them was the Duke, Abdullah spilling ash down the bosom of a plum-coloured velvet waistcoat. The other was a younger man, a Chinese-eyed chap with pince-nez and a medium-high collar and a necktie done up in a small knot. He had a quiet, thinking sort of feel about him; a doctor, perhaps. As I went in he got up from the table and came forward with his hand sticking out. I shook it. 'Captain Webb,' he said. So I knew they had been talking about me.

The Duke sat there and puffed his cigarette and looked up at his books. Without bringing his eyes down he said, 'Webb, this is Mr Carruthers. Mr Carruthers is, ah, a yachtsman.'

I sort of hoisted my eyebrows, quietly blasting this Duke for bringing me all the way to London to talk to a pleasure boatman.

'Not really,' said Mr Carruthers. 'I've done a bit of sailing with a friend, that's all. Hardly yachting by your standards.'

I said, 'Is that right, sir?' a bit surprised now, because in my experience a lot of yachting gentlemen would like you to think they fit in somewhere between Charlie Barr and Admiral Nelson.

'For God's sake, Chil— hrm, Carruthers,' said the Duke. 'Stop being modest for half a minute.'

Carruthers walked to the drinks tray, picked up the decanter and waved it at me. That was a surprise, too, for a paid hand.

'Doesn't drink,' said the Duke, rolling his pop eyes onto me and yawning as if he could see inside my head and was bored by what he saw. I was still standing. Carruthers said, 'Have a seat, Captain,' as if he wanted to please.

The Duke said, 'Lookee here, Webb, I've got a job for you.'

I sat down on the edge of one of the green leather chairs. I said, 'I'm sailing for Sir Alonso this year.'

The Duke took no notice. 'Now, then. Carruthers.'

'Quite.' Carruthers put his forearms on the table. He had a fresh, pink sort of face. But I thought that behind the pince nez his eyes had a burning gleam; trick of the light, perhaps. 'Now then,' he said. 'I'm going to spin you a yarn that you probably won't believe. But you'll have to take it from me that it's true.'

'He'll listen,' growled the Duke. 'He's being paid to.'

Carruthers frowned, a small frown, suitable for use on dukes falling behind with their *noblesse oblige*. 'Last year, I went sailing with a chum in the Frisian Islands. Chain of islands parallel to the Dutch and German coasts, just offshore. Funny place: wall of dunes, really, that the sea's broken through and outflanked, years, centuries ago.' I nodded brightly, wondering what he was on about. I knew about the Frisian islands—

Hello, I thought. And sure enough when I looked across at that damned Duke those pop eyes were half a yard inside my head.

Carruthers put his forearms on the table and looked down at his cuff. I could see notes pencilled there. 'You're a professional fisherman and yacht skipper,' he said. 'Of course I know you are, because I've seen you in the newspapers.' His face had a harder look now. 'I wonder, Captain. What are your views on the question of Germany?'

A lot of people seemed to be asking me this, nowadays. I had my mouth open to answer when the Duke butted in, smooth as cream. 'I think we're losing the thread. What we want to ask you about is whether you've any idea of salvage work.'

Carruthers opened his mouth and shut it again, as if he was swallowing something nasty. 'Salvage,' he said finally, and I swear he was blushing. 'Of course.' Pause, while he wound himself up. 'His Grace tells me you're a good navigator. We know you've learned surveying. It's important. In these Frisian Islands. There are gaps between them, y'know, seegats, they call them, same word as sea gates. The tide goes in and out of there at some speed, I can tell you. And when you get the wind over the tide, things can get pretty wild.' His voice was filling up with a sort of amateur yachtsman's excitement about what he thought was hard times and rough weather. Silly, but I found myself liking the man. 'Other times,' he said, 'it's a simply splendid place. The seegats lead you into the Wattenmeer, a shallow sea, sheltered, hidden from the outside, absolutely laced with creeks and channels that give communication from harbours on the land—'

'So it's a salvage job,' said the Duke, butting in again, as if he was pulling the conversation back onto lines already arranged. Carruthers shut up, Dukes having right of way over gentlemen, I suppose. 'Mr Chil— hrm, Carruthers was there last year. He got wind of a wreck on a sandbank off one of the seegats. French frigate, one of Napoleon's lot. Blew ashore with a million and a half of money. She's on a sandbank called the Schillplate off the western end of Juist, that's an island, for yer information. Wreck used to belong to Lloyd's. And in the view of some she still does. Lot of people have gone looking for her. Well, everybody knows where she is, actually, she's marked on the chart. But the banks shift, and now you see her and now you don't, and the gold's gone through her bottom years ago, gold being heavier than timber, and it's taking some finding I can tell you. Lot of people have bust themselves in the attempt. Last lot were at it last year, actually, between July and October. But times change, and machinery reaches a higher state of perfection. Some people at Lloyd's think it might be worth pursuing. So I've acquired an interest. There's a salvage expert I've come across, name of Dacre. Most authoritative man. He'll take a look, give me a report on what's possible and what isn't. Meanwhile I want things done quietly and discreetly. So you and your Samson Gidney can take Captain Dacre yachting, have a little spring cruise.

'Dacre?' I say. The name seemed familiar, goodness knew how.

'Late' – he gave the word a strange sarcastic twist of his mouth – '*late* ——th Lancers. You take care of Captain Dacre, and Captain Dacre will take care of business. He'll make a report. If there's anything to it, the lawyers can do their stuff. There's a boat waiting for you.'

I opened my mouth to remind him again that I already had a job. But of course he was already talking.

'You're an intelligent man,' he said. 'Tough as old boots. Which is important because you may not be the only chaps after the *Corinne*. As I said, last year some Germans set up camp on Memmert, next-door sandbank. Very dubious claim they had too. No need to let on what you're up to. There'll be birds nesting, I am informed. Terns and what not. You can make out that you're there to watch 'em. Captain Dacre'll be in charge. Just do as he says and you'll come to no harm.'

Mr Carruthers nodded, poker-faced, like they teach them at those schools they go to. But I could see he was miserable behind the pince-nez. Perhaps that Duke had diddled him out of a gold bar or two, I thought. Or more likely worse.

I said, nice and quiet, 'I'm fishing just now. And I can't see what we can do to dig up ninety-year-old gold off of a shifted bank—'

The Duke was not to be stopped. 'As for money,' he said, wrinkling his thick nose, scornful of the stuff, him who had so much of it, 'you won't suffer. You'll be back in a month. I'll pay you a thousand pounds. Five hundred now, five hundred when you get back.'

Well that was a stopper. Fishing, you would be pushed to earn a thousand pounds in ten years. Even as captain of a winning yacht that would take you three. There must be something wrong; some kind of foolishness about this. Still, a thousand pound . . .

'I'll ask Sir Alonso,' I said.

'Hardly necessary, is it?'

Here we go again, I thought. We had put a lot of time and effort into *Doria*, and this sounded like a wild goose chase. Plus we understood each other, me and Sir Alonso. 'He's the boss,' I said.

'Ah,' said the Duke. 'Well, if that's how you want it. But it would take six weeks of your time, maximum. You'd be back in the water in time for the season. If you change your mind, go and see my agent. He'll do the needful.'

'Best of luck,' said Carruthers, eyes blazing away behind the pince—nez. 'And one thing—'

'Never mind that,' said the Duke, a bit hasty, as if he knew what Carruthers was going to say and wanted to stop him.

But Carruthers would not be stopped. 'There's something else,' he said doggedly. 'There's a chap over there already. A friend of mine. Chap called er Wilson. He was keeping an eye on things. On the, well, competition. I'd like you to look out for him, help him if you think he needs it.'

'Treasure hunter, is he?' I had no intention of going along with this nonsense, but they would have their say before they let me go.

'Possibly,' said Carruthers. There was a sheen of sweat on his forehead, and in his voice the vagueness of a man born honest trying not to tell a flat lie. 'He went off, what, a month ago. We haven't heard from him since.'

The Duke said, 'Give Dacre what help he asks for, never mind this Wilson. We want you to start as soon as possible. If you change your mind, that is.'

Carruthers said, 'But if you see Wilson ... well, he's a great friend.' There was a doggedness in him I had not noticed before. You got the idea that once he had something in his head he would stick to it, no matter what. The Duke was looking at him with what was probably a curl of the lip under the moustache. Of the two of them, I was inclined to listen to Carruthers. Gentry he might be, but he sounded like an honest man.

But I had an honest employer already. Money or no money, this sounded like a wild goose chase. I said, 'I'll have to think that over,' meaning, not on your life.

'Please,' said Carruthers, pink as a boiled prawn.

'He'll see sense,' said the Duke, not even looking at me, his hand going for the bellpush on the table.

'Thankee, your Grace,' I said, and got up, and left.

CHAPTER SIX

Gloria in Excelsis

The footman Jeames conducted me down the gentry stairs and through the green-baize door into the linoleum and boiled onions. Emma was at the kitchen table, sewing, very demure. As I passed, she looked up under her lashes. 'In town tonight, Captain Webb?' she said.

'What's that to you?' snarled Jeames. A bell rang. High on the wall, a pointer quivered in a gold-leaf box. 'Morning room,' said Emma sweetly. 'Run along now.' Jeames gave her a look fit to light bladder wrack, and took his calves up the stairs. 'There's company this evening,' she said. 'So Albert will be standing behind a chair. And he can't expect little me to wait down 'ere all night, can 'e?' She hung onto my hand, stroking the rough bits with her soft London fingers. 'I think you're ever so brave,' she said. 'I like a brave man. Vesta Tilley's at the Alhambra, Captain. 'Ow about it?'

She was pretty all right, and I was pleased enough. But I was puzzled too. I said. 'What do you mean, brave?'

She smiled, a crafty sort of a smile. 'That Mr Childers,' she said. 'More to that one than meets the eye.'

'Childers?' I said. Then I remembered the Duke's stumble, as if he had known Mr Carruthers well, but had difficulty remembering his name.

' 'Ouse of Commons, 'e works in,' she said. 'But Mum's the word, eh?'

Well I still didn't understand what she was talking about, but she made a change from fishing up herring with icy water running down your back.

'Nother cup of tea?' she said, and she took me to a little sort of alcove where the teapot was and took my hand again, and her nails were working in the palm, scritch, scratch, and I could smell the heavy smell of the skin on her neck. She was very pretty. I had a sort of thought about Hetty, but only as it were a flash in the head, because she was long gone. And then unworthy as that might sound I thought, well, Hetty, you're not the only fish in the sea, girl, and here's a good one just longing to be caught. You must remember I was not yet twenty-five, and in London, and . . . well, perhaps all that is an excuse for what happened next, which is either not excusable or natural, depending on your point of view.

So she kissed me on the mouth, and I put my hand on her knee and moved that up towards her thigh, hearing her breathe heavy, feeling the opening of her legs, the whole of her opening up, and she said in a hot whisper, 'All the time you've been up there, I didn't know 'ow I'd be able to wait.' Then she pulled away. 'I'll find you a cup, then,' she said, in a strange, high voice. 'They're in the back pantry. Perhaps you'd like a wash. I'll show you.'

'Thankee kindly,' I croaked. Those big black eyes of hers were melting, and I should not have been surprised if mine had been similar.

Nobody looked as we went out of the kitchen. 'Down the corner on the right,' she said the high, don't-care voice. But even as she said that she was opening another door and pulling me into something that through the roaring of my blood I imagined might be a butler's pantry. She shut the door and shot a bolt and I took her waist and kissed her and she kissed me back, not those little flirting kisses but hungry ones, her tongue like a hot slippery animal, and her hands on my trouser buttons and inside, hot as fire, and my own hands bringing her skirts up until they found the skin above her stockings, and her moaning and shuddering as I pressed on, and she stuffed her face into the shoulder of my coat to muffle the sounds she could not help making and pulled me down on a bag of laundry and steered me in, and on in I went to the hilt, on and on, while she wound herself around me like a basket of hot eels and I felt her teeth in my jersey, and the shudder of her body like a hot bulb oil engine, and me beginning to shudder too.

And then we were both lying on the laundry bag seeeing stars, her purring like a cat, kissing my neck above the jersey, and I was stroking her hair, and her free hand was absent-mindedly working away, and that was all beginning to happen over again. But she suddenly sat up and shook off my hand and started pinning her hair back into place, looking flushed and big-lipped, and I was thinking how beautiful she was. As I buttoned up, that was hard to believe that had happened. Like a dream, as it were.

But that had been real enough, as I was about to find out.

'Well,' she said, very matter of fact. 'A duty can be a pleasure, and no mistake.' Before I could ask her what she meant, duty, she had kissed me on the lips again and let herself out.

I waited a moment and followed on. Nobody looked at me when I went back into the kitchen, but I felt that what we had been at was written a foot high across my coat. But there was Emma sewing again, and the cook browning stewing steak, and the kitchenmaids peeling potatoes and scrubbing the chopping block. So I went and stood between her and the light and I said, 'What do you mean, duty?'

She put up her chin and pushed an envelope across the table at me. 'You're to read that now,' she said, looking at me cool and hard, but after a moment her face pinkened and her eyes shifted. I took out my knife and slit the envelope.

The letter was in the handwriting of the Duke's secretary Theophilus whatever his name was.

Dear Captain,

I am glad you find my servants so much to your taste. Though if the pure-minded Sir Alonso were to hear about your corruption of the lovely Emma, I fear you might suffer in his esteem and indeed be forced to leave his employment.

Of course, what my servants do among themselves is their own business and is not bruited about outside this house. I suggest therefore that you enter my employ, as per our discussions this afternoon. A simple yes or no to Emma will suffice. Your silence will of course guarantee my own.

* * *

That was not signed. That did not need to be.

Emma said, 'Well?'

I could feel the blood hot in my face. I was irritated at Sir Alonso's rules, but rich men made rules, and Sir Alonso's were not oppressive, of their kind. What put me in a rage was a rich man who would have little enough scruple to use one servant's body to get himself another—

There was no use raging against Dukes. The error had been mine. I had fancied Emma. Or perhaps the perfume on the stairs had made me think about Hetty, and I had gone after Emma to blot her out. That made no difference now. Whether he knew it or not, the Duke had pressed the right buttons. Perhaps that was a gift God gave Dukes. But the long and the short of it was that a Duke would have his way, and so the world was ordered.

'Tell him yes,' I said, and took my hat off the peg.

She said, 'Where are you off to?'

'Business,' I said, hating myself.

'It's my night off.'

She was beautiful. I opened my mouth to say in for a penny, in for a pound. But I had my pride, and besides, Hetty was in my head now, and once she was there, there was no shaking her loose. I hardened my heart. I said, 'No, thank you.'

And her eyes filled up with tears, and she looked sort of desperate, because the truth was that damned Duke had made whores of us both with my willing help, and now I was taking away what would have made that better.

So I left her and Jeames to tread the path of true love, and carried my anger into the London streets.

I ate a chop in the Mile End Road, and took a room in a commercial hotel, and tried not to think about what I had done. Soon I fell to wondering why the Duke so badly wanted me to take this boat of his on a salvage reconnaissance, and why he wanted me to look after this Captain Dacre, and who this Mr Wilson was that Mr Carruthers had mentioned, and why the Duke had been so concerned to shut Mr Carruthers up. And why Mr Carruthers, who had seemed an honest chap, had looked like a man telling lies.

But of course there was no way of knowing; not with His Grace of Leominster.

I was awake at seven, with a greyish light coming in the window, and carts and hansoms clattering in the road. I got up and washed in cold water, and ate a pale London egg. At eight I was walking through a clear spring morning down Threadneedle Street, twisting my head around to look at the buildings. And at ten past I was in front of a brass plate that said Sulky Grigson and Lynch, solicitors.

The clerk told me Mr Lynch never came in till ten, so I sat and read *The Times*. I remember the Mad Mullah was acting up in Somaliland, and Marconi's wireless was transmitting to liners at sea. And that seemed that the Government had decided to build a Naval base in the Firth of Forth, to protect trade in the North Sea, against whom that was not said, but that did call to mind the *Kaiser Barbarossa* at Kiel.

Mr Lynch was an unmannerly old stick with a rusty black waistcoat and a panelled office full of used air. He spoke without looking at me. 'His Grace's requirements are as follows. A small sailing boat has been purchased, of the type known I believe as a smack yacht. It is called *Gloria*. It is lying at Limehouse in the Regent's Canal Basin. I am assured that you will find it suitable. P R Anderson of Medland Street are contracted to supply you with, ah, nautical necessaries.' He reached into a desk drawer, and pushed a fat brown envelope across the scuffed leather top. 'His Grace asked that I should give you this.' That was heavy, full of paper by the feel of it. 'I suppose you can read, my man?'

'A little, sir,' I said, knuckling my brow at the old idiot. 'Thankin' you kindly, sir.'

'Very good,' he said. 'You are to treat what is inside as a trade secret, not to be seen by anyone not a member of your crew.'

' 'ssir,' says I, wondering what he was on about.

'And what will probably interest you more than any of the rest of it, here's the money.' He reached into another drawer, pulled out a bag that chinked, and pushed it and a paper across the table. 'Sign this receipt. Hurry up, man. Haven't got all day.'

I looked at that for a moment, thinking of Emma; the wages of sin is death. I found myself getting cross again. So I counted the money very slow and annoying. Then I took the paper, dipped the pen, flicked ink on his collar and wrote a big, wobbly cross. He tutted and dabbed at hisself with a snuffy hand-kerchief, then wrote CHAS WEBB HIS MARK and sent me about my business.

I put all that money in Coutts' bank, except for twenty pound. Then I went round the corner and into a Lyons Tea Shop and called for tea and a pen and paper, and wrote to Mrs Huggett in Maldon to send on my sea slops. After that I opened the fat envelope with the trade secrets inside.

There were a couple of brand new charts in there, German, of a string of islands off a coast: the Frisian Islands, and the Wattenmeer. Outside the main shipping channels, there was very little detail. Beside the charts there were two black-bound note-books, filled with pencil scribbles in a small, neat hand. Inside the covers of each notebook was a stamp, like a library stamp, that said HM ADMIRALTY NOVEMBER 1902, and a number like the number you get on the back of a library book.

After two cups of tea and a bath bun I had puzzled out that the notes referred to the charts, being sketches and bearings that supplied the details the official charts left out – provided a key, in fact, to the tangle of creeks and channels between the islands and the mainland.

The only part of it that meant anything to me was on a louse-shaped sort of a sandbank called Memmert, where north of a beacon there was a diagram of two huts at right angles and a scrawl that said *salvors' camp*, and out on the three-fathom line to the northward a wreck symbol. As discussed with that damned Duke, and Childers, or Carruthers, or whatever he called himself.

I clapped the papers in the envelope and the hat on my head, and caught a train to Limehouse.

Limehouse Basin is where the canals of Britain meet the tidal Thames. That is a sheet of filthy water jam-packed with coasting ships and barges, narrow boats they call them. You can hardly see the quays under heaps of corn sacks and tar barrels and potatoes in boxes, not to mention the dirty fog of coal smoke that hangs over all.

The Basin is not a popular place with yachtsmen, who like to keep their darlings clean. But after hard inspection, I did spy a yacht mast in that forest of spars strung with sooty cobwebs of rigging.

That belonged to a tidy cutter with canvas protectors over her snow-white enamel sides. She looked like the kind of boat a Duke would think suitable for a job like the one we were being sent on. I shouldered my bag and walked over the lock-gates, and gave the men in the cockpit a hail.

'*Gloria*?' said one of the men, with a bit of a sniff. 'Not 'ere, mate.' He pointed into the press of masts down the quay. 'There you are, and good luck to yer.'

Now he came to point that out, there was another yacht mast in that higgledy-piggledy thicket. I walked on and looked down.

The object crammed between a Thames barge and two coasting brigs looked like the bastard child of a Broads yacht and a fishing smack. That was about twenty ton, forty foot long, not counting a long smack bowsprit. Out of a deck of dirty pine there stuck a coachroof that might once have been painted blue. There was a big hatch, skewbald where the paint had flaked off of it. There was a cockpit, big enough to work a net or a long line out of. And there was an iron tiller. The mast was black, the rigging weary, the sails bundled up any old how at the end of their halyards, the staysail awash in the bottom of the big, fishy old dinghy parked on the foredeck.

I stood there and let people bump into me and ask me where I thought I was off to in such a dooce of a hurry. I would say that my heart sank, except that was already on the bottom. She looked a real pig; everything above the water, nothing below. Handy in the islands, maybe, when the tide went out and she needed to sit on the mud. But if you wanted her to sail, you would make a foot of leeway for every two foot of headway.

For anyone who doesn't know anything about boats and doesn't want to know, what I am saying is this. That was an old boat, and a wore-up boat, and the only thing that fitted that for its work was that that would sail in shallow water like the water in the Wattenmeer, do we could get that to the other side of the

North Sea. Engine? Bless your heart, there was no such thing as an engine in those days.

Well, I stood and I looked and I cursed the Duke, and Emma, and most of all myself. I gazed upon the reward of my greed and fornication and I cursed us all until I was tired. When I was finished I balanced my traps on my shoulder and went down the ladder.

Now I have spent most of my life fishing, and fishing boats are no place for a man with a delicate nose. But the whiff that came up out of the *Gloria*'s cabin when I opened the hatch beat all. There was bilge, and mould. There was also paraffin and dead fish. But that was only the beginning of a whole rainbow of stinks unknowable. That was a living thing with teeth, hair and armpits, that smell.

I left my slops in the cockpit, took a breath, went below and lit the paraffin lamp. There was a saloon, high enough to stand up in if you bent double at the waist, with a thick varnish of rancid grease on all the paintwork and a rusty stove on the starboard side of the bulkhead. Bilge water was lapping over the cabin sole, floor to you. There was a pump on the bulkhead forward, where the mast came through the deck. I caught hold of the handle and I took out my feelings on that pump. When the waters had near enough abated, I took a closer look at this Purgatory to which I had been doomed by lust.

There was a saloon, with wet button-leather settees. There was another cabin forward of the mast with a pair of bunks, mattresses stuffed with kapok and mildew. Between the saloon and the fore cabin was a blocked and stinking head with a green brass pump, and a wardrobe with jammed doors. There was a door in the bulkhead at the forward end of the forecabin, but when I tried to open it, that was jammed as tight as the wardrobe. So I went back on deck.

The Limehouse air was mostly coal smoke and dead dog, but after the cabin that smelt like French scent. I walked up the deck, that someone had patched in places with cement, and gave a heave at the forehatch.

There was a sort of a forepeak down there, eight foot long, narrowing sharpish towards the bow. When the smack had been fishing, that was where the men would have lived. That was where Sam and me were going to live and do the cooking. The comforts now consisted of two plank bunks, a pile of rusty anchor chain, a dirty cooking stove against the aft bulkhead—

And something else. Something with arms and legs, collapsed in the runnel of dirty water in the bilges, with a head, a huge head, unnaturally round, gleaming in the light coming through the hatch.

My heart unsunk itself and shot right into my mouth. I dropped down, and turned that over. That was all floppy. And I started to sweat and giggle and tell myself I was a silly fool, wrought up enough to look for dead bodies when we hadn't even left the dock, and there was no reason for there to be dead bodies anywhere anyway.

Because what that thing was down there was not a corp, but a diving suit. The head was a brass helmet. And above the window, someone had written in chalk: GON TO GRAPES.

So I fired my slops down onto the port-hand bunk. I shut that hatch behind me and went up that quay ladder. Then I barged through the crowd like a whaler in heavy ice, and forced myself into the Grapes.

Light was trickling in through the glass doors behind the gallery, struggling against the smoke from a tug's funnel outside, and thirty-odd pipes inside. But I could see them, sitting at a table: Samson Gidney, pipe clamped between his teeth, and another man, stiff-built, with a big jaw and a thick head of hair and a gentry-cut blazer, who would be Captain Dacre.

Sam lifted his glass. 'Capting!' he cried. 'O my capting!'

'Dacre,' said the man, sticking out his fin. That was like shaking a wet board. He was a neat-looking man, fussily shaved, his gloves carefully arrranged next to his glass of whisky on the table. 'Drink?'

'Pussyfoot,' said Sam. 'Teetoteetal. Offer him tea,' by which I could tell Sam had been drinking port wine, and plenty of it, as usual when someone else was paying.

Dacre had a broken nose and a head the shape of a cannonball covered in that heavy thatch of black hair. He had a compact, tidy feel, but at the same time there was something dangerous

51

about him. There was a sort of a zone round him, fenced off. What was inside that fence you were not meant to find out, and you were not sure you wanted to. I had come across that in chaps who went in for fighting, boxing I mean, but never in a gentleman. That made me think of the sarcastic twist to the Duke's mouth when he had mentioned that he was late of the —-th Lancers. Still, I remember thinking, perhaps that's what you need if you're a salvage man and a diver. Perhaps that'll come in handy.

But I know I had my doubts about him. Even then.

CHAPTER SEVEN

The Famous Captain Dacre

So anyway, Captain Dacre said in a brisk and military sort of a voice, 'Delighted to have made your acquaintance. We sail in fifteen days.'

Sam said, 'That's Sunday fortnight. Easter Day.'

'Ten out of ten,' said Dacre, snappily. Cocky, he seemed, but uneasy in himself, too. Not quite the gent.

'Bad luck to sail of a Sunday,' said Sam.

'Bad luck be hanged,' said Dacre. 'Do what you can to that boat. It's only got to last a month. Leave me room for a few boxes of stores.' He smirked at us, consulted the gold watch on the slim chain, positioned the bowler hat carefully on that neat black thatch, and left, walking like a boxer.

Sam said, 'I wonder what is his favourite colour for window curtains,' sarcastic, like.

I said, 'Come you on,' and wheeled him back to the boat.

A respectable yacht skipper does not lash up a wreck. But there we were, and there was that dirty old *Gloria*, and she was the bed we had to lie in. So me and Sam we went around the Basin and found ourselves a dozen idlers, and bought up most of the paint and sandpaper and varnish in Anderson's. We housed her topmast and warped her round to the slipway, and dragged her into the shed. While the idlers piled all the junk and rubbish out of her cabin, we took a look at her bottom.

In case you are interested, she drew three foot six, with a long straight keel, shallow enough to be no use to windward and deep enough to make her heel something wretched when she took the ground. But when I dug around in her garboards with a spike, that didn't make much impression. Dirty she might be, but except for some bits of caulking adrift she seemed sound.

'Leave her,' says Sam. 'She'll pump.'

That was Sam for you: gloomy-looking chap with a big grey moustache, fond of his drink, sloppy devil, pure fisherman. He could get best speed out of anything from an ironing board to Noah's Ark, could Sam, and cook anything you liked as long as that was a herring. But he never had got the hang of the gentry, and he could never bear to spend money, even if that was not his.

'No pumping,' says I. 'We'll do her.'

So we patched her up. Forgive me, but this here is what we did. The yard boys put braziers under the bad spots in her seams to get the worst of the wet out of the planks so they would take paint. Then we caulked up the bad bits. Then we painted that over with one of the narrow boat chaps' patent mixture of tar and horse muck that we boiled together in a cauldron – tar for waterproofing, horse muck for binding.

On the second day of painting, the vile steam parted, and there by the pregnant bulge of *Gloria*'s side stood a sturdy-looking girl in a navy-blue skirt, tam o'shanter and peajacket.

She came up to me and said, 'Captain Webb,' and stuck out her hand. 'We met at Kiel.'

I remembered her fine. She was Clara Dollmann, who had been with that Gräfin. I remembered her as a nice-looking girl of about eighteen, with broad shoulders, a bright eye and a brown skin. Now she was pale, and might have been five years older – still pretty, mind, but with a look as if she had not had an easy few months of it.

She spoke with a soft German accent most pleasant to hear. I did my best to put her at her ease, showing her over what there was to see of *Gloria*. The cabin was bare and covered in wood shavings. But I got her to sit down, and being private seemed to encourage her. 'This is quite awkward,' she said. 'You are off to Ostfriesland, I hear.'

'Who told you that?'

'Mr Carruthers.' She flushed. 'I know it is supposed to be a secret. But Mr Carruthers is one of the best friends I have in the world.'

That crossed my mind that that was a peculiar thing to say. But someone was yelling my name on the slip, and that sounded like the smith for the rudder straps, that I had been waiting for all day. 'So what was you after, Miss?' I said.

'I believe Mr Carruthers mentioned a Mr Wilson.'

He had indeed started talking about some such person, just before the Duke had cut him off like a slice of ham. 'I believe he might have,' I said, mindful of the promises of secrecy I had made, and what would happen if I broke them.

'Mr Wilson went to Ostfriesland in February,' she said. 'We know he arrived safe. But for a month now there has not been a word.' She went quiet. This much Mr Carruthers had told me.

'Yes?'

'Please make sure he is well.'

I was puzzled. That was Germany, not Khartoum, and there seemed no reason this chap should be anything but in the pink. 'On salvage business, is he?' I said.

'My father was killed in the islands last year.' She would not look at me. 'Mr Wilson is making enquiries.'

She stood up. 'Mind your head,' I said, for the deck beams were terrible low.

'If you see him, please help him,' she said. Then she blurted, 'It is awfully dangerous.' There were tears in her eyes, that seemed to me. She took my hand and gave that a squeeze. She had a good-sized hand and a firm grip, the grip of a practical girl. Perhaps if I had grilled her a bit, that would have saved everyone some trouble. But the smith's sooty head came down the hatch and started about inch iron, and by the time I got clear of that she was gone. And I must say that at the time, I gave her and her Wilson no more thought.

The idlers rubbed and scrubbed, sandpaper for the spars and brightwork, caustic for the grease in the cabin, carbolic for the bilges. We got the cabin stove lit, and a rank chemical steam came rolling out of her hatches. I took the sails off and bowled them up to Jones's loft in a stable barrow, and he washed them and patched them and sewed up the seams. The running rigging and the cordage in general I left to Sam, who renewed what needed renewing, complaining the while about the thievish prices they were charging at Anderson's. That was dear, of course, but that was the Duke's money. And I had learned on the yachts that with organization and plenty of money, you could work wonders in hardly no time at all.

By Good Friday morning we had her back in the water, with red lead in the bilges, the cabin sole back in, and we were bending on the washed and mended sails. As we warped her through the press of hulls and back into her berth, that was definite that she had changed.

This is the last of the gibberish, I hope; but here goes. We had painted her topsides black, and gold-leafed her coving line, and varnished her brightwork. We had rubbed down her mast and boom and bowsprit, and given them six coats of varnish, and painted their ends white. We had rove new running rigging, and whited the seizings on her deadeyes. We had patched and caulked and sanded her deck. We had even done her name board. *Gloria, RYS*, that said, in new gold leaf. The Duke being a member of the Squadron, you understand, and apparently Captain Dacre too, though I confess I never heard of him at Cowes.

All of which means that she was looking smart and tidy. Even if you neither know nor care about boats you can't help noticing that, the way that even if you know nothing about horses you can tell a well-turned out hack from a ragman's screw. Beauty is beauty.

Well, then.

Next day we laid her under the hand crane with all her gear on board, according to instructions delivered per letter that morning. As we were making fast a cart comes jingling along the quay and behind it a hansom, and out of the hansom and down onto my clean deck in his dirty bootsoles steps Captain Dacre.

Half a dozen chaps come out of nowhere, burly chaps who did not work at the Basin, and they wound up the hand crane and started a lot of boxes down at us. Sam had took one in his arms, a strong wooden box, with FRAGILE – THIS WAY UP stencilled on that. 'We'll need to stow this safe,' says Dacre, as if there was any risk of stowing that different.

Well Sam was a bit huffy about all our work not being noticed, so he says, 'This one?' and tosses that up and catches that, casual like. Captain Dacre – Dacre, I'll call him from now on, looking at what came later – Dacre, I say, he went white as a sheet and he say, 'Be careful with that, you bloody fool.'

Well this is not the way to talk to Sam. 'Pardon?' he say, and drop that slam, right on the deck.

I thought by the look on his face Dacre would smack him one, at which that would have been all over with our voyage. So I move in and I say, 'Sam, do you take more care. Where do you want this here stuff stowed, sir?'

There was a glaze of sweat on Dacre's forehead, though that was blowing coolish from the east. He dabbed that with a clean white handkercher. 'If you treat it like that,' he said between those short little teeth of his, very nasty, 'you won't have any-where to stow it at all.' He looked around, and said, 'There,' pointing at the forepeak.

'Crew's quarters, sir.'

'All right,' he said. 'Put it in my bedroom. I'll do it myself.'

Well we stored up these things up in our hearts, as that says in the Bible, and kept stowing.

Those crates came swinging out of that sky most of the day. Near the end was something that looked like a concertina that was a small-size diver's air pump. That and the diver's dress we stowed in a little locker we made at the bottom of the chain locker, underneath six shackle, which is ninety fathom, of three-quarter-inch chain. Legal this treasure hunt might be, but Dacre seemed not to want that gossiped about.

The last thing to come down the crane was too big to go down the hatch. Twelve foot long, that was, a boat like a canoe with a little foredeck. I might be hazy on diving dresses, but I knew what this here was. I had used things like this here in creeks of the frozen marshes, creeping up on knots of teal till you were close enough to loose off with the four-bore muzzle-loader mounted on the little ferrule on the foredeck.

'What the *hell*,' said Sam, breathing stale port wine over me. 'Whoart in the name of *hell* do he want with a duck punt?'

That is what I mean about Sam. In those days gentry was

gentry, like spoiled children really. If they wanted to take duck punts to the Frisian Islands on a salvage trip two months outside the duck season, that was their lookout. As paid hands our lookout was to shut our mouths and sail the boat, never mind what we thought.

So I shut Sam up and we lashed the duck punt on deck by the starboard chainplate, and snugged all down, and soon enough that was six o'clock, and Dacre gave a shout.

He was in the saloon, on the new-cushioned settee, by the new-blacked stove, under the new-polished lamp, drinking a glass of whisky out of a new bottle, resting his black thatch on the new white paint. 'What o'clock do we sail?' he says.

'Tide's at four,' says I.

'Then we've time for a spree,' says he. 'As your captain, I order you.'

Well, I was the captain and he was the passenger, but this was not the time to mention such matters. So we got our hats, and he led me and Sam up the quay steps.

We rattled west by the sun until the dirty streets got cleaner, and Dacre, who had been sitting tapping his fingers on his knee in a nervous way that he had, said, 'The jolly old Strand!' He rapped on the roof with his walking stick, and told the driver to set us down.

'The dear old Pelican,' said he. He took us in at a big green door and into a sort of lobby with caricatures on the walls. One of them was that damned Duke, of course, Abdullah in moustache, stomach sticking out of a fur coat, signed *Spy*. We put our names in a little book. The air smelt of drink and cigar smoke, and somewhere or other a woman was laughing fit to bust glass. Dacre led us into a room that was a bar, very smart. There was a nice looking girl behind the bar, in a low dress and a white apron. She was looking up at a big chap who was standing on top of the bar. The chap on top of the bar was wearing a lady's hat with a woodcock on it, and holding a revolver, which he was pointing at the barmaid. The barmaid was smiling a smile that was cracking at the edges. She was an awful pretty girl, and she looked proper frightened.

'Mix . . . me . . . gin'n'brimstone,' said the man on the bar.

'That's old Hughie Drummond,' said Dacre, as if the drunk chap was St Paul's Cathedral. 'Marvellous chap.'

'Killer,' said Drummond, hearing his voice and fixing him with a nasty yellow gaze. 'Go back S'Africa.'

No doubt about it, that barmaid was in fear of her life. I thought, well, if nobody else is going to do nothing, I better had. 'Scuse me, sir,' I said to the marvellous chap. 'Do you give me that thing before someone get hurt?'

'Foreigner,' said Drummond, lowering the gun. 'You be damned, woggy boy.'

'Ladies present,' screeched a woman with rouge and cross eyes.

'Blast that's Marie Lloyd,' said Sam.

I did not look because I was holding out my hand for the gun. Drummond shut one eye and pointed that at me, and I thought, dear oh dear, he's going to shoot. But shutting the eye un-balanced him, and he fell off the bar with a crash. I picked up the revolver and gave that to the barmaid, who blew me a kiss and looked at Drummond as if she would like to use that on him. Dacre laughed most hearty. 'Drink, before we dine?'

'Port wine, thank ye kindly,' says Sam like a flash. 'Why'd that chap call you killer?'

'Just his little joke,' said Dacre, offhand. 'Terrific wag, old Hughie.'

I went to get the drinks. The barmaid let her hand touch mine, and said, 'Where d'you live?'

'At sea,' I said. 'Skipper for Captain Dacre.'

She looked disappointed, and so I expect did I. 'D'you know the Captain, then?'

'Only just made his acquaintance.'

She went into a room behind the bar and came back with an envelope. 'Out of the members' book,' she said, and pushes that into my hand. 'You mind 'ow you go.'

I gave her a wink and tucked that in my pocket and said, 'Next time.' Then I went back to Dacre.

The bar filled up with chaps with stomachs and stiff shirts, and gels with too much rouge and too little dress, not a gentle-man in the place. I sat there pretty awkward while Dacre showed us off to his cronies and told them about his yacht, and that we were his paid hands, no mention of the Duke. He was making guys of us, that was plain. I decided to leave, and get back to the boat as soon as ever I was out of the door. So I stood up, and Dacre stood up too, which was not my plan, and the long and the short of it was that the three of us started to leave all together, stepping over the great Hughie Drummond, who was blotto in a puddle of sick in the hall.

There was a bit of a crowd on the pavement. Dacre said, 'The Gaiety!' or some such. And at that moment from out of the crowd there steps a little chap in a seedy coat and a cap with ear flaps, and glares in his face, and says, 'It's him!'

And Dacre moves. As soon as ever this chap looks at him, he moves, not hesitating, straight into him. Before Sam or I can rightly work out what is going on, Dacre has jabbed him in the belly with his stick, then smashed him in the jaw so hard you can hear his teeth and then his neck, click, click, and the seedy chap is down on the pavement. That was a terrible punch – not a boxer's punch, but the blow of a man who could kill with his hands. I found myself looking at him as if he was a dangerous animal and thinking, that is not fighting, that is smashing people up, and smashing people up is what this chap is good at.

Across the road, some other chaps started shouting. Dacre said, 'We'd better get out of this,' and yanks open the door of a hansom that happens to be there. In we get, and Dacre is yelling at the cabbie, and off we go, nobody knows where.

'Lost 'em, by God,' says Dacre.

'What did you hit him for?' I said.

'Damned dun,' said Dacre.

'Bastards,' said Sam, wagging his head as if he spent most evenings drinking with actresses at the Pelican and half-killing bailiffs for afters.

'Well, well,' says Dacre, rubbing his hands as if he had bought a bunch of violets, not committed assault and battery on a chap doing his job. 'Where shall it be, eh?'

'Back to the boat,' says I.

Dacre looks sulky, and stares me in the eye, and I stare straight back, so he will not be in any doubt about what I think. In the end his eyes drop and he hammers on the roof. 'Driver!' he howls. 'Drop me off in the Whitechapel Road. Take these fellows on to the Regent Canal Basin.'

And in the Whitechapel Road he hops out under a gas-light and darts into the shadows like a shrimp into weed. But even as he darted, I could see a couple of girls moving towards him. Not much doubt what was on his mind.

Dacre had called the bailiff a bastard. I had heard him called a killer, and watched him sneak and toady, and offhand smash up a working chap.

I knew who the bastard was. And that wasn't the bailiff.

CHAPTER EIGHT

A Fleet and an Ensign

I do not sleep well in harbour, even when I know just where I stand and what is to be done next. That night I did not sleep at all.

They were working cargo up the quay, and that gave a little ripple to the water, so as I lay in *Gloria*'s forepeak I could feel her snubbing against her warps, ready to be gone.

I took the envelope the barmaid had given me, and turned up the wick on the paraffin lamp. That was a newspaper cutting from the *Star*, dated a year before. I was not in those days much of a hand at reading newspapers, least of all the *Star*, which had no yachting to speak of and was thought by most to be a pro-Boer rag. But I read this.

The Piemburg court martial has at last reached a verdict. Captain Eric Dacre, 12th Lancers, was tried for the murder of Annie de Blank, who led an insurrection against the guards after her three children perished in the Piemburg stockade. The Court Martial found that Captain Dacre acted with reasonable force given the circumstances, and prevented further bloodshed among the women and children of the camp. The charge was that Mrs de Blank was shot unarmed and in cold blood, in the camp's punishment cells. This shooting of a defenseless captive was, it was held, an act of unjustifiable rigour. Defending Officer deponed that Captain Dacre was a soldier of the Empire, doing his duty to God and the King. Readers may further remember the gallant Captain as having done likewise at the sack of Pekin, where he distinguished himself in the liberating of many captive treasures. The opinion of Defending Officer is supported by *The Times*, the *Daily Mail*, and the whole pack of Jingo donkeys.

The *Star* points out that Captain Dacre, the hero of Piemburg, has however resigned his commission. And the question we must all ask is: did he fall or was he pushed? In case you meet him and would like to ask him, here is his picture. But readers! Remember not to turn your back on this hero – particularly if you are a woman, and unarmed!

There was a steel engraving of a soldier half-hidden behind the brim of a shako and a broad moustache. But that was our Captain Dacre, right enough.

I read that twice. That was not up to Sam and me to pick and choose. If they said you needed a hard man for a salvage reconnaissance, ours not to reason why. But nobody could force us to like it.

He came aboard at three. At a quarter to four we were up and on deck, Sam in the body only. That was raining, with the shadow of a breeze from the west. We got a cup of tea with the dockers and barge boys at the Grapes, and came back on board at ten past, high water. We hoisted the staysail, let off the warps and led her out through the lock gates and into the first of the ebb. Sam and I hauled up the main, him throat me peak, shoulder to shoulder in the dark, Sam giving out all the while about sailing on a Sunday. I went aft to the tiller. The sail filled with a bump. *Gloria* dug in her fat shoulder, and we were away.

I still recall the roar and suck of the tide round the ships anchored in the Pool of London, the black loom of the hulls and the yellow glim of their anchor lights. I recall looking up at *Gloria*'s sails, grey in a bloody port-hand light, and smelling the coal-smoke of a steamer coming up for Millwall Dock. That was a big tide, a fast tide, and by the time the dawn came up the rain had stopped and Canvey Island was on the bow, and the banks had drawn back, low and grey, pimpled with coal heaps and brickyards and timber stacks. At seven o'clock, Dacre came out of the hatch, wearing well-pressed green-and-white striped pyjamas, perfectly brushed hair and three red scratches on his right cheek that he had got between nine and two last night.

He stood in the cockpit and bleared around him at the flat grey water and the dirty scud of the clouds.

'Now where do we go?' he said.

'Go?'

'How do we get inside the islands?'

'Straight for the river Ems, that's the border between Holland and Germany, pop inside and turn left, and Bob's your uncle.'

He gave a doubtful sort of smooth at that thick black hair of his. 'Bit straightforward,' he said.

'Beg pardon?'

'I think,' he said, with a false sort of a smile, 'I *theenk* it might be better to make a more roundabout sort of approach. Don't want our German friends to cotton on too quick, eh? Bird-watching. Cruising in the islands. Ozone, shrimps. That's the ticket.'

'Very well, then,' I said. 'We'll go in from the east.'

'How long?'

'A week,' I said. 'Depending.'

'At the outside.'

'Very good, sir.' Of course there was no way of telling whether that would take three days or a month, but he could not be expected to understand that.

He took a walk round the deck, swearing very crisp when he barked his shin on the duck punt. Then he sat down and did what looked like Swedish exercises. When Sam came by with coffee and herrings he patted his hair straight and went below to eat his breakfast.

He did not come on deck as we went down Black Deep and out between the banks into the grey North Sea. The land dropped away. Somewhere about the Middle Sunk he put his head out of the hatch and asked if that was always this rough. Sam started to say something about Cape Horn before I stood on his foot, because that was flat calm, except for a little wind over tide, which *Gloria* was making hard work of. Then out on deck comes Dacre and announces he will lead prayers, that being Sunday, but suddenly he is sicking up herrings over the side. After that he took a bucket below and wouldn't eat his luncheon, and as for prayers they were heard of no more. At tea he said

64

the herrings were off, and wouldn't think of touching anything else. Then he up on deck and sicked up again and went below, sharpish, and the only thing we heard out of him before dark was a sort of a moan when he smelt the paraffin Sam slopped out of the running lamps when he was filling them. Later there was the clatter of a medicine bottle. Chloral, Sam said that was, a great big bottle of it he had; stuff to make him sleep.

The sun went down red as India rubber. The Sunk went by, and the Outer Gabbard, where Joe had been fishing that night he died. At midnight I called Sam to the helm and went down into my bunk. I lay and listened to the creak of the bobstay, and the crunch of the stem in the swells. Then I woke up and that was four o'clock in the morning, and she was hove to, and Sam had the kettle on.

'Breeze gone east northeast,' he said, while the kettle boiled on the coal range against the aft bulkhead, the back wall I should say, of the forepeak. I took a bit of bread and butter, and climbed into my clammy oilskins, and went on deck.

At dawn I hoisted the White Ensign to the gaff peak, as worn by Captain Dacre and the Duke. Shortly after, Dacre came on deck and looked round him quick and furtive, as if he expected to be fired on.

'Herrings comin' up,' called Sam from the forepeak. Dacre had lost a little of his neatness. The mention of herrings turned him greenish, so I told Sam to knock him up some toast and tea instead. After a while Sam came aft with the tray and wedged that in a corner of the cockpit. Dacre took a swig of tea, then spat that over the side. 'Haven't you got any China?' he said.

'That's what that is,' said Sam. 'Dint I boil that long enough?'

As I now said, that was Sam and gentry for you.

Not long after, an odd thing happened.

We were properly out in the middle of things, perhaps midway between the Swale and Ijmuiden, nothing showing but a topsail on the horizon to the south. As we ploughed on, even that vanished. Then after half an hour a sort of smudge came up ahead, like the mark an inky thumb would leave on a sheet of grey paper.

That is a tedious business, being a skipper on passage, trying to make life interesting for the passenger, so this was a bit of a Godsend. I pointed that out to Dacre. Up that smudge comes, getting thicker and blacker, and that is definitely smoke. Dacre bobs down the companion hatch and comes up with a set of binoculars, which he trains on that smoke, wobbling a bit like a man not used to using glasses off of a moving deck. And something happened to his face.

In about two breaths that went from pretty hearty to dead white, and for a minute I thought he was going to sick up again. He moved his lips, that had gone hard and thin. He said, 'Ships.'

Well, you get ships on the sea. But I took the glasses out of his hand, and had a look. He was right, that was ships, half a dozen of them, low-slung grey chaps with three funnels apiece, all of them blowing out coal smoke and pushing big white bow waves, little sticky gun barrels poking out of barbettes and turrets. They were too small for battleships, so that made them cruisers. You could see the ensigns on them, white, with black crosses outlined in white and a black cross in the top right hand corner.

'Germans,' I said. 'On exercise, by the look of them. Need all the exercise they can get, useless lot they are.'

He grabbed the glasses back, looked and set them down with a bang. 'Hide your charts,' he said.

'Do what?' I said.

He swore most unpleasant, and I saw him stuff the charts I had marked off of the notebooks the Duke's agent had given me into the crack at the back of the saloon settee. Then he came back on deck and screwed his neck round and looked up at the gaff peak, where the White Ensign was stretched out stiff on the breeze. 'Get it down,' he says.

'Get what down?'

'That flag. They'll think we're something to do with the Navy.'

'Well we are. You got your warrant to fly that thing so His Majesty can call upon you—'

'*Get it down*,' he said, in a cold hard voice. So I gave him the tiller and ran forward along the boom to the mast, and pulled that down. Orders is orders.

'What are you a-doing of?' said Sam, sticking his head out of the forepeak.

'Dacre want the ensign down,' said I – a little put out, I must say, because that is an honour to fly a White Ensign, and when you are up agin a foreign Power that pays to put on the best show you can.

Dacre was trying to steer, making a wake like a half drunk eel. He shouted, 'Put up whatever you fly on a normal yacht.'

So I dug a Red Ensign out of the locker and hauled that up to the peak. Then I went back and took the tiller before Dacre had us sailing back the way we had come. And I said to him, 'So what if they do think we're the Navy?'

He turned on me a face that had gone from white with fear to white with anger. 'Do your job,' he said. 'Or so help me I will smash you.' As you can imagine, that made me pretty cross. Then I thought about the bailiff and the newspaper cutting and I told myself, bide your time, boy.

The cruisers were hull up now, surging down on us at fifteen knots. We sat there, tooling along full and by, old *Gloria* trimmed up pretty as we could. The screws of those ships came ticking through the timbers, and the ticking became a whir and a moan of bearings, and then they were sweeping by, great proud monsters, half a cable's length away. I said to Sam, 'Dip that ensign.'

He dipped, and the cruiser that was in the van dipped back very mannerly, and Sam gave a bit of a wave. She was close enough so you could see the little chaps up there at her rail, above the grey wall of the ship's side and below the gasometer of her forward funnel. They must have seen Sam, but they stood there like stuffed ducks, not waving back. There was no call for them to wave as far as strict manners went, of course. But manners and friendliness are not the same thing, and that would have been friendly, at least. At the time, I was so irritated with Dacre that I hardly noticed. But I did think about that later.

Then they were all past, and *Gloria* was shovelling their wake up with her bow and chucking that aft down the decks and into the cockpit. For all she had a beam like a barge I never did come across a boat as wet as *Gloria*.

'Lucky we didn't meet that lot in the dark,' I said.

'Would have been better,' said Dacre. 'Far better.'

'Sorry?'

'None of your damned business,' says Dacre.

Sam gave me a sort of old man's look that said, take that easy, boy, don't you worry your head with this one, and he was right. Dacre sat down out of the breeze at the front end of the cockpit, and started writing in a little black artist's sketchbook, the kind you can tear the pages out of.

Funny chap, Dacre.

Letter from Captain Eric Dacre, late ——th Lancers, to Miss Erica Dacre, St Jude's, Eastbourne, Sussex.

At Sea

Dear Sis,

Well, it's me again. I wonder if you have felt hot liquid in your ears of late? If so, this may be proof that there is no secrets between twins, as yours truly is, in the soup I mean, up to the neck as usual. But swimming, dear Sissy. Swimming.

It has been the Dickens of a year, keeping out of the way of silly sentimentals who recognize me from the papers. Then at Christmas instead of getting down to see you my dear old Sis His Grace sent me to Whitechapel, to look for some Jew devils who were plotting to shoot policemen. So in due course a house caught fire, oddly enough with the miscreants and some of their womenfolk inside. The women are as bad as the men. The papers, right as usual, said it was an anarchist feud! The police are looking for an anarchist who answers my description, seen leaving the house the day before the fire; there was an explosion heard, and infernal machines are suspected.

So what with one thing and another, His Grace thinks the country a little hot for me now. His Grace has been good enough to lead me to conclude that we have a special understanding of each other. On secret service I may be, but nobody ever said I was not the gentleman, I think.

So I am on another job, and a deuced ticklish job it is too. A couple of paid hands are taking me across this horrible North Sea on a little yacht. Sam, the mate, is an impertinent chap with a big moustache. The skipper goes by the name of Charlie Webb and is quite the swell in yachting circles, if you believe what he tells you.

68

He is a stocky little ha'porth, very young, quite a one for the ladies but at the same time a frightful prig with a tremendous 'chip on his shoulder.' The night before last I took them to the dear old Pelican. Dear old Hughie Drummond started acting the giddy goat with a little gun. And this fool of a Webb actually took the gun away from him. He was half an inch from getting his head blown off, but he was too cocky to realise it. And then to put the tin lid on it on the way out we bumped straight into some chap who recognized me, from the Whitechapel job or South Africa – 'the pace was too hot to enquire.' Well I shut him up, but I was awfully shaken and I think the hands suspect something. Never mind. I have come a long way since the days when I cared what servants thought of me.

Darling Sissy. I know you are with me, whatever comes to pass. I shall post this letter – well, you know when I shall post it; you and I only know.

I am your – as you are my – loving Twin and only Friend
Eric Dacre

CHAPTER NINE

The Watcher on the Pike

At four the morning after next we were lying on an oily grey swell with everything slatting and banging. After breakfast that filled in westerly, and away we went.

Soon after that I saw a sail ahead, and we went and spoke her. She was the *Flieger*, a trading ketch out of Ijmuiden with wheat for Aberdeen. Once upon a time she used to come in at Wells, and Pieter ten Boom, her skipper, used to come along to ours and give my mother the family news, then go out round the pubs and sell tobacco that he brought in in his bunk mattress. He was old now, a jolly old dog with a grey and yellow beard and a rattling pipe, and a couple of grandchildren playing on the hatchcover. Wheezing, he asked us in Fries where we were bound.

'The Pike,' says I, also in Fries, and up went his eyebrow, the Pike being no better than a sandbank. Dacre had come into the cockpit when he had heard the voices and the clatter of the ketch's sails. I felt his fingers clamp on my arm. 'Bird-watching,' I said. 'You got a position?'

Pieter looked at Dacre's hand on my arm and sucked his pipe but said nothing. Then he went and fished up his deck slate and told us we were fifty miles west northwest of the Ems. I swapped a bottle of the Duke's whisky for a box of cigars, which brightened his humour. He said that trade was bad in Ostfriesland. 'Watch yourself up there, my friend,' he said.

'For why?'

'Lot of Germans around,' he said. 'Nosy Parker Germans. They search my ship, month back. How's that Hetty?'

'Haven't seen her,' I said, pretty curt.

'Women,' he said.

'What does he say?' said Dacre. I told him. 'What do you mean, searched?' he said, in German, very sharp.

'Naval ship,' said Pieter. 'Called *Blitz*. She's all over the place up there. Ask anyone. Captain's been passed over for promotion, they say, so he's trying to show what a useful chap he is by harassing the poor bloody trader. Asked us if we'd been foreign. Looked everywhere. Found nothing. You wait and see.' He unbacked his staysail and drew away westward.

Dacre looked after him, tapping his bottom lip with his finger, and I noticed that for all his dandy habits he chewed his nails. Then he fumbled a cigar out of the box and began to blow hard puffs of smoke like an engine. Not much showed in those slits of eyes, but I got the idea he was a worried man.

On we went eastwards. The westerly fell light under a high, cold sky, with showers of rain. A little after midnight we were ten miles north of the islands, with the flood tide starting under our keel. At about four Dacre came on deck in an oilskin over his pyjamas, and I could hear his teeth chatter. He looked over the bow, and I saw him jump. 'What's that?' he said.

For out of the murk on the port bow, in front and to the left, had come a great white flash of light.

'Helgoland,' I said. 'Lighthouse.'

'Shit,' he said, very nasty. I got the idea his nerves were bad. *Gloria* tripped on a wave, and the fall of one of the reefing tackles swept the cockpit at head height. I ducked, but Dacre did not, and that caught him on the crown of the head, a gentle slap really. I saw his hand steal up, furtive, and pat his hair straight, vain as a woman with a hat. Fussy little beggar, Dacre.

Helgoland was the first mark for entry into the Weser, on the starboard bow now, ahead and to the right, that is. The estuaries of the Weser and the Jade make a great bay in the southern shore of the German Bight. Between the two rivers has arisen a huge sandbank they call the Hohes Weg or the Pike, a triangle of sand ten miles across the base and fifteen miles high. The eastern margin of this bank is formed by the bed of the Weser, the western by the Jade. The plan this morning was to go up the

Weser, if we could find that, and approach the Frisian islands from the east, as if from Jutland or the Canal.

So I brought the boat across the wind till that was blowing in my right ear. The light was growing, and I could make out Dacre's face. He was looking at Helgoland still flashing over the transom. 'Folly,' he said, every hair in place.

'Beg pardon?'

'Giving it back.'

That had belonged to England till 1890; at least, I presume that was what he was on about.

'Giving away a fortress in the front line,' said Dacre. 'Handing it to the enemy on a plate.'

'The enemy?' I said. Because the Germans were not the enemy, not by a long chalk.

He paid no attention. 'Jacky Fisher was against it,' he said. 'His Grace was against it. But the Government did it anyway. Damn fools.'

Admiral Fisher was the First Lord of the Admiralty, always seeing wars where there were none. As long as Helgoland light was kept lit and spinning I could not care less who that belonged to. I gave Sam a hail and told him to get breakfast going. On we went, the plates and roils of the tide gurgling round the hull. Ahead and to port the Alte Weser beacon was sticking out of the grey water. The wind was dropping. All you could see in front of the mast was a cold grey sheet of water that faded into haze at its edges. That was a place with no beginning and no end; hardly a place at all, unless you knew better.

I knew better.

One minute the world was shades of grey like a photographic print. The next the eastern horizon became a lemon-coloured streak that grew a fiery bulge and the sun bounced pop into the sky, and suddenly all that one-colour world was blue and green and yellow, with a string of Eider duck trailing across the bow, and round the rim of the sea the grey-green line of Germany. Dacre did not appreciate the beautifulness of that. He gave that a look like a Gatling volley and took himself below.

The tide was turning, the breeze scarce enough to blow away the smoke from the galley stovepipe. *Gloria* lumbered across the greasy blue water in a tangle of grey fumes. Helgoland had been washed away by the tide of light. Ahead was our new mark; a long, low hump of dun-coloured sand crowned with white birds: Alte Mellum.

Alte Mellum is nothing more than a big sandbank, the only part of the Pike that is above high water mark. We moved out of the main flow of the estuary and into the swatchways, the channels the tide has routed out of the bank. Not for fun, mark you. There was a reason.

Dacre came on deck and scraped most of his breakfast herrings over the side as if he hated the sight of them. He swept his narrow red eyes across the flat blue water. He said, 'What's happening?'

'Tide ebbing,' I said, offhand, because I was listening to Sam calling the depths, feeling for the edge of the channel with his lead. Then from the corner of my eye I saw Dacre's face change as if he had seen a ghost.

Over to port, the top of the sea had been seized by a mysterious convulsion. That writhed for a moment, then fell into white-edged ribbons of breaker. And out of the sea, slow but smooth, there rose a sweating brown hump – not high, but remarkable because apart from Alte Mellum that was the only feature in all that great sheet of water.

'What the bloody hell's that?' excuse me, said Dacre. He was hard, but he was jumpy. Brave chap with a woman or a bailiff, but water he did not like.

'Bottom of the sea,' said I, pretty short. 'Tide ebbing.'

We moved through the morning at the pace a horse would walk, while all around us, slow and silent, the banks rose. Where *Gloria* had been ghosting across a sheet of glass, she now glided up an alley of water between banks of sand smooth as a woman's flanks. The dun hump of Alte Mellum slid above them as if over a range of low hills.

Into a tangle of channels we moved, following the charts I had drawn from the black books the Duke's agent had given me, Sam calling the depths from the chains. And I have to tell you that whoever had made that survey was so far spot on.

After a mile or two we anchored. The wind was getting up

again, but behind our screen of banks we were as sheltered as we had been in Limehouse Basin, and a good deal more peaceful. Once the hook was dug in we got our heads down.

As I lay in my bunk I felt the first soft touch of keel on bottom, the heel of the boat as she ceased to be a creature of the sea and became a creature of the land, and all those bits of string up there began to tap and click and rattle, the weary frames to groan under the load of gravity. I woke a couple of hours later and went on deck. The pool we had anchored in was a dry dip in a sandy desert. There was only the scream of the terns, and far in the background the mutter and roar that would be the breakers on the outer banks of the Hohes Weg. Dacre was standing in the hatch, looking out at the sand with his blank little face. You could tell he found that strange, and even a bit frightening. He started to ask questions. He did not know which questions to ask, of course, so I helped him out, as was my duty. I explained as how there was high water about every twelve hours, how the phases of the moon decided where that was neaps or springs, and how the tides were shrinking at the moment but would be getting bigger again in a little more than a week's time. He pricked his ears up at that, and started to chew his nails, and scribbled something in his notebook.

I thought, fair exchange is no robbery. I summoned up my courage, and said, 'Did you ever hear of someone called Dollmann?'

'What if I have?'

'Young lady came on board,' I said. 'A Miss Dollmann. Said a chap called Wilson was over here looking for her father.'

'Dollmann's's dead,' said Dacre.

'So she said. That was Wilson she was worried about.'

Dacre looked at me like he was going to hit me. 'Now you listen here Webb,' he said. 'You forget what the girls tell you and what an important chap you are. You are asking questions whose answers you would not understand. If you do not stop poking your nose someone will cut it off.'

'Yessir,' I said, pretty cross, but interested in what that was that made him jump at this Wilson's name so violent. ' 'Spectful duty, sir. Sorry you was bothered, sir.' And I sort of backed away.

I suppose a sensible person would have left it at that. Not me, though. I was a racer, you see, trained racing against Joe Smith and educated in socialism and anarchy by Hetty. And with that kind of education, you wait, and do your work, and look for your chance.

For the moment I picked up the chart and went over the side. I walked up the bed of that dry river in the sand – to cool off certainly, but out of professional necessity too, to test the charts we had been given.

After 200 yards the river deepened into a pool that still held water. Out of the pool there led another channel, marked with birch poles with the twigs still on; withies, we called them at home, though they were marked on the chart as booms, which is what the gentlemen call them – marked correct, I may say, in the right spot according to my compass and what I stepped out. Whoever had done the survey had done that proper, gentleman or not.

From the top of the banks you could see the sands of the Pike stretch away in all directions, pricked here and there with little combs of withy marking other channels. Down to the south was the Kaiserbalje, the main channel across the base of the flats. There were more pools down there, and a bristle of masts that would be trading boats waiting for the tide. I stepped out three more of the channels – *watt* passages, was the name they went by in these parts. Two of them were good high water routes across the bank. The third was a bit of a lesson, though. The withies were there, but the channel was no more than a dint in the sand, a good way away from its markers. That was like at home in the Wash; in the space of six months a channel could squirm off into the sands and vanish.

As I started back the way I had come the mutter of the banks was more urgent, and the breeze had freshened, cold and north-northwest now, with plenty of winter left in it. I pulled my coat around my ears and quickened my pace.

I had been away longer than I had meant; the tide had turned, and was making briskly. My studies had taken me away from *Gloria* in a sort of curve, and now I headed back towards the leaning whisker of her mast in a straight line. As I crossed the first dry creek, a tongue of water swept up its bed, a grey, liverish tongue edged with yellow foam. I splashed through that and on to the next slight rise of the sand, which was like a low island between the creek I had just crossed and the next one along.

There was a line of footprints lying diagonal to my path and diverging, that I took vague notice of, there being no other footprints out here that I had seen. Sam, I supposed, or Dacre, out taking the air. I crossed the rise of ground and started down towards the creek, the strange footprints moving away and to the left—

I stopped.

The next creek, the last one before *Gloria*, was already a ribbon of water swept with small tidal waves. That was not the water that got my attention, though. That was something that was lying dark and bundled in the sand by the side of the creek.

Nothing had changed. The breeze blew, the tide flowed, and over Alte Mellum the gulls danced like sparks over a bonfire. But all of a sudden I was half perished with fright. I up and ran over the sand to the creek, and stood there with my breath in my ears and a chill in my bones.

The dark thing lay half-in, half-out of the water. What was out of the water was a pair of legs, in jackboots. What was in was a head, with brown hair cropped short and a mottled-purple face with open red eyeballs, and an open mouth the water flowed into then out of with a nasty little gurgle that fair to made me sick.

What that added up to was a German soldier.

A dead one.

CHAPTER TEN

Gloria Clears Customs

I caught hold of one of the legs and tried to pull him up out of the water. His boot came off, and I sat down plunk in the sand. Then I grabbed but he was a big chap, and try as I might I could not shift him. As I pulled, the thoughts skittered in my head. How's he dead, when did he die, what are we to do? He had not been under water yet, by the look of him. So he had died since the banks had dried out. What of, though? An apoplexy, perhaps. Bluish face, mottled. Sure to be an apoplexy.

I hauled away at that fish-cold hand. There were marks on the neck that did not look like apoplexy. To tell the truth they looked more like fingers. But who would strangle a German soldier?

All of a sudden my right boot filled up with water. I could see *Gloria*'s deck, Sam moving about. I waved to him, half-frantic. He waved back and went about his business. My other boot filled up. The tide was gaining on me, and there was the best part of half a mile between me and *Gloria*, and a great part of what had just now been sand had become water. If I did not get a shift on, there would be two bodies out here instead of one.

So I took myself off and splashed and waded back to *Gloria*, and stepped myself up on the bobstay.

'What you got?' said Sam, seeing me shiver I suppose.

I told him.

'Pore devil,' said Sam, very philosophical.

When we went back in the dinghy he was gone; the tide would have rolled him away, and a corpse will not float for the best part of twenty-four hours after that drowns.

Dacre's face stayed hard and neat when we told him. 'We shall

77

report it,' he said, 'to the appropriate authorities.' He did not look too worried, but that was his way, of course. So Sam and I upped anchor and hoisted a staysail and moved on along the line of withies.

I said to Sam, 'Did you see anyone out there on the sand?'

'Couple of chaps on Alte Mellum,' said Sam. 'Sojers, I thought. Lookin at us with glasses. While you was asleep, that was. No more 'n you'd expect.'

'Then what?' I was looking at all that innocent water, with somewhere a purple-faced body rolling around.

'Paid 'em no mind,' said Sam. 'You went off walking. I had a bit of a leg stretch myself; hour, two hours. So did Dacre. What did you say he died of, this poor beggar?'

'Apoplexy,' I said. Dacre came up through the hatch. You could see by his face that he had been listening. 'When did you want to inform the authorities, sir?'

'When we clear Customs.'

'There's Hooksiel just over the water—'

'It'll keep till Norderney. He's in no hurry, poor devil.' He did look a little stirred up, Dacre; a little shiny about the forehead and frantic about the eye. I was thinking about the marks on the man's neck. I was thinking about Dacre and the dun, hit first ask questions after, the hardness of the man, the way you could never tell what he was thinking—

But that was just foolishness. What would be the reason for killing a soldier in a country where you had arrived for a bit of a salvage investigation, confidential but by no means illegal?

Absolutely no reason at all. Webb, I told myself. You are in danger of getting yourself into a stew about this here Dacre. Steady on, boy.

Ahead, the withies writhed like an eel in a pan as we crossed the middle of the Hohes Weg. A little later we put her hard on the wind, and started to beat out of the deep-water channel of the Jade, Yellow Jack fluttering from the starboard shrouds.

That was a cold evening, with a churchy feel that came from a poor dead soldier, and a ribbed grey roof, and a blackish floor, and tomorrow Good Friday. A gunboat was going up the tide for Wilhelmshaven, and a couple of *muttes* were running goosewinged like rusty nuns. They would have pitied us, I expect, thrashing up that channel with the wind and the last of the tide in our teeth while *Gloria* made her two points of leeway. Twice we tacked under the mainland, the huge rampart of dyke at its edge dividing the heaven from the earth. In the dusk we turned away and slid westward, inside the Frisian Islands now, along a line of withies that took us south of the island of Wangerooge. We slunk across the banks and anchored for the night in a pool at the hub of a vast desolation of purple mud. Dacre rested his eye on a flock of greenshank. 'Perhaps we'll get Customs here,' he said.

But there were no Customs that night, only a couple of trading boats sliding by on the new flood. Good Friday morning started rainy, but cleared as we thrashed through the wind-over-tide past the Westturm, a great church tower that stands on the west end of Wangerooge with its feet in the sea. Once outside, we caught the ebb west for Norderney.

That was two o'clock in the afternoon when we ploughed the last of the ebb down the Dove Tief and into the Riffgat. A seal humped down a bank and sank away. There was no sound except the gurgle of the wake and the groan of the mainsheet as that stretched in a puff.

And all of a sudden, the tick of a ship's screw.

A grey gunboat had fallen in astern, a sharkish sort of an object with a tall funnel and a low bow that would be a shovel on a lumpy day. *Blitz*, said the letters on her wheelhouse: Pieter ten Boom's nosy devil. We ghosted past the fishing harbour pierhead, and tied up. As I put a spring round a bollard I saw that the gunboat was hovering close outside the entrance.

'That body,' said Dacre. 'Leave all that to me.'

I nodded, and started getting ready for Customs.

The usual routine was a bit of conversation, a form filled in, our tobacco smoked pretty heavy and perhaps a glass or two taken. So I told Sam to put out the whisky and cigars and light the stove, and get the salt ready for exhibition, salt being for some reason a thing they took a great interest in.

Then we got an idea of what had shocked Pieter.

We had not been alongside three minutes when they came down the ladder: two sharp-faced chaps about my age, an older one with a gullwing moustache and various chins, and about two hundred buttons between the three of them. They frowned at the Red Ensign on its staff, clumped into the cockpit without wiping their boots, and walked straight past the whisky and cigars and into the saloon. Moustaches hit his head on the way in, which did not improve his temper. He did not even mention salt. He gave me a long form to fill in and started burrowing away through the passports and the ships' papers, while the sharp-faced chaps began crawling round the saloon lockers. They finished with the saloon and went through the little door and into the fore cabin.

I went after them. I said, in English, 'Okay, gents?'

They stood there – well, crouched, because that was what you did in *Gloria*, her only having five foot-odd of headroom. What they saw was a bunk, all made up neat, with sheets, blankets and hospital corners all complete. They went to work, never a smile between them, prodding the mattress, whipping up the deck boards, squinting at the corned beef and beer. All the while Dacre sat in the cockpit, puffing at his cigar with a face like stone. And I wondered what on earth had could have happened to change things so.

That took those ardent lads the best part of an hour to go through everything. But they did not find the diving dress under the big dirty pile of anchor chain in the locker, nor anything else of importance. At the finish we all went up into the cockpit, and Moustaches stood to attention and yelled at us, or rather Dacre, in German with a powerful Fries accent.

That was an odd speech for a Customs man. The burden of it was that of course the German peoples welcomed the British gentry and their yachts to the islands. But (he yelled) there were rules, and in particular rules that forbade any access to the mainland except Norddeich. Norddeich was a large size of a port and indeed perfect in every respect, he said. The other ports were insignificant, ugly, and above all closed, owing to works in progress to extend the sea wall and the coastal polder, for the benefit of coastal defenses and the general agricultural improvement of the region. Moustaches was sure Herr Dacre would understand.

Dacre gave him solemn undertakings and offered him a drink. For a moment a small, stout man with a liking for spirits showed around the edges of the moustache. Then he clicked his heels and said '*Nein*,' the sweat of self-denial trickling into his collar. He gathered together his lads and left. I saw Dacre pull out a handkerchief and blow his nose, and when he thought nobody was looking pat his brow. Then he went ashore, to report the dead soldier to the police, I supposed.

Sam and I spent the afternoon cleaning ship, then went ashore. That was a place like Cromer or Eastbourne, full of big hotels with a clean, empty look, and a promenade with old folks getting pushed around in Bath chairs. There were a couple of nice-looking nurses, but Sam dragged me off to a street behind the hotels where there was a shop at which we bought fresh stores. When we went back to the boat I got my head down, and waited for the police to arrive. They did not come. I was woken some time after seven in the evening by Sam frying bacon and herrings, for a change.

'Good smell,' said a voice from over the side. I stuck my head out of the hatch. That was dark, of course. There was a punt alongside. The black shape of a tall man was standing in its sternsheets, made taller by a high-crowned cap with a badge that gleamed faintly in the saloon lights. Behind him, split and dancing in the black water of the harbour entrance, shone the anchor light of the *Blitz*.

'I am coming aboard,' said the figure, in a German with none of the singsong of Fries. He stepped into the cockpit without so much as a by your leave. But he was like that, as we later found out: active, friendly, but pushy – never pushy enough to offend, but always confident he would get his own way, and getting it. 'Von Brüning,' he said. 'Leutnant commanding His Imperial Majesty's gunboat *Blitz*. And you are?'

I told him. He was five years older than me, with a chestnut beard and very sharp eyes. In fact I straightway got the idea that this von Brüning was a very sharp chap all round. That and the general oddness of things made me uncomfortable enough to keep an eye on him. So after I had showed him into the saloon I sat in the dark cockpit and turned my ears and eyes to that little yellow slot between the hatch cover and the cabin doors.

I could see their heads over the saloon table, Dacre's black thatch, von Brüning's high forehead and clever eyes, creased about the sockets as if he did not get enough sleep, or was under strain of some kind.

Von Brüning admired the boat a bit, and used that as a pretext for having a good look round. Then he said that was early for a cruise in these waters.

'Oh, I don't know,' said Dacre, and I could see he was going to play the silly toff. 'Haven't got much time, week or two . . . Good chance of an easterly to blow us back home, this time of year, I am told.' He smiled, a silly sort of smile. 'New to this,' he said. 'Doctor's orders. Get out of the office, he said.'

'The office?' said von Brüning.

'Lloyd's,' said Dacre, and I was astonished because if that had been me I should have kept that quiet. 'Insurance, you know.'

'I have heard of Lloyd's,' said von Brüning, very patient. 'When did you arrive on this side of the North Sea?'

'Night before last,' said Dacre. 'Seems a lifetime.'

'And what have you seen?'

'Alte Mellum. Terns. Hoping for a Caspian.'

'Ah,' said von Brüning. 'The Pike, eh?'

I waited. I waited for Dacre to say, we found a body out there; or for von Brüning to say, the police tell me you saw a body on the sand.

But neither of them so much as mentioned it.

I sat there with my mouth hanging open. I did not believe a dead body was not worth a mention. And as the moments slid by, I came to a conclusion.

When Dacre had gone ashore, he had not gone anywhere near the police.

Von Brüning had the chart drawer open now. He had pulled out a chart and spread that on the table.

I craned forward, in case he said anything useful about the survey I had marked on that. Then I thought, Hello.

The chart on the table was identical to the one I had marked up. But that was not the one I had marked up. That was as that had come from the printers, without detail.

Why on earth would Dacre think that necessary to switch them?

'An interesting bank,' said von Brüning, with his finger on Alte Mellum. 'Black terns, I believe.'

I wanted to shout, because any fool knows that black terns are marsh nesters, not sandbank nesters, and that was a trap.

Dacre said, non-committal, 'I'll look out for them next time.' He was doing a very clever thing, I suddenly realised. He was not telling the truth, but without ever committing himself to a lie. I had the sudden thought that while Sam and I were on *Gloria* because we were high-class sailors, Dacre was there because he was a high-class liar.

'Well,' said von Brüning heartily. 'Now you are here, what are your plans?'

'Beauties of nature,' said Dacre. 'More birds. You know.'

'And is that a shooting punt on deck?' said von Brüning.

'Duck punt,' said Dacre. 'Yes. But not for shooting. It's not the season, you know.' He said this with the air of a man stupid enough not to realise that von Brüning would know very well when the shooting started and stopped. I thought he was overdoing it. 'Ornithology. Mount for telescope. Know nothing, of course. Hoping to learn.' Again the silly laugh. 'My skipper. Old Charlie. He knows.'

'He didn't look very old to me.'

'Well no,' said Dacre. 'He's not. But he knows a lot. So that's how you think of him, old, I mean. You know, what, eh?'

Von Brüning nodded. 'Curious you should work for Lloyd's,' he said. 'There have been salvage operations close by. On Memmert. An old bullion ship. I had a share in her myself. But they could find nothing. The sands move constantly, of course.'

'My word,' said Dacre, glazing over convincingly. 'Now look here, that Customs chap was saying that one can't go to the mainland harbours. That's a pity. I should have loved to take a look.'

Von Brüning shrugged. 'I am sorry,' he said. 'I am sure Herr Gruber explained. We are taking the opportunity of the spring to embark upon a comprehensive improvement of our coastal defenses, and at the same time try to improve trade for the farmers inland. It is good land, but much in need of drainage. So for the next four weeks, they are closed to all traffic. Except Norddeich, of course. But I think you will not find many nesting birds in Norddeich.'

'Oh, dear,' said Dacre, crestfallen.

'You would be better in the Dutch islands,' said von Brüning. 'All the harbours are open. Also the weather may be better.'

'Oh, I don't know,' said Dacre with a vagueness that was nothing like his normal self. 'We'll wait and see.'

Von Brüning shrugged, looking not altogether pleased. 'Well, if you are determined I will find you a local man as a guide.'

Dacre laughed. 'Wouldn't dream of it,' he said. 'Charlie's good enough for me.'

'I insist,' said von Brüning. 'So far you have been lucky. The channels are difficult, and the weather is not always so kind.'

Dacre said, 'Oh, we'll rub along.'

The two men smiled politely, definitely at cross purposes. 'I must be off,' said von Brüning, and rose to go. I turned away. Von Brüning came into the cockpit. I saw him on to his punt.

'You have done well with your pilotage,' he said from its sternsheets.

'We get by,' said I, unaccountably nervous of him.

'The charts are not good.'

'We've got a lead line.'

'You speak excellent German.'

'Thanks.'

'Is that a Fries accent?'

'Dunno.'

Like opening an oyster with your bare hands, he would be thinking. He gave an order to the oarsmen, and the punt thumped smartly across the black water towards the *Blitz*.

I went forward to the black hole, where all this time Sam had been frizzling up dinner. I sat down in the greasy fug. I said, 'He didn't tell them.'

'Tell who what?'

'About that dead soldier. He didn't tell the police.'

Sam chiselled away at the frying pan with a rusty knife. 'See his point,' he said.

'But he was dead. Strangled.'

Bacon started hissing. 'Apoplexy, you said.'

'There were marks on his neck.'

'What was Dacre doing while I was asleep?'

'Not a lot. Had a kip. Went off for a leg stretch, I believe.

I looked inside my head at the footprints in the sand. There had only been one set. But the body had been in a creek. The murderer could have come off *Gloria*, walked up the creek bed, done the deed and come back, without once putting his foot on dry sand.

''Scuse my asking,' said Sam. 'But presuming you are imagining that sojer was murdered, why would Dacre want to do that?'

There was no reason. Except the newspaper clipping about Annie de Blank, and the way he had smashed up the bailiff, and the anger of the man. But what I said was, 'He never reported the body.'

'Hell,' said Sam. 'That is Germans you are talking about.'

'Did he give you his trousers to dry?'

'Matter of fact he did,' said Sam. 'But we all had wet trousers, so that don't prove nathen. Now look you here, you are getting all steamed up for no reason. That pore chap died of an apoplexy, and if you mention him to these here Germans we'll be here till hell freeze.'

That was Sam for you. Hated the police, Customs, anyone in a uniform. I did my best to believe he did not have a point.

'Pore chap's dead. Can't get no deader,' said Sam, summing up. 'Now are you going to jabber on all night or do you want your tea?'

As soon as I had my knife in my hand, Dacre was banging on the door. 'Come aft,' he says. 'I want to talk to you.'

A proper gentleman would have smelt the bacon and waited. But Dacre knew what Dacre wanted, and that was up to others to fit in. So back to the saloon I went.

'What did he say?' I said.

'Mind your own bloody business,' he said.

As I now said, I was young enough for the idea to flit through my mind that that would be pleasant to give him a good spanking. But I had been at sea long enough to know that sort of thinking can turn a boat into a hell afloat. He said, 'I want to be out of here early in the morning. Very early in the morning.'

'Where to?' I said.

'Closer to the wreck,' he said. 'And, er, look here, I don't want any gunboats watching. Salvage is a private matter, that's the ticket. I thought Memmert.' He fumbled in the settee cushions. 'I took your charts,' he said, handing them over.

'I'll thank you in future to ask first,' I said, for revenge really, childish that was.

When I stuck my head out of the hatch the tide was making quickish, and the breeze had dropped to no more than a breath. I ran up the slimy ladder to the quay as if I was checking the warps. I made as if I was slacking them off a bit, but really I put them on slips, which means once round the bollard and back onto the deck, so you can cast off without troubling anybody such as gunboats. What Dacre wished for, Dacre would have. The *Blitz* was nice and quiet beyond the pierheads. My bet was that her furnace would be banked, and that she would take half an hour easy to get up steam.

I set the green brass alarm for one. Then I put my head down and went to sleep.

CHAPTER ELEVEN

Moon over the Sands

The clock got one bang out of its guts before I put a hand to it. I could feel that we were afloat, and a bit of a breeze was blowing, and my head was aching. But a head will ache if you give that a long passage and not much sleep, and the only way to stop that is to go on deck and work.

So I gave Sam a shove, and I swear he did not stop snoring until his feet were halfway into his boots. Up we tumbled on deck.

The breeze had brought in a marbling of high cloud that threw a ring of cold colours round the moon. The *Blitz*'s anchor light twinkled in the crisp black ripples like a yellow star. Sam pulled the jib topsail into clear air, and the bow came off the wall. I held onto the stern line till she had pivoted, then let go and hauled in. *Gloria* ghosted between the pierheads and into the roadstead. My headache was already gone.

The *Blitz* slid by to port, the tide gurgling loud round her anchor chain. There was a dim light in her wheelhouse, but no other sign of life. She shrank astern, and Sam and I hauled the mainsail up the mast. *Gloria* leaned her shoulder in and ploughed on across the *seegat* between Norderney and Juist. I was watching the compass and trying to judge the speed of the ebb and the rate she was sagging across the breeze, and point her bow according, and get that right . . .

The reason, if you will pardon a little lecture about matters already touched on, being this.

I now said the Frisian Islands are a dotted line of big sandbanks, with grass on top and gaps called seegats between. Outside is what Admiral Tirpitz was in those days pleased to call the German Ocean, which behaves the way you would expect a German sea to behave, cold and stiff. Inside the islands that is different.

What happens inside the islands is that when the flood tide comes up the North Sea, that sweeps round the east and west ends of each island, the east a little after the west. When the tide has swept round an island that moves in behind it like the pincers of a crab, the west pincer a bit longer than the east. As the currents start to run into each other head to head, they slow down, as I now mentioned on the Pike. And at a certain point they balance each other out and come to a dead stop.

Now you must remember that this is dirty old North Sea water, loaded up with sand and silt and rubbish. And the slower that dirty water moves, the more mud and sand that lets fall.

So if you looked at the whole business from the side, that would look like a low sort of a hill. The valley is the *seegat*, the deep channel the tide scours out between the islands. And the mountain pass, the *wattenhoch* or as I shall call that from now on the watershed, is the place where the tides having met stand still and drop their mud. You can see that easy enough as the tide ebbs. The watershed dries right out. On either side, the main channel becomes a river, drying as the ebb proceeds; so you have two rivers, back to back, running away from each other and shrinking, so that a channel with twelve foot of water at high water springs vanishes to a dry gulley at the ebb.

So now, one-third down the tide, I was staring down *Gloria's* deck and along her bowsprit, and what I was seeing was mostly night over water, black as your hat and to all appearances deep as a dungeon. But as I hope you will have noticed, appearances are deceiving. Most of that water was between no foot and seven foot deep. Which was convenient, given that what the boss seemed to need was a place deep enough for us, but too shallow for the *Blitz* and her steam cutter.

On through the night we sailed. All you could see was the yellow glim in the binnacle, and a faint red and green loom from the running lamps—

Sam said, 'Withy.'

Juist was well up on the starboard bow now, a long black whale of a thing, no lights. And ahead, standing a eight foot out of the water, was the black wraith of a tree branch. We swept by, hearing its cold shiver in the tide. I looked for the next one, but did not see it.

'Sound,' I said.

From astern there came the flash of the Norderney light. Up there Sam was heaving the lead, hoarse with sleep. 'Two fathom,' he sang. 'No withy.' Haul, splash as the lead went in, hit the bottom, swung vertical. 'One and a half. No bloody withy. What they done with 'em?'

We were fighting the tide here, three hours after high water now. We moved on, slow, sailing blind over the twists and turns of that channel, weaving around so Sam could knock his lead against its sides, squinting at the chart by the binnacle glim. 'By the deep, one,' sang Sam. 'By the deep, four foot. By the Christ, ent no water—'

There was a slight check underfoot, a tremor of the deck and a rough slithering. The wind seemed to freshen, and *Gloria* lay over on her side, pressed down by her sails. Everything was quiet except for the hiss of the breeze, and somewhere out in the dark a curlew whistling. We were aground.

Dacre came on deck like a jack-in-the-box. 'What's that beastly noise?' he said.

Sam and I soothed him, then laid out a kedge (which is an anchor) with the dinghy, and hauled on the cable with the windlass. But the tide was dropping, and we were stuck fast.

In my sleep I heard the tide gurgle down the side and fade away to nothing. Beyond my eyelids I could feel the moon rolling round the sky. When I opened them that was three o'clock. The breath-steam on the hatch scuttle was grey with the false dawn, and the moon was hanging low over the flats.

Dacre was wearing a nightcap, snoring. The chloral bottle was in the shelf above his head. I put the chart in front of him and tapped my finger on the watt a third of the distance west of the east end of Juist. 'Gone aground here, sir. You can walk to Memmert. High water at nine. I'll come along of you.'

'I'll go by myself,' he said.

'Tricky tides, sir,' I said, thinking I would go along and see what he got up to.

'Oh,' he said, a little nervous, I thought. 'I'll want a sandwich.'

As I went on deck I heard Sam clanking away in the galley, and Dacre cursing as he tried to hit his trouser legs with his feet. I went into the foc'sle to fetch my water boots.

The lamp was lit, hanging at a mad angle on its gimbals. Sam had the kettle attached to the stove with lengths of gardening wire. He had sawed off a couple of slices from the loaf he had bought in Norderney, and was slapping on butter. He opened a tin of corned beef, dug a knife in that, and said, 'What the *hell* is this here?'

Well I was paying very little attention, because I was trying to jam my feet into my water boots with two extra pair of socks on. When I glanced up Sam was standing there snorting into his moustache and holding up on his knife something that looked like putty. 'That's off,' I said. 'Hull that over the side and give him the bacon from last night.'

'What about you?'

'I'll look after myself,' I said, for that was early, and I was cross, thinking, blow you Sam you are my mate not my mother.

So Sam fired the bad tin over the side, and I put the bacon sandwich in a canvas bag with a bottle of beer, and Dacre told me I could carry that. Then he slung a pair of glasses round his neck and dropped over the side, and I went after him.

We marched off over the grey sand, treading on the heels of shadows a hundred yards long, heading for a black rise of ground a long way ahead. Behind us I could see the black mass of *Gloria*, very small already on those moonfrosted flats.

Me and Dacre we walked along the south side, the landward side that is, of what started off as a groove in the sand and became with distance a fair-sized limb of the sea marked on the chart as the Juister Balje. The sun rolled up, and our shadows turned from black to brown. In two and a half hours we had walked seven miles, and were coming level with the end of the island of Juist, and the Balje was opening out so you could see where that merged with the open sea. There was open water to the south of us, too, so that the sand we were walking on was a sort of a peninsula between two tongues of water; the Nordland sand, that was marked on the chart. Forming the westernmost tip of the sand, not much more than a mile away now, was Memmert, the rise of ground we had been aiming at. That was an overgrown sandbank like Alte Mellum, but with an iron beacon at its southern end and a bit of marram grass on a low line of dunes. A mass of gulls and terns wheeled above it, kicking up a great screaming.

The tide was flowing in good earnest, licking into the low spot we were crossing, and for a while we were splashing through water up to our ankles. Dacre had started walking very fast. His face was pale, his eyes darting about, and you could see he was only just stopping himself running. Hard man he might be, but that did look as if he was proper scared of water. Pretty soon the ground started to rise, and the sand changed from wet and solid to dry and blown, with bits of crisp bladder wrack and gulls' feathers. Then there was marram grass round our ankles, and we were up on the dunes with the terns bouncing round our heads.

That was a lonely place, made lonelier by the fact that when I looked back for *Gloria*, she had vanished into that huge sky. Across that low spot I was now talking about, a sheet of water was spreading.

The island was no more than half a mile wide. As I passed over the middle I could see a couple of sheds on a patch of ground covered with sea pink and wiry grass. Beyond the sheds was the bluey-grey Osterems, with beyond it Borkum, a low green hump in a fortification of sandbanks, and beyond that the Westerems and the Dutch border.

Dacre walked out onto the flat patch by the sheds, batting with his hands at half a dozen terns diving on his black head. I expected him to have a look round, then train his binoculars north, to the bank where his blessed *Corinne* was meant to be lying. Not a bit of it. He looked through his glasses, all right, but he was pointing them south, where the mainland sank away into the grey bight of the estuary. There were a few ships down there, a couple of *muttes* and a flock of what might have been tugs grinding up from Emden under black plumes of coal smoke.

I followed him down to the huts.

They were almost at the southern end of the island: two of them, set at right angles. The windows were boarded up, and on the roof loose bits of tar paper fluttered in the breeze. Sand had drifted against their tin sides, and against one of the half-dozen piles of railway sleepers stacked just above the high-water mark. Several pairs of terns were making agitated swoops above their nests in the patches of shingle between the tufts of grass. Anyone with eyes could see that if this had been a salvage base, that had not been used this year.

I tugged a yellowed piece of newspaper from under one of the piles of sleepers. *Emdener Zeitung*, said the Gothic script. *Juli 1902.* Last year's.

'Think they'll come back?' I said.

He shook his head, looking proper grim, which I remember thinking at the time was odd, because if you are racing for a wreck and the other chap pulls out, then your life is suddenly twice as easy as before. He went on down to the iron beacon at the south tip of the bank, and climbed up into its rusty iron struts, and gazed through his glasses a bit more. Then he came back to the huts and sat down on an old petroleum barrel that was lying in the grass, told me to hand him the bag and fished out his sandwich and his beer and demolished them in a hurry, not offering me any, of course. His bit of lunch seemed to brighten him. Half of that would have brightened me, too, because I was starving. But that was Dacre for you: out for what he wanted, and never a word to nobody. 'It's all here,' he said. 'Splendidly well-set-up operation. Exactly as I'd heard. She's sunk in thirty feet of water, apparently. You can't dig her out by normal methods. So what these chaps have been doing is sending down divers, blowing the sand away from the bottom with hoses, and putting in shores, sleepers or what have you, to stop the excavation caving in. Then the sands shift, and the timbers sink, and the gold, in bars according to the manifest, would sink further than any of the rest of it. Terribly expensive business, of course.' He looked at me with those narrow eyes, just as if he was checking to see if I believed him. Above his head a lark was singing fit to bust, telling everyone to keep clear of his patch.

We searched the sheds. They were empty, swept clean and boarded up. When we were done I went back to the top of the island and stood in the screaming birds with my stomach rumbling and the sand hissing round my boots. By the beacon at the southern end of the island Dacre stood looking down the river, making notes in his little black book. Looking the wrong way, as I now said.

He was all wrong, this Dacre.

Letter from Captain Eric Dacre, late — —th Lancers, to Miss Erica Dacre, St Jude's, Eastbourne, Sussex.
Juist
Frisian Islands

Dear Sissy,

Well here we are in a sort of prairie of sand and mud. One day it will be reclaimed as a useful part of someone's farm, I make no doubt. But for the moment it is an inexpressibly dreary place, torn by the ghastly cries of birds. We have cleared Customs, and advanced with the plan.

Just now we are conducting a preliminary reconnaissance, purpose to determine the lie of the land and to reassure the men. I must say that matters are less bad than I had feared they might be. Certainly we are being watched. But one of the watchers has already come to a bad end. And the Customs search was laughable. For the moment, the vigilance exerted upon us is at least remote – though I expect it to become less so. Frankly, there was a part of me that expected we would sail directly into a prison cell or worse. I can only assume that the enemy believe that any sign of hostility towards us will be taken as evidence of their guilt. Which means that they have no inkling of the reconnaissance undertaken last autumn, or Mr Childers' attractive romance, and that the ridiculous Wilson is dead or departed. As for Dollmann, we know that his fate in the book was invented. I am sure however that he is dead; as to how this came about, I neither know nor care.

At any rate, we now have a chance to drive a wedge between their wish to lull us in to unconsciousness, and their fear that action on their part will have diplomatic repercussions that may endanger their venture.

Meantime, I am coming to know the men. Sam the elder is steady, I think, though he will cook herrings which I abominate dear Sissy as you know. Webb is more complicated. He does possess a rudimentary form of intelligence and is a ladies' man, which means that he has been 'got at' by Clara Dollmann to determine the whereabouts of Wilson. Furthermore he has been trained to win as efficiently as any racehorse, which makes it hard for him to accept orders in a spirit of due deference. But I fancy I have used the powers of leadership inherent in one's sort, dear Sissy, to remind him of his station in life – and that the innate habits of our difference in rank will outweigh his impatience. As the man in charge of fetching and carrying one, one's life is in his hands, and I have no choice but to put my trust in him. Pray God he will show himself worthy of this trust.

Here it sounds as if I am doubting His Grace's choice of servant, which of course is not the case at all. His Grace as we both know is gifted with those powers of insight so often bestowed in heaping measure upon members of the Purple.

Tonight, we sleep in the islands. Tomorrow we must send telegrams from Norden, where I am told there is an office. And then – to work! I shall be taking a luncheon to Norden Creek, and we shall see what we shall see. And should I – no, when I – succeed, we shall see who it is who will stand up and point at Captain Dacre as the assassin of the widow of Piemburg. I rather think that soon there will be great events to occupy the public attention – in which will be pre-eminent the name of
    your loving Brother
    Eric Dacre.

CHAPTER TWELVE

Ships in the Night

———————————

Sam put *Gloria*'s bows in the sand on the island's north shore. As I walked down the beach Dacre came trotting over the dunes, all brisk and military. He said, 'I want to get some stores up. Put 'em in bags. Then we'll have a look at that wreck.'

'What for?' I said.

'Do as you're bloody told,' he said. Then he sat in the cockpit and whistled, very unlucky, while we did the work.

We took the chain out of the locker and pulled out the diving dress and the compressor. Then we went under the forecabin floorboards and started pulling out tins.

'You want to watch that here corn beef,' said Sam, who was in no very good humour, having shifted six shackle of chain and got himself well slimed with black mud. 'That's off.'

'What d'ye mean, off?' says Dacre, from the cockpit.

'Rotten,' says Sam, pulling up a bulgy-looking tin and chucking that out of the skylight, which was open. I heard that land plunk on the sand outside. I put my head out of the hatch and glanced at Dacre to see how he would take this imperence, and I was surprised to see his face turn suddenly stiff as a plank and greasy with sweat.

'No,' he says, and I swear his lips were white.

'Bloody was,' said Sam. 'Pale brown and stank. I tried to put that in your sandwich. But when I opened that that was off, so you got bacon and pore Charlie got bugger all.'

Dacre said, 'What did you do with it?'

'Slung that,' says Sam. 'Over the side. Bloody hell a bad tin 'll give you botulitis. Some bugger could get kilt.'

Dacre began to shake, most unearthly that looked, until I

realised he was laughing. He laughed and laughed until he was roaring and screaming and I thought he was going to hurt himself. So I left him to it and went to get some bags, sail bags we used, and filled them with all those stores, except for a few tins that Dacre kept back.

Once we were finished we floated her off on the tide and I got some breakfast, Sam muttering all the while about madmen and me with my own thoughts, which were not far different, except there was murder in there too. That was Sunday, but Dacre seemed to have forgotten about prayers. He would have us sail onto the Schillplate, and sail up and down lines of bearing taking soundings. After a while he looked at the sketch chart I had made and took bearings off the tail of Juist and Borkum. Then he hauled off his clothes, pulled on a big wool jersey, and started to struggle into the diver's dress. 'Anchor,' he said. So we anchored in about four fathom of water, just about on top of the wreck sign on the chart, and ran up a black ball.

Sam had done work with divers on Sheerness docks, so he knew his way around the straps and valves and what have you. Dacre sat there in the greenish-grey suit, a little stiff in the face he looked, and eyed the helmet, which seemed to eye him back. For a man who did not like water he was about to do a brave thing, you had to give him that. 'Right,' he said, and when he ran his tongue round his lips you could practically hear that squeak. 'Listen carefully.'

We listened. That was, as Sam pointed out later, like listening to fairy stories. He wanted a big yellow can buoy to mark the spot, with a couple of dirty great lumps of iron on that to stop that floating away. Then he wanted a half hundredweight of iron in each of the bags of stores we had made up. He wanted all this lowered over the side, and then he would go down after that.

'Preliminary survey,' he said. So Sam screwed on the helmet, and he did up the butterfly nuts on the faceplate, and down went Dacre into that cloudy green water, trailing bubbles and bits of string. And there we sat pumping away at the compressor levers, with the tide running and the small breeze blowing, and the yellow buoy bumping against the hull. Sam lit his pipe and watched a cloud of smoke go into the compressor intake. He said, 'What do he think he's playing at?'

To which there was nothing I could answer. He might be looking for his wreck, of course. But what he intended to do with that if he found that, as one man with a diving suit, that was very hard to tell. Nor did that account for taking two hundredweight of mixed supplies to the bottom of the North Sea.

'Feeding bloody mermaids,' said Sam. 'Hope they got tin openers.'

Which was all very amusing, of course. But Dacre was the kind of chap who shot bereaved mothers in the back of the head, and that is not necessarily the kind of chap that believes in fairies.

I said, 'Do you keep pumping,' and went down the main hatch.

There was Dacre's cigars, and Dacre's hair brushes, and Dacre's chloral in the sleeping cabin. And Dacre's Norfolk jacket and knickers folded neat and military on the buttoned leather settee.

I picked the jacket up, and started to go through the pockets.

There was a horn-handled clasp knife, a box of matches, and a cigar case. And in the breast pocket, the black notebook.

Through the porthole I could see the blue horizon, cut with the safety lines and the tubes. I sat down on the settee and opened the notebook. I had never done anything like this before. I must say I felt a proper sneak.

That was full of writing in faint pencil. Some of that seemed to be letters to someone called Sissy, which out of haste I did not read.

There were a lot of notes, sort of shorthand stuff about sight lines and bearings, and once what looked like a list of tide times. Another said W – *'tides shrinking, start to increase in 6 days'* –? I seemed to remember we had talked about tides yesterday morning, and thought W might be me. Then I looked for remarks about dead soldiers, but found none. On the whole that was like doing crossword puzzles, something I have never given any mind to. So I turned to today's entry. *Mt*, that said, meaning Memmert I suppose. *2ht abndnd*. You did not need to be a genius to work out that was the huts. After which he had walked down to the southern end of the island, and spent a long time watching the mainland through binoculars. *A*, said the next scrawl. *4 tug, train stop. Leybucht?* On the chart, Leybucht was the little place where Norden Creek joined the sea, just about where he had been looking with his glasses from the beacon. I started back through the book.

Once you started looking, there were other entries of that kind. The first one came shortly after the note about the tide. *G*, that said. *Collier? Smoke*. There were spots of rain on the page. That had rained yesterday morning, as we came through the Harle Seegat by the Westturm—

Not a word about salvage. Not a single solitary blessed word.

Sam said, 'Hoy!' I picked up the coat and put the notebook back in the pocket. As I did so my hand brushed against something hard, a little pocket on the left-hand side, over the heart as it were, in the lining, a ticket pocket, they call that. There was something in there. I dived in and pulled that out.

That was a little leather wallet. Inside the wallet was a little blue booklet, with black Gothic writing on that, and a German eagle.

Suddenly I was freezing cold.

That was a German soldier's paybook, in the name of Albrecht Schussmeyer, a corporal of infantry. The leather was damp, and had the little white tidemarks of dried out salt.

That was exactly the kind of paybook the dead soldier would have carried.

So assume Dacre had killed him and taken that off the body. Why?

'Oi!' said Sam, more urgent this time.

Numb-fingered with shock, I put things back as I had found them and went on deck.

Up towards Norderney the *Blitz* was cruising. She took a sweep to within half a mile of us, and as she showed us her side I caught the flash of the sun on a pair of binocular lenses. Dacre's safety rope started to jerk. 'Pull him up?' said Sam.

The *Blitz* was steady in the water, watching. There was no evidence the paybook belonged to the dead man. Sure, Dacre had killed before. But that was not what you would call evidence. And even if he had, why take the paybook?

'Pull him up?' said Sam again, impatient.

'Not just yet,' I said, dragging myself back.

'Could be he's in trouble,' said Sam. 'Could be he's got a toob round a bit on that wreck.'

So there we were, first day into what I had been told was a secret salvage survey, body in the sea, diver down, chap watching who was not only the German navy but had also been a shareholder in the last lot after this wreck—

More jerks on the rope. 'Come you on,' said Sam, running out of patience. So we hauls him up, heavy, he was, in that suit, and planks him on the deck streaming water, and unscrews his face plate, and pulls him out of the suit. He was blue and shaking. I pointed out *Blitz*. He said, 'Fine,' not at all bothered as far as I could see.

'Find it?' I said, looking into his face, thinking, are you a murderer?

'Early days,' he said. He did not look like a murderer. He looked like a man in need of a cup of tea.

'Where now?'

'Memmert's as good as anywhere.' He went below. You could hear his teeth chattering from the cockpit. I told Sam to pull up the anchor. When he was done, he comes aft and stuffs his pipe and lights it, and by the way he rams the tobacco home with his thumb I can tell that there is something eating him, too. So I waited, and out that came.

'One of them *mutte* boats,' he says. 'She'd be about the size of a Thames barge, eh?'

'Probably,' I said.

'Definitely,' says Sam. 'I had a job on the *George and Henrietta*, what belonged to Wellington Hicks.'

'Old Wellington,' I said, mind not on that.

'We was carrying shores for the Underground, Inner Circle,' says Sam. 'They was digging these here dirty great shafts and lining them with these here railway sleeper size of things, the navvies digging the holes and then jamming in these here sleepers to stop that caving in on em, if you follow. Well there was this shaft bloke, a Dutchy. He wanted them shores stacked just so. Eight across, sixteen up, running alternate directions every layer, so that made a sort of a square square.'

'Cube,' I said.

'Ah,' said Sam. 'Well, that's what they had on that there bank.' He jabbed his pipe at Juist, sharp as a paper cutout in the afternoon sun. I worked out that he was talking about Memmert. *'Exactly.'*

I pulled in a couple of inches of mainsheet to bring the boom off the shrouds. 'What do you mean, exactly?'

'They never did no salvage there,' said Sam. 'Not with them shores, anyway. There was six piles, that's what you'd carry. Six by sixty-four railway sleepers. All on 'em sitting at the top of the slip. One load, exactly. And they was supposed to have been salving away all last summer. But they didn't use any on em.'

The bit of newspaper stuck underneath the pile had been dated July. A whole summer season, and not a shore used.

'And something else,' says Sam.

'What now?' I said, squinting up at the topsail.

'That channel,' said Sam. 'Someone's been down there with an axe.'

'With a *what*?'

'Axe,' he said. 'They've gone along and they've chopped them withies down. All across the hard bit of the channel, where that start to wind. Cursed is he that moveth his neighbour's land-mark, that say in the Prayer Book.'

I said, 'What in the name of goodness are you on about?'

'They've left in the first and last,' he said. 'To show where the channel start and finish. But they've been and gone and chopped the rest of them off. You can see the axe marks, fresh as fresh. That ent even black yet.' He took the pipe out of his mouth and spat at the gulls again. 'Now you tell me, why would anyone do a thing like that?'

Well, that was a good question, along with all the other good questions.

We arrived back in the Juister Balje as the sun was going down. I went to the fo'c'sle to think some more, but fell asleep, I am afraid, having been up since three. I was woken by a crash of breaking crockery, and Sam, coming down the hatch like a bolted rabbit. 'Bugger that,' says Sam, excuse me. 'Slung 'is nice dinner into the cockpit plate and all.'

'Herrings, was it?' says I.

'In course,' says Sam.

I crope down the deck in my socks, and start to clear up, and get a bit of china in my foot. While I am looking for that, I hear a voice from off and over the water. That was dark, of course, but the sky was a carpet of stars, and the air no worse than cool. Over against Juist, a mast was moving. The gaff peak was scandalised, which is to say dropped, to shrink the area of her sail. The mast slowed, and the mainsail came down. She moved up against the ebb under headsails only. There was a sploosh and a roar of chain as they let go the anchor, and the clack of the gypsy as she fell back to her scope. She was a big cutter, one of the blunt-nosed Frisian kind, flat-bottomed, with leeboards. An acetylene searchlight waved over the water, which meant yacht, not working boat. By its beam I saw that Dacre was standing in the hatch. 'What's that?' he said, very chill and quiet.

'Nother yacht come in, sir,' I say. 'Dinner not to your liking, sir?'

He ignored me. A voice from over the water said, 'Englisch boat.'

'That's right,' said I.

'We come wisit,' said the boat.

'Christ,' hissed Dacre, and dived below.

'We come across,' said the voice in its broken English. 'Also we will present our compliments to your owner.'

Down in the cabin, Dacre seemed to be sweeping something off the table. He stumbled back into the cockpit. 'With the greatest of pleasure,' I heard him call, in his excellent German. 'Whenever you wish.' He thrust a small satchel into my hand. 'Get rid of that,' he hissed.

'Now,' said the familiar voice, jovial enough, but it was hard with the confidence of someone who did not know what it was not to be obeyed.

'I'll come too,' said another voice, a woman's. I had the notion that I had heard that one before.

I got rid of his satchel for him. Then I went scooting round the saloon with a rag and a dustpan and brush, trimming the lamp wick, riddling the stove, setting out the tantalus on the table, drawing the green baize curtains, tidying the bird books and the pilot books in their shelves. I went into the fo'c'sle and put the kettle on. In a minute or two I heard the knock of oars, and Sam saying, evening, sir, evening, madam.

'You must say, "My lady," ' said the man's voice.

'Sorry, your Ladyship,' says Sam to the man, with a grovel I knew to be worse than sarcasm. 'Thought you was a bloke.'

Then there were four new feet on board, and Dacre was offering them a drink, as good manners demanded. Sam came back down and said, quiet like, 'Nice piece in the saloon, bor.'

Somewhere aft a door opened and closed, and I knew they were getting the usual tour. They went through the heads, exclaiming with delight, proper gentry, able to find something to coo over even in a toilet. Then they came through to the forecabin.

Well, curiosity killed the cat, but I put my eye to the keyhole. I saw Dacre, who seemed to be wearing a striped blazer and an Old Etonian tie. Alongside him, two faces came out of the shadows. Faces I had seen at Kiel, the day the Kaiser rammed *Doria*. One of them had a shaved head, pointed, like a starboard-hand buoy with duelling scars. He was von Tritt. And the other one, the one I could only see part of because she was tucked away behind old Tritt's beefy shoulder, had heavy, dark brows and an eye that even in the lamplight was a deep, late-evening sort of a blue. And she was the Gräfin von und zu Marsdorff.

CHAPTER THIRTEEN

An Infernal Machine

They went out into the cockpit, and I heard Dacre shout for a light, and I pulled a hurricane lamp off the bunch on the bulkhead and took that aft. I hung the lamp on the patent hook someone had installed under the boom. Von Tritt did not look at me, so he certainly did not remember meeting me before. As I went to fetch the whisky, the Gräfin asked in good English for a cup of tea.

'Yes 'm,' I said. Our eyes met in the yellow lamplight. We remembered each other all right. She had used me to tease this Baron, then made that up to me quite handsome. Call me silly, but I thought there was still something there – a little hitch as the eyes slid apart, the kind of hitch you would get if a silk dress slid past the callouses on a working man's hand.

I took her her tea, then went and sat on the cabin top forward and put a whale knot in the end of a reefing pennant, and watched the three of them in their yellow egg of lamplight. Von Tritt had a heavy voice that he liked listening to. He seemed curious. What, he enquired, were we doing here? Cruising, watching birds, said Dacre. Well the *Blitz* must have spotted us diving on the wreck that very afternoon, but apparently von Tritt had not talked to the *Blitz*. We had chosen the wrong time of year for the birds, he said, snappish as if we had done it out of deliberate naughtiness. They were all on their nests. That was the only time the boat had been available, said Dacre. Available? said von Tritt, and Dacre told him as how his friend the Duke of Leominster had lent that to him.

'Not a very big boat for Leominster,' said von Tritt, as if that confirmed his suspicions that the Duke was a bit of a peasant at heart.

'You are acquainted with His Grace?' said Dacre.

'Of course.' Von Tritt managed to cram into his voice the implication that he thought nearly as little of Dacre as of the boat.

'I shall be telegraphing him tomorrow from Norden,' said Dacre. 'I shall remember you to him.'

Von Tritt bowed. The Gräfin sat and sipped her tea with the little yellow lamp flames reflected in her eyes. She was directing the eyes into the dark, where they caught mine.

And held.

Again I felt the jump as they caught, the tug that you get. And I knew she felt that too—

Rubbish, Webb. You were a weapon in her war.

Rubbish or not, I was twenty-four and I had raced against the Kaiser of Germany and beat him hollow, and I knew what that meant when a woman looked at you like that—

'Herr Gott!' said von Tritt. He stood up suddenly, and glared at the shore like a pointer dog.

Gloria was lying head to wind and tide, and both of them had pulled her stern to westward. The Gräfin and von Tritt were sitting on the port side, looking towards the mainland, with Dacre opposite.

Something had happened on the mainland.

Before, the coast had been a low black line between the pale sandbanks and the paler sky. Now there was a red glow down to the southeast, well east of Norddeich, perhaps as far as Nessmersiel or Dornumersiel, the little harbours where the next two rivers along met the sea. 'Something's on fire,' I said.

'*Dummer Kerl*,' said von Tritt, by which I understood that he had worked that out for himself. That was not a particularly warm night, but his face was shiny in the lantern-light.

'Biggish fire, by the look of it,' said Dacre, in a sort of smooth drawl. 'Captain von Brüning said you were making harbour improvements. Perhaps it's a works going up. Looks as if there's oil in it, too. Tar maybe.'

'Ja,' said von Tritt, and you got the idea he was ready to explode. 'A timber yard. Very probably. Heavens, is that the time?' Suddenly he seemed to be a man in a panic. He switched into English, for my benefit. 'Please my boat bring. We now return must.'

'So soon?' said Dacre.

'We must.' The man was fair dancing with impatience.

I pulled their dinghy alongside and took the Gräfin's hand to help her down into it. The clasp of it was warm and dry, very pleasant indeed. She said, 'I am sorry you have forgotten your German,' and I heard her laugh, a secret sort of laugh between her and me. Then she was gone, and von Tritt was stepping down after her. She rowed, I noticed. When they got the other end a sort of rumble of German came across the water and their anchor gypsy started to clack, and the last we saw of them the pale triangles of their sails were sliding down the Balje on the ebb, behind Memmert and down towards the mainland.

Dacre draped his arms over the boom. 'Woodyard on fire,' he said. 'Hah!'

I could still feel the clasp of the Gräfin's fingers, and I suppose my mind was in a soft sort of state. 'Poor devil that runs it,' said I.

'Poor?' said Dacre. He was excited, there was no doubt about that. 'I wouldn't call him poor. Not the All-Highest bloody Kaiser.' He laughed again, very loud. 'Damn fine woman, too. I like 'em thin, long as there's plenty *au balcon*, wha? Couple of nice handfuls there. Wouldn't roll over her to get at the candle, eh? Eh? Now where's that satchel?'

I do not like that kind of talk, specially from a primped-up little bounder about a woman I am sorry to see go. I looked him in his hard narrow eye, and said, 'You said get rid of that. I dropped that overboard.'

'You *what*?'

'As per orders,' says I, like a good employee. Then I walked away from him up to the foredeck, and sat on the hatch and watched the clouds roll across the stars and told myself to calm down. I heard Dacre scrub his teeth as if he hated them, the clank as he worked the head and the clink of the chloral bottle on the medicine glass. Why would a chap take chloral in all this fresh air? To keep his conscience down, perhaps. Down to the southeast, the glow waxed and died. That was a big fire, all right.

After a while Dacre started to snore. I went down into the foc'sle and lit the lamp and took the satchel out of my bunk, where I had hidden it, and emptied that into the lamp-light.

There was a bundle of tins lashed together with string: three bully beef and one cocoa. The cocoa tin was the only one with a detachable lid, so I took that off. That had been greased, to keep the water out. Inside was a drum, a small one, with a keyhole in the top. That was a small barograph, by the look of it. From out of the top of the drum there stuck a bit of ropey looking stuff, that joined the works to the square-sided one-pound bully beef cans, lashed together with marline, very neat.

I unclasped my knife and cut the lashings. The ropey stuff went from the top of the drum into a hole in the side of one of the tins.

Gloria heaved a little, creaking at the lanyards to the small flexing of the tide. The other side of the bulkhead, Dacre was snoring like a drowning pig. I took out my knife, that I keep squared off at the end. I cut the ropey stuff, and gently I began to explore the interior.

You cannot spend much time as a yacht skipper without taking a barograph to bits, on account of the salt. So I knew what to expect. This one had all the usual wheels inside it. There was something else, though. A little spike, neatly sprung, with a brass disc beside that. On Wednesday, when the movement brought the spike round, that would hit a bar and spring back onto the brass disc . . .

I took hold of the drum and turned it to Wednesday. My hand was shaking, I will admit. Perhaps that was why I turned that too far. The spike moved. That moved about as far as the catch of a mouse trap. Suddenly the works jumped in my hand, and something made a sharp *crack*, and I dropped it because the ropey stuff coming out of the drum had caught fire and burned all at once with a fizz and a whoosh, scorching my hand. Sam sat up suddenly, blinking like an owl, saying, 'What's a-burning? What the hell's a-burning?'

Dacre had stopped snoring. I waited, holding my breath. There was a grunt and a rattle, and that started up again.

The air was full of a sharp fireworky smell. That was gunpowder, from some sort of cap set off by the spike. That had lit the fuze, and that would have gone into the tin can strapped to it, if I had not have cut the fuze with my knife.

I pulled open the cutlery drawer and found myself a tin opener.

Two of the cans bore a picture of a bullock standing up to his hocks in a flowery meadow. BUTTERBLUME, said the name on the scroll underneath. Buttercup brand. The third had no meadow, just a bull's head with a ring in the nose. BEEFSTEAK, said the lettering.

Very gently, I opened one of the buttercups, and the beefsteak.

The Buttercup seemed to have a glass jar inside it, packed tight with something grey, like putty, with water round it. Gingerly I unscrewed the top of the jar a couple of turns, sniffed, and hastily screwed that back on, laid that down carefully, and picked up the Beefsteak.

There was no jar. There was just a buffy, fibrous sort of substance, the same stuff Sam had tried to put in Dacre's sandwich. But that was nothing to do with bad corned beef. That was faintly oily to the touch. The ropy stuff went right through the side of the tin and buried itself in the oily stuff. The dirty little foc'sle filled with a strong smell of marzipan – the same smell I had noticed earlier in the saloon. Now you came to see that with a timing device and a fuze, that was no difficulty working out what that was.

The blood began to pound heavily in my skull, the way nitroglycerine will make that pound. The stuff in the beefsteak tin was dynamite.

And the stuff in the buttercup tin, I was inclined to believe, was phosphorus.

Into my mind's eye there wallowed the blue and bloated face of that soldier.

Next Friday that would have lit the fuze, which would have set off the dynamite, which would have blown phosphorus all over the place, which when that met the air would have set fire to anything that would burn.

'Bit of a bomb,' I said.

'Bit of a *what*?' says Sam, muzzy

So I told him what. I reminded him about the two hundred-weight of dynamite and phosphorus we had dropped overboard by the yellow buoy on the *Corinne*. I pointed out to him that there was no salvage use for that stuff. I further pointed out that Dacre had not minded that the *Blitz* had watched him diving on the wreck. The salvage business, in short, looked like a red herring. Add this to the dead soldier and the notebook, and you had . . . well, there was no knowing what you had, but I did not like that at all.

That woke Sam up, but he was not impressed. 'That Duke's the boss,' he said. 'He say take this Dacre where he want to go. I am a working chap that works for rich chaps when they pay me. I do what I am told. That bring on night. That's that.'

I said, 'He wants to blow something up. We should turn him in.'

Sam said, '*What*?'

'Listen you here,' I said. 'He's killed that poor Boer woman, we know that. You saw him hit that bailiff. He went nearer that dead sojer than anyone else, and he's got his paybook. And now he's supposed to be salving for the Duke, but he's running round with firebombs in his satchel. What do that add up to, boy?'

'Bugger all,' said Sam, excuse me.

'Oh for goodness sake,' I said. 'Just look at the man.'

'I look at him,' says Sam. 'I sees a gent. Nasty gent, but a gent. You got a terrible rushing sort of a temper on you, Charlie, and you want to keep that down. Keep an eye on him if you want. But don't you go telling nothing to no Germans, or they'll hang us all.'

I looked at that hard. The blood began to cool in my veins. I thought about von Tritt, and the more I thought on him the more that became plain that there was a man would hang you soon as look at you, if you gave him an excuse. I hated to admit that, but Sam had a point.

'Now if you have finished,' said Sam, 'I am going to sleep.' And he went, bang, like a door shutting.

I took the infernal machine on deck and lowered the tins one by one into the tide. Then I pulled the clock apart and dropped the bits after the tins.

After which I lay on my bunk and stared a hole in the deck, but saw no daylight anywhere.

CHAPTER FOURTEEN

Light and Mud

An hour after dawn the breeze had gone westerly and freshened, tumbling in dirty grey bolsters of cloud. That was Easter Day. Where the fire had been last night, a smear of black smoke was crawling across the horizon. I took a bearing. From the chart, that looked like Nessmersiel.

When Sam had made tea I gave a rap on the hatch and went below. Dacre opened his eyes. 'We'll go to Norddeich,' he said.

The Norddeich channel was a mud-gulley half a cable wide between training banks they call *leitdamms*. We stormed up that on the last of the flood, white water roaring from under the bobstay, highly impressive. I had hauled up the White Ensign, and that snapped at the gaff peak chesty as a battlecruiser. We shot round the pierhead and came head to wind in the patch of muddy water inside the breakwaters, carrying our way long enough for Sam to jump ashore with a long line and run that up to a warping post. Five or six idlers came out of the mud and helped haul her alongside halfway up the wall. Dacre stuck his head out of the hatch and looked around. There were grey bags under his eyes, and the smell of marzipan came with him. 'Webb,' he said, 'you can go to Norden. Try and send a cable for me. It's just down the road. Pretty town, one hears.'

That would not be hard to be prettier than Norddeich. The harbour was a lot of mud and a few *muttes*. What there was of it on land did not look too beautiful either, unless you could find a way to admire a grain silo and a railway siding, and what was probably a bit of a canal, a *tief*, they call it in Friesland, with a sluice or *siel* that took that through the sea wall, dug out and made navigable so they could get a barge inland.

110

A dumpling in brass buttons came and nodded at the Customs form we had signed in Norderney. Dacre gave him an eye-opener of whisky and led him on to gossip about the fire last night. According to him that had been a yard over at Nessmersiel where they were making improvements to the sluices. Big fire but nobody hurt, thanks be to God. And no doubt heavily insured, so nobody none the worse off. By the way, were we aware that the mainland ports were closed pending sea wall works? We were. He wheezed off to a second breakfast.

Once he was gone Dacre said, 'I'll be back early in the afternoon,' slung his haversack on his back and went up the ladder. I watched him stride out in his brogues, spacking his walking stick on the quay timbers and up the road over the green dyke. I knew what was in his haversack. I did not know what he was going to do with that, but I was anxious to see. I gave him five minutes, then went after him.

That was a couple of miles' walk to Norden, heart in mouth, up and over the wall and down an unmetalled road that ran straight as an arrow between trees pale green with new leaf. I could see Dacre ahead, the size of an ant. That was a blustery morning, full of the smell of wet grass, and ordinarily I should have enjoyed that after a week on the sea. But there was no means of enjoying anything until I had found out what Dacre was up to.

There were plenty of soldiers on the road, foot and horse, marching by squads like clockwork. They paid no attention to me, nor should I have to them, soldiers being a very usual thing to see in Germany; except that every time I saw a soldier I saw that blue face with the red eyes, and I felt they must see that too.

I kept Dacre in view as he skirted the town. Then that got awkward. The road ran long and straight, with no hedge, only a ditch on either side. Halfway along was a level crossing. Beyond the level crossing was a clump of trees. I had to wait by a sally bush until he had rounded the corner. As I came to the crossing the gates closed. A goods train rumbled by, closed waggons and flatbeds with loads shrouded in green tarpaulin. I fair to hopped with impatience. That seemed to take hours. At last the gate opened, and I went through.

There was no sign of Dacre. In the trees at the end of the straight I ran into a squad of soldiers under a sharp-eyed sergeant. The sergeant stopped me, asked me who I was, looked at my papers and when he saw I was foreign made me turn out my pockets. I did so in a sort of agony, for if they had done the same to Dacre, we would all hang. 'What's that all about?' I said.

'Harbour defences,' says he, civil enough. 'Spies, y'know. Can't be too careful.'

I sort of nodded, feeling the sweat running inside my clothes, thinking of Dacre's bomb.

'On yer way,' says he.

And on I went, knowing I had lost Dacre now, looking left and right over the marshy fields. Of course there was nothing. Just marsh and pasture, and the sea wall dragging its shadow across the morning. Cows and sheep there were. But no Dacre. And nothing worth blowing up.

That made no sense at all.

I turned, and was soon walking through the first villas of Norden.

That was a busy little town, with black and white cattle lowing in the market pens, and a vast belfry that jangled in my ear like the saucepans of Satan while I asked directions to the telegraph office.

The office was a barred cubby hole with a shirt-sleeved clerk and a tiled stove blasting out heat in the corner. I unfolded the paper Dacre had given me, and wrote out the form. *Birds marvellous*, that said. *Safe arrival. General von Tritt sends his kind regards. Shall cable Wednesday. Dacre.* I passed that over to the clerk, who frowned, holding that at arm's length. '*Vas ist das?*' he said.

'*Englisch.*'

A lounger with a greasy trilby and a drinker's nose peeled himself off the wall. 'Hey,' he said, in a horrible blend of Hamburg and Hull. 'Zat right?'

The clerk looked at him with a sort of recognition, as if they worked together, and I was suddenly sure that the man was a spy, posted to oversee any suspicious cables – though that was hard to imagine what material there would be for suspicious cables in Norden. '*Auf Deutsch,*' said the clerk.

'He say read please in German,' said the trilby helpfully, leaning on my shoulder and breathing old gin in my face. 'Excellent chickens,' he said. 'Strongbox here—'

I interrupted him, and did that right. 'You speak good German,' said trilby, piqued. I nodded and tried to leave, but he clung to me, asking where had we come from and why, what were our plans, how many were we, why we were yachting so early in the year. Finally I told him to go to blazes and started back on the Norddeich road. When I looked over my shoulder he was talking to a policeman, who was writing in a notebook.

I trudged uneasily back to the boat, pursued by the wind-chewed strains of *ein feste Burg* from the belfry. That was just before noon when I walked over the sea wall. There was another yacht on the quay ahead of *Gloria*: a big lemsteraak sort of thing, cutter rigged, blunt nosed, with leeboards. In the cockpit, sitting by the tiller with the gold-leafed dolphin, was the Gräfin.

When I looked down at her she raised a hand and smiled, not too much of a smile but enough to remind me of the way she had held my eye last night. I went down the ladder and gave her good morning, and one thing led to another, and before I knew what was happening we were nattering on at some speed. A big blond deckhand hung around, polishing the brass on a porthole, and I could tell he did not like paid hands talking to his mistress. But she did not tell me by word or look that I should go away, or indeed that I was a paid hand.

'I had a visit from Miss Dollmann, that was with you at Kiel,' I said eventually.

'Clara,' she said, with a lightening of the voice.

'She came to see us in England while we were getting the boat ready.'

She lowered her eyes, and the blood came into her face, and for a second she looked flustered. 'Hans,' she said to the deckie. 'Tell Elly to bring my sketching things.' Hans shuffled below. 'Perhaps you would care for a walk,' she said.

I had already walked six miles that morning. 'Nothing I'd like better,' I said. Hans showed signs of wanting to come too, mentioning the name of von Tritt. But this had no good effect – rather the reverse, in fact. So I caught hold of the sketching bundle and off we set, the Gräfin and Elly the maid and me, up the quay ladder and onto the quay. As the Gräfin went up, Elly shouted something and Hans and his mate turned their backs so as not to see the mistress's legs. Sam did no such thing, so I kicked a bootful of grit in his face to teach him manners, and followed the women along the quay, the Gräfin walking very elegant in a narrow red flannel skirt and blue fisherman's jersey, Elly plodding along in a black dress that flapped on the wind like a parliament of rooks.

We walked down the quay and turned left, east, that is, and onto the sea wall. 'Excuse my asking,' said the Gräfin, 'but what are you doing here?'

'Working,' I said, because I did not want to tell her I had not got a clue. We moved onto the sea wall.

'Captain Webb,' she said, with a sideways glance and the lift of an eyebrow. 'Who beat the Kaiser at Kiel. In Ostfriesland, on a tarted-up smack yacht.'

Not much got past this Gräfin. I was feeling most uncomfortable. That had been a peculiar last night, and a peculiar morning, with questions buzzing thick as flies, and not an answer in sight. Now that someone else was asking them, that was worse. I shrugged my shoulders, and said, 'That's a job.'

And she got that wrong. She thought she had reminded me that I was poor, and had to take any job that came along, while she was rich and could do as she liked. As I now said, we had been getting on as two people the same age but different sexes. But now there came a sort of embarrassment between us, as if she had pricked a bubble and regretted that. She went a little pink, and said, to get back on safe ground, 'What is this about Clara Dollmann?'

'She found us in London,' I said. 'She said a friend of hers called Wilson was over here, and she'd lost sight of him, and would we keep an eye out for him.' As I said that, I was suddenly worried I had made some sort of bloomer. Just because I had seen her and Miss Dollmann together at Kiel did not mean they were confidential friends.

'Her friend Wilson,' said the Gräfin. 'Poor Clara.' For a rich woman she had a very straightforward way of talking. The way she said that, I knew I had no worries.

'Scuse me,' said I, 'but who is this Wilson?'

'Clara's father made a mistake.' He had been killed, Miss Dollmann had said. Some mistake. 'He was a man disgraced, it doesn't matter how. Mr Wilson is Clara's fiancé. He felt he should come to Ostfriesland to put things straight.' She did not sound as if she thought that was a specially clever idea.

'An affair of honour.'

'That is how she and Wilson see it.' Again the sense that that was not how she saw it, not at all.

We were on top of the wall now, walking through coarse grass turned silver where that was flattened by the wind. She was looking out to sea. I thought she was a strange one, I must say – half-world-weary, half-innocent. And one hundred per cent tasty, if you will excuse the expression.

She seemed glad to talk, as if she was saying things that she had kept bottled up for a while. She had a Danish mother and a German father, some sort of nob in Prussia, a Junker she called him. She told me right out that her mother had been rich and pretty, and her father had been a fool with a title and a castle. Any road, she had been brought up in a castle – pine trees, she said, sand dunes, brick battlements overlooking the Baltic – and married off to some Graf when she had been eighteen. Six months after, he had fallen off his horse while he had been hunting deer, and come home dead. That might have been only me hoping, but she did not sound as if she minded too much. From what she said he had been a stuffy sort of chap, and reading between the lines that sounded as if she had spent her childhood locked up in one brick castle, taken the first chance she had seen to get herself out of it, and landed up in another one as bad as the first. Anyway after he had died she went off to Berlin and Paris and such like spots, to practise her painting, she said, and got rid of most of her houses, except for one here in Ostfriesland, the Carolinenhof she called that, because she liked the light, found that interesting to paint I suppose. And there was *Delphin* of course.

I said, 'And Baron von Tritt?'

'He was appointed military commander of the district six weeks ago. You have met Leutnant von Brüning, I think. He was in command here until the Baron was brought in over his head.' She made a face. 'Poor Brüning, he has great energy but not many friends in Potsdam, at court, you know. Anyway, my father-in-law instructed me to make my boat available to von Tritt. You met him at Kiel. Baron Schwering.' I remembered him; old boy with a face like a sheep. 'My father-in-law thinks I am a dangerous liberal and that Baron von Tritt is an influence for the good. Actually he wants me to marry him.' She looked at me, no expression except a sort of polite enquiry, as if she was going to ask me if I thought that looked like rain. She said, 'Do you think I should?'

'Don't know the gentleman,' I said, blank as a plank. I should have liked to give her a straight answer. But that was not my place.

She gave me a scrutinising look with those dark blue eyes of hers. 'Lucky you,' she said. 'So what do you really think?'

'I think people should follow their inclinations.'

'My father-in-law controls two-thirds of my property.'

'That leaves a third.' Never having had any property, that was easy to say. And the way she looked, if I had had any I should have given that to her. 'If there's anything I can do to help,' I began, then realised what I had said, and waited for the horse laugh, the set down, the who *do* you think you are?

But that did not come. In her face I saw not scorn at a servant who had stepped out of station, but the desperation of someone who was stuck, trapped. I said, 'Don't you worry,' and took her hand.

She gave that a squeeze and said, 'Thank you, Captain Webb.' And what was in her eyes was not hoity-toity, but the relief of someone lonely who all of a sudden feels less alone. For a moment there, we were practically hanging on to each other. Then the moment passed, closed out by the shutters such people have, even the best of them. In a backwards way I found myself thinking of Hetty – which is to say I was surprised I was not thinking about her, because there was no room in my mind for anyone but this Gräfin. She pulled back; perhaps she thought she had said too much, and she was probably right. She said, 'Now if you will excuse me I should like to draw.' I unfolded her easel for her, and she started.

I walked away, trying to get my head clear. The one thing I had set myself to do was follow Dacre, and I had failed to do that. That was all very well walking with countesses, but I was walking in fog: fog in which the landmarks were horrors, dead soldiers and infernal machines. My feet took me down onto the foreshore, it being a natural instinct of those bred up in Dalling and such places to keep an eye on what the tide might have washed up in the way of wreck.

That was a strip of clumpy bushes and rough grass above the wrack left by the big spring tides. I wandered along, eyes down. Perhaps I had been brought out here to be given messages. Perhaps the world was full of signals. But I did not have the code book, so I did not know what was a signal and what was not—

Hello.

I had walked a quarter of a mile. Norddeich had vanished behind a curve of the dyke. To the north the sand flats rustled under a dirty roof of cloud.

Ahead, there was something in the wrack.

CHAPTER FIFTEEN

The Ragged Man

To most people, what was down there in the dead weed and old branches and bits of cork was a mere bulge, halfway between a dead horse and a ship's boiler. To anyone bred up in Dalling, that was a boat.

I walked on over, and started pulling the weed off it.

That was a boat all right; or rather, half a boat. The aft half – back end, to you. Once, that had been a yacht. Now that was bashed and walloped and ground into the sand until that looked like nothing on earth or sea. I was not the first to her, either. Where the cleats should have been, the fairleads and all the other useful little bits of bronze and galvanized you find on pleasure boats, there was nothing but screw holes and mud.

She had been a converted lifeboat, by the look of it; a double-ended hull with a counter stern grafted on by someone with at least half an idea of what he was at. Inside, she was a mess of weed and splinters. The rudder was gone, for the pintles, no doubt, the bronze hinges that hold that onto the sternpost, a nice find for a fisherman used to fighting for his life with a rudder held on with rusty iron. About the only thing still on her was the nameboard, blasted clean of all but a few specks of gold leaf, the letters still visible because of the way they were carved into that little plank of cedar. That was a nice-looking thing, done no doubt by a man to whom boats meant pleasure and delight, not hauling freezing nets in a blizzard.

Well I hate to leave anything on a wreck. So I out with my knife and I unscrewed that with the flat end of the blade and I stuck that down my trousers at the back. Then I walked one more time around, just to see if there was anything I had missed.

118

And this time, I noticed a funny thing.

She had come in half just about in way of her main hatch. The plank ends of her were broken and splintered, but not much. They were charred, but not much. They had a sort of a *shattered* look, is the only word that comes to mind—

'My goodness me,' I said, out loud.

For the reason that was in half was that someone had blowed that up.

I looked back at the Gräfin. I saw the white oval of her face. She was watching me. She turned away to talk to Elly. She had led me here. I was getting messages.

But I had no code book.

I walked up the dyke, and cooled my head in the wind, walking up towards Hilgenriedersiel. On the chart that looked a hopeless little place, a mere trickle of water butting up against the dyke. What I saw did not correspond. There was a group of long, low roofs behind an embankment, and a couple of brick chimneys dribbling smoke at the sky. The roofs looked like a works of some kind, perhaps to do with the sea wall improvements and coastal defences von Brüning had talked about. I stopped, watching a new plume of smoke draw up from the south, moving towards the roofs. A train.

That is a skipper's job to get the rail connections of a cruising ground in his mind, in case his gentry should require transport. The chart marked stations at Norddeich and Esens, but none at Hilgenriedersiel; and that chart was in date as of October 1902. But a lot could happen in six months, specially if there were Germans behind it. I started to walk on, then stopped.

Not more than a hundred yards away a figure had appeared on the dyke, a vertical tick among all those huge horizontals. That was a man, spidery and disconnected, as if the parts of him were trying to fly one from the other and tumble away on the breeze. Then I realised that was just his coat, a big oilskin in rags, and he was waving at me, a full-armed seaman's sort of wave. He had a blackened look: a *burnt* look, even. When he saw the flash of my face, he pointed straight out from the shoulder with his right hand.

He was standing next to a sally bush that was growing in the dyke. At first I thought he was pointing at the tree, a thing that would have been in keeping with the ragged and crazy aspect of him. Then my eye passed beyond.

Far away down the sea wall, five or six cables away, the dyke took a jink. A ray of sun on was turning its face bright green, but the jink was in shadow. Out of the shadow a group of men was spilling onto the dyke – a group with corners and straight edges, and something about their heads that had a gleam to it, and something else was gleaming, too. And I felt a new chill, not because of any ghostliness about them, but almost for an opposite reason. For I knew straight off that this was a platoon of soldiers, and the gleam was *pickelhaubes* and fixed bayonets. And rightly or wrongly I got the idea that the reason they were walking along the sea wall was me.

When I looked back, I saw that the man in the ragged coat had vanished. Taking one thing with another, I decided to vanish too. But down there among the soldiers someone raised a hand, and I saw a puff of grey smoke and heard the report of a gun. I had been seen.

I walked into the cover of that sally. There was a patch of mud alongside the bush, and in the mud the impression of a foot shod in one of the wooden-soled boots they wear hereabouts. I stood there scuffling for a minute, to spoil the footprints. The ragged man had not felt like a hunter. Hunted, was more how he had seemed, and I was never one for hunting. I strolled back along the top of the dyke towards the Gräfin. To tell the truth, what I wanted to do was run. But I strolled. I strolled.

I got back beside her and looked over her shoulder. The painting was a lot of blue and green and black, a seascape but not very like, to be honest, with a figure in the foreground. I said, 'There are some soldiers coming.'

She looked at me as if she was thinking about her painting, not soldiers. 'Ah,' she said.

'And that chap on the dyke looks as if he knows you.'

'Chap?'

'In a coat.' She could not have avoided seeing him.

'Elly,' she said. 'Did you see a chap in a coat?'

'No,' says Elly, stolid as the wall itself.

I opened my mouth to argue. But the Gräfin was dabbing away at the figure in the foreground, with a red splotch at its neck that was a handkerchief – the handkerchief I was wearing. Her brush moved quick as a flash, and suddenly there was another figure, a charred-looking man in a flapping coat, highly skilful. The two figures were shaking hands. Then there was a little flurry of the brush, and the figure in the flapping coat dissolved into the mud, and the soldiers were upon us.

There was some kind of officer out the front. '*Ausweis!*' he barked, meaning identity card. He had a long nose with a red end that twitched as he talked. I reached for my passport. The Gräfin did no such thing. 'Who exactly are you?' she said without looking up, and you could have iced champagne with her voice.

'*Ausweis*,' said the officer. 'Or you are under arrest.'

This time she did look up. 'Go away,' she said. That was not just your aristocratic *froideur*. That was who-the-hell-do-you-think-you-are-I-live-here-and-you-don't. The native talking to the trespasser.

But he was not having any. 'Arrest them,' he barked. Then a sergeant stepped forward, a red-faced chap with mutton-chop whiskers and the look of a man who knew his way around. He whispered in the officer's ear. The officer looked suddenly as if he had been shot. The red end of his nose turned I promise you as white as bone. 'Your ladyship,' he said. '*Mein Gott* . . . how can I ever . . .'

The Gräfin carried on painting until he had spluttered himself quiet. Then she said, 'You must remember that this is a part of Germany you do not know, with inhabitants who have their own lives to lead. So if it would not be too much trouble, perhaps you could leave me and my people in peace?'

He stood juddering on the slope of the dyke. He said, 'My lady . . . that is . . . we are looking for a man. He is dangerous.'

'I have seen no man. Elly?'

'No man,' said Elly. 'Worse luck.'

'Captain Webb?'

'Indeed not.' If that was good enough for her, that was good enough for me.

'So there you are,' said the Gräfin. 'If you have any complaints, I shall be visiting the yards at Hilgenriedersiel tonight, with the Herr General.'

'Frau Gräfin . . .' The officer was telegraphing at me with his nose and his eyebrows.

'Bah!' she said. 'He hardly speaks a word of German.' She had said something in front of him she had not been meant to say. Yards at Hilgenriedersiel. What kind of yards could they be?

The officer bowed, and scuttled away down the sea wall. I was watching the Gräfin's face. She grinned at me, a conspirator's grin, two lonely people, all that. Then she put herself back together. 'Well,' she said, 'that's the morning spoilt. Shall we go back?'

Before we left Elly went down to the wreck of the boat; call of nature, I assumed. She was carrying her brown hessian bag. When she went down, the bag looked full. When she came back the bag looked empty. So I pretended a call of my own, the wreck being the only bit of privacy in all that wide landscape.

The weed on one of the shattered lockers in the saloon looked as if that had been disturbed. So I crawled inside and pulled that open.

Inside was a little basket, of a size to fit into Elly's bag. In the basket was a loaf of bread, half a round cheese, a sausage, a pie in a napkin, four apples, a bottle of Hock, and a seed-cake. None of that had been there last time I looked. So Elly had put that there. And the odds were that she had put them there for the ragged man on the dyke, who was also the man the soldiers had been looking for.

We walked back down the wall to the harbour. There were a couple of squads of soldiers there, hanging about on the quay. I did not like the look of them. 'Well,' said the Gräfin. 'Thank you for your company, Captain.' She put out her hand. I took that. She wanted reassurance. So did I. That was more a holding than a shaking—

'Katja!' yelled a voice from the quay. 'What the devil do you think you're doing? We're to be at luncheon with the Burgomaster in seventeen minutes!'

That was von Tritt, jowls mottled with fury. The look he was giving her had nothing to do with lunch, and everything to do with jealous rage.

The Gräfin took her hand away from mine, slowly. She said, 'He'll have to wait.'

Von Tritt started screaming in German. I stood there and wanted to punch his nasty bald head for him. The Gräfin said, 'Thank you,' and gave me a last private smile, and went down the ladder to the *Delphin*. Von Tritt gave me a glare that filled me with satisfaction. I had been noticed as a human being. Better still, as a human being of whom he was jealous. He climbed back into his carriage. I sat on a bollard and waited.

Five minutes later she was back on the quay, all dolled up in a green gown and a hat, the complete fashion plate except for a smudge of crimson lake on the side of her hand as she pulled on her glove; the crimson lake she had used for my handkerchief, in the picture. I could hear von Tritt's voice start grinding away as the coachman opened the door. As I think I have said before, when I was with a woman I liked Hetty was always there, in the back of my mind like a ghost. But this time she had not been there at all. When they were gone, I went down the ladder to *Gloria*, took the nameboard out of my trousers, and nailed that up over the foc'sle stove. Sam was asleep, and the hammer did not stir him. But when I made tea he opened an eye, and focused on the new decoration.

'Kiel,' he said. 'Larse year. In the summer. Day we smote the Kaiser.'

'What?'

'That boat,' said Sam. 'Little yawl.'

And as he said it, I remembered.

I remembered a yawl with a ragged Red Ensign and a dinghy a couple of sizes too big, wallowing out under the ram of the *Kaiser Barbarossa*. And the chap on board, who had thrown something over the side, watched the bubbles rise, and settled to his tiller—

Last time I had seen the nameboard on the wall, the gold had been chipped, but there had been enough of it to set up a gleam in the July sun. Now there were only a few specks of leaf left, but the letters were clear, carved in firm but amateur script.

123

Dulcibella, she was called. And I would have bet a thousand pound her captain had been a man called Wilson.

I spent that afternoon being anxious about Dacre. I could not stop myself fussing about on deck, making little jobs to do, watching the soldiers hanging about on the quay. The tide was making fast.

Then about teatime a figure in Norfolk jacket and knickers walked over the sea wall. He came quickly down the quay, nodding at the soldiers. His face was flushed, the eyes narrow as gun slits. He squelched down the ladder onto the deck, and I could see his knees shake in his knickerbockers, which were soaking wet and covered with black ditch mud. 'Away,' he said, unslinging his knapsack.

'Where to?'

'Anywhere. Did you send the telegram?'

I said, nice and easy, 'Come you on down into the foc'sle.'

He looked at me very wild, as if he wanted to tell me to go to hell, but he saw that would do no good. I sat him on the bunk and Sam poured him tea. 'Now then, Captain Dacre,' I said. 'We wants a bit of truth out of you.'

Very jerky, he was. Very frightened. He started to shout. He damned my impudence, and told us we were being paid to sail the boat, not ask him questions, and that he would have us arrested for mutiny if we carried on this way. 'So help me,' he said, and his face was that hard and frantic I knew he believed himself, and that any argument would just goad him on. 'You remember your place,' he said. His eye went round that nasty little fo'c'sle, two bunks, stove, bucket, and assorted deck leaks. Look at the way they live, he was thinking. Like pigs. And of course that was their own fault, for being born servants—

'What's that?' he said. His eye had lit upon the nameboard above the stove. He was up, shaking with fury. There was a look on his face that made me certain sure that was him had strangled that soldier. He pries the nameboard off the bulkhead and breaks that over his knee and tosses that in the stove. 'Now if you have quite finished interrogating yer betters,' he says, 'you will make preparations to leave this place.'

'Plenty water now,' I said, blank as a plank and steady as a rock, like all good servants who are making plans of their own. He stood up, banging his head on the hatch, and left.

'Dear oh bloody dear,' excuse me, said Sam. 'What's eating him?'

'We'll find out,' I said. 'Never you fear, we'll find out.'

Letter from Captain Eric Dacre, late — —th Lancers, to Miss Erica Dacre, St Jude's, Eastbourne, Sussex.

Dearest Sissy,

Hello there! from your brother, still in the Frisian Islands and . . . well I will tell you Sissy from whom I have never had any secrets, wishing he was anywhere but. The fact of the matter is that things are going a bit shaky hereabouts. Last night someone set fire to what proves to have been Nessmersiel, which you may think is all to the good. This morning, seeking to take advantage of the confusion, I tried for Norden Creek. But instead of causing confusion, the Nessmersiel fire has got everyone on his toes, and if there is one thing worse than an ordinary German for nosiness it is a German who is on his toes. Really they are marvellously well organized – frighteningly, one might almost say.

Well what happened was that on my way to Norden Creek I ran slap into a detachment of police. As soon as I saw them I knew the game was up. So I pretended to slip and fell into a ditch, a great big ditch full of beastly black mud, and dropped the [here a line is crossed out] what I had with me into the bottom and stamped it well in. By the time I was done the police were standing in the reeds shouting that spies would be hanged, and I was, I would not tell anyone this but you my darling Sissy, I was in a blue funk. They searched me pretty thoroughly. And thank God I was soaked to the skin, for I was trembling so badly I could scarcely stand, and only for my saying I was cold they must have suspected something.

Dear Sissy, I hate myself. I am deathly afraid of this terrible place that we are in, where there is no such thing as land and no such thing as water, and the two change places at the drop of a hat. Yesterday I was looking over the side of the boat at a line of footprints where a bird had landed on the mud and taken wing again. I wished I had wings myself, instead of this horrible tub.

But lacking wings, I find myself as usual far more reliant on Webb than I should like. He is a man not without intelligence and resource, but one has learnt it is never wise to entrust responsibility to a class used to being taken responsibility for.

Heigh-ho; there are no rights without duties, and one must do one's duty. So tonight, we shall try again, and we shall see what we shall see.

There are a couple of rays of light in this sea of mud. One is that by intrusting me with this mission His Grace forces me to conclude that he feels a deep and real regard for my powers. The other is that we have met quite a jolly gel here, a Gräfin, rather 'greenery-yallery-Grosvenor-Gallery'(!) but pretty enough!! She is it appears a widow, so who knows!!??

Dear Sissy, remember while you Sleep
Your loving Twin
Eric

CHAPTER SIXTEEN

Deep Sleep of a Subby

I was out on deck, pulling up sails as if I hated them, when hooves came on the quay, and all of a sudden the Gräfin was standing up there in her green dress. I remember thinking, the state I was in, that's not lucky to see something green when you are casting off. 'Back the jib,' I said to Sam. He backed that, and the nose came off the breakwater, swinging out into the harbour, pivoting on the quarter line slipped round the bollard on the quay. I kept my eyes on the Gräfin. As she turned to watch us go our eyes met again. She raised a hand, at waist level; a hand with a yellow kid glove on it now, masking the smear of crimson lake she carried like a token. I nodded back, wishing we were staying. There was that bitter taste in my mouth that only the Duke had managed to produce, till now.

At the moment she waved, Dacre's head came up the hatch, so I was standing behind him and he was looking at the quay. He caught the wave and the little smile right between the eyes, and thought that was for him; there was nobody else on the boat, after all.

He took his hat off quick as a flash, and bowed. The Gräfin disappeared behind the jib as the bow came round.

'Leggo aft,' I said to Sam.

Gloria moved ponderously into the middle of the harbour, turning, as I brought the wind down her port side. Dacre smoothed his chin with the flat of his hand. 'Damn fine woman,' he said, licking his nasty chops. 'Like to make that one squeak between the sheets, what? *Hell* of a filly.'

I hauled the tiller over so the wind came round the stern and flapped into the wrong side of the sail and brought the boom

127

over with a flap and a crash, missing his pate by a couple of inches, worse luck. 'Have a care,' he snapped, then turned back to wave at the Gräfin. But she had gone below.

Dacre blew a kiss at her boat. I thought of wrapping the boathook round his red neck, but only for a moment. We moved out of the harbour and between the *leitdamms*. The glass was up. The clouds were going high and peaceful, and the wind was dropping. I said, 'We won't get far against the tide.'

He glanced at the dinghy, trailing astern on a slack painter. 'We'll anchor over there.' He waved towards the Riffgat, down inside Norderney. And on we drifted, limp-sailed, through the satin and scum of the water.

There was a lot of smoke in the Norderney gat. I counted a dozen plumes and the stacks that made them, hull-down in the dusky fringe of the night. Tall stacks, they were, with a yellow band. Tugboat stacks, heading for Wilhelmshaven or Hamburg. And between us and the distant smoke was another lot of smoke, close and getting closer, that came from a grey ship with a silly low bow pushing a pile of water tinted reddish-gold by the sinking sun. The *Blitz*, coming to have a look.

She came alongside, rocking us in her big wake. Von Brüning was on the wing of the bridge. 'Nice evening,' he said. 'How are the birds?' There was an ironical glint in his eye. Not surprisingly; that was the eye that had watched us deep-sea diving over the *Corinne*.

'Splendid,' said Dacre. 'Absolutely marvellous.'

Von Brüning stroked his beard. 'Where are you off to?' he said.

'Doesn't matter,' said Dacre.

'You won't get anywhere like this,' said von Brüning. 'You will permit me to tow you back to Norderney.'

'I say—'

'I insist,' said von Brüning, steely under the smile. 'It is no trouble, really. And this time I will leave you a guide. A pilot, really. So you will not have problems.' He smiled his nice smile, but there was no doubting that was an order, not an offer. A sub-lieutenant was already climbing down *Blitz*'s side, a pink chap with pale blue eyes and yellow hair cut peg-top, like a shaving brush that is. 'Not into Norderney,' hissed Dacre, so only I could hear. A couple of matlows with ribbony hats hove us a warp, and we made that fast round the bottom of the mast. *Blitz*'s funnel belched steam. And off we went.

Von Brüning seemed to be in a hurry. He cast us off at the harbour mouth with a wave and a line to the pierhead. The Subby said, 'Now we will go in to harbour.'

I said, 'Sorry?'

'Go!' said the Subby, using the sort of voice I expect you learn if you have been bossing fishermen about since you left your mother's lap, which in his case had not been long ago.

Well, I had had enough of being told what to do for that day. So I stood on the foredeck with a silly grin, holding the warp from the pier, two turns round the samson post. When the *Blitz* was safely out of sight, I let that go. 'Dearie me,' I says.

'Butterfingers,' says Sam.

That was nearly dark now. The lights inside the harbour were sliding by as the last of the flood took us east up the Riffgat. The Subby galloped aft and started bellowing away at Dacre most disrespectful, and Dacre was spreading his hands, and Sam and I stood and listened to the beautiful music of Dacre getting the dirty end of the stick for a change. Meanwhile *Gloria* had slid past the harbour mouth, and what with the lack of wind and the state of the tide, there was no getting back.

The Subby yelled himself silly. After five minutes or so, Dacre had to admit he understood him, and by that time the harbour mouth was a good cable's length away, and shrinking.

'He says drop anchor,' said Dacre.

'Too deep,' I said. 'Too much tide. Get the lead, Sam.'

So Sam started to cast the lead, very slow, getting the line round his foot and taking a terrible time untangling himself. And the long and the short of it was that by the time we dropped the hook we were in two fathom of water, the best part of a mile southeast of Norderney, on what amounted to the northern slopes of the Hohes Riff, the big sandbank that prods out from the mainland hereabouts.

'What about some dinner, Sam?' says Dacre, very chummy, for the Subby's benefit.

'Got a nice chop in Norddeich,' says Sam.

129

'Capital,' says Dacre, and takes the Subby below.

As I hung an anchor light on the forestay the smell of burning grease began drifting up from the fo'c'sle hatch. I sat up in the cockpit and looked at the stars in the black water; all right, I was eavesdropping. Dacre had the whisky out. But at the start the Subby was not having any. So Dacre made himself charming, the serpent. He was the older man, well along in depravity and vice, and I am afraid he played on that Subby like a stringed instrument. He flattered him, and jollied him along, and built him up till he felt just like one of the boys. Through the slot in the hatch I saw the poor child accept a glass of whisky and try not to screw up his pink face at the taste. But he was a game one, and he drained that, and tried not to look horrified when Dacre filled that up again.

After half an hour, that Subby had loosened up considerable. He wanted to know if Dacre thought his collar was in the English style, and whether his pea jacket would pass muster on the *Ark Royal*, and Dacre said that the King had one just like it.

After a bit, the Subby lurched off to the head. Through the slot in the hatch I could see his glass, half-empty on the saloon mahogany. As soon as the head door was shut Dacre whips a quart medicine bottle from his pocket and sloshes in a dose. I knew that bottle. That was chloral hydrate. He took a little belt himself, then slipped the bottle back into his pocket and swirled the glass to mix the stuff in. When the Subby comes out of the head, Dacre says, in English, 'Down the hatch, eh?'

'Mud in ze eye,' says the infant like a true Briton. And they drink their glasses down.

So there was Dacre, who I had just watched first win the trust of and then poison an officer of the High Seas Fleet. And here was me, captain of a yacht, keeping quiet while my boss went round drugging juveniles belonging to the navy of a friendly power—

I heard a noise. That was a strange noise still in those days, when most things had sails, not engines: a lot of high drumbeats beating across one another, with in the background the moaning of thrust bearings. The noise of plenty of big propellers. I looked away from whatever Sodom and Gomorrah was about

130

to crack loose in the saloon. And I saw the tugs.

There must have been a round dozen of them, sweeping in from the open sea on the first of the ebb, port lights shining like rubies in air and water at once, steaming lights casting a pale glow on the coal smoke pouring from their funnels. Their wakes came down on *Gloria* in long, shining billows, setting her rolling like a tub. There was the crash of breaking glass from the saloon, the slat of block against block, halyard against spar. Before the rolling had stopped they were gone, sweeping into the dark towards Norddeich.

Dacre's head came out of the hatch. 'Decanter gone,' he said. 'Be a good chap and get down here with a dustpan and brush, would you?'

The saloon stank of spilt whisky. The Subby was propped up in the corner. His eyes looked glassy, and his eyelids kept clattering down.

'Took a bit queer,' said Dacre airily. 'Whisky on an empty tum-tum.' He was down to his long underwear, pulling on a pair of navy-blue flannels. When his feet popped out of the end, they were wearing black canvas shoes. He stuck his head into a dark blue gansey. 'But he'll sleep well, anyway – steady the Buffs!'

For that poor Subby had at last given up the fight. His eyelids came down so hard you could practically hear them, and his head rolled across and hit the bulkhead a terrible wallop.

'Best get him to bed,' said Dacre, frowning as if he was worried for his guest.

Murderer, I thought. Assassin, bomber. Now poisoner. We were decent chaps, Sam and me. A little smuggling was one thing. This was too much and he could not be let get away with any more of it.

'Call Sam, eh?' he said.

We lugged that Subby into the sleeping cabin and pulled some blankets over the remains. He had a lump on his head, and his breath smelt like Hicks the chemists' shop in Wells. When we had him tucked up, Dacre popped his head round the door. 'Word with you, Webb?'

'Dinner's ready,' said Sam, and whacks the plates on the table.

'Ah,' said Dacre, mind not on it. Sam went huffily back to his grease fumes. 'Now then. I want to go and look at some, ah, nightjars in Hilgenriedersiel.'

When Hetty and I used to go up on Kelling Heath of a summer there had always been nightjars whirring away in the gorse. There might even be nightjars at Hilgenriedersiel. There were also, according to the Gräfin, yards, whatever that meant.

'Cursed nuisance, and sorry to trouble you,' he said. 'But I want you to put me down on the Hohes Riff.'

'Could do,' I said. 'Tomorrow morning, when the tide's fit.'

'Tonight. Now.'

'What if that chap wakes up and asks where you've gone?'

'I don't expect he'll wake up. Sleep like tops, these young 'uns.'

He had that look that they give you when they have forgotten that you are human, with curiosity. I said, oily as you please, 'All right. We off, then?'

As I now mentioned, he was dressed top to toe in dark colours. On his head he wore a little old stocking cap, black. He looked like a nasty little French acrobat. He shouldered his pack and ate a mouthful of bread and burned pork chop while I took a squint at the chart. Then we went on deck.

Here he hummed and hawed for a bit as I hove the dinghy up short on her painter. 'I . . . that is . . .'

'You don't want nobody to know you've gone for a little row.'

'That's the ticket.'

All right, I thought. This time, no mistake, I will wait until you are in the middle of whatever nastiness you are planning, and I shall turn you in.

I muffled up the dinghy rowlocks with bits of rag. He struggled down and plumped on the after thwart. I let go and found a transit with *Gloria*'s anchor light and a bonfire someone had lit to boil shrimps on Norderney. Then I started to row.

High water was about an hour gone. The sea was like a great black field sown with stars, with a quarter moon wavering in the ridge and furrow of the dinghy's wake. The yellow lights of Norderney fell away and left us hanging, the sea huge and the land low, so you could feel the curve of the world, and us cocked up on the top of it.

Dacre felt that too. That made him uneasy. He hated water.

As we moved east along the south shore of the Riffgat, that was just about possible to tell where we were by the pull of the tide; strong in the Riffgat as the ebb got going, less so on the south side of the channel. The withies had been chopped out here too. After about four miles, I took a bearing on the light-house and began to pull south south-east.

'What are you doing?' said Dacre.

I did not answer, because I was concentrating, crabbing across the tide. According to the survey in the notebooks there was a little creek, the merest finger of a tributary, beyond the Lutets-burger Plate, on the south side of the main flow of the Riffgat. I found the side of the channel with an oar, pushed off, heading north now, rowing against the current still, navigating by the knock of the blades on first one side then the other of that little drowned river.

'Where are we?' said the anxious voice of Dacre.

I was feeling my way, fully occupied as you might say. Then the blade of my right oar crunched sand, and the left at the same time, and I gave one pull, both together hard, and the nose hit bottom.

We sat there, proper motionless now, while the great moving sheet of water passed us by.

A steamer chugged up-channel, a green starboard light in the black Riffgat. Her wake swept up the creek and rocked us, bumping the bow against the sand. 'Well?' said Dacre. 'What are you waiting for? Row on, man.'

'You're ashore,' says I.

As the steamer's wake went past us, the waves sharpened and collapsed with a small roar. When the sea settled again, the shining glass was streaked with black lines like tar.

'What's that?' says Dacre.

'Sand,' says I. 'Tide's going out.'

He laughed, a nervous, high laugh. He was planning some-thing, all right. 'Well I must say,' says he. 'Moses at the Red Sea again, eh? You are a trump, Webb.'

'Straight inland for Hilgenriedersiel,' says I, blank as a plank.

He stepped over the stern of the dinghy. I watched that jaunty little shadow splash through the puddles and march inland; a soldier's gait, not a birdwatcher's, carrying that pack of dynamite for the nightjars. Then I tripped the dinghy out into our little creek, and made the tripping line fast to a bit of a stick I had brought along. After, I pulled out a bit of bread and liver sausage and ate that. When I had swallowed the last of the sausage I started after him.

CHAPTER SEVENTEEN

The Nightjars of Hilgenriedersiel

The sand was firm underfoot, with a pale gleam in the moonlight. Behind me, the dinghy merged immediately with the darkness of the horizon. When the tide went out that would be below the level of the sand, and nobody who was not looking for it would be able to see it. The night was still as well water, the only sounds the breath in my ears and the big rustle of the sea.

Dacre seemed to be going straight for the northward bulge of the sea wall to the west of Hilgenriedersiel, where I had first seen the group of soldiers. For a moment I laid myself flat, putting my eyes close to the sand. Ahead, the little black figure was still stumping along against the stars, trending to the left now. Above the wall was what looked like the glow of lights; nightjars, perhaps, putting on illuminations.

I kept about three hundred yards behind him. He did not turn his head; he had no reason to think that anyone would be following him out of the dark sea.

So I tramped after him, skidding and sticking on the mud, grim and sick and to tell the truth in a miserable state of fright. There had been too many lies told, and too much dynamite packed. Paid hand I might be, but I bled when cut and choked when hanged, just like the gentry.

You could smell the shore before you saw it – the rotten whiff of the wrack, mixed with the tang of sea lavender and thyme. And behind that, a raw, bad-eggy smell that some folk might think was sewage, but anyone marsh-bred knew was fresh-dug sea mud.

Fresh-dug sea mud, and a new railway. Dredging, perhaps,

and a railhead. Yet on the chart Hilgenriedersiel looked like nothing at all.

Samphire whipped at my boots, then brush and coarse grass. The sea wall cut the stars. For a moment I lost Dacre. Then I caught the twink of a star on the buckle of his rucksack. He was walking fast, along to the left. I went after him.

The wall turned suddenly right, sloping away into a big muddy ditch, half-full of water and a hundred feet wide, from which rose that waft of raw mud. A dredged channel. Blocking the channel was a blank-faced mass that looked like lock gates. Running away on either side of the gates was the dyke, with at its foot a wire fence. From the far side of the dyke came a surly hum, like a lot of bees in a room. Somewhere close ahead a train whistle shrieked long and loud. Dacre had vanished.

I could not imagine what had become of him. I stood still as a stone and listened to my heart pound, and scanned the line of the wall.

Something moved against the glow of lights in the sky. That turned into two soldiers, wearing long greatcoats, with rifles on their shoulders.

Very slow and quiet, I lay down.

The two chaps on the wall marched off solemn and steady. My dark-accustomed eyes caught a movement on the wall behind them.

That was Dacre, creeping like a serpent towards the base of the wire. I saw him struggle with the meshes, hands in front of him. He was trying to break in, that was plain. My heart was thundering in my chest, the way that thundered when you saw the float start to bob when Hetty and me were children fishing for eels off of the quay at Blakeney. I drew breath to shout to the sentries; look out, here he come, he's a murderer, a burglar. But the thing about the eel fishing was that the bobbing was just play. You had to wait for the float to go down and away into the murky water. Then you took your action.

So I thought, not yet. He hasn't done anything yet. Give him enough rope to hang himself proper.

Seemingly he had been through fences before. He gave a sort of struggle and a wriggle, and then he was through the fence and over the wall. You silly beggar, I told him. Oh, you silly beggar, what are you taking us into? My mouth was dry as dust. But at the same time I noticed I was getting closer to the wire my own self.

And the next thing I knew there I was, right up against the fence. That was wire mesh, on high concrete posts, with barbed wire at the top. As I felt along the coarse grass with my fingers, I came to a bit that felt scuffed up, and sure enough when I pulled at the base of the wire, that lifted easily in my hands. I remember thinking, you can't go in here, not with a fence like this, and those sentries, not even to catch Dacre at whatever he is up to. But by then I already had my head through, and was squirming my shoulders under.

Up on the dyke, someone coughed.

I could hear the marsh empty at my back, and the tick of an insect in the grass, and the little jingle of the meshes of the wire around me. And I could hear the sentries' boots, thump, thump on the wall.

And all I could do was lie there and hold my breath, and think, I am not part of this, but that is going to be hard to explain to the sentries.

Thump, thump went the boots. The men were grumbling. All leave had been cancelled.

'After,' said one of them.

'*Scheisse*,' said the other one, gloomy as hell.

The first one said something about English girls that made no sense. They were so close I could smell tobacco and sweat on them. That's it, I thought. Now they will see me—

But they had already walked on.

Run away, said the sensible parts of Charles Webb.

But Charles Webb shoved the base of the wire back into the ground, and wriggled up and over the dyke.

The huts came right up to the base of the wall. Beyond them was what looked like a big yard, with men thronging in dim yellow pools of electric light, squads of soldiers marching, the flame of a match illuminating a heavy grey beard as a workman lit his pipe.

But no Dacre.

I took a couple of steps forward, between two huts. Something hard and heavy knocked me over and flattened my face into the mud. I half rolled towards it, but that pinned my arms and legs, and I remember thinking, hell, this is a person who has been taught to fight, because I can't move a bloody – I did actually say bloody, I remember that, and the frightening crush of those hard fingers on my windpipe, like that was last week – a bloody muscle. I said, 'You—' then ran out of breath. There was a train chuffing, or perhaps that was the blood in my ears. My mind filled with blood and that mottled blue face in the creek, water gurgling in the mouth. The stars began going out.

Then the fingers went away, and the stars came back, with Dacre's thatched cannonball of a head blotting out the ones in the middle. He said, in a voice like a wet thumb on a hot stove, 'I told you to stay with the boat you silly interfering little bugger.'

I was furious. I should have shouted, except his thumbs had crushed the voice out of my throat. I croaked, 'Murderer.'

'German,' he hissed, and that filtered into my mind that he was scared out of his wits. 'Speak German.'

'You can have my notice,' I said, but I said that in German. 'I'm not sailing you round while you kill people you nasty murdering little twerp.' That was silly. All I can say was that I was half-dead, and I meant every word of it.

'Go back to the boat.'

'No.'

'Do as you're told.'

'Not bloody likely. What do you think you are up to, Mr Dacre?'

'You don't need to know.'

'I'll be the judge of that.'

I could feel him staring at me. I could smell the whisky and tobacco on him. He was thinking, I could tell. My throat was coming back to me. I could have shouted out, then.

But I didn't.

'All right,' he said. 'You won't like this.'

'That's up to me to decide what I like,' I said.

'Ah,' he said, sounding sort of puzzled, as if the world was turned upside down now that servants were asking questions gentry had to answer. 'Well, you'd better come with me. If anyone asks, you're a shipwright from Emden. If they find out different it's a hanging matter.'

I sat there and rubbed my neck. A silly little voice said *Curiosity killed the cat, Charlie*. The train's chuffing had stopped, and that was hissing steam from its valves.

'*Komm*,' said Dacre. '*Schnell*.'

I followed him out of the dark area behind the huts and into the yard, which was a sort of gravel square. Dacre had his hat off and his hair was sticking out like the spines on a sea urchin, which made a good disguise, him normally being so neat. I shambled along beside him, rubbing my aching neck, grinning at nothing. The lamplight ended on the muddy faces of more sea walls. The place was a sort of hollow square of sea wall, a space between the inner dyke and an outer dyke, walled in with more dykes so that was invisible from the sea, and invisible from inland and on either side. On a sort of earth platform behind the square were the sheds whose roofs I had seen in the afternoon. There were many more of them than I had thought – streets of them, in fact. The streets and the yard were full of soldiers and workmen and carts and horses. Midnight that might be, but that was as crowded as Yarmouth of a bank holiday.

Dacre led me through the crowd to the platform where the train was hissing, up to its hubs in a carpet of steam. That was a single-track spur, the sort of thing they built out to Wells to take whelks to the Cockneys.

The train was the same sort that had held me up that morning on the level crossing west of Norden. Some of the waggons looked as if they were meant for passengers. Others had little high windows, barred, too high for men but about right for horses. The rest were flatcars bearing odd-shaped loads covered with green tarpaulins. The tarpaulins were coming off, and men with handspikes and tackles were working on the loads, very fast and efficient.

When I saw what was on those flatcars I stood with my mouth open and I could not move. Dacre yanked at my sleeve. 'Let's get finished,' he said in German. 'Then we can get some sleep, in God's name. Down here.'

He led me to the edge of the quay.

They had dug the *tief* out into quite a basin. There were steps down, and ramps leading from the train's platform so what was on those flatcars would roll down here with no more pulling and hauling than necessary.

But that was what was in the basin itself that stopped my breath and turned my knees to jelly.

The basin was full of barges.

You have to understand that when I say full, I do not mean just tied up alongside the quays. I mean solid, jam packed, shoved in there like fish-boxes in Grimsby market in the middle of herring time. They were big barges, too; 120 foot long, twenty foot wide, built to go to sea, with a bit of sheer to help them ride and a flare to the bows to keep them dry. They were moored six along the side of the basin, then ten deep, though I might have been mistaken, because my eyes were actually watering with shock. Any road, there were about sixty barges in there. Some of them were empty, but some of them had been loaded.

I stood there with my knees shaking in my trousers. Dacre's knees had shook that afternoon, when he had got back from Norden. Now I understood why.

Sorry, Dacre, I thought. Not that I would have said that. But I thought that, all right. I will admit I thought that.

The empties were at the bottom of the ramps, waiting for their cargoes to come rolling down from the train, which was not the first train, and would not by the look of it be the last. What they were waiting for was guns. Big guns, little guns, middle-sized guns. Enough guns to blow a country to kingdom come, with limbers and ammunition all complete.

Military manoeuvres, I told myself. But I knew different. All those men. All those guns.

Military manoeuvres, my left foot. This was the real thing.

Dear, I wished I had stayed on the boat.

'Coil those ropes,' said Dacre, in German. There was sweat on his forehead. 'Those ones,' he said, pointing to a tangle of old hawser on the stones. '*Dummer Kerl.*'

Odd as that may sound, that was almost a relief to get an order. I bent down and started sorting and coiling with a will.

Dacre strutted off down the ramp and onto the dock, among the barges; same jaunty walk, lighting a Meerschaum pipe as he went. He found a barge with no one anywhere near it, hopped on board as if he owned it, and disappeared under the little bit of deck that had up in its bow—

'Hey!' yapped a voice. 'Who are you?'

That felt as if all the blood had drained out of my head. I found myself looking at a chap in a dark uniform with a plainish looking spiked hat. A policeman.

'Georg Schlumpf,' I said. 'Who does that look like I bloody am?' begging your pardon, in the broadest Fries I could dig up, still coiling.

He took a step back at that. He had an awkward, long-nosed face, and I saw with a sinking heart that that might do for an English bobby, but Germans were different. His nose was twitching, his curranty little eyes burning with trouble. 'Imperence,' he says, or words to that effect. '*Ausweis*?' Which means pass, of course. Well I went numb all over, but not as numb as I was going to be when they hanged me, which they would do for certain definite.

Then there rang upon the scene another voice. That was a familiar voice; a voice to stop your heart beating, but just now the voice of an angel. 'Constable!' that said. 'Your orders were to watch the loading, not harass labourers doing their duty.' That was a woman's voice, clear as a bell, lofty as a church on a mountain. From the top of my eye I could see her, tall and slim in a dark skirt, smart little hat tipped forward over her eyes, nose in the air. My neck was hot with blood, but I kept my head down. That was the Gräfin, and she was saving my life. Then up alongside her came another man, cap crammed over his little pig eyes, neck bulging over his collar. Baron von Tritt.

'Well?' he said. And I knew that this time I really had had it.

But I was a member of the working class, doing my work and therefore invisible. That was the policeman he was looking at. The policeman was standing there like he had a poker up his behind, if you will excuse the expression, stammering about duty and not making any sense at all. And I knew that if I did not get out of this by going full ahead, I was not going to get out of this at all.

So I said in heavy Fries, anvils heavy that was, 'I am a mindin' of my own business when this hair owd fule of a carper start throoin his white about, and I still ont know what the hill he want or what the hill I done to git wrang a him—'

Von Tritt ignored me. 'As Her Ladyship says,' he said. 'You do your job, and let this oaf do his.'

'*Jawohl*, Herr General Baron,' said the policeman. 'As the Herr General Baron orders.'

If that had been von Brüning, that would have been it. But to von Tritt I was a servant, not a human being, and, besides, he was showing off to the Gräfin. I could have kissed his nasty scarry face. He walked on, talking to a Herr Bohm about steam dredgers. Behind him, the Gräfin caught my eye, and held that a second as the air thickened up between us. Then without changing her expression she walked away.

I put my head down and coiled like a ropewalk finisher.

The footsteps moved off; gentry footsteps, dawdling, scuffing, clicking their new-cobbled steel heels on the paving.

I was running with sweat, and the coil was spilling round my feet like a live serpent. I picked that up, and started again. Beside me, Dacre's voice bellowed, 'All done. Let's get a glass of beer.' The policeman, standing to attention twenty feet away, did not even turn his head.

We walked back in to the crowd. The stevedores had stripped the train. Dacre led me through clouds of steam and broken light and the blowing of whistles. I was dazed, like a man who falls off a high mast and finds himself still living.

'Here,' said Dacre, and shoved me smartly between two wagons. I stumbled into the shadows, barking my shin on a coupling. Dacre was balanced on a sort of step, whistling. Suddenly there was a pant and a jerk and the carriage behind me struck me in the back. Dacre's hand grabbed my collar, and hauled me onto the step. The train drew out, the electric lights flicking past one by one. A sentry stared at us. Dacre waved. Then we were through the fence and in the dark of the night.

'Jump,' said Dacre, and was gone.

I jumped myself, and hit the ground hard. The compound was a box of light in the sky. Near at hand an owl was calling. I hardly knew was I dead or alive.

Well, we skirted across some swampy fields and through a couple of cold drains, and got over the sea wall and onto the flats. By the time we reached the dinghy we had been gone two hours.

We rinsed off the mud with cold water, and I let the ebb carry us till *Gloria*'s mast cut the stars ahead. Sam and the Subby were snoring like bull seals, and the tide bubbled cheerily round her counter. She was a horrible old pig of a thing, painted up like a Heybridge bicycle that everyone rides and nobody marries. But when I climbed up her side that particular night, that felt like coming home.

I went down into the saloon without being asked. I sat down like a tree falling. 'Now, then,' I said. 'Perhaps you would be so good as to explain what the hell you are playing at.'

CHAPTER EIGHTEEN

A Riddle Explained

Dacre tipped whisky into a glass and took a gulp. He looked tired, and the slackness of his flesh showed him harder, more weaselly, with a nasty glint in his eye, half-energetic, half-mad. He still looked like a murderer. But what we had seen tonight was all murder. Perhaps that was a case of fighting fire with fire.

He said, 'Look here, how much do you know about the German naval buildup?'

I thought straight away of Mr Childers, sitting behind the table in the Duke's library in Mount Street. The Duke had cut in on him, because what he had been going to tell me could not be trusted to servants.

'It's like this,' he said. 'They haven't had a Navy worth talking about. But old Tirpitz has been building battleships hand over fist. I hear you've raced against the Kaiser at Kiel. Few years ago, he used English crews. But you've probably noticed, his crew are Germans now. Training. Experience. And why d'you think they're doing this? Getting 'em up to snuff, eh? But what for?'

That sounded familiar so far. In my mind I could see the grey director towers of the cruisers that had frightened the life out of Dacre last week, black and white ensigns stiff in the breeze. But I could also see our North Sea Fleet on manoeuvres, ship after ship in line ahead, a bulwark of guns and armour trailing smoke from horizon to grey horizon, unbreachable. I said, 'They'll be a while catching up.'

He gave me a good-boy nod. 'They say there is no intention of going to war with Britain, their old friend. They're looking to

France, and further east: Japan, Russian coaling stations in China, you name it.' He put his hands on the table. 'But it's all rubbish. Of course war at sea with England is out of the question. So they're planning an invasion by stealth. Three hundred men in each of those barges, with horses and guns. Motors, even. War motors.'

Sixty barges, there had been in that basin inside the lock gate. 'Eighteen thousand men,' I said. 'They won't get far.'

Dacre reached into the drawer, and pulled out the chart, my chart, and unfolded that on the table. 'Seven siels,' he said. 'All closed except Norddeich. That's what they told us, isn't it?'

I looked down at that chart. In the Ems estuary, there was Greetsiel. Then there was the Norden creek. Then came Hilgenriedersiel, Nessmersiel, Dornumersiel, Bensersiel, Neuharlingsiel, Carolinensiel, and round the corner in the Jade estuary Hooksiel and a cluster of others.

'Look how the railway runs,' said Dacre.

The railway ran parallel with the coast, linking the *tiefs*, the tidal channels that joined the sea at the *siels*. The Greetsiel *tief* stopped well short of the railway, as did the Hilgenriedersiel *tief—*

Not any more.

Dacre said, 'You want an invasion fleet at sea, marshalled on one tide. Which harbours would you choose?'

That was a question that answered itself. I put my finger out, and drew it along the coast from Norden creek to Carolinensiel.

'That's what we think too. Seven of 'em. Each one with a collection of barges the size of the one you saw tonight, if not bigger.'

That drew me in; the innocent black and white coast-line, with the hatched line of the sea wall. But in the shadow behind the wall, provisions and equipment brought up on the railway, and a quarter of a million men waiting in their mud-holes for the signal. And how would anyone ever find out, unless he could fly?

The saloon was full of the clop of the tide. I said, 'So what's to be done?'

Dacre was looking at his hands. He said, 'We've got the

145

greatest Navy in the world. And the stupidest Admiralty. A couple of chaps got a whiff of this last year—'

'Mr Childers,' I said.

'He was one,' said Dacre. 'There was another chap. Wilson. Your Wilson. Fumbling bungling bloody amateurs, both of them. Funny. Most of this was started off by amateurs, on both sides.'

'Dollmann?' I said, at hazard.

'Goodness me,' he said, with a sneer and a lift of the eyebrow. 'Very acute. Dollmann was an Englishman, actually. Good family.' He licked his lips and ducked his head, and for a moment Dacre the toady showed through Dacre the . . . well, secret agent. '*Excellent* family. Naval man. Royal Navy, I mean. He spotted the weakness in our defenses, laid the plan. Bloody traitor. But the Germans never trusted him, you see. Once a traitor, always a traitor, I suppose they thought. So they quietly had him killed.' The eyes were on my face. 'Good God, man, it was war. All this is war.'

Mrs de Blank with her dead children was war. So was the strangled soldier.

'Wilson and Childers started it,' he said. 'They did a decent job of work, for amateurs. Particularly Wilson. Quite a genius, in his way. They saw what we saw, in its early stages of course, and came straight home and went to the Admiralty. Well, the Admiralty thought, silly beggars, but they said, most interesting. But a decent warship draws better than five fathoms, and everyone knows that sea battles are fought between decent warships, not overgrown canoes sneaking about in the shallows. Trafalgar is the Admiralty's idea of a good sea battle. England expects its admirals to charge in line ahead, and sporting enemies to do likewise.

'So the minute these fellows I was talking about were out of the room the Admiralty filed the report under *T* for tommyrot, and forgot about it. And here we jolly well are.'

'Where's that?'

'Use your brains, man. About a week away from a surprise invasion of England by way of the Wash.'

Someone in the cabin said, 'The Wash, eh?' using my voice.

'It goes like this,' he said. 'The railway brings the troops to the barges. The troops embark. The tugs tow them off on the high tide. They marshal here, where we are now, for Heaven's sake, behind the screen of the islands, where nobody can see them. The Kaiser is smiling, the Chancellery obliging. England suspects nothing. An escort of the High Seas Fleet meets the barges and their tugs outside the seegats. Forty hours at sea; a dawn landing on the beaches between Boston and Skegness. If one of our ships sees their smoke in the daytime, they will assume that it is merely the High Seas Fleet on manoeuvres. And the following dawn, the the hammerblow. Two hundred thousand highly-trained Germans marching from Lincolnshire inland, smashing at Nottingham and Manchester and Birmingham and Sheffield, the workshop of the world. Opposition? What opposition can there be to such an army? They will blow the railway lines as they march. Clausewitz, as usual. Speed and decisiveness. Classic Prussian stuff. It will take us a week to organize ourselves. And by that time the manufactories of the kingdom will be blazing wrecks, and the heart of the Empire will have ceased to beat.'

I noticed that 'would' had become 'will,' and that little thing just about froze my blood. I could see that mass of barges and tugs jammed with men under the spring sky—

'Never,' I said, not because I did not believe it, but because I did not want to.

'They're amazing, the Germans,' he said. 'The things they can do when they put their mind to it. Good God!' he cried, 'they've only been a nation these thirty years, and look at them!' He took a gulp of whisky. 'Anyway. Childers has written a sort of penny dreadful. *The Riddle of the Sands*, he calls it. If the Admiralty won't listen to him, he says, the public will, and there will be a mighty stink. I think he's right. It's all there, in that book. Names changed to protect the innocent. Bit of love interest crammed in for the ladies, bless 'em, and . . . well, things tidied up, if you know what I mean. Things he doesn't know written about as if he does. An ending more exciting than real life, because after all he wants everyone to read this book, failure if they don't. And of course he has to make out that the Admiralty are already impressed with his arguments, when you know and I know that they aren't, the donkeys. But they will be. They will be.'

'So why are we here?'

He smiled, a corpse's smile. 'It's in the presses. Ready in May. But the Germans are ready now. They'll sail any time after the tides start getting bigger again.'

I nodded, very matter-of-fact. That meant any time after two days from now. They had a better than average chance of easterly breezes at this time of year, too. I said, 'Excuse my asking, but what's in it for the Duke?'

'He's a patriot,' said Dacre. I could feel a sort of confusion in the man. We had been on opposite sides of the fence. But he was a servant of the Duke, and he did not know the Duke's mind any better than I did.

'And he probably owns factories in places this lot would set fire to once they were ashore?'

'Look out for number one, that's the ticket,' said Dacre. 'All wars are about that. The Empire's a matter of trade, which is the flow of money. The Germans want to control the flow. Our Government wants to do the controlling itself. That's why people keep an Army and a Navy.'

I said, 'There's more to life than money.'

'Can't think what,' said Dacre.

Well, the world was never going to be the same place again, but I was beginning to be able to think straight. I said, 'If they're planning an invasion, why are they letting us hang about here?'

'Wouldn't do any good if they threw us out,' he said. 'We might talk about what we have seen. They don't know how much we have seen. Far better to keep us here, under their eye.'

'So why won't they lock us up?'

'That's what you were doing in the telegraph office,' he said. 'I told von Brüning I'm telegraphing progress reports to Lloyd's every couple of days without fail. You can be sure he's taking a look at them. The bonus from his point of view is that if Lloyds is getting salvage reports from a sharp-eyed investigator in the Frisian Islands, and said investigator says nothing about invasion preparations, then it won't enter anyone's heads that invasion preparations are being made.'

I thought of the drinker with the trilby in the telegraph

office. 'I send the cables, you plant the bombs.'

'That's right.'

'But not at Norden.'

The smug look went off his face as if I had let him have it with a bucket of water. He did not like the idea that I had eyes and a mind.

'They chased you off,' I said. 'Didn't they?'

'How do you know?'

'Stands to reason. You wouldn't get in in daylight. You ran away, dropped the bomb in a ditch, I don't know.'

He stuck his nose in the air, and I knew I was right.

'How long till your bomb tonight goes off?' I said.

'Three days.' That made him feel clever again.

'And who lit that fire last night?'

He tried to look superior, but he lacked the equipment. 'Accident,' he said.

'Or Mr Wilson.'

He laughed out loud. 'Oh, yes,' he said, very sarcastic. 'Him and his box of matches.'

'And why not?'

'The age of the amateur's over,' he said, very smug. 'We're professionals now. Professional yacht hands. Professional secret agents.'

Professional cads, I thought. I said, 'That was the nameboard off his yacht that you burned this afternoon.'

'How do you think it would have looked next time von Brüning came aboard? There's no room for sentiment in this world, man.'

As Mrs de Blank discovered. 'Sentiment's why you're here,' I said.

'Beg your pardon?'

'The Gräfin was there tonight,' I said.

'Von Tritt too,' he said. 'I saw 'em.'

'And she saw me.'

His face went quite blank. 'She *what*?'

'She stopped a policeman who wanted to see my pass. She saved my bacon.'

But he was not listening. His face had turned cruel and

wooden. The bottom fell out of my stomach. Soldiers got strangled, and dynamite and phosphorus made big bangs and big fires, in which humans were blown apart and roasted alive. You did not stop invasions without taking lives. Perhaps the Gräfin was now someone Dacre had to keep quiet.

I said, 'She won't say anything. She did that to help.'

Dacre said, 'And since when are you an expert on what Countesses think?'

'Countesses are women,' I said, and looked him in the eye. He flushed and looked away, and I saw he knew that master or servant, what we were was men, and he did not like the idea.

He nodded, as if he was already thinking about something else, but I could see that was still in his mind. 'Now if you have quite finished,' he said, 'I should like to turn in.'

I sort of screwed up my courage. I had not finished. I said, 'About the Gräfin.'

'What?'

'She won't say anything.'

'Webb,' he snarls, every inch the murderer, 'you have been reading women's novels.'

Well I started to get cross then. I said, 'Mr Dacre, if anything happens to that lady I will go ashore and tell them where you have hid your bombs and leave you to get home on your own.'

He stared at me. 'But your country,' he said.

'Working chaps haven't got no country,' I said, which I did not mean. 'We're professional. We look out for number one. Like Dukes, but smaller scale.'

Well he could see I meant it. He looked at me out of his nasty narrow eyes. Then he said, 'They told me you're a lady's man. But don't you think you've set your sights a bit high?'

I said, 'That's a chance you'll have to take, isn't it?' We looked at each other, and that was man to man, not master to servant, and I could see he was jealous, but a bit amazed, too. 'She's only half-German,' I said. 'The rest of her's Danish. She's got Wilson ashore, and she's feeding him. She's best friends with Clara Dollmann, who is Wilson's fiancée. So apart from anything else he is dead keen to undo what her dad did. An affair of honour, they call that.'

'I thank you kindly for the information,' he said with a sneer. That was as if I had let the air out of him. Then he said, more or less to himself or his whisky, 'Why didn't she tell me this herself?'

Well if he could not work that out for himself, nobody was going to be able to teach him. I went to bed.

I lay there and thought about dukes who wanted to stop invasions to protect their fortunes. Of an empire like a lion with a noble face whose arteries ran money, not blood. And about wars fought to protect such empires.

The same tide knocked against the overhangs, and the same stars hung in the porthole.

But everything had changed.

CHAPTER NINETEEN

An Anchor Watch

I awoke next morning to find that blowing a fresh breeze out of the west. I dimly heard Sam frying a breakfast and hauling that through to the saloon. When he came back, I was crouching at the basin splashing warm kettle water on my neck. 'Blast you look rough,' he said. He waited for me to get my face out, tipped in the crocks and started washing up. 'Hell knows what they was up to last night. That here Subby's asleep in his brekfuss. And Mr Dacre got a face on him fit to stop a steam tug. He want to see you, boy.'

I filled my mug out of the washing up water and began to shave. I had watched the gentry amuse themselves everywhere from the Fastnet to the Faeroes. Sir Alonso, now; he was the real thing. So was Mr Childers. But this Duke was a cold and slimy one, up to all dodges. And Dacre was the kind of chap you would expect to find working for him. Devious, really. I mean if he had said, look you here boys, here is a quarter of a million Germans polishing up their bayonets to stick in British guts, me and Sam would have said, all right, here we go, right behind you, and we might even have called him sir. But instead, he had kept that from us as if we were children, but brought our necks into the noose just the same.

I said to Sam, 'Sit you down, boy, and I will tell you a story.' And I told him, quiet like, while he sat there behind his moustache.

When I was done he stared into his mug like Gypsy Petulengro at Fakenham Races. Finally he looked up. 'We got to get to sea,' he said, and from the glint in his eye I knew he did not mean run away. 'We got to find a bloody great battleship of

152

ourn and tell him blow the living shite out of these here sneaking Hun devils.'

'Battleship'll draw five and a half fathom of water,' I said, and I noticed I was talking very reasonable and steady, as if that was about where to haul a net, and not the end of the world. 'Plus if we went to sea, how do we know we'd find one? And if we do, how do you plan to persuade him to open fire on a country that belong to a nevvy of the King on the say-so of a couple of fishing boys?'

'Bugger me sideways,' says Sam, a remark for which there is never any call. 'Then what about this here Duke of yours? He'll have friends in the Government that he can tell.'

'He's already got the brushoff from the Navy.'

He said, 'So that's up to us, then,' knocked out his pipe, and went on with the washing up.

About two minutes later there was the hiss of steam and the whoop of a whistle, and the *Blitz*'s steam pinnace was alongside.

I now said the breeze had gone westerly. That was kicking up now, whining in the shrouds and raising a sharp little sea that was no amusement to man nor beast. I climbed into my peajacket and went aft and stood to attention next to the ensign drumming on its staff, and received those I now knew to be my enemies. In the pinnace von Brüning was standing to attention himself, cap-brim well down over the eyes, beard fluttering in the wind.

Well I tried to hate him, but he was an ordinary chap, that was all. 'Morning, sir,' I said. He looked straight through me; cut me dead.

As he stepped aboard, Dacre's head popped up in the hatch, and very terrible he did look, black under the eyes, stubble on his chin, hair like an explosion at an upholstery works. A blast of old whisky and stale underwear rolled up with him, and I saw von Brüning's nostrils twitch as they caught it, and I know mine were twitching too. 'I have come for my sub-lieutenant,' said von Brüning. 'You did not go into Norderney.'

'Me crew let go a rope or something. We anchored as you see us. Made an evening of it.' He laughed. 'Only thing missing was the billiard table.'

'I hope you have not been teaching him nasty habits,' said

von Brüning, not bothering to soften the remark with a smile. Enemy or no, you could not help liking the man.

'Just a glass or two,' said Dacre, with a bounderish grin that made von Brüning wince. 'Fritz! Get yer arse up here!'

The Subby came up the companionway and staggered into the cockpit under his captain's sharp eye. I felt almost sorry for the poor devil. His uniform looked slept-in, and a runnel of dried spit linked the side of his mouth and the silly too-high collar. Von Brüning said, 'Mr Dacre, I must speak to you.'

'Fire away,' said Dacre. 'How 'bout a bit of breakfast?'

Von Brüning just straightforward ignored the offer. He said, cold and scornful, 'It is time for you to go home.'

My heart went into my boots. But you had to hand it to Dacre, he could keep a straight face. 'Home?' he said. 'Why's that?'

'The weather is deteriorating,' said von Brüning. 'We fear for your safety. This is a bad place in a blow. And you have seen Norddeich and Norderney. Come back when the other ports are open.'

I saw Dacre's eyes sort of haze over. He laughed, a bookie's laugh. 'I assure you that my company's claim to the *Corinne* is well established.' He looked grimmer. 'Do I understand that you are ejecting us from German waters?'

'That is correct.'

'On what grounds?'

'Your activities here are not in keeping with your stated reason for visit.'

'Excuse me?'

'Your investigations of the *Corinne*,' said von Brüning. 'You have been less than frank about them.'

'If you want to check our title,' said Dacre, and made to go below for his papers.

'That will not be necessary,' said von Brüning.

'I regret to inform you that you are in breach of international law,' said Dacre, stiff as a post. 'I demand to telegraph my principals immediately.'

'I fear the telegraph office is closed.'

'It was open yesterday.'

'It is closed today.' Von Brüning frowned. 'If I might have a word in private?'

'By all means,' said Dacre with a face like stone, and ushered him into the sickly fug of the saloon.

Well I did not like the sound of this at all. So I left the matlows holding on to *Gloria*, and went below to the foc'sle, and put an ear to the bulkhead.

The door from the forecabin to the saloon was open, so their voices came low but not much muffled, except by the creaking of *Gloria*'s timbers.

Dacre started talking about salvage, technical stuff that was Greek to me, and to him too I should think. Then he asked straight out to what he owed this change of attitude.

At this point von Brüning's voice lost its hard edge. But what he said was clear enough.

'How long have you known your captain?' he said.

'A fortnight. Since we sailed from England. Why?'

Was he aware, said von Brüning, that this man Webb was an enemy of . . . had offended some very influential people at Kiel?

Dacre did not sound amazed. If von Brüning meant that Webb had beaten the Kaiser in a fair race, he said, and lost his job as a result, and landed up in a place beneath what he was used to, namely as skipper of *Gloria*, then yes, he knew. But in that race nobody had broken the rules of yacht racing except the Kaiser, something the Kaiser himself had admitted. So was that a difficulty? From what I knew of Dacre he was not a man who often found himself doing the honourable thing, and he sounded as if he was enjoying the experience.

Von Brüning now began to sound embarrassed. No difficulty, he said; or at any rate not to him. But there were those . . . not to put too fine a point on it, General Baron von Tritt had recognized this man Webb, and wanted him out of the islands, his presence being an offence to all loyal subjects of the Kaiser. That did not take a genius to work out why von Brüning had not wanted to meet my eye when he had come aboard just now. He was ashamed to have to do the dirty work of von Tritt.

A thought struck me. Von Tritt had been fair cross when he saw me holding the Gräfin's hand. His little problem might have something to do with the Kaiser. But that probably had more to do with the fact that he was jealous.

'What are you grinning at?' says Sam.

I shushed him.

'Following your explanation I have no objection to this salvage,' von Brüning was saying. 'But what I think you must do is take this man Webb from German waters, get a replacement on the Hook of Holland packet. It cannot take more than a week.' You could almost hear him shrug his shoulders. 'This is at the orders of Herr Baron General von Tritt. My superior officer. In so far as yacht racing goes . . . well, I do not necessarily agree with him. But orders are orders. So I fear I must insist that you discharge this man. Then you can come back and continue your work.'

'We'll put him on the train,' said Dacre. 'I'm terribly sorry. Had no idea.'

'The Herr General Baron insists that he leave the islands with the boat. It will take a week, at the outside. The weather is deteriorating. Conditions will be unfit for diving for some time, I think.'

I sat there with my hair standing on end. Von Brüning had just revealed the invasion timetable. In a week the barge fleet would have sailed. With England invaded, perhaps Dacre would want to come back. Then again, perhaps he would not.

They wanted *Gloria* out of there, and no mistake. But if they tried too hard, we might smell a rat, they would be thinking.

Then Dacre said, in a voice much darker and more like the real Dacre, 'I must object in the strongest terms to this unwarranted ejection. If I leave these waters it will be under protest. General von Tritt is perpetrating an outrageous breach of international law. It will most certainly be taken up through the highest channels.'

Von Brüning said, 'I am sorry you are taking this line. The General insists you leave tonight. Can I assume you will comply?'

'Assume what you damned well like,' said Dacre, and started yelling my name.

When I went on deck the pinnace was leaving, and Dacre was scowling after it.

'What was all that about?' I said, to test him.

'Mind your own damned business,' said he, slapping down my free-and-easiness. 'We're being thrown out.'

'Do they know what we're up to?'

'I'm up to.'

'Beg pardon,' I said. 'They can't know, or we'd be in jail already. They just want their privacy.' I shut up for a minute, watching the tiller kick against its lashings. Then I said, 'That would be a terrible thing if we was to get put ashore. We'd be neaped, wouldn't we?'

'What the hell do you mean, neaped?'

'Go ashore at high water. Tides get smaller for two days yet. Then bigger again. So we'd be stuck for four days, minimum.'

Dacre stared at me with his tired narrow eyes. He looked like a man who had run out of ideas. 'Tonight?' he said.

'We'll go and wait at Memmert. That'll blow tonight. They'll think we're sitting out the breeze. We could be waiting to leave tomorrow, if that's fit.'

He looked blackavised and grim, sulky at not having thought of that himself. 'Carry on, then,' he said.

So Sam and I hauled up some sails, while *Blitz* watched us from a distance. Sam pulled up the anchor. As we beat down for Memmert, the sun shone silver on the heavy surf walloping the outer beaches. That was not the night for running boats ashore.

Von Brüning had been right about the weather. The glass dropped steadily as we took her across the *watt* on the tide, and came to off Memmert with two anchors in tandem. The breeze went southwest and began to blow. That evening we snugged down as if for sea, and hove the dinghy onto the foredeck. And at last light the *Delphin* came in and anchored a quarter of a mile off. There was no sign of the Gräfin or von Tritt. There was only Hans in the cockpit, and a couple of heavy boys I thought I had seen at Norddeich. They did not look at us. At eight o'clock that was dark and raining now, proper westerly rain, coming aboard in bucketfuls and finding its way everywhere. That was a good night for an anchor watch. I sat in the cockpit and squinted down the bowsprit into the eyes of the wind. Beyond the rainy globe of the anchor light that was black as a coal cellar, and four times as wet. The nose was going up and down like a woodchopper's axe. Every time that hit bottom the spray came bursting up and down the decks. Every time that came up that jagged at the anchor chain and sent a horrible jolt through the samson post and into my bones. Norderney light was a dull sort of glimmer down to the east, and sometimes you could not see that at all. The only bright spot was that I could hear Dacre sicking up his supper down below.

After about an hour I went down to the foc'sle for a cup of tea. Everything was dancing about in mid-air, and there was no chance of keeping the fuel in the stove, let alone the kettle on the hob. But at least that was out of the wind, and even on the dry side, if you stayed out of the way of the leaks in the deck. So I decided to stand my anchor watch in my bunk. I lay there and thought about the Gräfin, and listened to the plunge of the bow and the clank of the anchor chain as that snatched on a new crest—

There was a bump against the hull by my head. Bit of driftwood, I thought, half asleep as I was. Then the bump came again, as if that was hung up there, a chunk of tree stuck in the bobstay perhaps. I got my feet onto the deck and stood up and made ready to go out of the hatch.

Then everything started to happen very fast indeed. There were a couple of bangs on the deck, and I was very surprised, because there had been no hail, but that was definitely the sound of feet coming aboard. I went for the companionway and out on deck, but I was a fisherman, not a secret agent nor a soldier, so I did not look first or do too much thinking, I just went. And as soon as I got my head out of the hatch and into the shining ball of rain round the anchor light, something hit me a terrible whack somewhere around the top of the neck, and I fell straight down the companionway again, with all the bees that had been in Dacre's bonnet inside my skull. I heard a crash, which was me hitting the locker where Sam kept his pots and pans. Then there was another slam, and another, and a sort of fiddling noise, and a splash, and more fiddling. I lay there like a fool and thought, someone is putting padlocks on the hatches, as if that was happening to someone else. Back in the saloon, Dacre started shouting and banging. Then just forward of where my head was, a new noise started; a rattle at first, that grew to be a big horrible clattering roar.

Sam woke up then. He said, 'Chain's going out.'

I could lift my head now, but otherwise that was hard to move. He was right. What was ahead of the forepeak was the chain locker, which is the little cellar sort of place the anchor chain lives in, or that part of it not stretched between the hook and the samson post. What had happened, I thought through a steam-engine throb in the head, was that whoever had kicked me below decks had now let the anchor chain off of the post, and that was roaring out, never to be seen again—

That stopped. That stopped with a bang that shook every nail in the boat, and for the space of a head's throb that went quiet. Then I heard a shuffling on deck, and a sort of slithering. Something hit the bobstay a twang. Then there was proper silence.

Whoever had been up there was not up there any more. I climbed a few hundred feet into a sitting position and held my head. The boat was easier, the jerky pitch of her gone, her motion a gentle corkscrew, as if she had stopped fighting the weather and decided to go along with it instead.

Stopped fighting, because she was going to die.

Someone had let out the anchor chain until they had come to the long lashing of small hemp at the bitter end, that ties the last link of the chain to an eyebolt in the chain locker. Then they had cut the lashing.

Let me run over that again.

We were battened down below decks. That was blowing most of a gale. We were adrift in shallow water, and blowing towards shallower.

I had wanted to stay in the islands. That looked like whoever had been on deck had granted me my wish. And as an extra, free, gratis and for nothing, there were three headstones thrown in.

CHAPTER TWENTY

Moonlight and Daisies

Dacre was shouting and banging still, proper panicky, using a lot of horrible language. Well he had a point, but yelling never helped. So I began to think, slowish, because of my head, but as far as I could tell reliable. First out I thought I would smash open the fore hatch. But that was a bad idea, because once I had bust that open there might be no way of shutting that again, and any water that Gloria shovelled up on her foredeck would come straight below. So I fumbled a hatchet and a tommy bar out of the tool kit, shoved open the door by the stove and crawled aft, holding my head, which was trying to bust open like a box of mud. There was no light in the saloon. I waded through books and charts flung out of their racks by her pitching at anchor. Something that must have been Dacre walloped into me and began yelling. I found the side of his head and grabbed an ear and yelled, 'Shut up, sir!' hoping that the shock of hearing me call him 'sir' would do the job. Then I knocked out the window in the washboards with the back of the hatchet, shoved my hand out into the wet and found the padlock. That was a big, heavy German thing, but *Gloria* was old and English. I jammed the end of the tommy bar through the hasp and gave that a twist.

The padlock held. But *Gloria* was put together with silly little screws driven into poorish timber. So the hasp came away with a pop. I took out the washboard, slid back the hatch, clambered on deck and wished I hadn't.

Gloria was thundering under bare poles into a night no less black than when I had last seen it. The wind felt softer, which is always the way when that is blowing you along. There was a dirty square sea running, which is to say the waves were six foot high and six foot wide and not a lot more than that apart. And needless to say *Gloria*, that had her mast just about in the middle of her sail plan, was not lying easy, head to wind or tail to wind. She was lying as close as she could get to beam on, which is to say sideways on, to those potato furrows of water, and she was rolling forty degrees one way, forty the other, scooping up buckets of water with her side and sluicing that down the deck and into the cockpit until she was more like a floating washtub than a gentleman's yacht. I hear Dacre shout, and I gathered that the water was getting below, too. Then I heard Sam's voice, and Sam was on deck, a sort of darker blur in the sheets of rain and spray driving across the boat.

I had the tiller unlashed, and I was hauling the helm over, trying to point her nose downwind, anything to stop that rolling. Sam was trying to ask questions, but there was nothing he needed to know that he could not find out for himself. 'Get us a staysail,' I yelled in his face. 'Bend on the spare anchor.' He lumbered off down the deck, trudging down that bucking arrowhead of planks as another man might walk to work in the fields. After half a minute I heard the rattle of canvas and the groan of shrouds as he sheeted that in.

At once she became easier, and started to answer the helm. I hauled her off of the wind until we were piling across the waves instead of along them. Her bow reared up at the scud and plunged into the deeps with a booming like the hammers of Hell, kicking up water by the ton and sending that feet high down the decks. But she was moving through that now, not wallowing. Which was a better state of things altogether.

So there we were, charging east in front of a westerly gale. There was no way back into the wind, not for a boat that made as much leeway as *Gloria*, with one sail up in the teeth of the wind and the tide. There was no way out one side or the other, because of Juist to the north and the Nordland Sand to the south. There was only east. And blast we did go east, pounding along at between six and eight knots, I should think, along the Juister Balje—

At least, that was what you had to hope. The Norderney light had gone behind a lot of rain or fog or goodness knows what, and we could have been in the horse pond on Dalling Green for all I knew. A gust came screaming over the stern, and *Gloria* stood on her ear. I hauled the tiller up to the weather gunwale, and she came back upright, and roared on into the dark and the shallow water. The rain faltered a moment. The sky off the port bow paled and darkened, which was the Norderney light back again. And in that paling I saw the gleam of wet oilskins as Sam trudged back down the deck.

Well I was pleased to see the light, and Sam coming aft. Now we could anchor, and if that held we might not land up on the high ground and get thumped to splinters by those nasty square waves—

'Gone,' bellowed Sam's voice close to my ear.

'What's gone?'

'Spare anchor. Bloody gone.'

That was when I recalled the fiddling noise on the foredeck, and the splash. The sound of someone unlashing an anchor and dropping that over the side. Someone who wanted to make sure that we left the islands, even if that meant leaving the earth in the process.

'That's not right,' yells Sam, and he did sound proper aggrieved. 'Not bloody right at all,' excuse me.

'Yes,' I said, thinking, get on with it.

'They got no business to do a thing like that.'

'No,' I says. 'Get—'

'We'll be running out of water,' bellows Sam, very helpful.

'So get the kedge,' I yell back at him.

The kedge was the fourth and last anchor. That was a silly little thing, forty pound, not much bigger than a toothpick really, with a third of a shackle of small chain, meaning thirty foot, and some rope on the end of the chain. Well of course Sam started to say what was right, namely that in a breeze like this that would be no sort nor manner of use. But I said, 'Get that overboard, and get out your lead, boy.'

A washboard popped out, and Dacre's voice said, 'What's happening?' very shrill.

'Go away,' I bellows, above the roar of the wind.

'Carry on, then,' he says, and pops back below. Sam hauls the kedge out of the locker and lumbers up forward, and I pay out the chain into the dark.

Two minutes later there is a bit of a splash, and the roar of chain going out, and I remember I sort of shifted my hands on the tiller, because I had an idea of what was going to happen next.

Sure enough, that happened, and more besides. Dark as that was, I could see that in my mind's eye.

The kedge warp would have run out like a scalded serpent, first the chain, then the rope. Sam would be standing there on the foredeck with four turns on the samson post, waiting to haul that tight so the friction could do its stuff, stop the rope going out, tighten that up so that would drive the flukes into the sand, bring the boat's nose onto the wind, keep her safe and sound until the wind dropped and the tide went out, and the sea calmed down, and she settled to her anchor if we were in the channel, and onto the bottom if were out of it.

But when you are in a howling gale in the middle of the night, with a twenty-ton boat and a forty-pound anchor, the above is a terrible lot to ask.

So the chain roared out, and then all the rope, and Sam took up the turns, as I now said. The boat gave a sort of a tripping lurch, as if the anchor was holding, and the nose started to come round until we were broadside on to the sea again, and the tops of waves were flying over the side and the cockpit was full of water.

What should have happened is that the nose should have kept on coming up into the wind. What actually happened was that having got halfway round she stuck, and began a sort of shuddering that anyone with half a brain could tell was the kedge hopping along the bottom, as might have been expected. Well either that was going to catch or that was not going to catch, you might think. And sure enough after what must have been half a minute but felt like a couple of years, that caught. That caught with a bang, as if that had hit a rock or a cable, and as the warp came tight that sang like a 'cello. The nose yawed round and the wind blew a blast in my face that made my eyes water.

We took a big wave in the cockpit, and the binnacle light was drownded out. Then all of a sudden the motion eased off and the Norderney light swung down the side and took up position on the port bow. And Sam came spluttering aft and told me what I already knew.

'Warp's bust,' he said.

I could have said, that was your job to look after that. I could have said, with all that damned Duke's money you could have bought a mile of brand new rope and nobody would have said you nay. But that was Sam, doing his best to save money for the Duke, who would not even have noticed. There were things you could not expect from a fisherman, and sound ropes was one of them.

So we tore on into the black and the shallow water, with no anchors left, no way of stopping. We stood there, Sam and I, the wind battering our sou'westers against our collars and the rain roaring in our ears, while ever and anon the Norderney light loomed in the sky. I could hear Sam's teeth chattering, and I was not feeling any too warm my own self, not counting the aggravation from the lump on my head. 'Two hours to high water,' said Sam.

He was not just talking for talk's sake. Ahead was the high ground, the place where the channel wriggled over the *wattenhoch*. There would be six foot of water there at high tide, four foot six now, if you could find that in the twists and turns of the channel. We should be getting into shallow water in half an hour. If we could get over the watershed, that would shelter us from the worst of the sea. That was a biggish if, of course, seeing the withies marking the channel had been chopped off. But there was no way round it.

So I said to Sam, 'Get the lead.' I passed the binnacle lamp down to Dacre, and I saw the match shake in his fingers like a withy in a strong tide, and when he passed that back lit I took the chart and refreshed my memory by its feeble glimmer. The Juister Balje headed east, narrowing, and then followed a line of withies west, then a point north of west, then curled and fiddled until that was heading a point south of west and into the next deep water, inside the Norderney Seegat, which God willing we should reach not long before high water. So I stamped into my mind as much of that as I could, and pushed the tiller until I heard Sam cry the depths shoaling. Then I took her west and a half point south, until the sand began to fall away again. So now that was plain where the north slope of the Balje was, and all I had to do was follow that until that gave out and turned into the *watt* channel.

All, I say. As in all or nothing.

Over to port there was now a heavy sort of muttering rumble, and a distance off, that could have been ten yards or ten cables, the sea was white and foamy where the waves were rolling into the shallow water and busting into surf.

'Be the mark, two,' sings out Sam. 'One 'n' a half now.'

There was spindrift coming aboard now. That feels different from rain on your face, softer and lighter with all the air that gets whacked into water when that trips and falls flat on its face on the hard sand. There was white to starboard as well as to port. This was a very silly thing to be doing, not that there was any choice.

'One,' said Sam, meaning one fathom, six foot to you, remember. 'Here we go, boy.'

Gloria swept on, lifting her arse to those waves as if she enjoyed them, and maybe she did, but that just went to show that the old fool had no imagination about what that could lead to. She was charging down a bumpy black road between two great white fields of foam that thrashed and shone like a hay-meadow full of daisies. Beyond the bowsprit, the road became an alley. The stern slewed to port as a breaker hit, and I eased up for mid-channel before she could broach.

But by now there hardly was any mid-channel. Sam was still flinging away with the lead, coming up with depths between six and eight foot, but the breakers were thundering and crunching all around us and the cockpit was full of their uncanny greyish light. Then bowsprit plunged on into the last of the black water. Then suddenly the sea was all white, and there should be a starboard kink to the channel up here, found it, then a couple of points to port, and the wind heeled us away from the breakers; that was the worry, getting knocked down and filled by a breaker. 'Six foot here,' says Sam. 'Four.' Then the broken remains of a wave lifted us and when that dropped us this time there was not the wallow and the roll, but a crash fit to jar your bones, with a lot of breaking china in it and a burst of yelling from Dacre. The next wave lifted us and hooked the stern round and brought us down again *crash*, and she went right over, almost on her beam ends, and I remember thinking, this here is where she break up and we drown. But the staysail pulled her nose round and she gave a sort of long, dragging slide, and she fell into deeper water and was away again. And then we were in the middle of a wave, a big wave, that was spilling white water down the smooth black slopes on either side of us, and I suppose that was carrying us along, because everything seemed to have gone quiet, except Dacre, who was complaining in a squeaky voice about being wet—

I felt the tiller go useless in my hand as we and the water moved on at the same speed, waited for the stern to break away and the roll and pounding and the breakup. I said to Sam, in that quiet, 'Hang you on, boy,' and I found myself thinking about Joe, Hetty's brother, and thinking, well, that had to happen really, never mind how much care you take, but this is too soon—

Then the wave broke.

That came down around us like a thousand of bricks. Our heads went rattling round the lockers, and there was water up my nose and down my neck inside and outside. But that went away, and I climbed up, back to the tiller, and from the way Dacre was yelling he was still alive. The deck was stretching away forward, streaming water, gleaming in what was now the white flash of the Norderney light. The rain had suddenly gone, and the light made a long, thready path down the sea. And far ahead, standing out of the water in the middle of that path like a witch's hand, was a withy.

The water that was standing in was practically calm. Maybe we are dead after all, I thought, and gone to heaven. Then I turned round.

CHAPTER TWENTY ONE

Neaped

Over the stern, the surf was a line that seemed to stretch from horizon to horizon, and the thunder of it on the breeze was enough to judder your teeth in your head. But we were past it. We were over the watershed, that was hard to say how, and out of the fetch of the sea. We had that lone withy marked on the chart. So with the tide still flooding, and the cloud breaking into big man o'war squalls, we moved out of the *watt* channel and into deeper water. Alive. Grinning, even.

Dacre put his head out of the cabin. He said in a shaky sort of voice, 'Everything's wet.'

'And my arse and all,' said Sam, forgetting his manners, and who could blame him.

'It's up to my knees,' said Dacre, almost timid.

So I told Sam to hold on to the tiller and keep the lighthouse in his portside eye, and I went below and lit a match to have a look.

The yellow matchlight shone on water above the cabin floorboards. In that water was a sort of porridge made up of crockery from the lockers, and a few books that had escaped the shelves, and a lot of Dacre's clothes, and goodness knows what else, all clanking and crunching in the trench between the settees. That was almost a mercy when the match went out.

I caught hold of the pump handle and gave a few swipes. Then I gave two hundred more. If I pumped until my arm hurt, I could get the water below the floorboards. But pump as I would, I could not keep that there.

'See?' said Dacre, as if he had done something clever.

That was plain we had knocked some sort of hole in her when

we had hit the bank. I said as much to Dacre.

'What are we going to do?' he said, and I saw that he was not a hard man any more, just a frightened one. 'Run her up the beach,' I said, very consoling. 'Now do you pick your stuff up and get that drying.'

'So we're stuck,' he said.

'As per plan,' I said, making a virtue out of necessity. He nodded, as if that was him that had made the plan. I went back on deck.

By the white blink of the Norderney light we were crossing the bar south of the *seegat*, it being just about high water now. The breeze was hard and steady from the west, but nowhere near as fresh as that had been. We thrashed on into the *seegat*, no lights, pitching and walloping, water everywhere. Norderney harbour channel buoy loomed black to port and fell astern. We pounded further into the Riffgat, past the place we had anchored last night, and on into the narrows of the next *watt* channel.

This *watt* was easier than the last. There was less wind, and no breakers, and more water, and a moon now, dancing in a black sheet of sea. Sam found the withy at the beginning of the channel, and we felt our way through till the keel was catching on the mud at the top of the pass. But *Gloria* gave a long pull and a strong pull, and over we slid, thank goodness, and started downhill.

We were past Juist and Norderney now. Somewhere across all that water ahead was Baltrum, smallest of the German islands, a quietish spot by all accounts, with a harbour at its western end, and a bit of a town inland. That was a wildish place, not a halfway holiday resort like Norderney. We could take the ground there. And that was bang in the middle of the islands, so if Dacre wanted to go visiting, that would be easy.

Sam said, 'What now?'

'Run her ashore.'

'What then?'

Thar was a good question. Whoever had set us adrift had meant us to drown. When they found we were not drowned, they were going to be very upset.

I was tired, and with the tiredness I became discouraged.

Perhaps that was the Gräfin. Perhaps she had led me on, reported seeing me at Hilgenriedersiel. Very likely she had let us go then so as not to cause a rumpus, let us think we were safe, so she could tell her friend von Tritt and he could arrange for us to disappear nice and tidy, no trials . . .

Sam handed up a cup of horrible tea. That chased off the megrims. The Gräfin was fine. One thing Webb knew about was women, all twenty-four years of him, as long as you left out the awkward bits, like for instance Hetty. We thrashed through the wind-over-tide in the Wichter Ee, which is the gap between the east end of Norderney and the west end of Baltrum. Though that was not long gone high water you could already see breakers on the banks that fence the channel in at its seaward end. Then we were passing Baltrum town, a couple of lights over to port, and heading for the watershed.

The Baltrum *watt* is a shallow one, and the tide was leaving us now. The tea had worn off. The whole German Navy could have come by and I would have tipped my cap to them and wondered what time was breakfast. When the lights of the town were well past, I heaved the nose up to norrard, and let out the mainsail until that was only half drawing. About a mile along the shore from the island, well south of the high-water mark, *Gloria* took the ground with a scrape and a bump. Then we turned in, ignoring some noises Dacre was making about lookouts.

When I awoke the sun was coppery in the eastern sky, the wind a little breeze from the south, the horizon hazed in so the mainland was a long blur like smudged pencil, no detail visible. I hopped over the side and onto the sand.

That could not have been better if we had done that on purpose. There was a great big crack along the garboard, which is to say the plank next to the keel, on the starboard side, which was the side that was up. I grovelled on the hard brown sand and watched that leaking a shine of water over the bulge of her bottom. That was bad enough to keep us still while we fixed that, but not bad enough to be proper dangerous. I told Sam to keep his eyes open, and set off across the sand for the pale fringe of marram grass that marked the beginnings of the shore.

169

I had a mile-and-a-half leg-stretch under wheeling gulls and larks ascending to a tidy little village of houses built of brick and wreckwood, each with a sandy patch of seedling vegetables hedged in with rugosa roses, and women in caped coats and wooden shoes cleaning up after the night's blow. I sought out the harbourmaster, a bony chap with yellow hair and drinker's eyes to match, and he directed me to a sort of rag-and-bone chandler with a clay pipe under his nose and a silence that meant money. The long and the short of it was that at half past nine o'clock he and I were rolling back along the sand on the perch of a species of cart, pulled by an elderly mare with a perverse lust for seaweed. Behind us in the cart was an anchor of ancient design weighing the best part of a ton, and a hundred fathom of best three-inch manila, and two shackles, which is thirty fathoms, of slightly used three-quarter-inch chain.

Gloria was canted over in a golden waste of flat sand, with the flood tide stalking her half a mile away. A wisp of blue smoke crawled down the breeze from a fire beside her. As we got closer, you could see clothes and charts fluttering as they dried along her boom. Somewhere in this golden morning people were looking for our wreckage, but that might as well have been on the Moon for all the sign you could see of that. Dacre gave the chandler a fill of tobacco and paid him from a bag of money that made his eyes stick out like organ stops. *Gloria* would get a high billing in the Baltrum gossip, today. We hauled the bitter ends of the cables onto the deck and used the mare and the cart to lay the anchor up the beach. The chandler cast a shrewd eye on *Gloria*, and started a professional interrogation. I took him underneath the hull, and looked at the garboard and explained how we were going to neap her while we mended that. Which was the same as explaining into a megaphone that here we were, and here we were stuck for the next three days.

As the tide came in we warped *Gloria* in to the beach until we could warp her no further. The breeze came up and blew away the haze. The mainland was a sharp green slash across the southern sky, with Dornum spire standing up behind the wall south by southeast. Dacre had pulled himself together. You could see that now he had had his moment of weakness, he had decided there was a job to be done, never mind how frightened he was. You could almost admire him for that. He said, 'Give us a hand down with the dinghy.'

'What for?'

'I'm going to the mainland.'

'To do what?'

'My duty,' he says, fumbling at the painter knot with his ignorant fingers.

'They'll see you coming,' I said.

'Day like this, like the bollocks on a dog,' said Sam, excuse me, but he was right. But Dacre said, very stubborn, 'I'm going,' and began to haul at the dinghy, with no success of course.

That really looked as if we were going to have to stop him making a fool of himself by not helping him drag the dinghy down, which would have led to unpleasantness. But just then I looked over his shoulder, down towards Norderney. And I said, 'Not just yet you aren't.'

There was a grey dot down there, with a wisp of smoke above it and a smear of white under its nose: the steam pinnace of the *Blitz*, coming towards us full steam ahead.

Letter from Captain Eric Dacre, late —-th Lancers, to Miss Erica Dacre, St Jude's, Eastbourne, Sussex.

Oh my God, Sissy. Oh my God. Things are going, oh, going so wrong. So wrong. Will you believe that it has taken the arrival of a German gunboat to stop me from making a most utter fool of myself? And all because I feel so powerless. It is all slipping away from me. If the Duke were to find out—

They have tried to kill us. The Germans. Not with fire, or guns; easier than that. They simply cut us adrift in a gale. All night we rolled and tumbled. I was most dreadfully sick, of course. The bottom of the boat is smashed in, everything soaked, I half-drowned. Now we are on the sand above the reach of the water. Webb says we are neaped, which I believe is like being moored on the beach for a few days. I know we are wrecked.

In every sense.

171

I am useless in this place. I must breathe air, I know nothing of boats. My terror paralyses me.

Not Webb. Not he. With increasing peril, Webb finds increasing strength. So does Sam, who is impertinent in ways he thinks I do not notice. He has the right, though. Whatever the circumstances of our birth, I am forced to the admission that they are the better men. From their filthy little cave up in the bows, wet and stinking and black with soot, they come bright and brave and calm. Yes, they are better men . . .

In all respects but one. As one closer to the Duke's eminence, I have His Grace's ear. And I think I can make him listen to whatever version of events I put forward. It is not perhaps an honourable thing to say. But the proof of the pudding is in the eating.

If we succeed in making any sort of pudding. Most of the ingredients are sunk by the wreck, and we shall not be able to retrieve them. Very little remains . . . If, if, if.

And for success, I depend on these fishermen.

Pray for your brother, who loves you,
namely
Eric

CHAPTER TWENTY TWO

To the Carolinenhof

The pinnace came straight for us, up to the beach. Von Brüning walked up to us. There were grey bags under his eyes, and he moved stiffly, like a man badly tired. He said, 'Please may I come aboard?' and scrambled over the side before anyone could give him leave. He said, 'I must ask you to remember that I ordered you to leave the islands.'

'We were trying,' said Dacre, with an indignation that was not hard to put on. 'And while we were waiting for the weather, someone cut us loose from our anchor and dropped the spare over the side. I must protest at this outrage,' said Dacre, 'in the strongest possible terms.'

Von Brüning looked taken aback, something you did not often see. He would not have known about that. Von Brüning was a seaman, and an efficient one. If he ever decided to murder someone, they would stay murdered. 'When was this?'

'Last night.'

'In the Juister Balje?'

'You are very well informed,' said Dacre nastily, and I saw he was getting the upper hand, the injured innocent complaining about the inefficient policing of the islands.

'You came over two *watt* passages in the night, in that weather?' Von Brüning was a seaman before anything else, and, he looked almost impressed.

'And made a hole in the boat.'

'Even so,' said von Brüning.

'It was Webb,' said Dacre.

'And Sam,' said I. I decided to tell him the truth, and see what he would do. 'Couple of chaps clocked me one, let us go, sank

173

the anchor. Could have lost me my ship. That's not right.'

Von Brüning frowned. They said von Tritt had been brought in over his head. That was a landsman's trick, to cut us adrift, not a seaman's. A seaman would know boats float, even in weather like last night. A landsman would assume that was certain death. That was von Tritt's kind of trick, not von Brüning's.

Von Brüning covered up, as was his duty. He said, 'I am afraid our people are poor. They take their chances where they see them. I shall make enquiries.'

I pointed out that we were neaped pending repairs. 'So that'll be a bit hard to move as per orders,' I said, and I hope that did not sound smug. 'I'll get back there in the dinghy and have a drag around for me anchors.' For in those days, before motors, an anchor was your brakes and your lifeline and your engine. Nobody moved without at least two manageable anchors.

Well, he who is smug last stays smug longest.

'I think you will not find them,' he said, and I knew that if someone had not picked them up already on the day's low tide, he would have them up just as soon as he could steam back round Juist. 'And I think yacht anchors will be hard to find in the islands. But at least you are safe.' He was beginning to look more cheerful, and I could see why. Neaped and tied to that big anchor, we could be watched by anyone with a decent set of glasses. 'Anyway, I am not here to talk about anchors. The Gräfin saw you here this morning, and asks that since you are neaped you will dine with her. Your men will doubtless appreciate some home comforts after all this time on board. She has an excellent cook. We shall all be there. I am longing to find out what you have achieved.' He gave Dacre a roguish sort of smile, into which you could read what you liked.

I felt a sort of jubilation. If she had tried to kill us, she would not be asking us to hers. So that was von Tritt. And if that had been von Tritt, the odds were that he had done that at least partly out of jealousy. But you cocked that up, you bald old devil, I thought. That's what you get when you tangle with Webb—

'Delighted,' said Dacre, with a look in his eye that said he was anything but. I started to think with my brain, not my trousers.

This could be the deliverance into the hands of the enemy. 'I shall be most interested to see over her boat.'

'Not on the boat,' said von Brüning. 'So you will not be able to ask her crew why they have done what you say they have done.' His tone was light, but his face was grim. 'Please rest assured that I will do that myself. At any rate, we are dining at the Carolinenhof. Her house here. I shall collect you this evening, when the tide serves; eight o'clock, shall we say?'

The pinnace thumped away towards the Wichter Ee.

'*Jesus*,' said Dacre, for which as with so much he said there was no call. 'You'll stay on board of course.'

'Hell no,' said Sam.

'Language,' I say.

'They'll search the boat.'

'And find nothing.'

'You can't just leave her.'

I said, 'If we do, von Brüning's going to think we've got nothing to fear by going.'

'A test, eh?' said Dacre. 'I see. I see. Very well, Webb, have it your way.'

'Aye, aye, sir,' said Sam, teasing him. But of course he did not notice.

Now that was decided, the cold clutch at the belly was here to stay. Last night someone had had a very good try at drowning the three of us. And tonight, we should be walking like Daniels among the lions.

So we spent the rest of the day very innocent at make-do-and-mend, during which we took Dacre's ready-use stock of bully beef tins from under the cabin sole and buried that in the dunes above the anchor, the main part of it now being beyond recall. On the last of the tide the pinnace came back with the Subby at the tiller, very stiff after the fool he had made of himself off the Hohes Riff. Dacre had done himself up in the full soup and fish, and Sam and I had rigged ourselves out in our Sunday blues.

'All of you?' said the Subby.

'Fancied a run ashore,' said I.

'Ah,' said the Subby, and blushed bright red, bless his guileless heart; and I knew I was right, that von Brüning had told him, all right, boy, they got you drunk last time and dear knows what they got up to, so this time I want you to search their boat, and I don't care how you set about that long as you get that done.

So we marched across the sand to the pinnace, and that chuffed us down to Dornumersiel training bank, where a little carriage was waiting on the sand, the harbour being dry at this time of tide. And away we bowled towards the high green dyke.

Dacre had read us a lecture that afternoon. 'Tell the truth,' he had said. 'Leave things out, don't invent them. Speak when spoken to. You should be used to that.'

'Aye, aye, sir,' says Sam, knuckling his forehead humbly, and of course as usual Dacre did not notice a thing.

The cart clattered up a track cut athwart the dyke, and down the other side. The breeze off the land smelt of grass and stagnant water. The road ran between drains green with young reeds, and into a thicket of new-leaved ash and willow. Among the trees slanted the red tiles of a great low-eaved Frisian barn, set into the sea wall at its northern end.

We passed through a pair of smart white gateposts and onto a drive of cobblestones. Farm that might be, but that was a farm you could eat your dinner off any part of. The house was a stern-looking thing, tacked onto the southern gable of the barn so the ridge of its roof was a continuation of the barn's. Its flat windows looked out over a bit of garden, and a pond where a Mandarin duck was taking her ducklings for a swim, very tidy and springlike.

Also tidy, but not at all springlike, were the two soldiers in jackboots, greatcoats, *pickelhaubes* and fixed bayonets standing one on either side of the front door.

The coachman opened the door. Dacre swallowed, shot his cuffs, and strutted tails flapping between the soldiers and into the house. Coachey jerked his thumb at a back door.

As we went round the side of the house we passed a drawing-room window, from which came cigar smoke and the pop of a champagne cork. I caught a flicker of diamonds, but did not raise my eyes, because of the blood hot in my face.

There were no soldiers on the kitchen door. If there was a secret war on, that was going to be a war of gentlemen against gentlemen. The talent of the lower classes was dying, not think-ing. Inside the door was a kitchen, darkish, floored with red tiles, with hams and bunches of herbs hanging in the ceiling. After the hellish reeks Sam knocked out of *Gloria*'s fo'c'sle stove, that smelt like paradise. There were three women in white aprons clattering between stove and chopping board in wooden shoes, and a fourth at the table, and Elly the Gräfin's maid sewing in the grey light that came in through the single window. When we said hello she dropped her sewing and sat us down and brought Sam a jug of beer and me a glass of milk, and then began chattering away in Fries with Sam. I sat there and sipped the milk, which was nice and fresh after all that time on the tinned stuff, and tried to add up this homely uproar with those barges lying in the *tiefs* like shells in a magazine.

Suddenly I noticed that Sam and Elly were jabbering at a new pitch, and they were grinning and grabbing each other, and then Elly picked up his beer and drained it. 'Blow me down,' said Sam. 'This here is my Aunt Lisbeth's niece by her second husband. Blast we're as good as cousins.'

'*Ja*,' said Elly, and she looked as pleased as Punch, poor deluded thing. 'And you are the Captain. Ah, Captain.' She laid her hand on mine. 'How cruel is Life.'

'Pardon?' I said.

'My lips are sealed,' she said. 'My poor mistress has a heart soft as herring roe.' She looked sort of arch. 'My Lady has a weakness for Englishmen. But the Herr Baron will have his way, more's the pity.'

I could feel myself turning reddish. 'We'll see,' I said.

'Pardon?'

'Nothing.'

Sam had his jersey off now, and Elly started darning a hole in the elbow, though I happened to know that he could darn perfectly well his own self. All of a sudden the place filled up with menservants and the cooks were yelling and banging smoked eel onto plates, and I recollected that out there in the dining-room our fate was being decided, and the person who was deciding that was Dacre, face to face with von Brüning and von Tritt and the other chaps, and the Gräfin.

I could not just sit there. After a bit I got up and wandered out after the footmen. There was a sort of corridor, and an open door at the end of it from which a shaft of light fell into the gloom. With the light came voices.

Some of them I recognized. There was Dacre's drawl, and von Brüning clipped and precise, and the champagne-and-cigars bellow of von Tritt. Then there were a couple of others, sharp and soldierly.

A flurry of footmen passed me. Plates were cleared, silent in the dining-room, clattering on the sort of pantry table next to which I was standing. The next courses went in, dozens of them. The gentry started to help each other to this and that. Under cover of all the life and movement, I moved up to the door.

This was not a normal farmhouse, and that was not a normal farmhouse room. There were big odd pictures on the walls, fuzzy things with bright colours. There were chandeliers that shone lights at you through coloured glass in the shape of leaves and grapes. After the bright flat lights of the outside, that was a green pasture for the eye.

Von Tritt was at the head of the table, and the Gräfin at the outer end. She looked pale, her eyes big and brilliant, as if something had given her a scare. Dacre was on one side of her, von Brüning the other. Also at the table were a couple of soldierly-looking chaps, and the old boy with a sheep's face who had been at Kiel, and another woman with brassy hair and a face brittle with paint. A lot of attention was being paid Dacre, and he seemed uneasy in the limelight. They seemed to be talking about birds. Von Brüning was teasing him, a jolly grin on his weary face. 'So, Mr Dacre,' he was saying. 'Have you found your Caspian terns on Memmert?'

'All the terns on Memmert are German,' barked von Tritt.

'Haven't seen any of them,' said Dacre. 'Not to my knowledge.'

'Perhaps because you have been too busy looking in the *Corinne* salvage sheds.'

Dacre grinned sheepishly, as if von Brüning had rumbled him.

'Mr Dacre has some very unusual ideas,' said von Brüning.

'He has invented a new system in which he puts on a diving dress to watch terns.'

Dacre's eyes went down, and he shook his head, and addressed himself to his glass of champagne. You had to give it to him, he did a good imitation of a man found out undertaking a secret salvage reconnaissance. 'Well,' he said. 'Someone must think we're getting close. They cut us loose from our anchors last night.'

Von Brüning frowned. 'So you say,' he said.

Von Tritt had been round-shouldered over his plate, shovelling beef into his great flat face. Now he swivelled his pig eyes up at Dacre. 'You should not be surprised,' he said, chewing with his mouth open, and I thought I had never seen a worse mannered nor a more bullying man. 'This wreck is in German waters. *Ergo* it is a German wreck.'

'Not according to international law,' said Dacre with a sort of shifty meekness.

Von Tritt snorted. 'International law is only international as long as England benefits by it,' he said. 'Does it really surprise you that a German patriot takes against you sniffing around?' That was you, boy, I thought with complete certainty. You cut our chain, and you will pay.

'The law's the law,' said Dacre, with a doggedness you had to admire in the face of this bully.

Von Tritt made a noise that closed the subject and sprayed beef over his half of the mahogany. The Gräfin watched with her luminous eyes. I wanted to be out there, telling her that was all right, fighting him for her. An uneasy silence fell.

'So,' said one of the soldierly chaps eventually. 'How long do you stay in the islands?'

Dacre counted on his fingers, too elaborately for my liking. 'Depends on the weather,' he said. 'We're neaped. Hole in boat. When she floats again, I'll be leaving for Holland.' He grinned, a grin that was meant to be frank and disarming. 'Got to report to a shareholders' meeting on what I've found. Chief shareholder's coming from England. The Duke of Leominster. With whom it is wise to keep appointments.'

There was a general nodding of heads. Face had been saved.

Calculations had been made, and proved satisfactory. 'And what have you found?' said von Brüning.

'You must allow us our secrets,' said Dacre with a smooth grin. He was getting his confidence now. 'I was hoping there would be time for someone to show me these sea wall improvements.'

For a long second there was a silence like death. Then von Brüning said, 'Yes, that is a pity. But I don't think you would be very interested. It's just a matter of improving communications; agricultural goods, that kind of thing. The difficulty in this landscape, like a sponge it is, is transferring produce from the farms and the markets to the harbours. And while we are at it, we are taking the opportunity to improve our harbour defenses.' He smiled. 'You must allow us our secrets, Mr Dacre.'

'*Touché*,' said Dacre. 'Bit weak on farming anyway. Bright lights for me, what?' Von Tritt looked scornfully away from this non-member of the landowning classes. 'And the company of the Sex, God bless their lovely hearts.' He kissed his hand to the Gräfin, and leered. But he got no chance to go further, because at that moment Elly the maid whisked past me and practically rushed over to the Gräfin and whispered something into her ear. Judging by von Tritt's looks, this was not etiquette. But the Gräfin stood up, said, 'A disaster in the kitchen,' with an urbane sort of smile, and turned to leave the dining-room. And I went back to the kitchen, fast, and got there twenty seconds ahead of her.

She did not stop in the kitchen. She picked up a lantern and went straight through a door next to the range. I caught the gleam of light on the worn wooden handles of garden tools hung neatly on a wall. Then the door closed behind her.

The fat cook looked after her with a sort of well-worn curiosity. 'What now?' said the fattest, a scarlet-faced woman with a hairy mole on her great cheek.

'There'll always be something with that one,' said the butler, to a wagging of heads.

The door opened again, and the Gräfin swept out. She was wearing a low dress of blue silk, looser than the fashion, so that gave her a look of freedom not a bit like the trussed-upness of most ladies you saw in evening dress. She paused, to brush away a couple of stalks of straw caught in her skirt, and as she did her eye met mine. That was the same blue as her dress, but fierce and hurried, so there was no time for admiring its colour. 'You,' she said, in a voice like cut glass. 'I don't expect you have seen one of our great German generals before.' Well I expect the whole kitchen knew I had been watching, but that was not the same thing at all. So I said, 'No'm,' and looked at my boots, confused.

'Then come with me.'

She led me up the corridor to the dining-room. When we were in the half-dark she took my arm; she actually took my arm. I could hardly breathe for the scent of her, the faint breath of champagne on her breath close to my face. Her hand was trembling.

Then we were approaching the dining-room door, and she pulled me to a stop. I felt her hand pushing something into my pocket. Then, wonder of wonders, her lips brushed mine, light as a feather, and gone quick as a feather in that gale of circumstances. 'Help me,' she said.

I put my hand on her waist, and through the silk felt a waist of muscle and skin, not whalebone. But she pulled away. The door let out a quick flash like the blink of the Norderney light, and she was the other side of it, and I was alone in the dark, with whatever that was she had pushed into my pocket.

Ears ringing with blood, I walked slowly back to the kitchen.

'Nice looking General?' says Sam.

'Beautiful,' says I.

And the cook starts talking about how many wars the General has won, or something. I got myself another glass of milk, and sat down so the rest of them had their backs to me, and took a look at whatever that was the Gräfin had shoved in my pocket.

That was a little piece of paper, with writing on it. The handwriting was the same as in the notebooks the Duke's agent had given me in London all that time ago. The note said: *Back barn. Now. Please. Wilson.*

CHAPTER TWENTY THREE

In the Bull Pen

I had a quick word with Sam, in English. Then I got up and put my hand over my mouth as if I was yawning. 'Breath of fresh air,' I said.

'Make that quick,' said the cook. 'They'll be finished dinner in ten minutes, and they don't sit around much afterwards these days.'

I slid out into the night, fumbling at the front of my trousers to give them the idea.

That was dark outside. The sky was clear and starry, with a half moon. I could hear boots on gravel, the clink of soldier's equipment. When I followed the barn wall round to where that ran into the dyke, I saw a soldier silhouetted against the sky. There was a door in the barn wall. But as I walked towards it the soldier on the dyke said, '*Wer da*?'

'Boatman of Gräfin's dinner guest,' I said. 'Private, er, business.'

The sentry laughed and said something not called for about lucky beggars who were allowed to drink beer on duty. I went round the barn. There was a field on the other side with no guard in that. I went back indoors.

Nobody paid me much mind in the kitchen. The fat cook was reading the *Ostfriesischer Kurier*. The maids were in the scullery, washing up by the sound of it. Sam and Elly had their heads together over glasses of beer. I walked past the lot of them and through the door the Gräfin had taken.

There was a sort of lobby, with tools hung up and big bins of potatoes and carrots and swedes. A lantern burned on a hook over the door. I took that down and carried that through the next door.

I was in the barn. That was huge, and smelt of cow. And cows there were, ranged down one side, great black and white things dim in the lanternlight, munching hay. There was no sound except the crunch of jaws and the drowsy *chuck* of a chicken in the roof. The lamplight played on the high rafters. I said, 'Who's there?' My voice fell dead in the straw.

'Here,' said a voice; a hesitating sort of voice, as if the chap that it belonged to did not want to commit himself to speaking. An English voice.

I went towards it, holding up the lantern. 'Mr Wilson,' I said.

There was a sort of shed in the corner, a solid little affair of heavy planks and beams, the sort of thing you might keep a bull in. The door was bolted on the outside. The voice came from behind the door. 'Who are you?' that said.

'Captain Webb,' I said. 'Yacht *Gloria*. Wait.' I drew the bolt.

Inside was the ragged man who had warned me away from the soldiers at Hilgenriedersiel. Now I saw him close to he was a smallish man, about my height, standing there looking awkward, dressed in mud-coloured clothes. His hair stuck out like hedgehog's spikes, and what you could see of his face behind the scrub of beard was dark, the sort of darkness you get from living rough. 'Jolly glad to see you,' he said. The voice was gentry, very odd coming from that weatherbeaten ragbag. He had a half-gnawed leg of lamb in his hand.

'They'll be out of their dinner in five minutes,' I said. 'What happened?'

'I was asleep in a shed, like a silly fool,' he said. He had a serious, rueful kind of look, and a self-deprecating tone, as if for all his roughness he was detached from life as lived by the general run. 'They think I'm a tramp. No tramps allowed round here any more. They want to question me. My German's not up to much. Look here, I've got to get out. I've got news. And I can't be seen by von Brüning.'

'News about what?'

He frowned. He did not know if that was safe to tell me.

'About barges,' I said.

'How did you know?'

'We were sent,' I said. 'By the Duke of Leominster.'

'Ah.' He had never heard of the Duke, that was plain.

'Mr Childers' friend.'

'Dear old Childers,' he said, and the warmth was back in his voice, the warmth of a man who sees help at hand not just for himself but for his country. 'How many of you are there?'

'Two men beside me.'

'I see.' He sounded hollow and defeated, all of a sudden. As who would not, once they had seen seven *siels*, a quarter of a million men and their guns, and opposing them a mere four men. 'Well then,' he said, in the voice of a man making the best of a bad job. 'Someone's got to get away and warn the Fleet.'

'We've got a dinghy,' I said. 'We're on the beach at Baltrum.'

'I watched you.'

I went back to the toolshed, found a bar, and started to pry one of the door planks loose. While I worked, he talked.

When the plank was loose I put the bar back. Wilson went to the eastern wall of the barn. He moved awkwardly, as if he had to think about his body all the time to make that work proper. I heard the discreet squeak of a rusty bolt being drawn. Then I went to the waggon door of the barn, and knocked.

A German voice outside said, 'Who's that?'

'Me. Captain Webb. Yacht *Gloria*.'

On the far side of the barn there was a rustle in the straw, and a window-shutter opened and closed.

'Only someone said there was a tramp in here,' I said. 'But I can't find him. And someone went out of this window here as I came in.'

There was a frozen silence. Then the door opened. The soldier's face was white and shiny under his *pickelhaube*. He pushed past me and tore open the bull-pen door. He opened his mouth to shout. Then he said, 'Which way did he go?' I could hear the cartridges in his pouch rattling as he shook. This was a soldier terrified for his life.

I pointed past him, into the night.

'Took the plank off,' said the soldier, in a voice packed with doom. 'Oh, my—'

'Hell of a lot of generals in there,' I said.

The soldier was too busy watching pictures of himself

being skinned alive to do more than nod.

'But he was only a tramp, you said.'

More silence, this time filled with the creak of wheels turning in the poor fool's mind.

'What the eye don't see,' said I, 'the heart don't grieve over.'

He frowned. 'What do you mean?'

'If the generals want to see this tramp, you can say he was only a tramp, so you let him go. If they don't ask to see him, then don't say nothing about him.'

His face turned warm and relieved in the lanternlight. Then his eyes narrowed. 'You're being very helpful,' he said.

I looked at my fingernails. That was like yacht racing, really. The more there was at stake, the foggier people's minds got and the more nonsense you could get away with. ' 'Bominate violence,' I said. 'I saw a chap flogged once. Sojer, like you. They hit him till you could see his ribs and all the little pipes and tubes and that inside him, like chitlins in a basket.

His face was white and stiff-looking. 'Shut the door,' he said. 'Not a word.'

'Not a word,' I said, and strolled back to the kitchen. The cook was still reading her newspaper. Sam and the maid were still flirting. I hissed in Sam's ear, and sat down at the kitchen table. Feet crashed in the corridor outside, and the gentry appeared in the kitchen in a block, von Tritt with a face on him as if he had never been in such a place before.

'Where is this man?' he said.

'Man?' says the cook, wiping her hands on her apron, all of a flutter. 'I don't—'

'In the barn,' says Sam. 'Was, anyway.'

Von Tritt did not look at him. 'Was?' he said.

'That was Pieter Wugsma,' said Sam. 'From Lewsum. Him that married Gerda Mausbutte the year—'

'Silence, oaf!' roared von Tritt.

Sam looked pained. 'No call to be rude,' he said. 'Hey!' For that gaudy lump of a Baron had stepped forward and given Sam one round the ear with a sort of a swagger stick he was carrying. I could have told him that was a poor notion. Sam sort of gripped the edge of the table and put his hand to his ear and said, in

English, 'You are going to get wrong a me, chubby cheeks,' and started looking about him, and took hold of a big black-iron frying pan.

Well Dacre stepped between them, and so did von Brüning, and the Gräfin put her hand to her mouth. Brüning looked that tired you could see straight through to his thoughts. What I read in his face that moment was that he was tired, and that he thought the Baron was a fool, but he could not say nothing about it because the Baron was his superior officer.

I took Sam by the arm and said, 'Pay that no mind, boy.'

Von Tritt said to Dacre, 'You should do something about the training of your servants,' very nasty. I could feel Sam's arm sort of vibrating, which was not surprising, because whatever they may get up to in Prussia, that is not wise to hit a true-born Englishman with a stick. 'Drop it,' I said, and took the pan off of him.

And the Gräfin spoke. 'It's true,' she said. 'It was Wugsma. Elly saw him.' And in the background there was Elly nodding away, bless her faithful heart.

Von Tritt looked at the Gräfin, equal to equal. 'You are sure?' he said.

'That is why I spoke.' She had a fierce look in the kitchen lamplight, pale face, glittering eyes. She looked like a woman on her way to war.

The Baron clicked his heels. Dacre grinned his keen-to-please grin. Von Brüning's clever eyes moved among the faces, and you could tell he knew something was not right, but could not put his finger on it. I very much feared that he would make enquiries. But later. For now, his superior officer was satisfied, and that meant that he was satisfied too.

'Shall we have coffee?' said the Gräfin, and the spell was broken. They went back, Dacre falling behind the party, playing over-polite after-you games, and making sure everybody noticed. I stood there listening to the thump of my heart, thinking what a creepy crawly thing he was, and how I was not the only one who could see that. Give me von Brüning any day, do we were on the same side.

'Bastard,' said Sam. He was getting the vinegar and brown

paper treatment from a white apron well rounded out at the front, and not looking too unhappy about it, bar the odd wince.

'We'll talk about that do we get back to ours,' I said, because the fire-cheeked cook was looking as if she wanted to know what was being said in her kitchen.

But he was wounded in his pride as well as his ear. 'You listen to me,' he says. 'You think you are saving the bloody world. We've got a bad boat and this silly fool Dacre and us boys from Norfolk, and if you think that's going to make any difference to the whole bloody German army you are bloody foolish, boy.'

I said, 'Shut up, Sam.'

'Don't you shut up me,' he said. 'You got such a big head you can't see what's in front of your bloody face. You think now you've stopped that silly Dacre you're in charge. Balls you're in charge,' excuse me. 'Nothing nobody can do will be any damned use and if you was to use your brains you would see that plain as day.'

Blast I was cross. But there was no point being cross with Sam, because he didn't notice. So I sat there and stopped myself telling him he was a foul-mouthed drunkard who had never made nothing of himself, because that would do no good, and also because that cook might not speak English but she knew a row when she heard one, and her tongue was roundabout her knees with anticipation. So I held my peace and watched him get patched up, and sipped milk, and listened to the wheels grind in my head. The night felt like a boiler coming up to pressure. You could just about feel the men and the machines pouring in to those barges, the whole of Friesland gorged and creaking at the seams with war stuff. And against it, Wilson's fire at Nessmersiel and Dacre's bomb that might or might not burn a tier of barges at Hilgenriedersiel. In my experience, what could go wrong would go wrong.

You be blowed, Sam, I thought, and I was proper angry, because there is nothing more annoying than to be give out at by someone you know to be right.

Also, I was thinking about that chap Wilson.

I had been working away at the bull-pen door. I said, 'What are you doing here?'

'I was sailing,' he said. He had an odd, jerky way of talking, as if he was not used to company. 'I had an idea . . . well, I had an idea, that's all. I was here last autumn, with Childers. Awfully clever chap. He's written a book, you know, about what we did. To warn people. Bit of a story, awful rot really. Calls himself Carruthers, me Davies.' I realised that even here, locked in a shed and like to hang, he was actually proud to have been put in a book. 'The message is there,' he said. 'Except that I'm afraid it's too late. I came back to keep an eye on things. Von Brüning's a white man. But this von Tritt fellow arrived. Worst kind of Prussian. He had my boat blown up.'

He said it flat as a pancake, as if he had thought about that for a long time, and there was no shock in that any more, only sorrow and disgust, as if at the loss of a dear friend.

'*Dulcibella*,' I said. 'I saw you leaving Kiel last year.'

His face brightened. 'Did you? I remember that.' He spoke as if that had been years ago. That did feel like years, actually. 'Splendid lot of boats. Bit smart for me, of course.'

'And after that you came down here and made the charts.'

'Me and Childers,' he said. 'Childers was a tremendous help. We worried von Brüning, of course. They were all out on Memmert, making believe to do salvage on the bullion ship: Bohm the engineer, von Brüning, chap called Grimm, nasty piece of work. Of course they were using it as a base to do surveys of the *siels*.'

'And Dollmann.'

'Yes. Didn't I mention him?'

'Father of your fiancée,' I said.

He was trying to cover up for her, in his way. His oak-coloured face had reddened to the colour of best Honduras mahogany. 'How d'you know that?'

'Miss Dollmann visited us before we sailed.'

'Clara? Was she well?'

'Anxious about you, sir.'

'Bless her dear heart.' He fell silent, refusing to meet my eye. 'Sorry,' he said at last. 'Where were we?'

'Miss Dollmann's father.'

'Yes.' Another pause. 'I'm afraid von Tritt killed him. Held

188

him under while he drowned, the brute. Childers didn't write it in his story, of course.' He smiled. 'Loves a good story, old Childers. Awful rot. Dollmann's buried in Esens churchyard.'

'Dear me.'

'Man was a traitor, of course.'

I waited.

'Still,' he said. Then, with passion, 'Von Tritt's an animal. Von Brüning was officer in command until von Tritt was brought in over his head. He's a white man, von Brüning. Tritt's a – oh, Lord, we've already been through that.'

All this time I had been working away at the door. In his face I could still see the innocent pleasure of the man in his boat, heaving a stove over the side and eying the bubbles with satisfaction. But now his death was waiting, two rooms and a corridor away.

'That was you set fire to Nessmersiel?' I said.

'That's right. They've tightened up now, though. Can't get a cigarette paper between the sentries. Look here, we've got to get out. Get to Holland. A telegraph office. Alert the Fleet.'

'We can't move,' I said. 'We're neaped. Watched, all the time. And if you could get out, how would you convince the Admiralty?'

'Childers'll know,' he said, a bit wild. There was a sort of blind trust in his voice, the note of a man who understood one world talking about a man who understood another. 'Have you got a dinghy?'

'Yes.'

'I'll steal it. Sail to Holland. Do whatever else I can do. All right?'

'Of course.'

He had grabbed my hand and shaken it, hard. 'Thanks, old man,' he said.

And that had been that. He had rounded up some useful bits and pieces from the barn. Then he was gone, and I was in the kitchen.

The milk was at an end. Frightened or not, my eyelids were sinking. The butler was slumped in the corner behind a flat-faced bottle of gin. The ring of a bell had him out of there like a ferreted

189

rabbit, and he was back as quickly. 'Webb, you're wanted,' he said.

I went with my stomach full of butterflies. They were in the drawing-room, full of cigar smoke, under some more of those hazy paintings – one was of some haystacks, I recall, quite unlike but at the same time somehow very like. Von Tritt was plumped on the sofa next to the Gräfin, bulging over the edges of his uniform and looking horrible smug. The sheep-faced old party looked smug too. The soldiers seemed to have left. Von Brüning was slumped grey-faced behind a thicket of cigar smoke. And Dacre was sitting on the edge of his chair with the smile of a corpse anxious to please. 'Baron von Tritt has kindly offered us a guide,' he said.

'Guide to what?' I said.

'The banks. The birds.'

'Don't need a guide,' said I. 'Not much space. That's a small boat. We can find our way round—'

'This is an impudent swine,' drawled von Tritt to the Gräfin. 'If he belonged to me, I'd have the hide off him.'

I looked at him, and said, 'I don't belong to anybody, boy, and just you remember that.' Silly you may say, but I had had enough. First Sam, and now the Gräfin looking at me like a servant getting a dressing down.

The scars on Tritt's face began to stand out like electrical bulb filaments. I kept my eye on his, and try as I could I could not keep my feelings out of it, and that was plain to me that he knew what was passing through my mind.

Even Dacre could tell what was going on. He looked nervously at the ceiling as if he expected chunks of plaster to be falling out of it, and said, 'I'm sure we can find room for this chap. Now I think we'd better be off.'

'Yes, you should,' said von Tritt, his pig-blue eyes fixed on mine. 'It has been pleasant to have your company. In this I speak for myself. And also—' here he gripped the Gräfin's hand in a paw like three pound of sausages – 'for my fiancée.'

There was a silence that rang like Dalling church belfry. I looked at the Gräfin. She was staring at me, eyes wide open. They did not look like the eyes of a brand new fiancée. They looked like the eyes of a woman stark terrified and asking for help.

But what could I do?

Von Tritt said, 'Is something wrong?' and smiled a great lippy smile.

'Wish you joy,' I said, very sarcastic. Then, somehow, we were out in the cool, clear night.

CHAPTER TWENTY FOUR

A Frightful Deduction

I was hardly thinking about invasions any more, nor barges, nor railways. That had narrowed right down to the Gräfin.

'Funny thing,' said Dacre. 'That Tritt bounder and that splendid gal. No accounting for taste.'

The carriage rattled off the sea wall and onto the stones of the training bank. I said, 'He's not her taste.'

Dacre laughed. 'Ladies, who knows?' he said. The state I was in I could have gone for him, except that I felt Sam's fingers grip my arm. So I realised that he had spotted what was going on between the Gräfin and me. And if Sam had spotted that then the rest of the world would have picked that up years ago.

We climbed into the steam pinnace straight off the *leitdamm*. Steam hissed, and the cylinder panted, and we began to move slowly out into the *watt*. The moon was behind the clouds, and the night was black as a coalhole. The breeze had turned westerly again, and there was a raw, rainy feel to it that made you think that might develop into something powerful. And there was that chap Wilson, who was going to get hisself over here and steal the dinghy and sail that to a telegraph office in Holland . . .

Not if that blew a gale he wasn't.

They took us out with their acetylene searchlight gleaming in the pale birchwood of the withies. Before long the beam began to sparkle with rain. After twenty minutes the shore loomed, and *Gloria*, heeled over on the beach, touched with faint gold from her anchor light.

The petty officer in the sternsheets was a bruiser with a look of Bob Fitzsimmons, the boxer. He eyed *Gloria* pretty dour, and so did I; but for different reasons. Fitzsimmons thought of her as his floating prison for a few days. I was thinking of that chap Wilson, at liberty in the wet black night, with a Dutch telegraph office in his mind. Wilson was the only thing that stood between England and the barges. That was silly, I suppose. But at dead low water you can walk all the way from Bensersiel to Baltrum. I half-expected him to have pinched the dinghy and be on his way, like you expect Father Christmas to pop down the chimney when you are a kid.

But there was no Father Christmas. There was only *Gloria* on the beach, and the dinghy on its tripping line in the channel as before.

We climbed aboard and knocked the sand off our feet and tumbled into our bunks, leaving the bruiser, to whom the name Fitzsimmons had stuck, to bed down in the saloon. Sam made a cup of tea and tipped it on all the beer in him. Then we put the lantern out.

I was tired, as I said. But Fitzsimmons was a sleep-talker, something you do not necessarily want on a small boat, on account of thin bulkheads. And I suppose my nerves were pretty well twanging. So I lay there and listened to him raving about parades, and the rain on the deck nine inches in front of my nose, and the thoughts went marching through my head, larger than life and much odder-looking. I started off thinking about the Gräfin – remembering, to be exact, that soft brush of her lips in the corridor outside the dining room. I was weighing that, really. On the one hand, the kiss. On the other, Tritt with his blowed-up neck, claiming her as his fiancée.

Well, I thought, one I heard from her own mouth, in a manner of speaking, and the other from his. And I know which one I believe.

But that got me thinking of that damned Duke: specifically, the stupidity of him having kept the truth from us, us being servants and not to be trusted with that. If I had opened my mouth to the sentries at Hilgenriedersiel, that would have been that . . .

The more I thought, the more puzzling that became.

I said, 'Sam?'

A snore, a splutter, and he was awake, 'Wha?' he said. I

stopped him before he could fall into his boots and tumble out on deck. 'How long have you known that Duke?' I said.

'I don't know no bloody Duke—'

'Known of,' I said, before what he thought about dukes could burn the paint off the bulkheads.

'He's been there, down Dalling . . . hell,' said Sam. '*You* know.'

'So he knew of you. He knew about your mum and your cousins over here and all that.'

'Spose,' said Sam.

'Did he know about Elly?'

'On't know how he could have. Now I'm going to get some kip, boy, do I'll get lines round my eyes.'

'Think.'

He thought, groaning. Finally he said, 'Yes.'

'Yes what?'

'He called me in for a talk,' said Sam. 'He mentioned that he knew about her. "You might get to see your cousin Elly", he say.' He was sounding sharper now. 'Why do you ask?'

'When you started that tenant's strike,' I said. 'Who was the landlord?'

'Sir Albert Birkbeck.'

'Friend of the Duke?'

'How would I know?'

Into my mind floated a picture of two men with guns, in front of a pile of pheasants laid out on the lawn at Sandringham. That had been in the *Daily Mail*. One of the men had been the Duke. The other had been Sir Albert. Shooting with the King.

'He knew about me, too,' I said. 'He knew I knew the Gräfin. I was with him when we met her. So he knew that they would be here, and the Gräfin would be here. He knew that you and me would get recognized. Racing hands both, off of crack boats, on this old tub of a thing. If he wanted us not to be noticed he might as well have painted us bright yellow and given us Red Indian headdresses.'

I found I was grinning at the deckhead, concentrating hard, so as not to think of the Gräfin. I shoved aside the picture of those great sausage fingers on her hand. Instead I began to think of reasons the Duke had for sending us here. He did not like me because I had been a friend of Hetty, and had given him cheek as a boy, and more in the Canal, and rammed the Kaiser at Kiel against his orders . . .

And suddenly I was staring into the dark with my eyes wide open, thinking of the Duke's, pale blue and bulging and calculating. Some time or other, I suppose I went to sleep. When I woke up the scuttle in the hatch was greying with dawn.

The wind wailed in the shrouds, a long howl that rose and trailed away. That was getting up, and getting up proper. We were stuck. Spectators, really, held in the grip of those sausage fingers that had clutched the Gräfin's hand. But was that all we were in the grip of?

The wind howled up again. Fitzsimmons' snores faltered, then steadied. You could hear the busy tap and clang of halyards and runners, the roar of the waves on the beach; the ordinary sounds of a breezy morning—

Not quite ordinary.

There was a new sound in to my ear. Anyone not familiar with *Gloria*'s natural racket would have missed it. Certainly, Fitzsimmons' snores went on untroubled. Very quietly I sat up, unlatched the hatch, pushed that upwards and stuck my head out.

That was a good hour off dawn, but after the fug of that little coop, that seemed actually light. I looked towards the mainland, across the beach, and the metal-coloured edge of the sand. That was cold and wet and raw out there, drumming with rain. But I did not pay any attention to the rain. I was looking at the dinghy – not flat-topped and empty on its anchor, but with a man in it.

I knew from the shape of him that this was Wilson. And by the look of the weather, he was on his way to the bottom of the sea.

I would have shouted at him to stay where he was, but Fitzsimmons was snoring steady down there in the saloon, and shouting would have woken him.

So I watched him move around the dinghy, without any of the awkwardness I remembered him showing on land, sure-footed, a man back in his element. There was a short roar of canvas as he pulled up the sail. Then I was up and out of the hatch, going down the beach in my bare feet, waving. Not that he could not have gone by hisself, you understand; but I was tired of being a puppet, and I wanted to have had a hand in his going.

He gave me a wave back. The sail filled with a snap. I saw that he had double-reefed it, strange sail, in the dark, by touch: not bad. Then that was taut with breeze, pressed to leeward in the rain and the darkness, sliding westward down the ebb. I saw him tack, tack again, fading in the muzzy trails of rain until he popped out like the flame of a lamp when you turn that down.

He was away in a dinghy twelve foot long, too big for *Gloria* but too small for the banks and rips of the Wichter Ee, never mind forty miles to windward in the direction of Holland. Good luck, boy, I thought.

You are going to need it.

I went back to my bunk. And the funny thing was that though he had gone to drown hisself, and we were as good as in jail, that one shred of hope was enough. I slept like a baby, and did not wake up until that was well daylight: grey, true, with the wind lashing across the sand carrying dirty clods of rain; but light.

The first thing I did was to give Sam some instructions about luncheon. And the second was to go and see Mr Dacre.

I found him in the forecabin, and gave him his tea. 'Dinghy's gone,' I said.

He started up, and banged his head on the deck beam.

'With Mr Wilson,' I said. He put his head back on the pillow, and held that with both hands. 'Good luck to him,' I said.

There was a stirring from the saloon. Fitzsimmons stuck his head round the door, gummy-eyed and creased with suspicion. '*Vas?*' he said.

'Get out of here,' I said. 'The *herr* is asleep.' And I chased him up on deck.

Straight off, he noticed the dinghy was gone, and began to look angry and nervous, his hair tore about his head with the breeze, which was still blowing great guns.

'Terrible thieves round here,' I said. 'They got our anchor the other night.'

'Not possible,' he said. 'These are good Germans.' That was all my eye, because last night he had told me he came from Hamburg, so he did not know anything about the islands.

'All right,' I said. 'We stole our own dinghy. Now if you will excuse me, I got work to do.' I could hear the cold drum of the surf in the Wichter Ee.

Sam lurched past us as we went into the cockpit, flapping with oilskins and carrying a pail. I went down into the saloon and did some repairs while Fitzsimmons sat up above in the bluster and the rain. Then I swabbed the deck, and managed to tip a fair old bit of water into his boots. He even offered to help after a bit, but I would not let him. I wanted him cold and bored and sore-headed with breeze.

Meanwhile Sam was a mile away on the sand; sand that was not gold, like yesterday, but greyish brown, the colour sucked out of that by the stone-coloured cloud driving over from the west. He came and went between flurries of rain, a little figure, stooped over, the colour of earth in his stiff, stinking oilskins. Raking cockles.

Dacre had shut himself up in the fore cabin. I sat down in the saloon and banged with a hammer at a frame while I looked at the chart, and in particular at the rivers and drains that snaked in solid black lines across the fenny parts behind the sea walls. Then I knocked on Dacre's door, and went in.

He was lying on the downhill bunk, wedged in to the angle of the berth and the hull, writing in his notebook. He put it away quickly when he saw me. His face looked pasty and bad. 'Can't get at 'em,' he said. 'Can't do a bloody thing – sorry,' he said, noticing my looks perhaps, '– a jolly thing. We'll just have to hope Mr Wilson gets through.'

I nodded and tried to look bright, for even down below you could hear the boom of that surf. I said, 'Scuse my asking, sir, but how do you come to be here?'

'You brought me.'

'Before that, I mean.'

'Sorry?' He tried to look disdainful, but that is a hard thing to do upside down in a bunk.

'The Duke,' I said. 'How did he find you?'

'I am a soldier,' he said. 'Experienced in secret service. A natural choice for service of this kind.'

'Yes,' I said, patiently. 'But what did you do wrong to put you here?'

His face went stiff and hoity-toity. 'I don't think I—'

'Look you here,' I said. 'Sam's here because he's a socialist and he got across His Grace. I'm here because I rammed the Kaiser. Both of us stick out like sore thumbs, were chosen for it. So I think you stick out too, and I should like to know why.'

He was red and hard. 'I don't have to explain myself to my crew,' he said, that angry I knew I was onto something.

'No,' says I, and to be fair he was quite right. 'But do you know why they sent us over here?'

'Of course I know,' he said. 'Don't be a d— jolly fool, man. And so do you, now.'

'Well I know what you think you're doing,' said I. 'And you are doing a good old job, and so are we all. But I don't think that's the job the Duke wants us to do.'

'Oh, for goodness' *sake*,' he said, very impatient and angry. 'This is a complete waste of time—'

'Excuse me Mr Dacre but just you listen to me a minute.'

'Excuse *me*,' he said with a bit of a sneer. 'What is it that Captain Webb has found out that is so important?'

I gave him a nice smile, to aggravate him. Then I said, 'I think the reason we were sent over here is that we are meant to get caught.'

CHAPTER TWENTY FIVE

Chicken and Cockle Sauce

'D o *what?*' he said, and I could see he was proper stumped from the way he was staring at me, not so much with his eyes open as with the flesh of his face fallen away from his eye-balls.

'Birdwatching,' I said. 'When you don't know a bird's beak from its behind, excuse me. Salvage diving, in three knots of tide, just you and your diving suit. Sam and me, we've met these people before, and the Duke knows it. He also knows that Sam and me wouldn't be on an owd tub like this in the normal course of work. So I was wondering if you could explain to me what is going on.'

Dacre was gazing at me with a sort of set hate on his face. And all of a sudden I realised what I had done, and I would have cursed myself, except that I do not curse, as you know.

He was a proud little brute: look at his preening, his airs and graces. Hobnobbing with a Duke would be meat and drink to a chap like Dacre. And what had I done, Cap'n Webb, hired hand, but tell him that all the time he had been hobnobbing with that Duke, the Duke had been bowling him around like a wheel-barrow. I had stamped on his pride when pride was his widow's mite. There was no chance he would let himself believe me.

'So you've worked it all out in your clever little head?' he says, very sarcastic. 'Perhaps you are under the impression that just because you have allowed yourself to be led on by Her Ladyship you understand more about this situation than anyone else.' He smiled, his fierce, angry smile, the smile of a man who might have spent his life winning little races but had lost all the big ones. 'Not so, Webb. And if you take my advice you will follow your damned orders and cease allowing that gal to lead you round by the prick.'

Call me naïve, but I did not know anyone had noticed. The fact that was Dacre gave the whole thing a dirty peeping sort of feeling that made the blood roar in my head, as you can imagine. At that moment there was the wallop of a bucket on the deck, and Sam's voice saying, 'There you are then, my old Hamburger. *Kokkeln. Gut, ja?'* Fitzsimmons grunted, but that was not a grunt of a man who did not like cockles. 'Leave 'em spit till teatime,' said Sam. 'Get all the nasty grit out on 'em.'

Hearing Sam's voice talking sense calmed me down a bit. I said, 'What had the Duke promised you, may I ask?'

'I don't understand.'

'You shot a woman in the head,' I said. 'They chucked you out of the Army. Has he told you he'll get you put back in?'

He went red as fire. I had pulled his string for him, and no mistake.

'So we're all hired hands,' I said. 'And we've all done things that mean the Duke won't be too sorry if we get throwed away.'

He opened his mouth. No sound came out.

'He thought we should get caught as soon as we arrived, with our dynamite and our charts and all. What we're here for is to tell the Germans someone knows what they're up to. If you get caught blowing up their barges, they'll know the barges is known about. They'll think we're here sent by the Government, not no damned Duke. They'll never let their barges out of the islands, because they'll think that if we know enough to make secret missions, we know enough to have the Grand Fleet waiting out there to sink the lot of them. We're a diplomatic hint, that's all. Nobody would have said anything, not ever. That would have been an understood thing between governments. We're here to . . . embarrass them into keeping quiet.' I was speaking low, now, and Dacre was listening with a hand on his forehead, straining to hear over the wail of the wind.

He sort of sneered. But his heart was not in it, you could tell.

'But that didn't work,' I said. 'We were too good at what we were doing, or they were too clever. Perhaps His Grace didn't think we were that bright.' I saw him wince. 'But he was wrong.

So here we are. One dead German, one bomb planted, one yard burnt. Perhaps the Germans are too bright for his Grace. They aren't throwing us out nor arresting us; don't know whether they can see what we're up to and won't rise, or they just plain don't know. Whichever way, they've got us wrapped up now. They're the oyster, and we're the bit of grit. They've built a pearl round us; very smooth, very civilised. And there's nothing we can do till after those barges are away, unless Wilson gets through.'

'What are his chances?'

I did not answer. He got the message. He looked down at his hands as if they had handcuffs on them. He had seen what his precious Duke thought of him, and his life had gone to smash round his ears. He said in a small voice, 'What are we to do?'

'Not a lot we can,' I said. 'If we get off the boat, they'll lock us up.'

'Yes.'

'I have got a slight idea,' I said.

He did not like other people having ideas. 'It had better be good,' he said.

'You stay put,' I said, thinking, here we go, flattery will get you everywhere. 'Tritt knows me and Sam are simple seamen. He knows you're a gentleman.' Dacre's shoulders squared. Ah, he would be thinking, yes; could have been wrong about Webb. Far-seeing chap. 'So you stay on the boat, and take care of Fitzsimmons. I've got a bit of a notion.'

'Take care?'

'Sam'll do the cooking,' I said, grinning to myself but thinking at the same time, give me strength. 'And do you show me how your corned beef tins work, eh?'

'You sure?'

'Chicken and cockle sauce for dinner,' I said. 'Speciality of the *haus*.'

'You had better be right,' he said.

Sam went to finish the repair on *Gloria*'s bottom, poor bored Fitzsimmons trailing behind. The tides were getting bigger as from tonight, and we should soon be afloat again. While they were over the side, Dacre showed me his own brand of cookery.

Then I had forty winks, which was very welcome in view of

the last few short nights, and by the look of it another to come. I was nervous, I must say; nervous, and thinking about the Gräfin. Wondering, I should say. Wondering how far I had got with her, and how far that look in her eye would let me go.

Towards teatime, Sam and Fitzsimmons went into the village. I put the duck punt on the staysail halyard, and hauled that up and onto the sand. That had been rained on and sprayed on enough to be swelled up and watertight, which I was pleased to see.

At six o'clock Sam came back from the village with two chickens. He had wrung their necks, and as he walked over the beach he was plucking them, letting a plume of feathers off down the breeze. The rain was still falling, but softer now, and the breeze was blustery, no more. But as I looked to the southeast there was nothing to be seen but beach and tossing grey, merging into murk and rain. No mainland to be seen, just shallow sea and high bank. Going over there would be like going over the edge of the world.

I cleaned up the saloon, and put that into good cruising order. That gleamed and sparkled, though I do say it myself, green baize curtains and brass lamp and bright varnish, and only for the corrupt whiff of bilge you would have said she was a tidy little gent's cruising yacht. Sam was doing his famous *sauce velouté*, that he had learned off of a French girl he had had designs on in Dinard one year when he was with Sir Thomas Lipton, and tipping in the cockles. The chickens were fizzing away in the oven, and there were a few leeks and potatoes and carrots and whatnot he had picked up in the village, too.

At six o'clock, Dacre offered Fitzsimmons a drink of whisky, which Fitzsimmons refused; no doubt von Brüning had warned him not to follow in the wake of that poor Subby. At six-thirty, when I went down to light the cabin lamp, Dacre was discoursing to Fitzsimmons on the joys of small boats, while Fitzsimmons kept a wistful eye on the level in the whisky bottle, which was dropping. At seven, I pulled a bottle of white Burgundy out of the bilges, spread the tablecloth, and said, 'Dinner is served.'

Well, that was not what you expected on a small boat, but

Fitzsimmons did not turn a hair. He just sat there with his fists on the tablecloth, letting Dacre's lecture sweep over him. When the dishes arrived, he sort of grunted, and a hungry glint came into his narrow eye.

Dacre carved. I watched him ladle the cockle sauce over Fitzsimmons' chicken. I watched him say, 'Enough?'

'More,' said Fitzsimmons, and dug in like a miner at the coal face.

They both had two helpings, big ones. Sam and I crouched in the sooty little fo'c'sle and had a blowout of chicken and potatoes, no cockle sauce. Sam drank bottled beer, and I drank tea. Up above the rain was still falling, a small, thick, warm rain. The wind had dropped.

After the chicken I got into my bunk, and looked at a chart. Then I dozed off.

At eleven o'clock, I opened my eyes, and lay there for a second, wondering what had woken me. We were nearly afloat, for the first time in three days. But that was not what had woken me. I listened close, and heard that again: the sound of someone being ill.

'Dear oh dear,' said Sam's voice in the dark. 'Must be them cockles I shouldn't wonder.'

'Sam,' I say, stern, like. 'Did you pick them things above or below low water mark?'

'Why above of course,' says Sam. 'Else I should have got my hands all wet.'

'That never would of done,' I said. The back end of the boat was full of horrible noises. That certainly sounded as if Sam's cockles were highly unreliable, like most cockles you get above low water.

There are more ways of putting a chap out of action than drugging him with chloral hydrate.

I told Sam to move the boat into deeper water when he had a chance. Then I pulled on my socks and jersey, and picked up my boots and the bag I had packed earlier. After which, making no noise at all, I put my head out onto the deck.

The anchor light shone pearly in the Scotch mist. I found a couple of pails, and took one to Fitzsimmons and the other to

Dacre. The smell down below was horrible. Then I went up into the empty cockpit, untied the duck punt from its cleat, and lowered myself and my bag in. There was about three foot of water, now. I cast off, and let the tide sweep me gently away. *Gloria*'s light became a golden globe on the black face of the night, then a glimmer, then went out.

I set the oars and began to row.

The duck punt is twelve feet long and two wide, half-decked like a squat version of an Eskimo canoe. That is low and fine in its lines, painted grey so that will not show up in the eye of a duck, which is a lot sharper than the eye of a man. That was a pleasure to row.

What tide there was took me east and south, over the southern fringe of the Steinplate. After a while I found a withy, not that that mattered now I only drew six inches, and worked out where I was. The rowing got harder, because I was rowing against the tide now, over the Dornumer Nacken and across towards the Neiderplate, inside the island of Langeoog. Between the Accumersiel Balje and the Damsumer Sand was what I was looking for: a two-mile horn of deep water that led to within half a mile of the sea wall.

And I needed to hurry. There were pale patches showing in the clouds overhead, and the rain was easing up. Soon there would be a moon, and come morning that would be clear and bright, sun and showers from the west or nor'west, and even in a duck punt I would be standing out like a lighthouse.

So I rowed on into the tide, feeling the starboard oar touch mud from time to time, using that to keep me on the edge of the channel. I could feel the rise of the sea wall at my back now, the way you know someone is standing behind you in the dark without actually hearing them speak or breathe.

That was an hour after high water when the punt's nose touched bottom. I hopped out. That was still drizzling, and I was wet, and I found myself shivering.

Not that shivering was anything to do with the wetness. The shivering was because *Gloria* was five miles out there, on the ground by now, occupied by my friend Sam and two gentlemen giving out at both ends of theirselves. She might just now be a hell afloat, but she was a heaven to what was waiting behind the black loom of the sea wall . . .

The bottom brushed mud. I stepped out of the punt and into the wind, stowed the oars, and put the painter over my shoulder. Then I began to drag that towards the sea wall.

That is a light thing, a duck punt, flat-bottomed. That drags easily through shallow water and over mud. I hoped that the groove in the mud and the footsteps would not show come morning. That was too dark to tell.

The sea wall was high above me now. There was a low cliff of grass and mud, perhaps three feet high, gnawed away by spring tides into a series of coffin-shaped grooves. I pulled the punt into one of them, and put my head on the ground so I could see the slope of the sea wall against the sky, checking, in this lonely place, just in case there was a sentry—

There was a sentry. In fact there were two, bulky black shapes with spiked heads and greatcoats, standing just below the crest of the sea wall. For a moment I thought they were watching me. Then a match flared between cupped hands, and there was the glow and darkening of a pipe lighting. Well, one of the things I had against smoking was that that spoils your night vision; I have known men take twenty minutes to get their sight back after they have lit a pipe. So the chaps up there would be blind as new kittens.

I lay there and listened to my heart and the small hiss of the rain, and hoped that I was right—

The sentry got his pipe going to his satisfaction. Him and his mate moved on down the dyke, leaving me lying there with my face in a pile of old seaweed and the sweat running out of me like water from a tap.

I picked myself up and scrambled over that low cliff, hauled the punt's nose after me and started to pull that across the foreshore. That dragged across the wet grass even easier than that had gone across the mud. I went up the sea wall on my hands and knees. On the top, I looked left and right. The sentries had disappeared into a thickening of the rain. I paused to calm my breath, and went down the inland side.

You could smell the marsh now, greenness and flat water, the same smell there had been last night when we went over the dyke in the Gräfin's carriage, five miles west of here, beyond Bensersiel. The wind was less powerful here, only the odd puff, rattling the reeds at the dyke's inshore base. I moved on, faster now, downhill, getting heedless. A shape rose from the ground beside me. My heart jumped and my knees slackened, and I was halfway to the ground, falling away, before I heard that baa and worked out that that was a ewe with her lamb, taking shelter in the night.

That was consoling to think there were things as commonplace as sheep in this land that was getting ready for war. I crept the rest of the way to the bottom, the rattle of the reeds getting louder, like sticking your head into a boxful of grasshoppers. I stowed the oars in the punt and took out the little hand-paddles—

I am sorry. Looking back, I see I never explained what I was up to. The thing is that along the foot of the dyke there ran a species of ditch or drain, ten foot wide, with what I guessed would be three or four foot of water, and black mud going down to the earth's core. That was marked on the chart, and so were others connecting in. And all of them, as is the nature of drains, arrived eventually in the rivers, which if you remember turn into the *tiefs* or channels that lead to the *siels* or sluices. In this dead flat land, they were a way a chap could travel without being seen – or so I had to hope.

There was a patch of thinner reeds to my right. I slid the punt through and in, and climbed in myself. Bubbles rose, and the night filled with the smell of bad eggs. I began to paddle west.

Letter from Captain Eric Dacre, late —th Lancers, to Miss Erica Dacre, St Jude's Eastbourne, Sussex.

Dearest Sissy
  Dreadful news. News so dreadful I can scarcely convey it, even to you. Harrowing, galling, deadly—
  Judge for yourself.
  I have sat through the worst of dinners, with the German

command, while they pumped me. There was von Tritt, a bully, and
von Brüning, who is worse, for he sees into your head, and what he
saw this evening was no gentleman, I fear. The Gräfin was there too,
but she paid me no attention; none at all. And now we are back on
board, Webb has shown me things as they are.

The truth is that I am betrayed. The Duke my patron has sent me
here so that I may be thrown to the lions to blunt their appetite. How
he has deceived me! Dear Dacre, my old friend, he would say. Fellow
Pelican, dear chum, such rare times we have had! We understand
each other, now if you could do this leetle thing for me I might just
be able to arrange with the Colonel that the Regiment look favourably
upon the restoring of your commission . . .

All trash. All vanity. He has played upon me like a stringed
instrument, Sissy, and all the while he meant to feed me to the
Germans as a sign that their intentions were known, their fleet
doomed. He was banking on my incompetence, Sissy, my snobbery,
my blindness. And the most dreadful thing is that I now see that he
was right. What will save us, if anything will, are the actions of the
man Webb; a servant, but a clearer thinker . . . in fine, a better man,
Sissy . . . than your brother will ever be.

That damned Duke has hooked us like fish – Webb and Gidney
only by the lip, for they are sensible men, wary of the bait. As for
me, I believed. And I swallowed the hook. I feel it now, turning in
my belly. I shall never be rid of it, I think; whenever I hope or confide,
I shall feel it turn.

Put not your trust in Princes, it has been well said. But not well
enough believed

by

Your loving Brother

Eric

CHAPTER TWENTY SIX

Voyage in a Duck Punt

What a punt is for is creeping up on duck. Duck do not like the sound of oars, or anything else man-made for that matter, and that is hard to blame them when you think that up on the front end of a duck punt you will normally have a four-bore muzzle loader with the best part of a pound of old nails and black powder up the spout

So for the final creep up on your raft of duck you use a couple of little paddles not a lot bigger than gardening trowels, and with the same length of handle. With a bit of practice you can drive that thing along a creek or a drain at a goodish speed, without much of a wake at all, and nearly invisible because the bluey-grey that is painted is the colour of sky reflected in water. Marsh water, any road; the water you get in the creeks in the freshes, which is what they call the marsh round Dalling. I just had to hope that would be right for round here too.

Once I had the punt over the wall and past the sentries and in the water, I pulled the watch out of my weskit pocket and waited for a pale patch in the clouds. Half one, that said. I ate a bit of black bread and cold chicken left over from supper, and took a swig out of a bottle of cold tea, though that was fair to say that was more medicine than food as the state my nerves were in I did not want either. Then I checked the skyline and shoved off.

I paddled west at first, as I now said. The rain had stopped, which was a nuisance, but the wind was still up, bowing the ghostly reeds and whipping up a ripple on the water, and I soon began to ache and puff.

I now mentioned that I spent some time on the chart before I came. After a couple of hundred yards, I saw a sort of a dip in

208

the drain's bank on the left-hand side. I steered over there, very quiet. That was another drain, and now I saw that I knew where I was, from what I had read on the chart. I gave a push of the arms, and slid the punt into that. That fitted like a shell in a gun barrel, and the reeds fair to met over the top. When I looked back I saw the dark loom of the dyke, that had been with me so long, sliding astern.

Pretty soon I came to a right-angled bend. Then the little strip of water stretched away ahead like a Fenland lane, which come to think of it was what that was. And I paddled on down it, the splash of my progress masked by the rattle of the reeds.

A few hundred yards on the drain came to an end. Somewhere nearby a dog was barking. I slowed, pulling in to the side, keeping my head down. There was a jingling clatter, and across the grey sky at the ditch's end there stamped and rattled a stream of mounted men. A squadron of cavalry, at a guess. They charged through the night as if they owned it, to pile into their barges and head for poor old England. The outrage drove out the fear. As the sky ahead cleared of horsemen, I paddled on up the drain.

The dead end was not a dead end, but a junction with the big ditch that ran along the side of the main coast road. That had been marked on the chart. For some good German reason the old reeds and bushes along its banks had been cut hard back, so the drain ran broad and deep and straight, but without enough cover on its margin to hide a dabchick.

There was no help for it, though. I turned right, and paddled on.

The wind was right in my face now, funnelled between the high, clean banks. Each yard forward was like lifting myself and the punt up a cliff. There were houses ahead, bulking sharp against the sky. There were no lights – that was late for marsh folk to be showing lights – but there was that dog, barking in shortish bursts, that its owner would be used to but that would drive the neighbours mad, I thought.

Then there came that rattle and jingle again, and I pulled in under the bank closest to the road, and lay sweating with my head down until the cavalry had gone past, squadron after squadron, most of a regiment by the sound of it. The dog was yelling and swearing at the horses. The clattering faded away ahead. The dog calmed down. When all was quiet but the hiss of the wind, I went on.

The drain ran between the house and the canal. That was a tidy looking house, that from the glimpses I had of it looked as if that might belong to someone richer than the general run of small farmer, a cattle dealer perhaps. Whoever lived there had thought the usual plank bridge across it was not grand enough. So there was a full-scale culvert, which as I drew nearer I saw was faced with some sort of stone or more likely brick. That looked very narrow: about the same narrowness as the punt, in fact. But there was nowhere to go but on, now, and at least the dog had stopped barking, secure in its mind that it had sent the cavalry packing. So in I went.

The mouth of the culvert swallowed me up, and the nose of the punt broke out of the far side, and I remember thinking, well, that wasn't so hard, was that?

But that has been well said that the race is not won until that is finished. And a bit more than halfway through, with the roof six inches above my head as I lay in that punt, there was a scrape to the left and a scrape to the right. And the next thing I knew, I was stuck fast.

At that moment I can promise you I did wish that I was a swearing man. If I had been, I would have cursed the mason who built his culvert narrower at the middle than the mouth, the man who had built the duck punt half an extra inch wide, the man who had marked this drain on the chart—

But I realised that this was panic. So I forced myself to think. The punt's greatest beam or widest point was from rail to rail, which was what that had stuck on. What was necessary was to reduce the beam. And that was easy done, by tilting.

So I wriggled over to the port side of the punt. For a reward the port rail went down and the starboard rail went up, and there was a great big graunching of wood on stone, and the good part was that I felt the punt come free and float again.

But there was a bad part, too, in the shape of that dog. That dog heard the sounds and galloped down the side of the ditch and next thing I know there is a dirty great head in the half-round mouth of the culvert and that is barking fit to bust your eardrums, biting at the nose of the punt, close enough so I could get a nasty whiff of the horse meat that had ate for its supper.

Well, I pulled back into the culvert, which was just long enough to hide all the parts of the punt at a time. That was horrible uncomfortable, because I was squeeged right down into the curve of the punt's hull, and the bag with all those corned beef cans was somehow under my hip and I thought I felt something crush, which was not what was wanted. Then over the noise of the dog barking came a noise that really did freeze my blood: a man's voice, shouting in Fries. The dog's owner, the cattle dealer as I now thought of him, who would come and look for his dog, and find me instead.

He sounded angry, all right. I heard the shuffle of his feet and his long, wet cough. He kept yelling, and I suddenly realised that he was not only angry, but drunk.

That did not seem long since Hetty's brother Joe and me had dusted Vicar's sheets with icing sugar and Vicar had discovered that as we stood one behind each of his bedroom curtains. Vicar had yelled like that then, except he had been drunker if anything. There was a grunt, and a yelp, and that seemed the cattle dealer had kicked the dog, because the dog stopped barking and ran away, and as that ran there was another grunt as the cattle dealer aimed the next kick at it, and then a big yell and a thump and a splash that made the punt rock in the culvert, and framed in the the culvert's end I saw a fat man in a white nightshirt with ruffles, shoulder deep in the water, clawing his hands into the grass of the bank and dragging himself up, scrabbling with his bare white feet, and not for one moment did he stop swearing at his dog. He was no more than six feet away. I lay there with the bombs digging into me, very frightened now. He clambered out, still bellowing, and I heard the dog yelp as he kicked that into its kennel and slammed the hatch on it, and the bigger slam of the house door.

Then and only then, I scrabbled that punt out of the culvert and shifted my weight off of the bombs and commenced paddling along the ditch beside the road. That could not have taken more than five minutes. But I was soggy with cold sweat and I felt as if that had aged me twenty years. Still, I had learned how to go through a culvert in a duck punt, and as the ditch passed more houses that became useful knowledge. So that had not been time wasted.

After ten or fifteen minutes, the drain lost its man-made straightness and departed, waving and wriggling, from the road. That had become the Pumptief, not much more than a drain itself, but what passed for a stream in these parts. The interesting thing about the Pumptief was that according to the chart, in a little less than a mile that straightened out and ran between two dykes, the main sea wall and a sort of spare built behind it. That was a similar looking arrangement to the one at Hilgenriedersiel: the widened canal in the dead ground, invisible from outside. A most interesting place.

I paddled on, under the now overgrown banks of the Tief. That was easy to worry about what lay round those corners—

Suddenly the stream ahead widened out into a broad grey channel. That was empty, except for some ducks. But ahead was a glow in the sky, and that buzz again, the sound of voices and hooves and engines coming on the hiss of the wind, the beehive sound we had heard at Hilgenriedersiel.

The ducks paid me no attention as I crept along the west bank. Either I was invisible, or they were used to seeing men. I put my head down, took a sweep of the eye along the sea walls, inner and outer. There were people. A lot of people, and what looked like a wire fence.

Ahead, the *tief* curved left behind the inner sea wall. There was a clump of trees there, willows, overhanging the water. Very carefully, I made my way along the shadow of the bank and into the trees.

Between the branches you could see the rest of the Pumptief. The rest of the Pumptief was not empty.

Between the two sea walls, the rest of the Pumptief was jammed with barges. From water level that was not possible to see how many, because the sterns of the first tier stood up big and black as headlands, eight across. There was light further down, men and horses, that hum like a swarm of bees. There was a railway line too, by the hiss of steam, and I fancied I could hear the rumble of gun carriages on ramps.

I stayed under the willows, hardly breathing. A couple of mallard sat on the water. I watched them paddle away, sleepy, no doubt, edgy about their ducklings. I looked at my watch again. Quarter past two. That felt as if my stomach was full of live mice. Through the curtain of hanging branches the stretch of water between me and the first barges was flat as a black mirror. I had never seen anything so naked in my life. The punt's wake would stand up on that like a tidal wave. Why not leave that to Dacre? That was his problem, after all. His business—

All our business.

> Oh, we don't want to fight
> but by jingo if we do
> we've got the Sam and we've got the Webb
> and we've got the duck punt too

But here was Webb, under a tree, feeling not real, looking at the big fat barges that would go ashore in England unless someone did something.

The mallard, not liking the company under the tree, began to swim away. They swam down the left-hand center of the *tief*, the west centre, the whole family of them. The ripple of their wake spread in overlapping arrowheads that interfered with each other, making a little robble on the water, spoiling the flatness of the black mirror.

Brushing the willow branches gently to one side, I went after them, by jingo, a duck punt and a flotilla of German mallard in the service of dear old England Home and Beauty, not to mention that damned Duke. I took that punt so close to the edge that I got grass in my ear, paddling with the inside paddle only. On the other side of the *tief*, the wire fence came down to the drain. A man was standing next to it, greatcoat, *pickelhaube*, the usual. A voice above my head said something, and I nearly jumped out of the punt. But that was saying, '*Quake, quake,*' which being interpreted is quack, quack. Talking to the ducks. Then we were past him, and the barges were tall as buildings ahead, spanning the *tief*.

213

Like I now said, they were seagoing barges, not river lighters. Whoever had designed them had made sure that whoever and whatever was in them would stay dry. So there was a little sheer to their sides, and a little flare to their sides, too, so that when they plunged into a wave the spray would be squoze outwards and not upwards. Moored as they were, side by side in tiers, their rails were touching, but their hulls at the waterline were three feet apart, so between them there was a tunnel about the right size for a duck punt, hidden from anyone looking out above.

I crept down the bank until the barges' sterns loomed seven feet above my head. There I left my escort of ducks, and entered the realms of darkness.

That was proper dark, black as ink, a tunnel with another little patch of light ahead where the bow of one barge met the stern of the one in front. There were voices, and rumblings that came through the timber, and the groan of mooring warps and the rub of strake against strake. They were loading up, fast as they could go. That was a noisy place, but private, and privacy was what I wanted just then.

I stayed there a moment, fending off from the barges with a hand either side, trying to keep my knees from knocking against the punt's hull. I could not believe what I was about to do. I could not believe I had got this far, Charles Webb, twenty-four, yacht-hand, secret blessed agent. So get that over with, I thought. Haul out that bomb and fuse that up and whack that in the nearest barge you can see, then get out of here just as fast as ever you can. You will have done your duty, boy, which is more than what you are being paid to do anyway.

But putting that in the back end barge would be a terrible slapdash job. The way they were packed in here, that was no use at all. What was needed to do that properly was to blow up one of the tiers closest to the sluice gate, so that would block that off for the rest of them, and take dear knew how long to clear. And if you got that right (I thought, getting excited now, the way you get excited in a race, when you have seen the way to give the other chap your port side) you could block off not only the Pumptief, but also the lagoon at Dornumersiel into which that flowed, and which would no doubt be full of barges itself.

That was a very nice picture. All those barges, aimed at England, full of men and guns. And all bottled up behind a pile of wreckage, while von Tritt worked with steam cranes and goodness knows what else, trying to get that clear before the tide turned. And having to explain that to that mad little Kaiser of his. Blast that would blow the scars right off of his fat face—

Language.

But I sat there with the mice playing tig in my belly, and I fair to laughed myself overboard at the idea.

When I had had my laugh out, I paddled on.

Those barges were moored eight across, as I now said. At the second tier I crossed over from the bank, and went between row four and row five. I went slow, and saw nobody, counting barges as I went. After half a dozen their sides seemed to get lower. Those were the ones that had already been loaded. At Hilgenriedersiel the night before last, they had hardly started. The time must be getting near. After ten more tiers the barges turned a corner, and I knew I had moved out in to the lagoon at Dornumersiel. Something low and black showed up ahead, barring the path. The transom of a tug.

That was quiet out here now, the barges being already loaded and the troops not yet aboard. So I stopped at the back end of the first tier behind the tugs, and stood up.

I found myself looking down a pair of broad side decks moored rail to rail, with a pair of coamings running away from me, coamings being the little walls that stop the water coming into the hold when a wave splashes over the decks in a seaway. They were high coamings, and out here in the middle of the *tief*, the light was poor. So I slung my haversack around my neck and I tied the painter of the duck punt to one of the bollards on the back end of the barge, and up I went onto the side deck, staying flat as a dab, to keep below the level of the coaming. There was a cover over the well of the barge, a stout tarpaulin with a good hard lashing. I whipped off the knot, and hove up a fold, and slid under that like a seal going off a bank.

I had with me a stub end of a candle, which, the tarpaulin

being thick and heavy, I lit. That showed a huge deck, seventy foot by twenty as I said, with at its point of balance a sort of huge crate or bin sheeted in with more tarpaulin. So across I padded, funny, but that felt quite safe really, in this barge, in the middle of all those other barges, but invisible. I started the lashings on the bin, and held the candle up to look, and pulled that back again right sharp.

For what was under there, throwing the yellow candle flame back at me, was a steel cylinder gleaming with grease, but no matter how much grease anybody put on that there was no hiding that that was a field gun, or that by the markings on the crates stacked around it that they were shells or charges or something. I am not a soldier so I could not say for sure, but that did not look like something to be waving lit candles about near.

So I set my candle on the deck on the tinlid I had brought, and opened the haversack.

Like I now said, I am not much of a hand at bombs, never having had the practice. So my fingers were all of a tremble as I pulled the tins out: the buttercup, the bullock, and the cocoa. I pulled off the top of the cocoa, which was the barograph mechanism as you might remember, and set that, and tugged the fuze cord free. I took off the top of the buttercup, which was the dynamite, and shoved in the little points on the ends of the fuze. So far so good.

Then I started on the bullock.

The bullock, you will remember, was phosphorus in water, in a glass jar inside the tin can, the top of the glass running a quarter of an inch below the top of the can, to allow space for the opener. Dacre had said to open that, to leave a glass container which would smash on explosion and fling phosphorus far and wide.

But this jar did not have a glass top.

CHAPTER TWENTY SEVEN

Pale Fire

I was nervous, remember. I was that nervous my brain was not working too well. So in the flickering shadows of the candle, what had happened took a while to sink in. I put that tin up to my nose and sniffed, thinking I suppose that might be meat, a mistake, the wrong tin. But that smelt of match heads still. That was still phosphorus. And the smell of the match heads went right up my nose and into my head, and I sneezed.

That was not a loud sneeze, but loud or soft, that did the job. That blew out the candle. And that jerked the tin in my hand, so stuff went flying out of that and across the deck.

I would have swore, if I had been a swearing man. I knew what had happened, then. I had lain on the knapsack in the culvert with that dog yelling in my face. I had felt something give. What had given must have been the tin, and the glass inside had broken. And now there was phosphorus all over this here deck—

The sleeve of my jersey was burning with a greenish-white glow that moved when I moved my arm and stank of burning wool. I started to yell, then remembered where I was, and tore that off, and started for the exit. The candle was out. But there still seemed to be enough light to run by. The light was coming from a line of green-white splotches on the deck, like luminous blood out of a big fish you would gut, brilliant splotches, becoming even as I glanced at them edged with red. Not that I watched for long, because I was running.

Dear I did run. I left the jersey and the haversack lie, and by the dead green light of the burning phosphorus I made for the corner where I had come in. I went up and over, and for a second

I wondered about making fast the lashing on the cover, but decided there was nothing to be hid any more. I untied the painter, dropped into the punt with a crash, and began to paddle back through the barges, telling that dog what I thought of it to stop myself thinking about that a bargeload of artillery shells burning a hundred yards away.

But that would have taken more than a dog to stop me imagining those red sores of fire eating at the corner of the tarpaulin, running along the canvas, busting through into the night—

Shouting filtered down into the tunnels. There was open water ahead. I stopped in the shadow of the barge's bow. The water was full of the reflections of the red sparks blowing down the sky. The sentries were still at their posts at the butt-ends of the fence, one on either side of the *tief*. They stood stiffly, looking back at the fire, nervous, on their toes. In between me and them swam the mallard, the flames like little rubies in their eyes.

Someone must have given the sentries an order, for they both trailed arms and trotted down the path, one on either side of the *tief*, until they had disappeared from the field of view. I gritted my teeth and gripped my paddles and scooted out of there and under the willow trees, neck crawling, expecting yells or bullets, there was no way of telling which—

Then all of a sudden I was in the slab of darkness under the willows.

There was the distant sound of a steam engine, a blast of boiler sparks. The sparks were beyond the black mass of barges, and the bonfire spewing orange flames at the black sky. By their light, little figures in greatcoats were running, stumbling across the barges to the banks of the *tief*. They had been on the barge that was burning. Brave chaps.

I started to paddle, hard, for the corner of the *tief*, away from that burning sky, into the cool black ahead. My reflection went in front of me, fading with distance from the flames. The banks narrowed down. Well, Duke, I thought. One yard burned, one bomb placed, another on its way to kingdom come. I wonder if that was what you wanted, you popeyed devil—

Then the black water and the green banks and the grey sky

turned the colour of day. Everything stood out sharp and clear, every blade of grass, every whorl of the water, in a quiet that was like Creation holding its breath. Then came a bang fit to drive your eardrums together in the middle of your head. And after that there were only ringing ears, and paddler's breath—

And a new sound, a sort of roar that you could feel as much as hear. For a moment, that was hard to say what that was. Then I knew, but that was too late to do anything about it.

That was a wave, of course. There was a sort of whoosh. Then there was just time to glance over my shoulder and see the face of it, a six-foot wall of water pinched up by the narrowing banks, its front black and grey, tumbling and roaring. Then that was on me, and the crest collapsed with a boom and a roar over the punt and plucked me out and took me away until something caught me and I stopped, trapped, praying, waiting to die or come alive again, I knew not which.

But that seemed I yet lived; for as in Noah's flood, the waters abated, and I was in the fork of two willow branches in the night. Over the dyke, the lower parts of the sky were hot orange. Everywhere but there, the sky was black velvet. Of the punt there was no sign.

I unwound myself from the tree. On the ground again, I saw that my troubles were only beginning. My matches were wet, and even if they had not been, this was no place to be showing lights. There would be no finding the punt, unless I were to trip over that, of which there was little chance. I was alive, certainly. But I needed somewhere to go.

East, I thought. Back to the place where I had come ashore.

No boat. No point.

At low water I might be able to walk. But low water was well after daybreak; one man walking would show up like a Christmas tree. Anyway, the duck punt had gone, and that would lead to questions being asked on *Gloria*, to which there would be no answer.

Wilson had found shelter at the Carolinenhof. So the Carolinenhof that would have to be. Headquarters. The last place they would look for a saboteur. Or so I told myself, to banish the nasty hollow of fright under my breastbone. That was not more than a couple of miles away. If I could pick up the sea wall, I could find the Hof.

Where that was just possible that the Gräfin would take me in. That was a lot to ask of her. Still, I told myself, faint heart never won fair lady. Blast that sounded stupid.

But off I set anyway.

I went at a lively clip towards the village of Dornumersiel, at the head of the lagoon. There was a bridge there that would put me on the western side of the *tief*, with no obstacles between me and the Carolinenhof. After five minutes I came upon a metalled road. There were houses here, black and lightless. I went past them gingerly, listening out for dogs. But what dogs there were were either asleep or hiding from the fireworks. There was a tramp of feet, and a biggish lump of infantry came past. I lay in the ditch and watched the serpent of marching shadows, packs on backs, campaign order. When they were gone I got up again.

The road bent left. I went around that, and saw I was coming to a bridge – the bridge over the *tief*, more than likely. I stopped still – I had been walking on the grass verge, to hide the noise of my footsteps – and watched.

There were two sentries on the bridge.

They were looking nervously towards the orange glow in the sky. Beyond them on the road were more marching boots. Marching in time, I crossed the road. When I was out of the houses I started to walk south, in the wrong direction, towards the bank of the *tief*, hearing the soldiers behind me break step as they crossed the bridge. After five minutes I connected up with a cobbled track that might have been a towpath, with beyond it a grey glint of water.

I followed that inland, waiting for the *tief* to narrow, or for a bridge of some kind. As far as I remembered from the chart, there was no bridge till Dornum, and anyway, that seemed likely that if the bridge at Dornumersiel was guarded, the bridge at Dornum would be too. As for narrowing, that was a fond hope. The *tief* looked as if that had just been widened, for use as a canal. That looked too deep to wade, and as for swimming, well, you know what they say about fishermen and swimming, and Charlie Webb was no exception to the rule. That looked as if I was going to have to chance Dornum, or nothing.

But I never got that far.

Behind me, I heard horse's hooves. I jumped off the bank along which the track ran, and into a little thicket of bushes. And only just in time. A horse and rider thundered past, coal-black, the rider low in the saddle, the horse's hooves going hard enough to strike a blizzard of sparks out of the cobbles. There was no way of connecting them to my own case, of course. But I must admit they frightened the life out of me.

When they were past I got up and started once more along the road to Dornum. I had fallen into a sort of panic. The glow in the northern sky was a guilty flush, and the terror of messages passed through the night was heavy upon me. I was a fisherman, for goodness' sake, a man who squashed tins flat when he got treed by a dog in a culvert. Not a soldier, or a secret agent, or a rick burner. But to the whisperers in the night I was all those things, and they would hang me for them.

But what if they thought the explosion was an accident?

That was the second accident in a week. They would be rounding up strangers. That was only thorough. Only German.

Drat that dog.

As I walked trembling on, I came upon a couple of barges tied up in the *tief*, ordinary barges, these, innocent carriers of lime and turnips, not the seagoing type. I looked at them idly, the wind in my face, thinking that would have been a good place to hide, except that everyone else who saw them would be of that mind too.

The wind was in my face as I looked across the *tief*. The barges were perhaps sixty feet long, the *tief* a mere fifty wide. As the Germans were showing, a barge could be a bridge as well as a cart.

Suddenly I was a man again.

I went down that bank like an avalanche. I untied the back end of one of them and stepped on. Then I kicked that away from my bank, so that slewed out towards the far bank, the one I wanted to cross to. But the kick was nowhere near powerful enough. So I rummaged around in the bottom till I found a young treetrunk of a pole, and I lodged that on the bank as a quant, and I heaved on that thing until the sweat ran down my face. And inch by inch, the back end of that barge began to creep across the water.

That took what seemed like an hour. But finally that touched the far bank, and I jumped off, and chucked the quant back in the bottom. As I hove that out into the breeze and that started to swing back across the *tief*, I heard the tramp of feet and the jingle of harness. I lay down on the bank, and pressed my face into the rank grass. From the corner of my eye, I could see the barge fall into its mooring, rocking faintly. A frieze of men marched along the skyline above it, dark and silent and full of purpose, heading north. They marched past, and were gone.

I shall not dwell on the next couple of hours. That is enough to say that I floundered through reed beds and scrambled through ditches, and trekked across hayfields and skirted shelter-belts, and was reduced to a state of gibbering terror by a barking dog in a reed-cutter's hut. And all that time the red glow in the sky moved from the starboard bow onto the starboard beam.

Finally I began to see the dyke in front of me, a tall black wall separating this sticky place of mud and bushes from the graceful engines of the wind and the moon. That was drizzling now. Over to the left, backed up against the dyke, was a pale patch, lamplit windows diffusing among trees. The Carolinenhof.

I took myself towards that through the fields, keeping low, along a stretch of tall dead grass that stood up between the road we had travelled the previous night and the ditch. The sea rumbled on the other side of the wall, and the wind hissed in the aspens. There were a couple of men on the gates. I crept round the back, through a hole in the hedge, and into the grounds.

Then I straightened up and started to whistle *Deutschland uber Alles*, and walked across to the wicket in the barn door. As I put out my hand for the latch, I saw a soldier, standing under one of the trees. Well, if I ran away that would get me shot. So I made my hand keep moving, sprang the latch, shouted a cheery '*Morgen!*' and walked in, pouring sweat. Nobody came after, though I waited. Now I was here I was tired, terrible tired, so my knees were not working and there was a buzzing between my ears. I needed somewhere to rest and think, and decide whether I could risk throwing myself on the Gräfin's mercy to keep me hid until Wilson got through to the Dutch, assuming he was still alive. Which we had to, or give up now . . .

I blundered about till I came to the hay mow. A chicken squawked, and a cow changed feet, crunching hay. I climbed to the top. There I lay down. Wilson knew the islands. He might well have got through. The Fleet might even now be heading for Helgoland. The bombs in the yards would certainly hold things up. Even if not, I could walk across the sand to *Gloria*, and we could get out somehow and raise the alarm . . .

Somewhere in the middle of this foolish and hopeful pipe-dream, I fell asleep.

I fell into a silly dream of being chased across flat ground and falling into ditches in the dark, and all the time the person chasing me could see where I was because my shirt was on fire. Then a voice started yelling and I woke up with a sneeze, and the voice was still yelling, and that was not a dream at all.

'Out of that!' said a loud Frisian voice from down below.

I held my peace.

'I hears you snore!' said the voice. 'Now you ain't snoring, which mean you're awake. Come down, you warmint, or I'll blow a hole in you.'

Well, there was nothing else for it. I slid down and into the light of a lantern. Holding it was the old butler, with his bald head and his mutton-chop whiskers, and a short muzzle-loading-looking gun pointed at my fifth waistcoat button.

'What you doing here?' said the butler.

'Trying to get some sleep,' says I.

He eyed me nastily. 'Come you in here and we'll see what we makes of you,' he said. He frowned. 'I knows your face.'

I did not much want to be known. 'From Wilhelmshaven,' I said. Last time he had seen me, he had been drunk and I had been in my Sunday blues. This time I was crusted with mud, in my shirtsleeves. 'Go easy, squire. I'm looking for work, is all. On the tramp.'

'Funny way of going about it,' he said. 'Breaking into people's barns.'

'When the weather is good,' says I, 'I sleeps under God's good stars. But on a night like this here I thought the Herr farmer would not grudge a chap a roof—'

'You should have asked first,' said the butler. 'And it's not a Herr. It's a Gräfin. Now get along and let's have a look at you.'

I did not like this idea at all. 'No,' says I. 'I'll just be on my way, that's morning now—'

He jabbed me in the ribs with the snout of his blunderbuss. 'No you don't,' he said, surprisingly brave. 'You get along in there.' And so doddery was he, so tremulous the hand that held the gun, that there was nothing for it but to let myself be prodded through the toolroom, past the potato bins and up to the kitchen door.

'Open that,' he said.

I opened that.

The kitchen was as usual, with the high beams, the hams on their hooks, the bunches of herbs. There was a bracing smell of coffee, which having caught a whiff of I began to crave something terrible. There was the red-faced cook, and the scullery maids: the only one missing was Elly.

The one thing that was not as usual was that sitting around the walls, greatcoats unbuttoned, rifles propped, were a good twenty German soldiers.

CHAPTER TWENTY EIGHT

Love and a Court Martial

O f course the first thing that came into my mind was that they had hunted me down and now I should swing. All of them looked at me, all right. But I soon made out that they were hardly interested at all, really. So I said, chirpy as could be managed, 'Morning, all.'

A couple of them even gave me good morning back. And now I had started, that seemed to me that the cheeky chappie routine was quite a good one to carry on with. So I said, 'What are all of you a-doing of here?'

The butler said, in a self-important sort of voice, 'This is local Army headquarters.'

Well I knew that already, of course, but that seemed to recall a sergeant to his duty. He walked over, latched onto me with eyes like a plaice drag, and examined me from stem to stern in the greatest detail. 'And who,' he said at last, 'are you?'

'Tramp,' said the butler, in his glory. 'I apprehended him sleeping on the hay mow.'

'Very alert of you,' said the Sergeant in his nasty thin voice, and I knew we had a dogged one here, and that did not please me at all. 'So where are you from, then?'

I stood there and kept my mouth shut. The cockiness had worn off, and to be fair I was sproper frightened.

'Wilhelmshaven,' said the butler.

'Me too,' said the Sergeant, and my heart went right into my boots, for Wilhelmshaven was a place I had never been, and that would not take more than a couple of questions from a native to show me up for a liar.

'Where were you working before you went on the tramp?' says he.

'Naval dockyard,' I said, which was the limit of my information about the place.

'Which department?'

Well there he had me, of course, but when in doubt, charge. I said, 'If you want to ask me questions you can ask me questions when I have got a cup of coffee in my hand and not before. That is all very well for you sojers with your three squares a day. But I am a pore civvy on the tramp, and I must have coffee.'

'Which yard?'

'Coffee. I'm gasping.'

'Give him some coffee,' said the Sergeant, in the voice of a man with unlimited time.

I kept my head low as the cook slapped me down a cracked cupful, hoping she would not recognize in this mud-splattered wreck the trim English yacht skipper who had sat at the table in his Sunday blues two nights before. But she had no desire to examine such an unhygienic object. I took a noisy sup, and even in the spot I was in, that tasted like nectar.

'Which yard?' said the Sergeant, steady as a dripping pump.

All of a sudden the coffee went bitter. There was nothing to say. 'Bastards gave me the sack,' I said. 'Where's the lady of the house what you now told me about?'

'Which yard?'

'Do you mind your own business. I want to see Her Ladyship what that old boy now told me about.'

'Her ladyship is dressing,' said the butler, to impress me with his priviness to the household's doings. 'She have no time for the likes of you.'

The Sergeant was leaning on the post of the door into the passageway where thirty-six hours ago the Gräfin had kissed me on the lips. I walked over towards him. 'The yard that fired me,' I said, 'if you really want to know, was Schmidt's. I was a riveter.'

'Never heard of them,' he said.

'That's not my problem, mate,' says I, and I saw a tiny niggle of doubt in his eye, but doggedness, too, and I knew I had had it. There was only one way out, or perhaps I should say in, and that depended on blind faith and was most unreliable, meaning the testing of things I had not wanted tested. But faint heart and all that. So I opened up the door and went through.

They let me go; at least for the half a second that took to walk through, they let me go, I suppose because that was the door that separated the gentry from the servants, so that did not even occur to them that one of the lower orders would walk through that unless something needed cleaning or someone rang a bell.

When I was in the passage I started to run. As I came into the dining-room I heard the kitchen door open behind me, and boots and voices. The doors off the hall were open. Faces in the drawing-room turned towards me; faces I recognized as belonging to the generals who had been at dinner the night before last. There was the smell of cigar smoke, and a glimpse beyond the heads of a great blackboard with beside it a window flung open to catch the early air, and beyond the window the orange glow of Dornumersiel.

All that I saw in a couple of seconds. Then the door slammed shut, and a voice above me said, 'What is going on?'

That was a voice of ice, or cold metal, the voice of a member of the people-owning classes routed out of bed before dawn by the rioting of the common herd. That froze everyone to the spot, including me. That was the voice of the Gräfin.

Her eyes swept the stairwell like the *Blitz*'s arc searchlight. The only eyes that met hers were mine. And as always there was that catch, the workman's hand on silk; except that this time odd as that may sound that was like the hand stroking the silk, and the eyes held, and her face turned pink, and I think mine did too. She said, to me, 'What are you doing here?'

Tell the truth, like Dacre said. Just leave out the bits that might get you hung. 'I was sleeping in your barn, milady,' says I. 'These people woke me up and wanted to know why I was there.'

She nodded as if that was something she already knew. 'In my own house, I ask my own questions,' she said.

The Sergeant was shocked. 'But the Gräfin will not . . .' His voice trailed away under those eyes. 'As the Gräfin wishes,' he said, nervously. 'But with such persons . . . the Gräfin should . . .'

'I am grateful for your concern,' said the Gräfin, and you could hear stately icebergs in her voice. 'But I must beg your permission to choose my own acquaintance. Now I am sure you have better things to do than stand around in my hall.'

I had the presence of mind to look shamefaced and start back to the kitchen with the crowd. 'You,' she snapped. 'Come up here.'

So I started to trudge up the stairs, doing my best to look like a man entering the lioness's den, not like one borne on wings of angels to a scarcely-expected salvation.

'So,' she said sharply, shooing me into her dressing-room door. 'What is your reason for being alive, my man?' She shut the door.

She had her black curls piled on her head, and a lace-trimmed *peignoir* nipped in at the waist that went down to the ground. Elly the maid was in there, looking at me, seeing a man in leather seaboots, blue serge weskit and trousers, blue flannel shirt and a short-peaked yachting cap, none of the above visible for more than a square inch here and there because of the mud caked on them. 'Stop staring, for goodness' sake,' said the Gräfin. 'You saw worse in Paris. Get the poor man a dressing gown, take his clothes away and clean them up.' Elly opened her mouth and shut it again. The Gräfin said, 'And run the bath.'

So Elly scuttled off, eyes cast up, resigned.

That was an enamel tub long enough to lie down in, and have brass taps, one for hot water, the other for cold. The dressing gown she left over the chair was blue tadpole sort of pattern, with quilted lapels. I should have been worrying. Instead I found myself jealous of whoever that had been made for, and whatever had happened in Paris too.

When I went back into the Gräfin's room she was sitting at a little table writing on a sheet of paper. 'Arson in His Imperial Majesty's Dockyards,' she said. 'Death by hanging.'

My face felt as if that was made from clean wood. This woman was the fiancée of von Tritt, and never you forget that. Secret agent and Countess we might be, but we were two people wearing dressing gowns, if you take my point. I could smell her; new perfume, bed, essence of woman. All of a sudden, without knowing how I had got there, I was close enough to hear her breathing. I could hear myself breathing, too. There was a thrush singing to the orange glow over Dornumersiel. I was looking into her eyes and she was looking back and some far distant part of my brain was saying, now she will turn me in to von Tritt, and I shall swing, but the parts of my mind that had my attention were paying that no heed at all.

'Gräfin,' I said.

'My name is Katya,' she said, and caught hold of the lapels of the dressing gown and pulled me towards her.

And that became quite plain that did not matter whose fiancée she was. All that mattered was that she was a woman who was finding life strange and lonely, and had tripped over a man who was finding that likewise. And now neither of us felt lonely any more.

Then I took her face between my hands, her cheeks like silk, the hard hands of a chap who works with them, and I kissed her mouth, and she kissed me back. She did not seem worried or shy. We moved over to that big bed, and somewhere along the line the dressing gowns fell off. I knew that would cause trouble, but that mattered not one tiny bit. Her body was white as milk, and her eyes were violet-blue, and outside, Dornumersiel was burning, and inside, she and I were burning up on that bed—

But I am here to tell you a story, not show you the inside of my head or bedroom, so I shall thank you to turn your eyes away for a moment; until, in fact, about an hour and a half later, and the pair of us tangled up in that bed like a pair of warps flung anyhow into a locker.

I could tell from her breathing that she was asleep. I looked at the curve of her cheek on the pillow, and had the feeling that this was not just a girl I had tumbled in clean sheets, but something bigger and better. Hetty turned up again, of course, but as history, not a present haunting. With Hetty, that had been all fire and youthfulness. With this Gräfin, that was . . . well, fiery all right, and neither of us was old. But we were both on the wrong side, she German, me English, her a lady, me a working chap, but we had done that none the less. I suppose that when you came right down to it, that was love. But what became of this kind of love? Nothing good, if that was found out about.

But there were other things that needed considering. I made myself consider them. Two *siels* out of action, and a third mined. Two-sevenths of the invasion fleet, possibly three. Little as I knew about invasions, that struck as something I should be slow to try, with between a quarter and a third of my fleet out of action.

Then there was Wilson. Wilson was not a great hope. But by now he would be drowned dead or at a telegraph office in Holland. So wait until dark. Walk back to *Gloria*—

There was a clatter and a jingle below the window, and things that had seemed straightforward in the quiet bedroom were suddenly not. There was an army out there, ready for war. That was borne in to the still air of the room by a hum of voices. Speaking one at a time, they were, sharp and clipped; military voices. This room was over the top of the room where all those soldiers had been round the table, with the map and the blackboard. That sounded like a meeting; a council of war, even.

Gently, so as not to wake Katya, I crept out of the bed.

The dawn was up now, and the day had a balmy feel. I pulled up the sash of the window. A faint smell of cigar smoke rose from below, and the voices became clearer. That was a lot of reports, by the sound of it. All would be ready and loaded at A, B, D, E, F and G. That rambled off again into a thicket of what I supposed were code words, hard to hear because of the words not making sense but also because of the worry. That stood to reason that the letters meant *siels*, as they had in Dacre's notebook. Six *siels*. But Wilson had burned Nessmersiel, and the black smoke over Dornumersiel showed that I had been out and working. I was fuzzy in the head from sleeplessness, mind; but fuzzy as I might be, two from seven still made five . . .

Down below, the discussion stopped. A single voice took over; a harsh sort of voice, with no tune in it, and a parade-ground carry. Von Tritt.

I found I was holding my breath.

'I will be brief,' he was saying. 'The All-Highest will be arriving by the eight o'clock train. This will enable him to watch the beginning of our venture. The hour is at hand! All is in readiness. Gentlemen, God will bless our efforts this day. *Hoch*!

'*Hoch*!' they all shouted back, and the crash of boots came up through the floor.

I stood there in my birthday suit, breathing the sweet air of that morning. Today was the day.

I was terrified.

I heard a body move in the bed. When I looked up she was looking at me with her head on her hand. She caught my eye that way she did, so there was nobody in the world but the two of us. The terror went. The hum below became unimportant as the buzz of a fly.

I went and sat down by her. 'Today,' I said.

'What can we do?'

That was half past seven in the morning. We were surrounded by a quarter of a million Germans. *Gloria* was on the beach for the next three hours at least. 'That's up to Wilson,' I said, with a confidence I did not feel.

Then all of a sudden there was a terrific rattle and a clatter in the yard. That had me off the bed like a flash, and across to the window.

Perhaps I felt invisible, or perhaps I was just not thinking clearly. Either way, I should have realised that he who sees may also be seen.

A squadron of Uhlans had come through the gate. They sat eyes front, back straight, their horses down to slow ahead as they brought them alongside. They were bunched around someone whose face I could not see; someone out of uniform, slumped in his saddle. A door slammed. Out onto the gravel, cigar in mouth, strode von Tritt.

The cavalry dismounted. The man in the middle stayed in his saddle, and now you could see that the reason was that his boots were lashed under the belly of the horse.

The boots were seaboots. Seaboots that should have been rolling around the bottom of the Wichter Ee, or treading the parquet of a telegraph office in Holland.

Wilson's seaboots, with Wilson in them.

Von Tritt pulled his watch out and frowned. His face was the face of a busy man, a man waiting for something or somebody, getting on with things. Then as a man will do at the house of his fiancée, he looked up at her window, to see whether the curtains were drawn, whether his beloved was awake.

Well, the curtains were drawn, all right, and the beloved was awake. But so was her lover, stark naked, standing in that window staring numb with horror at the hope of England frapped to a horse.

So the first thing that Baron von Tritt saw in his fiancée's window was me.

Katya's hand grabbed my wrist and pulled me back. But I could see from the frozen shock I had glimpsed on his face that he had seen me, all right. And a moment or two later, jackboots were thundering on the stairs.

I had my clothes on by then, and Katya was in a dressing gown, making believe to sip cold coffee. The door opened. Von Tritt was standing there like a ticking bomb, but quieter.

'Morning, Baron,' I say.

He did not look at me; beneath his notice, I expect. He looked at Katya with eyes that if I was a ladies' novelist I would say burned with an icy fire or something, but seeing as I am not I will only say looked very cross and bloodshot. 'What is the meaning of this?' says he.

Katya was watching him most chilly, one eyebrow in the air. She said in a voice like cut-glass, 'It is usual to knock.'

'What is this . . . person doing in your room?'

'Minding his own business,' said Katya. 'And setting you an example by so doing.' He did look at me then. I smiled at him, man to man. That made his forehead veins stand out like down-pipes on a house.

'Now please leave,' said Katya.

Von Tritt clicked his heels, and that was amazing the blood did not come shooting out of the top of his head. 'Not until I have told you some . . . news,' he said.

'One fears that your manners leave something to be desired,' said the Gräfin – I cannot think of her as Katya, not when she was like this.

'Whore,' said von Tritt.

I saw her face flush blood-red, then turn white as ceiling paint. He saw he had got one in. But of course what he had said could not be stood for. 'Mind your manners, Baldy,' I said.

He turned upon me with his bloody eye. 'Your time will come,' he said. 'Soon. I shall find you, and kill you slowly.'

I said, 'Is that not legal to go yachting in Germany nowadays?'

He smiled a crocodile's smile. 'Of course,' he said. 'It is not, however, legal to be a spy.'

'A spy?' Katya was still white.

'This man Wilson,' said von Tritt. 'He was apprehended by the gunboat *Blitz* – in the dinghy belonging to this man's yacht, curiously enough – leaving German waters north of Borkum. I think we shall try you next.'

'The dinghy was stole,' I said. 'I reported that to Captain von Brüning.'

'What exactly makes the man outside a spy?' said the Gräfin.

Von Tritt smiled. 'Before he was boarded and questioned by the *Blitz*, he attempted to evade Captain von Brüning.' He let his eyes rest on the pair of us; nasty, cold, knowing eyes. 'There was a woodyard fire last week. It caused much damage. This area is under martial law. This Wilson is guilty of arson. Now,' he said, 'I am busy.'

'So this . . . Wilson,' said Katya, and if I had not known otherwise I should have sworn that this was the first time she had used the name. 'What will become of him?'

Von Tritt was already showing us the bristly folds on the back of his neck. 'He has been tried,' said he, 'and found guilty. So he will hang, in twenty minutes. You can watch, if you like. I shall deal with you later. Just now I have an appointment.'

His jackboots thundered on the stairs, and he was gone.

CHAPTER TWENTY NINE

The Glittering Horsemen

They put Wilson under the ash tree at the side of the barn and slung a rope over a branch. They had dug up a priest somewhere, a bald chap who looked dazed, as well he might, this not being the kind of thing you got a lot of in a country parish, I suppose . . .

The reason I am going on like this is that remembering it, I think that everyone there was dazed; me, the soldiers even, and most of all Wilson.

He stood under that tree, poor devil, wrists tied behind him, and watched as they brought a stepladder out of the barn, a homely sort of stepladder, the kind you would use for painting walls and picking apples, not killing men. You could see him sniff the wind, as if to work out what the weather was going to do, then realise that in ten minutes he and the weather were going to have nothing to do with each other no more.

We stood around him in a ring. There was me and the Gräfin, and half a dozen soldiers, and von Brüning, and the Parson. Von Brüning looked ill at ease. He had given Wilson a cigarette, and Wilson was smoking that hard.

I said, 'You can't do this.'

Nobody paid no mind, except von Brüning, who was standing off to one side now, his face yellowish over the auburn beard. When he heard my voice his eyes moved and his mouth opened and I thought he was going to object. But he shut it again, and watched, grim as stone.

Then the Gräfin pipes up. 'It is wrong,' she said.

The Parson started praying. Wilson was looking round him like an animal in a corner, realising now, white and stiff about

234

the lips. He smiled at me and the Gräfin, then caught von Brüning's eye. 'Sorry to have . . . put you through this, old man,' he said. 'You're a good chap.'

Von Brüning bowed, about an inch of a bow, the bow of a Spartan with a ferret up his shirt. The wind hissed in the leaves, and the sea rustled, and I thought, this poor devil is going to die, and nobody here wants him to.

I said, 'If he was a spy, what was he spying on?'

Nobody paid any heed.

'All right then,' I said; desperate now, and without much hope, as you will see. 'You can declare martial law until you are black in the face. But this is peacetime and in peacetime you can't go pulling Englishmen under trees and stringing them up without so much as a judge nor jury, thank goodness. I may be speaking out of turn but my king and your king are uncle and nevvy, and that is not the way you carry on between relatives, blast that is not. Begging your pardon Captain von Brüning.'

Von Brüning turned those horribly bright eyes on me, and they seemed to see right through the honest peasant business. But I held his eye, and said, 'Do you mark my words, if you go through with this you are going to get wrong,' and this time that was not playing peasants, but a promise, man to man, near enough a threat.

A sergeant walked up to Wilson and put the noose round his neck. Katya's fingers were wound tight in the lap of her skirt. That was the fiancé of her friend Clara they were going to hang; the reason she had brought herself to betray her country.

She lifted up her chin and said in a quiet voice, 'Leutnant von Brüning, this is not legal.'

Von Brüning said, 'Unfortunately, I have my orders.'

'These orders are illegal. And unnecessary.'

'Unnecessary?'

'The deed is done. The word cannot spread.'

She meant the invasion would go ahead whether or not Wilson was hanged. I stood there and held my breath and tried to look as if I did not know what she was on about. Von Brüning's head was bowed.

'Get on with it, would you?' said Wilson.

235

Von Brüning looked half-paralysed. He had been trained to obey orders, be loyal to his country, his class. But from what Wilson had said von Tritt had stolen his command off of him anyway. And now von Tritt had given these orders, and left him to kill a man out of pure spite, that seemed to me.

Never mind what von Tritt called it. What this added up to was murder, pure and simple. Von Brüning was a naval officer, not a murderer.

There was a long pause, with the breeze sighing in the ash tree. Then he said, in a voice that sounded as if he was choking his own self, 'Take the rope off that man.'

The Sergeant said, 'But the Herr General—'

'The first thing you learned in this Army was?'

'*Befehl ist befehl.*'

'*So.*'

The Sergeant looked as if he was due a bout of brain fever. But the noose came off.

'Go,' said von Brüning.

Wilson was greenish white, and his eyes were rolling all ways in his head. 'Go where?'

'Away. Back to England, if there is anything left of it.'

The sea rustled on the other side of the wall. Katya seemed suddenly to arrive at a decision. 'Come,' she said.

Wilson and I both looked at her.

'The *Delphin* is at Dornumersiel.' She said to von Brüning, 'You are an honest man.'

'I have done my duty.' And lost his job, and got his own self court martialled, if I was any judge of von Tritt.

Wilson spoke. 'This probably sounds silly,' he said. 'But I hope this doesn't get you into trouble.'

Brüning laughed, very hard indeed. 'It has been a pleasure to work with a real amateur,' he said. 'I can only hope that the events of the next few days will not remove your kind from the face of the earth.' He bowed and walked away, taking the soldiers with him. The priest looked relieved, and showed signs of wanting to shake hands with everyone. All of a sudden we were walking towards the sea wall, trying not to run. I said to Katya, 'Dornumersiel's blocked. Barges sunk in the entrance.'

'No,' she said. 'There was a fire in the night. But they towed the burning boats to one side after they exploded. Half the fleet was destroyed. But the rest can get out; the harbour is clear.'

'Oh,' I said, with a swooping feeling in the stomach. All that effort for nothing. That was why there were six *siels* still in action. Hilgenriedersiel might go, of course. That left five and a half. Would they still go with five?

Von Tritt had the wind under his tail. He would go.

But Wilson was glancing over his shoulder as if he expected said Prussian to come galloping out of the trees with a new rope. This was no time for fishermen to be hanging about making forecasts about strategy. We walked fast along the seaward slope of the dyke with the breeze in our faces.

That was a pure and innocent morning, a morning with the weather on the change, breeze gone east, sky blue as a baby's eyes, as if the Kaiser had arranged with the Devil to have his dratted fleet blowed where he wanted that to go. At the foot of the dyke the *watt* was a sheet of brown and blue with Langeoog and Spiekeroog standing up clear above their white beaches. The tide was still ebbing. When that had finished ebbing and started to flood again, there would be two hundred thousand soldiers in that holy bath of light, fuses burning, aimed at England.

Delphin was anchored at the seaward end of the Dornumersiel channel. We walked quickly down the dyke and onto the muddy sand, Katya, Wilson and me. Smoke was still floating up from the *tief*. We all looked back at the sluice, but nobody made no remark. There was enough to think about without talking.

Von Tritt, for instance.

After the crew had fetched us in the dinghy, Katya told them to go ashore. They looked at us and did not seem to like what they saw, but orders being orders, they trailed off across the beach towards the wall. 'Can't make traitors of the poor fellows,' said Katya.

I hauled up a staysail and Wilson cranked up the anchor. Katya put her blue serge hip on the tiller. The training bank began to slide. We were away.

Now Wilson had finished with the windlass, his face went suddenly waxy, and he sat down hard. Katya saw that first, bless her, the way she does. She fetched him a drop of schnapps, which he drank like an Arab in an oasis. That seemed to do him good. 'What now?' he said.

'We'll go to sea. Try for Holland. Telegraph. I'll land you near *Gloria*, if you like. So we get two chances.'

He said, 'There'll be a destroyer screen. Escorts,' as if he was pointing out a shower of rain, not sudden death. But there was nothing else we could do against all those men. We were too late, too late. We all knew that.

We were sliding down the Accumersiel Balje, deep water, the tide ebbing under us at a fair old clip, feeling that lightness underfoot, that what is under you is alive, not solid and grim like the dirty land. The channel was a strip of blue-grey water between brown fingers of sand. That was smooth water ahead, the mouth of the balje where that joined the Accumer Ee, the *seegat* between Baltrum and Langeoog. In the centre of the *balje* was the brown whale of a sandbank. I think she was not seeing any of it. If she was anything like us, that was the things inside her head that were filling her view: a full Wattenmeer, a sheet of water lapping at dune and dyke-foot: the swinging open of the great *siel* doors, the vomiting forth of tugs and barges and men—

The *Delphin* with a six-hour start.

'Straight out to sea'll be best,' said I.

Wilson nodded. That was too early to try a *watt* passage. Out between the islands was the way, then turn west for Dutch Friesland, with a foul tide and a light breeze, and steamships to chase us.

Katya made a sort of a gasp noise. When I looked at her her eyes were over the gold dolphin on the rudder post, looking at the land.

The green sea wall hung between heaven and earth, as always. The sun was up, but low, it being not much past seven o'clock. That shone full and flat on a group of horsemen who had come onto the face of the sea wall, to the west of the Dornumersiel sluice. That sparkled in the sun, that group, as if they were toy soldiers made for some mad potentate, all enamel and precious metal and diamonds. Soldiers they were, but not toy ones.

Wilson looked mildly interested, but his eyes were burning as he passed me the glasses.

There were aides de camp with nodding plumes, the stars of orders twinkling, dolmans and sabres and snow-white breeches. In the centre of them was a man in butcher boots and white tights, a frogged black tunic and a busby with a skull and crossbones on the front. A man I had last seen on the deck of the *Meteor* at Kiel, in a different uniform, but then as now favouring a withered arm, and with black moustaches waxed into two points that stabbed at the sky.

'*Herr Gott,*' said Katya.

Then we turned away all together. And all together, we shouted out loud.

For the *Delphin*'s bowsprit was not looking at open sea any more, but a low hill of sand, with a withy on its summit; in a peculiar place for a channel marker, actually, but I was not thinking about that just then. For before Katya could haul the tiller round again, there was the slithering crunch of her keel on the bottom, and that rising of the deck that meant one thing and one thing only.

We were not heading out to sea any more. Under the eyes of Kaiser Wilhelm of Germany, the three of us and fifty tons of boat were fast aground on a falling tide.

CHAPTER THIRTY

Whistling in the Dark

Nobody said anything for a while, except for the things you have to say as you drop the dinghy out of its davits and lay out a kedge and grunt and strain at the windlass. Ten minutes we hove and sweated, and all we achieved was to pull the anchor home twice. All the while you could see the water falling away from her copper, hear the echoes like knockings from the tomb as that sucked and clocked in the turn of her bilge. We strove like madmen, but to no avail, me and Wilson red and sweating, Katya pale and set-faced as a church marble.

'Look here Captain,' said Wilson at last, panting. 'This is no good. Where's your boat?'

'Same place as before.'

'You'd better get back to her. At this rate, she'll float first.'

I added that up in the mind. He was right. But by the time there was enough water to get *Gloria* over the watershed to the Accumer Ee we should be four hours into the tide, and the *siels* would be opening. There would be water enough for the Wichter Ee, between Baltrum and Norderney, a couple of hours earlier.

There came back to the ear of my mind the growl and thump of the Wichter Ee banks as we had come past on our way to Baltrum. Nobody who had not walked the thing could get out of the Wichter Ee.

Wilson had walked the thing.

'You know the Wichter Ee,' I said. 'You go ahead. We'll come out of the Accumer Ee when we float.'

He looked back at the sea wall. The group of horsemen still glittered on its green face. He looked worried; he would have been silly to look anything else.

'Two chances are better than one,' I said. 'Take the Gräfin.'

'I'm staying,' she said.

'Don't be—'

'You want me to move, you'll have to carry me.'

Well there was no arguing with her. Even Wilson could see that. He grabbed my hand and shook that, silly fool, and said good luck and God bless you and that sort of thing, which was a waste of time but seemed to please him. Then he went off at a trot, round the southern headwaters of the creeks, crabbing northwest, for Baltrum and *Gloria*. That was only five miles, a little over the hour if he kept going and did not drown. He shrank in the wavering air, became double, and winked out like a candle.

To tell the truth I longed to be with him, but there was Katya sitting there, and we were aground for a good hour yet, and von Tritt would be out here long before that. Call me stupid if you want, but I thought she would need help against von Tritt.

Which is laughable really I suppose, the way things worked out.

I turned back to Katya. I said something like, 'Here we are, then.'

She said, 'I'm sorry.'

I grinned at her, though I have seldom felt so little like grinning. I said, 'If the Kaiser of Germany comes onto the sea wall while you are steering down the creek that is an excuse for running aground.'

She said, 'I should have let you do it. You've beaten him once. Take the dinghy. Get to *Gloria*.'

'If you come.'

She did not answer. If I took the dinghy, von Tritt would come chasing after us, and catch *Gloria*, and that would be an end to it. The longer we sat here, the better chance *Gloria* had of getting away.

'All right,' I said. 'We'll wait. And when he comes I'll knock his block off.' But as we sat there and waited for the tide to turn, I knew I was whistling in the dark.

We sat quiet, holding hands. Then I saw her head turn towards the sea wall, and her hand went to her mouth. That is quite possible that my own hand was somewhere near my own mouth.

The sun was out, as I now said. The glittering little group of horsemen went up the wall and over the top. There were four little figures left, horses stamping, shining with bright metal, gold on the breast and silver steel in the hand. They came towards us at the gallop, the speed of the tide rushing over a beach.

I found a pair of glasses down below. They were three ordinary soldiers. And in front of them, sabre out and up, face gleaming like a tomato above the collar of his big cavalry greatcoat, von Tritt.

Von Tritt did not look happy.

If he had had the brains of a von Brüning, he would have gone after *Gloria*. But he had let himself be drawn away by his jealous fury. I guessed that he would not hurt the Gräfin, not with a sword anyway. What he would be wanting to see most, just now, was the colour of my own personal insides.

I said, 'Is there a gun on board?'

She shook her head. White as paper, she was, a thing I thought you only found in books. She looked at the sand, the water, the horses. The hollows around her eyes creased as she peered into that lake of light.

The soldiers were close enough so I could hear the rattle-*thump* of the horses' hooves. There was a flash and a bang, and something went past my ear like a bee with a steam turbine up its arse, if you will pardon the expression, and another bang, and another bee. Then von Tritt swung his sword round at the chap who had fired and I suppose he must have hit him with the flat of the blade because the chap tumbled off onto the sand and lay there, and I thought, hello, why did he do that there?

I had a nasty sort of feeling that was because he wanted me all to himself.

Of course all this time I had been waiting for *Delphin* to float again, being as the tide was flowing now. But you could still hear the water clocking away underneath, and the sad conclusion was that she was an easy half hour off floating yet, and that if Charlie Webb did not do something about this right sharp, that was not a half-hour Charlie Webb was going to be alive at the end of. This was life or death, not a yacht race. All of a sudden I forgot about being a hero and developed a strong desire to keep on living.

The dinghy was tied up on the seaward side, half-ashore and half-awash. Horses could not ride on water. So now I ran along the rail and untied the painter and those hooves were deafening, and I actually saw von Tritt's fat shadow flick across the dinghy, and there was something in his hand. A sabre. Oh dear oh dear, I thought. I dropped pell-mell on to the deck as the blade hummed over my head with a horrid swiping noise. I rolled away as he wound up for the next swipe. My hand landed on the boathook. I pulled that out of its clips, good bronze head on a two-inch ash helve, and turned to look at him and on the whole wished I had not.

He had a face on him like a Swiss flag, red with white duelling scars. His horse put a leg in the water and shied. I said to him civil enough, though actually I was that scared I wanted to go to the lavatory, 'Morning, you silly Count,' and took a poke at him with the boathook, a sort of prod really, which he dodged. And for a moment we stood there, him on his horse and me on the side deck by the *Delphin*'s deck house, just about eye to eye. They were clammy as oysters, those eyes of his. No doubt about it, Charles Webb was meant to die this morning.

Well there was no point just standing there, so I gave another jab with the boathook. Which was not a practical thing to do, because he took another swipe with that sword of his, great big heavy cavalry sabre sort of a thing that was, all sharpened up and ready for a hacking war. I felt a sort of whack in my hands and there was the boathook in two halves. Not being a fighter I was off balance, so that knocked me down and I hit the gunwale with my shoulder and fell overboard, flat on my back in six inches of water.

'Get up!' bellows von Tritt.

From where he was lying he looked about twenty foot high, which for some reason irritated me. 'Say please,' said I.

'This is an order.'

'Go away with you,' say I, very cross.

Well he took a swipe at me then, and I rolled away under the turn of the bilge at the back end of the yacht. That was safe under there for the moment, in the little wooden cave between the water and the bottom of the boat. There was a thump and a grunt, and he was off his horse, and any second he was going to be fishing around in here with his sword like a man hooking for crabs at low water. And now I was not angry any more, just frightened.

'Charlie!' shrieks Katya.

'Do you keep out of this,' I shouts back, and what choice did she have, with those other chaps up there holding the ring while the boss went a-butchering, but I had no time to think about that, because of these problems I had of my own.

If I went on the sand, he would come after me on his horse and slice me up. If I stayed under the boat, that was the crab treatment. If I tried to drag the dinghy into the water, he would chop me up for bait while I was at it.

Which left only one way out, and that was not a way that filled a person with joy and delight when that person could not swim.

I was on the water side of the boat. The creek stretched away in front of me, flooding now; twenty minutes off floating the boat, perhaps. Twenty long, long minutes.

I got down on my hands and knees and sprang out of there like a flea from under a cat. There was the blur of the sword, and I rolled in the water, and the steel clouted me but the water slowed that down and that bruised, not cut, and I was running along a mud bottom that clung at my feet, losing a boot and then another boot, getting into deep water, catching a faceful of salt, rolled over by the force of the tide, coughing and choking, losing my bearings, the way you lose your bearings when you cannot swim and you are in deep water, frightened out of your wits by a man coming after you with a sword.

I saw him as I rolled; I saw the whole thing. Von Tritt shin deep in the edge of the water, the skirts of his great-coat dark with wet, trussed up to the chin, buttons gleaming. Behind him *Delphin*, gold and white and lovely, lee-boards gleaming in the sun. And in the cockpit, stirring now, Katya—

But I did not see where she was stirring to. For von Tritt fixed me with his eye and started towards me, steady as death. I got my feet on the ground. The water was up around my armpits. I took a step backwards. The bottom dropped suddenly away. The tide grabbed me like a hand. Cold salt water closed over my head.

And there I was, drowning.

Between the devil and the deep sea no longer; for the deep sea had me.

All a normal man would have had to do was wait. But this was von Tritt, and I had laid hands upon his fiancée, and he wanted to cut me into strips.

My feet hit bottom. I was in about eight foot of water, and as they hit I gave a little jump that had me breaching like a whale, spewing spray. There was a sort of a shriek from the back end of *Delphin*, but I paid no attention to that, being occupied on the one hand by trying to breathe, and on the other by the fact that von Tritt was wading in after me.

But the tide was running pretty rapid, as I now said, and by the time I was back on the way to Davy Jones that had swept me a good distance downstream, back towards the mainland, and Tritt was running after me, keeping up well, with a sort of berserk snarl on his nasty fat face.

That should have been a relief to sink, after that. But that was not. Some of the water got into the breathing tubes, cold and wet and nasty, and the bottom of the creek was gone for ever, so I just went down and down and down and everything was turning slow and peaceful. Then I got one more touch of the bottom, hard slimy mud that felt like, and I gave that a little poke of the foot. And up she came, daylight, and then a suck of air, that I was just about certain would be my last.

And with the daylight and the air came a glimpse of von Tritt: von Tritt waiting, holding his sword out in front of him, ready. When he saw me come up he took a step towards me. Then his arms shot up in the air and he shouted something and went down with a splash, and the rest of that I did not see because I sank again, mouth open, and the salty water was locking up my throat and there seemed to be bubbles everywhere, and the world was a horrible panicky place that was turning from pale green to red to black—

There was daylight, and a pain in my head, and wood by my face; wood-planked clinker. The side of a boat. A dinghy. And as I coughed and sputtered I found that the pain in my head was a hand in my hair, and a voice was shouting at me to hang on. Well they say drowning men will clutch at straws, so I did not need a lot of persuading. The hand let go, and someone was rowing; the Gräfin, Katya, rowing across the creek, towing me away from the *Delphin*, that was on the other side.

My feet touched bottom.

'In,' said Katya's voice.

I tumbled in over the side of the dinghy. The coughing was getting less, making room in the mind for other ideas beside breathing. We should be being cut up, or shot. What was going on?

What was going on was that I was on the stern thwart streaming water, and Katya was on the bow thwart, rowing. The nose of the dinghy was pointed out between Baltrum and Langeoog. I turned round.

Three horses stood alongside *Delphin* on the sand. Two soldiers stood waist-deep in the flowing grey water of the creek. They looked lost and frantic. Except that was not them that was lost, as far as I could see. They were looking for something, groping in the water with their hands.

There was no sign of von Tritt. That came into what was left of my mind that that was him they were looking for.

Then in the middle of the channel something rolled. Something with a spiked helmet and an open mouth and bulging eyes, over a torso swaddled in the heavy folds of a wet greatcoat. Arms thrashed. The weight of the helmet took the head down. The feet came up. For a moment the thing floated, buoyed up by a bubble of air in the greatcoat. Then the air escaped in a great, well, fart, excuse me, and a boot with a spur came for a moment out of the water. Then the boot slid away, and there was a burst of bubbles, and after that nothing.

Katya rowed steadily to seaward. 'Aren't you going to help him?' I said.

'No.' Her face was hard and still – more than that, even; triumphant. Not lonely any more. I sat there shivering. You must remember I had been on the sea most of my life, and that went against the grain to sit and watch a man drown. The soldiers waded to and fro, losing hope. The horses wandered off towards the sea wall.

She must have guessed what I was thinking. 'He would have killed you.'

I did not answer. That was true. Still—

'I heard what he did to Dollmann,' she said. 'Clara's father. They did not trust him, because he was English. So von Tritt took him walking on the sand off Wangeroog. He knocked him down with the flat of his sword, into a pool, not much more than a puddle, really.' She pulled a few strokes, harder than was necessary. 'Clara's father landed face down. Then von Tritt stood on his neck till he drowned. One of the soldiers with him told Elly. He flapped like a plaice, they said. It took him ten minutes to die.' She rowed on, untidy strokes, looking at the bottom boards. 'He was a traitor,' she said. 'But he was a man, the father of my friend.' When she looked up again I saw her face was wet with tears. 'So now that swine has stepped into a mudhole and drowned, and I am very, very happy.' She started to cry in proper earnest.

I took the oars from her, and pulled on. The movement got the blood going in my body, perhaps even into my brain. We were making progress now, even against the tide. On the beach the soldiers were little figures, moving like swimmers, fuzzy with shock. One of them fired at us, but we were a long way away now, and there was no chance without their horses, but the horses were on the sea wall, reins dangling, cropping the wind-flattened grass. Von Tritt had been under water for ten minutes, and that was not likely he would still be blowing bubbles. So that was one worry out of the way; but only one. A drop, as you might say, in our sea of troubles.

The Gräfin had got herself under control. She smiled at me, sort of shy and nervous. We were out of her world; mine too, for the matter of that. But at least, that smile seemed to say, we were together.

There was in all conscience little enough to smile about. On or off horses, those chaps were going to spread the word that the C-in-C had been done in by the Gräfin von und zu Marsdorff and a rough-looking chap in a dinghy. And that was not all. There was an invasion fleet on its way out of port in two hours. An invasion fleet with no commander now, and reduced by fire and explosion. But still an invasion fleet. More immediate was the fact that if the tide got to *Gloria* before we did, she would be off down the Wichter Ee, and we would be left to make our way through the destroyer screen and into friendly waters in a yacht tender—

'Look,' said Katya.

CHAPTER THIRTY ONE

To the Wichter Ee

We were moving towards the *seegat*, the Accumer Ee. There were ships out there, not the usual fishing boats and *muttes* but low grey ships with high narrow funnels, with turrets and barbettes and the long, down-sloping chutes of torpedo tubes. The first escorts, shallow-draught gunboats and destroyers and torpedo boats, the first screen for the barge fleet. And behind the sea wall volcanoes of smoke were beginning to rise as the tugs got up steam.

The bank of the *balje* was trending west now. Katya had her glasses to her eyes. The breeze had freshened a little, though nothing to signify. That was still a nice day for a row, or an invasion—

'I see her,' said Katya.

'She afloat yet?'

'Still on the ground. Not far to go, though.'

The tide was flooding hard now. There was sweat on me, and not just because of the rowing. Sam must have managed to move her into deeper water. She was still a good mile away. If they upped and offed without looking back, we were in pretty sharp difficulty.

'Bank ahead,' said Katya.

A low rise of sand and mud ran across our course. There was water at its centre; the salt river that led up to the *wattenhoch*. *Gloria*'s mast was the other side of that, a leaning whisker, but only just leaning, visible to the naked eye. I aimed up the river. Wind and tide were with us now. The banks closed in on either side, seemingly as fast as a railway cutting will close in upon a train.

'Sails going up,' said Katya. 'She's off the ground.'

They were three-quarters of a mile away now. I saw the tan flutter of the mainsail crawling up the mast. My heart was beating like a steam hammer. 'Wave,' I said.

She stood up in the sternsheets and waved a red handkerchief. I gave two more strokes. The nose of the dinghy touched sand, and Katya was flung into my lap as we went aground. 'Out,' I said. 'Run.'

'The dinghy,' she said.

'Never mind the dinghy.' That was a nice dinghy, but not worth two lives.

'You run,' she said. 'I'll bring it. We'll need it to get out to *Gloria*.'

She had a point. I started to run.

Gloria had her main up all the way, and Sam was peaking that up, which means tweaking in just the degree of stretch to give the boat full power once that filled. In a straight line, she was not more than three cables away. But you could not run straight on this part of the *watt*, because the ground round the channel was soft mud. I blobbed about looking for a streak of sand. Katya plodded laboriously after me, shining with black mud, the painter over her shoulder, dragging the dinghy.

The mud reminded me that I had not been to sleep for twenty-four hours, and done plenty of other things instead. The heart banged in my chest, and the sweat stung my eyes until *Gloria* shook and blurred. I was over the hill now, looking at a sheet of sand penetrated by a broad wedge of sea, and in the middle of the wedge *Gloria*, sails up now, jib and main and staysail, topsail heading for the masthead, for if ever there was a topsail day this was it. Wilson was on the foredeck, winding at the windlass. I shouted. Blast, I shouted. But she was head to wind, of course, and all her sails were shivering, and I could hear the drum and thunder of them even up the wind, and the shoe on the end of the boom would be going like the cymbals of Baal, and Sam would be bellowing at Wilson because Sam trusted nobody but himself and me, and the chance of them hearing a shout over four hundred yards was a fart's chance in a gale, excuse me—

The sails stopped shaking. They stopped because the anchor

was up, and Wilson had backed the jib and brought the nose round, and the sails were full of wind. There was smooth water under *Gloria*'s fat stern. Wake. Slowly and silently she was moving down that vee of water, over the small ripples of the small wind over the small tide, towards the beginnings of the Wichter Ee.

Moving away.

I stopped still. I stood there with my feet planted in the sand, and I drew breath over my salt-scorched throat, and I shouted.

Wilson was working on deck, tidying up all the bits and pieces of rope you had on a yacht in those days. Sam was at the helm. There was no sign of Dacre or Fitzsimmons. Wilson hung the last coil on its cleat and started aft, jogging down the deck like a man whose natural walking was done on the deck of a boat. I raised a hand a full arm's length, the gesture of a drowning man going down for the third time.

The little figure stopped. Then he went to the cockpit at a dead run, and he must have said something to Sam, because I saw the pale specks of their faces as they looked back. Then Sam walked the tiller over, and the sails shook, and I heard the chain roar as she put her anchor back down.

I ran four hundred yards back to Katya and the dinghy, and tailed onto the painter and helped her drag that into the scummy edge of the tide. All of a sudden we were afloat, then rowing full chat towards Gloria; rowing across that calm grey water, boatman and Countess black with the same mud.

Then we were on board, and the dinghy was swinging up on the staysail halyard, dripping and the sails were drawing again, and we were moving, bless us, we were moving. 'Do you let Mr Wilson take her,' I said to Sam. 'Her Ladyship and me need breakfast.'

'Left that a bit late,' he said, as if we had just been for a leg-stretch ashore, and stumped forward. Dacre's head came up the hatch, pale green. 'What's happening?' he said. Then he saw Katya. 'Your Ladyship,' he says, all of a sudden smarmy. 'Can one invite you—'

'Thank you, I am well,' said Katya, and you could tell she did not like him.

I said, 'Where's Fitzsimmons?'

'In his bunk.'

'Throw him overboard.'

That was me giving Dacre orders, you understand, but Dacre did not even blink. That was turned around now, me the Captain, him the chap who did what he was told. Fitzsimmons came up on deck double-quick in a nasty twisting sort of a hold Dacre had on his arm. Dacre shoved him at the rail. Fitzsimmons give a sort of a roar. 'Wait a bit,' I said, for there had been enough drownings for one day. 'Can you swim?'

Fitzsimmons said he could. 'Over he go,' I said.

Dacre heaved him over the rail. He landed with a huge splash. Last we saw of him he was wading towards the patch of mud we had dragged the dinghy over.

Then for a moment that was almost like normal, getting inside some dry clothes and outside some breakfast, *Gloria* ghosting west down the inside of Baltrum, boom on her shrouds, staysail poled out. We drank tea in the cockpit like cruising folk, Dacre and Sam and Wilson, the Gräfin and me. That was a perfect spring day, high and blue, with little fluffy clouds, and the sea empty except a couple of lines of eiders dotted across that like those lines you get round the insurance coupons in Tit-bits; cut here. But if you cut here and now, there was no telling what black and bloody horrors would come spilling out from behind.

For when you looked round at those faces in the cockpit, that was only at first sight that looked like a cruise. That was more like the beginning of a race: a wound-up sort of feeling, but worse than a race, because this was a race in which the loser was going to die, and that was sail against steam with no handicapping, so you did not have to be a genius to work out who the winner was likely to be.

Wilson was at the helm, the chart weighted down with a bit of wood on the thwart in front of him. And on we went, into the Wichter Ee.

Well there was not much for me to do, so I went into the foc'sle and put the kettle on. A shadow darkened the hatchway; Sam's shadow. He said, 'What you been up to, boy?'

I told him, those parts that were fit to tell. 'All peaceful your end?' I said, just like we were on passage.

'All peaceful,' says he, very steady in that calm before the storm.

The kettle was boiling. I chucked the old leaves into the gash, put in a handful of new ones and tipped water on. I said, 'Matter of interest, boy, who told you what we were doing here?'

'Pardon?'

'Dacre hates water,' I said. 'He thinks the tide's going to come in and drown him out of spite. But that soldier we found strangled on the Pike. He was strangled by someone who went wading, so his footprints didn't show. That wasn't Dacre, and that wasn't me, and the poor beggar didn't strangle hisself.'

Sam sort of sighed, and pulled out his pipe, and made a noise like a main drain while he got that lit.

'So what I want to know,' I said, 'is why in the general run of things, if you thought we was here on salvage, you killed that soldier?'

Sam made his pipe gurgle most repulsive, but said nothing.

'We're going to croak, ten to one,' I said. 'You might as well get it off your conscience, do you'll have Saint Peter to worry about.'

'Had to be done,' he said. He would not meet my eye. Instead he looked down at his hands, at the dirty thumbs that had been in that poor sojer's windpipe.

'But you're not much of a murderer, boy. You left the paybook behind. Water or no water Dacre went and fetched that, so nobody'd know where the soldier came from.'

'I'm not a bloody murderer at all,' said Sam, and I could tell I had stung him. 'That's not murder if there's a war on.'

'So all the while you knew what we were doing here?'

'More or less.'

'Who told you?'

'Duke.'

I stirred up the tea to blacken that. 'So everyone knew but me.'

'He knew you'd find out for yourself.'

'He did?'

'That's what he said. He said you wouldn't take orders from

nobody, but if you saw that was win or lose you'd win. He said if I mentioned anything about that to you, he'd . . . well.'

'He'd what?'

'My old mum,' said Sam. 'She live in the almshouses down West Thornham. That belong to the parish. The church living belong to the Duke.' He whacked out his pipe into the stove. 'Well he was right about you, boy. Bastard he may be, but he's a clever bastard.'

I watched him ram more shag into the bowl, and thought, that is not nice language to use, but that is the only language you can use about a man like that. That damned Duke had made Dacres of us both. He had made sure we would come over into the lion's den, and made sure we should get ourselves caught, and here we stood, on the edge of our reward.

But he was a snob, that Duke. He could not see that chaps like us could be just as clever as him, even if we did not own our own houses. So Sam had gone murdering, and me and Dacre planting bombs, and the Germans had not found out about us, and the invasion was going ahead anyway. That was disappointing, really, whatever way you looked at it

I belted him on the shoulder. The Duke had made dirty devils of us all. 'Come you on,' I said. 'Up we go.'

And up we went. We took tea in the cockpit, three murderers, Katya from the wrong side, and Wilson the amateur. Dacre asked for extra water in his, to show refinement in front of the Gräfin, who incidentally took hers the colour of old oak, with three sugar. We were out in the *seegat* now, at the southern end of that, where there is a sort of a lagoon with no dangers or difficulties therein, these not coming upon you till further north, once you have passed between the islands and think you are clear into the North Sea. We were sailing north now, on just about a beam reach, which is the wind hitting the boat sideways-on, a nice easy point of sailing when there is any water under you, the wind a little fresher now, everything up including jib topsail, making about five knots into what must have been more than two knots of tide. In front of us was the open sea.

But nobody was looking out to sea just then. What we were looking at was over the stern, towards the mainland. The banks were sinking now, the *watt* a sheet of water, blue and green and brown, darkened here and there by the shadows of clouds. And onto that flat, wind-ruffled sheet there moved the Kaiser's fleet for the invasion of England.

The tugs led, of course, each one pouring grey-black smoke at the head of a raft of barges: four barges to the tug, coming out of the *siels* like eggs out of a queen ant, moving out into the channels then pausing, hanging head to wind and tide, waiting for the next raft out to catch up. That was horrible to see those flat square things slide out, full of death and explosions and traitorous surprises, and join up. There were fewer of them than I had thought there would be. Even so, they lay on that blue water in a dark and dirty carpet. After the first flush, they came out slower; much slower. 'Splendid,' said Dacre, and for once you could see his point. That was splendid, in a horrible way; the way a properly equipped slaughterhouse might be splendid. But once you started thinking what that meant, that was not splendid at all—

Then suddenly over to the southeast, there was a great flash, and a tongue of orange fire jumped into the sky, and a great swift billow of black smoke, and a little while after, a bang, or anyway a great shock you could feel in your eyes and your ears and your chest all at once.

'Hilgenriedersiel,' said Dacre. We all nodded. I think we all looked extra hard, to see whether his bombs had done anything to halt this terrible shadow of men and machinery spreading across the sands. And perhaps that did get thinner down towards Hilgenriedersiel, but there was no way we could be sure. It was the last hour of the tide now, and all inside the islands the smoke of their tugs darkened the sky and rolled off eastward in great banks. After a little, you could not watch that no more. But out to sea was as bad.

The grey boats had multiplied amazingly. There were shoals of them now, groups and singles, strung across the face of the waters in their prearranged positions. And further out to sea would be capital ships, waiting to steam alongside the barges and stand off the beaches of Lincolnshire to support the invasion forces.

And sandwiched between the barges inside and the escorts outside, fat as a washtub and plodding down upon the banks and wrecks that clog the Wichter Ee, the defenders of freedom, in *Gloria*.

I felt a hand catch mine. Luckily that belonged to Katya. She looked pale, which she had a perfect right to look, as did we all. I grinned at her as if everything was all right, and she grinned back. Dacre's eyes were on us, tentative, as that were. He was having a bit of trouble with the certainties of life, seeing me and her hold hands. Oh, yes. Everything was up in the air that day, and the world was made new. Still, that did not look as if we should live long enough for that to cause us much distress.

Letter from Captain Eric Dacre, late 12th Lancers, to Miss Erica Dacre, St Jude's, Eastbourne, Sussex.

Dearest Sissy

    This is the letter we all one day must write. Death is close; I hear the beating of his wings. I hope it comes by fire and not by water — there has been too much water.

    As to His Grace, I must conclude that if he is the model gentleman, the age of gentlemen is done. He has stripped me of my hopes for the future and my pride in the past, and left me naked in the dark. For this he will be cursed.

    Sissy, we shall soon be together, you and I. Till that blessed time, I remain

    Your loving Brother
    Eric

CHAPTER THIRTY TWO

Blitz Opens Fire

S o there we were, moving out to sea in a little bubble of quiet that had to burst.

There was pale water to port. Even as I saw that, Wilson leaned on the tiller and *Gloria* swooped off the breeze with a roar of wake. 'Banks moved since last year,' he said, standing away from the tiller a moment to let her nose seek the wind again. Another puff was heading at us across the water, thrashing up a small surf over the shadows of the banks. Further out, on the Othello-plate, the big bank that plugs the Ee like a stopper in a bottle, the surf was bigger and whiter. That is an odd channel, the Ee, as I said. In between the islands that is narrow, but pretty straightforward. That is only when you get outside the islands and think you are on your way that that sends the bottom of the sea up at you to whack you one.

But of course there was more than sandbanks about to worry us today.

Wilson was having the same kind of thoughts. 'I'll keep over to the west,' he said. 'Stay in shallow water, so they can't get alongside and board.'

I must say that being come alongside of and boarded was not a big worry in my mind, not while gunboats had guns on them. At the best, staying in the western banks would keep the Germans at long range for a couple of extra minutes – whatever good a couple of extra minutes would do. 'If we can stay out of the way for now,' I said, to encourage everyone really, 'these here gunboat chaps will have other things to think about.'

Wilson let off a few inches of mainsheet to stop the head coming up in a puff. He knew the essentials of making a boat

257

go, though that was not going to help us against steam. Katya said, 'They each have their position.' She spoke in English with an accent that even there and then I noticed was nice and soft. 'They won't drop out unless we are a direct threat to the barges, I think.'

That was the other thing, of course. Enemy aliens we might be, but bobbing around in *Gloria* we were no threat to anybody. Judging by the silence that fell after that, we all got the same idea at the same time.

The puffs were coming stronger now. Wilson had the nose close on the wind, heading northeast, heading up the west side of the channel for the nasty grey-studded horizon.

There was not much of a breeze, as I now said, but we were coming out into the open sea now. There was a swell running in from the northeast, nothing but a heave, really, but in a fathom of water, which was the most we had out here, a heave will break, and that was what that was doing in the brown patches of shallow water. The brown and white seemed to go all the way across the horizon, the way Germany went all the way across the horizon astern.

'Hilgenriedersiel's burning nicely,' said Dacre.

We paid no heed. Barges might sail or barges might burn, but we were trimming for dear life, Sam on headsails, me on the mainsheet and topsail, sticking those little blades of canvas into the breeze as if we were racing a match against the Kaiser—

Which of course was what we were doing, again. That flitted through my mind that this was where we came in.

So *Gloria* caught a better puff, a long, fresh easterly puff, and laid her blood-coloured sails over till her chain-plates tore plumes out of the sea, and the wake roared from the cheeks of her counter with a hissing roar, and we came up on that brown water and those breakers like we were reeling them in.

Katya gave me that great grin of hers, a flash of white teeth in her neat and lovely face. And that bubble of joy and excitement in my breast burst with a wet pop and in its place came a sort of dingy feeling, that what we were looking at here was death and destruction and the rotting down of everything beautiful into stink and mud.

At which moment the luff of the topsail began to shiver, faint as the quiver of a maiden's thigh, if you will excuse the expression, and I went and hauled in six inches of sheet until that was pulling again, and I seem to remember that the gloom went away because I was back doing the job I was meant to do, which was what I had been put on earth for, not feeling gloomy, which any fool could do. 'White Ensign,' I said, and Sam hauled that up to the gaff peak.

Then Dacre, looking out over the port bow under the boom and the headsails and over the breakers on the Othello-plate, said, excuse me, 'Jesus Christ.'

And there, hanging halfway down the coast of Baltrum like a pike in the weed, was the *Blitz*.

I saw Wilson's head turn. I saw him lean on the tiller, the nose swing, felt the mainsheet run through my fingers as the wind came on my right ear, saw pale water all the way across the bow. I said, 'What are you doing?'

'There's a sort of a cut through the bar,' he said, apologetic as ever. 'We might get over, this time of tide.'

I was going to ask him what he meant, might get over. But as I watched *Blitz*, her mast and funnel came in line until she was a tall, narrow thing balanced on the water. Smoke puffed out of the front end of her. The bang came a little later, the hard, dull sound of a fair-sized gun fired in anger. 'Heads,' I said.

Nobody ducked. I saw Dacre's hand creep to the lifebelt on the hatch – he truly did hate water, Dacre. There were a couple of seconds that felt like years. I expect we were all thinking the same thing. If we went on out to sea, we should get shot to bits. If we gave ourselves up, we should be locked up, then hung, sure as eggs, Katya too, because apart from everything else those two soldiers had seen her rescue Webb while von Tritt blew bubbles—

The shell went by with a sound like tearing paper, and hit the sea half a cable ahead with a bang and a yellowish splash of water and sand. The shot across the bows; heave to.

Dacre was about the same colour as the shellburst. I saw him look round at us, and open his mouth to say we ought to give up, then shut that again when he saw we had no plans to do that thing, and what he had to face was death by high explosive or death by water.

We were in pale water now, and to port and starboard our bow wave was breaking on the banks. Wilson had us in a channel of sorts—

The deck paused underfoot, there is no other way of explaining how that felt. The shrouds and runners groaned, and the topmast creaked very evil against its fid.

'Ground,' said Sam, which was not necessary. Then she dragged and shifted and jammed her nose through a breaking swell, and we were off and away again, all sail set, sweat running into our boots.

'Top of the channel,' said Wilson, in a voice that did not shake hardly at all.

Bonk, said the *Blitz*'s gun again. She was closer now. This time the sound and the muzzle flash and the rip of the shell came just about at the same time. There was a crash from aloft, and on a sudden there was a ragged-edged blue circle of sky in the middle of the topsail.

'He'll blow us to bits,' said Dacre, which was not helpful, but on the other hand no more than the truth. Wilson was steering, frowning at the compass and the waves by turns. Katya had a little sketch book out, but it must be said that she was chewing her pencil more than actually drawing.

'I think we're over,' says Wilson, apologising.

I had been thinking. 'Strike the ensign,' said I.

'You be damned,' said Wilson, very hot.

'Scuse me, sir, but do as you are told,' said I. 'Then heave her to.' And I told him why.

Well when I had done he looked at me as if what I purposed was horrible unsporting, which that was. But when I asked him did he have a better idea, he had no answer. So we struck the ensign and hauled the topsail down and hove to, and *Blitz* held her fire, us having struck and therefore (from my small knowledge of the rules of war) surrendered. *Hors de combat*, we were.

'What now?' says Dacre.

'Wait and see,' says I.

'What for?'

Well that was the point of wait and see, so nobody made him any answer.

The situation as I saw that was this. We were hove to in among some nasty banks, but fore-reaching a little, which means moving gently forward, out to sea, as that happened, by not quite accident. What we had to hope was that the *Blitz* had some part to play in the great plan, other than chase after sailing yachts. And of course we had to hope that she did not conclude that the easiest way to take us off of her worry list was to blow us out of the water, surrendered or not.

My guess was that von Brüning would not countenance this, being too much the gentleman. My guess was that he would think I was a gentleman too.

But there of course he would be wrong.

Anyway there we sat and there we waited for the shells to start landing, or *Blitz* to go away, or the steam cutter to come on over.

None of these things did actually come to pass. What happened was this.

She started to steam towards us. At first I could not believe my eyes. Then I saw that her steam cutter was not on the davits.

'She's never coming over the bank at this time of tide,' said Wilson.

But that grey shadow moved steadily on. Her cutter must be away on other duties. If she went round, that was five miles. This was a short cut, no more than a mile. She came steadily over the brown shallows, reining back from a canter to slow ahead. On she came—

On she did not come. She stopped suddenly. Her sternwave washed past her, drowning her low, unseaworthy nose. Her funnel belched smoke and the water at her stern thrashed white as cream. But she was stuck fast.

Wilson's mouth was hanging open. 'Not von Brüning,' he said. 'That can't be old von Brüning. He knows these waters like the back of his hand.'

I trained my glasses on the *Blitz*'s bridge. The chap up there had a yellow beard. Von Brüning's was a sort of auburn colour. Taken alongside the fact that the steam cutter was gone, that would mean von Brüning was not on board. Well of course he would be away on the land, where von Tritt was lying stiff and stark. There would be councils of war. The second-in-command would be taking over. Von Brüning knew the waters, and the plan of campaign. He would be needed. There would be some confusion, all right.

And that was the moment I remember my mind began to change. I now said that I had a cold, emptyish feeling. But they say hope blooms eternal, and I felt that bloom, spreading through me like they say whisky will spread through a drinker.

'Let draw staysail,' says I to Sam, and he let draw. The wake bubbled under the counter, a discreet bubbling, but music to our ears.

'You struck to him,' says Wilson, very shocked.

I could tell what he was thinking, gentleman that he was. Von Brüning had saved his neck by sticking to the strict rules of war. Now *Gloria* looked like getting away by breaking those rules. Any minute now, he was going to tell me that was not cricket.

Well, that would have been true enough. That was live or die, not bats and balls. 'That's not von Brüning,' I said.

'You still struck,' said he, glasses to eyes.

'Slip of the hand,' I said.

Katya's face did not change. She kept on chewing her pencil, looking back at the *Blitz* as if that was a painting in a gallery. I did feel sorry for whoever was in charge. I honestly did. But there were other things to worry about now. 'We might,' I says to Mr Wilson, 'put a bit of a weave on.'

He still did not approve of me, I could tell that, silly man. But he began a sort of pudding-stirring movement of the tiller, so *Gloria* became not only a target three yards wide, but one that shifted without pattern on the face of the waters, and was thus confusing for the *Blitz*'s gunners.

For although the *Blitz* was aground the best part of a mile away, she was still able to shoot.

We were heading northwest now, with the last little fag end of the flood running from the west and the wind from the east, so we were squeezed like you would squeeze an orange pip between your fingers, lee-bowing the tide they call that, moving out from the coast and away from the *Blitz* at six knots plus the tide wind, making that closer to seven. Sam hauled the spare topsail up there. There was clear horizon under the bowsprit, give or take a curtain of destroyers and gunboats—

Bonk, said the *Blitz*'s gun, and whizz went the shell, high and to starboard.

'Aim for the burst,' I said, as that flowered in the water a cable's length ahead. The gunners would still be rattled, correcting away like billy-o—

Bonk, said the gun.

This time the range was better, but the shell landed down to port, as I had expected. We were feeling the breeze over the tide now, so there was a steep little robble out here. Dacre was green as grass. Katya had thrown away her pencil, and I could see she was a bit nervous, but then so to say the least was everyone else.

'Port two points and show him the stern,' says I to Wilson.

As we went down the next shot hit close enough alongside to blast spray into the cockpit, but by the mercy of the Lord that bounced like a duck and drake and burst a couple of cable's lengths ahead. *Blitz* had not seen the bounce, so he lowered his sights, and the next one burst a cable length astern.

'Bominable shootin' ' said Dacre, shaking spray out of his thatch and making a bad stab at a smile.

So of course the next shell came in with a noise like a partridge and blew off the starboard rail forward of the chainplates.

Well there were wood splinters everywhere and a nasty smell and some yellow smoke, but when I looked round everyone still seemed to be in one piece, Katya with a thread of blood on her forehead, Wilson heaving on the tiller till the sweat shone on his face, Sam making a remark about Germans I will not repeat since I expect you are reading this in peacetime.

But Dacre was face down on the deck screaming like a woman.

I crouched down beside him and turned him over, not too gentle. There was hot wet all down the front of him, and I thought, blood, that has come at last to blood, and that will go further. Then I realised that was not blood, but sick. I wanted to laugh, and so I could see did Katya, but this was not time for mirth and jollity, plus Dacre was mortified already and there was no point in making that worse. So we lurched about in the shadow of death, snorting like children with the giggles, till we heard Sam shouting from up forward. And what he was shouting was, 'Fire!'

Now if there is one remark that will get your immediate attention on a boat that is made of wood and canvas and tar and varnish, that is it. We got up there, Katya and I and three pails. We hauled the dinghy (perforated not smashed, by a miracle) outboard on a spare halyard, breathing hot, burnt-paint-smelling air. The foredeck was jumping about in the robble as *Gloria* charged along on her reach, and a lot of air was getting into the hole in the deck by the rail, which when you came to look at that was four foot long and three wide, very evil indeed. The *Blitz* was still firing, but was not scoring no coconuts, and when I glanced back at her I was surprised how the range had opened. Three mile off, she was, if she was an inch, and three miles is a long way to shoot with a popgun like what she had. So all in all she was making good practice, von Brüning or no von Brüning.

But this was an idea that took up no more than a teaspoonful of my mind. Most of that was full of the idea that the shell had not only wrecked the fo'c'sle, but also blowed the top off the stove, and distributed the fire thereof, that Sam had been husbanding against lunch, sloppy devil of a fisherman that he was, all through the fo'c'sle and the head and by the look of that the saloon as well, and only for the washboards being closed into the cockpit too.

I kept dipping water up and out of the sea, and Katya, hair flying from its moorings, passed that down below to Sam, who was swearing and coughing most terrible and chucking water everywhere. After a bit the swearing stopped and so did the water, and seeing that the smoke was coming out of hatch and rail in a solid white column now I put a hand down and groped around there, and found something that felt like Sam's jersey, with Sam inside that, waving about very feeble. So between me and Katya we haul him on deck and as that were take stock.

On the boat we had a fire, now out of control. There was more bad news astern. That was not easy to see on account of the smoke pouring out of the front end and spilling down between the headsails and away to the west, but the seegats port and starboard were getting a crowded sort of look, which would be a result of the invasion barges making the best of the tide to start for England.

The plus points were what you might call short-term. One and foremost, *Gloria* was moving across the wind so tidy that she might almost have had an engine under her decks. Two and handyish the German Navy, though plentiful, seemed to have its hands too full shepherding barges out of seegats to worry about a yacht that was sure to sink soon any road. And three – this was the only plus point of any actual practical comfort – we had Katya's dinghy trailing alongside, holed, true, but only half-full of water. The dinghy was sure to be very important indeed—

'What's that?' shouts Wilson from the tiller.

That was between the grey upperworks of two great lumps of German battleships. That was something tall, and spindly; something designed for pleasure and elegance, not war.

'Give me your glasses,' I say to Wilson.

He handed them over. I trained them on that thing over there and my heart fair to bust out of my chest. 'Rockets,' I say.

'Wha?' said Dacre.

I pulled him out of the way of the locker door and placed the rockets and hauled on the lanyards. Up they whizzed, little red pinpricks against the bright sky. Down the wind rolled the smoke from *Gloria*'s front end. There were little feathers of it on the washboards now. If that thing out there did not pay us some attention, we were cooked.

I raised my glasses at that strange spindly superstructure. And I held my breath.

For the superstructure had turned itself into two masts. The masts of a huge black steam yacht with a clipper bow and varnished upperworks and a buff funnel. The masts came closer together until they were in line, heading straight for us. At the cross trees a little speck shone the colours of blood and surf in the spring sunshine. A White Ensign—

Whoomp, said something forward of *Gloria*'s mast, and a bright spear of flame jumped out of the deck and jabbed at the sky.

CHAPTER THIRTY THREE

The End of *Gloria*

The staysail caught straight away. *Gloria* wallowed upright as the pressure came off, bucketing in the sharp little sea. The mainsail darkened at the luff and I flung a bucket of water at that, but the time for buckets of water was past, and that went up like tinder, and suddenly everything in sight seemed to be burning, the tar bubbling out of the deck seams and catching, the varnish on the washboards lifting into bubbles, the very cockpit sole heating up underfoot.

That was a nasty moment, but not at all confusing, as a child of five could have seen that she was going to burn to the waterline, then sink. So I said, 'Abandon ship.' And we went over the side, Sam first with a bucket to bail the dinghy, which was pitching nose-to-sky, nose-to-Davy Jones. When he had the water under control I sent down Katya, then Wilson.

'Mr Dacre,' I said.

But Dacre was sort of hanging around, with a worried look on his face. 'My notebook,' he said, uncertain, like. 'My papers,' though I think what was really on his mind was the way that dinghy was pitching.

'Burnt up,' I said. 'Now come you on, Mr Dacre.'

'No, no,' he said. He was looking at those thin masts now, as if he was more worried by them than the whole German invasion. 'I've failed,' he said.

'Never,' say I, quite impatient, as that was getting really very warm and smoky.

'Excuses are neither offered nor accepted,' he said. 'Captain Webb, I thank you for your dedicated service.'

Well I had hardly served him at all, actually. He stood there in his brass-buttoned peajacket, framed as that were by the charred rags of the sail and the smoke and flame coming out of the front end, sick down the front of his coat, outlying parts of his hair beginning to smoulder. I could see he was half potty. So I touched my cap and said, 'Glad to have been of use, sir,' pretty brisk. 'Time to go now, sir.'

When he heard me call him sir, his face sort of smoothed out. 'Must get me writing case,' he says. And before I could rightly tell what was going on, he had turned and shoved back the mainhatch.

Well the flames came out of there like Hell with the lid off. He gave a sort of a shout: Erica, that sounded like, the name of a woman, but perhaps that was only a shout at that. I saw him catch light where he stood. He must have fallen forward, because I heard a cracking which could have been the washboards caving in, and a horrible scream, but I could not see because of the scorch of my eyeballs. The only thing I did see after I had blinked my eyes clear was a pair of brown boots sticking out of the fire with smoke coming out of their soles.

Then I was in the dinghy.

Things were a bit odd, in a centre-of-the-storm sort of way. There was no feeling that anything had happened, or would happen, just a sort of dream of being here, now: in the little white dinghy on all that blue-grey sea, jumping about on the chop that brought the islands hull-up and hull-down over their white beaches five miles away; and all around in the water the drub of engines like the beating of the hearts of a herd of animals, and down towards the land a straggle of barges. In the foreground, *Gloria*, her spars black lines drawn in an orange pyramid of fire. In the sternsheets, Katya with soot on her cheekbones. In the bow Sam, still coughing, bailing with his bucket. And on the middle thwart me and Wilson, scorched and rowing; rowing out to sea, away from *Gloria*, belching and fuming on the water.

You could not keep your eyes off *Gloria*, somehow. The flames went down her sides like lava. She took on a bit of a list. And then suddenly she was gone, leaving her long plume of smoke and a weird white puff of steam that hung over the water like a ghost before the wind took that away.

'Poor Mr Dacre,' said Katya.

'Captain Dacre,' said Wilson, which was about all the promotion he was going to get.

'His writing case, he wanted,' I said.

'I got that,' said Sam. 'When I was below.'

That was too late to say oh, dear, really.

And then the steam yacht was alongside, showing us the nameboard in the gold-leaf scrolls under her clipper bow: *Fata Morgana*, that I had last seen at Kiel last year, the day we won the last match against the Kaiser, the match before this one, that is.

A gangway came down, and we went up, Katya first, me last. And suddenly we were standing on white teak planks on a British yacht, while the might of Germany came pouring out from between the islands. And down the companionway from the wing of the bridge there came a chap in a peajacket and a Gieves yachting cap, a chap with a bay window and a big moustache with an Abdullah sticking out of the middle, and above the moustache a pair of codfish eyes that saw half a yard into your head. The eyes were on me and Katya, who was standing as close alongside as she could without touching.

'You've bettered yourself, I see,' he said, blowing smoke.

There was no sense paying any mind to this. 'Invasion commenced, your Grace,' I said.

'Yes,' he says. 'Ye-es,' drawling, lighting a cigarette from the stub of the last one. And there he was, a British yacht in the middle of that huge German fleet, and he did not seem bothered at all.

'Here she come,' said Sam.

'Gidney,' says the Duke. 'Ask the steward to get you a drink.'

But Sam did not move. The land was a line across the horizon. Towards us from the line the *Blitz* was churning.

I said to that damned Duke, 'You're agoing to get fired on.' And as I said that, there was a flash and a whizz, and one of these little trees of spray rose up from the sea ahead of the *Fata Morgana*'s clipper bow.

'So we are,' said that damned Duke. 'Stop her!' he yelled to a chap on the bridge. Engine telegraphs rang, and she blew off steam with a hiss. 'Scuse me, sir,' I said, 'but we should be getting a move on.'

The Duke smiled. He handed me his glasses without a word, and pointed back towards the islands. 'It's gone high water,' he said, and at first I had no idea what he was talking about. Then I put the glasses on what was happening behind the islands, and I saw.

There were three strings of barges out of the Accumer Ee; only three. Further east, where the Otzumer Balje should have been a black mat of lighters and tugboat plumes, the carpet had broke into untidy clods of black caterpillars on the silver face of the waters. Only down to the west, in the Norderney Seegat, was there anything like a concentration, and they had a hovering look, now, as if they could not make up their minds whether to go or stay. But why where they still there? The tide had turned. If the barges were not out of the *gats* by now, that was too late.

The invasion of England was dead in the water.

I lowered the glasses. I looked at Sam, and Sam winked. And a picture rolled unbidden into my mind.

I saw a young birch trunk, a withy, a starboard-hand navigation mark. That had been on the way out of Bensersiel this morning. Normally, your withy sat hard by the margin of the low water channel. But this one had been right on top of the sandbank, a hundred yards from the channel.

Where Sam had moved it.

There were not many withies in the Wattenmeer, since the Germans had chopped them down. Those that remained were important.

And Sam had been moving them around.

I said, 'How many did you move?'

'Dozen,' said Sam. 'I dunno. All uphill, though.'

In my mind's eye I could see him. I could see *Gloria* canted over on the sand, Dacre and Fitzsimmons retching down below. I could see that little black figure moving about in the half-dark before dawn, the flames jumping behind the sea wall. He had a spade over his shoulder, and he wandered across the mud and the sand like a man digging lugworms, except that he was digging withies, taking them out of the low ground and putting

269

them on the high. I saw the sun high and the channels full, the tugmen heading out on the flood, half their minds on the mighty loads they towed, distracted by the explosions and smoke from Hilgenriedersiel. Drafted in from goodness knows where, most of them; not familiar with these waters, steering by the thin birches that marked the channels.

Then the first touch, the slew in the channel, barges lurching sideways, colliding with others astern, evasive action by tugs provoking more evasive action, more groundings; until the roads to England lay clogged with grounded tugs and lighters, stranding as the flood ceased and the ebb set in.

Bensersiel had been damaged. Hilgenriedersiel was blown up. Half the channels were blocked, von Tritt lay dead, and most of the fleet had missed the tide. In the Carolinenhof the councils of war would be raging. The invasion was an animal with only half its complement of limbs, and no head. It was not an animal that could live.

'Thankee, Mr Gidney,' I said.

'Thank *you*, Captain Webb,' says he.

But meanwhile there we were standing on the promenade deck with *Blitz* coming on, a group of men round her bow gun, looking angrier than a hornet. I could feel Katya's fingers in mine, clutching hard, and I knew how she felt, up here on this great defenseless slab of a thing, stopped in the water, looking into the black eye of that gun. I suppose we had been close to death much of the last few days. But never had that felt as close as now.

Then that Duke said something or other to a matlow that was close by him and the matlow trots up to the bridge, and all of a sudden there are little bundles popping up to the yardarm and breaking with a snap and a flutter in the breeze: signal flags, two pennants and a square: EDV, which means Ambassador. Dirty trick, of course, the Duke being no more an ambassador than I was; and not necessarily a trick that would work.

But there are rules. We waited to see if the *Blitz* would keep them. She came on fast. I dare swear that after my false strike if von Brüning had been on board, he would have sunk us, flags and all. If von Brüning had been in command of the invasion operation, people in Birmingham would be eating Bratwurst and drinking lager beer by now.

But von Brüning was ashore. And the pile of white water under *Blitz*'s nose shrinks as she begins to lose way until she hangs grey and hesitant on the sea. Beyond her, on the horizon, there is all of a sudden a twinkle of electric lamps as the escorts broke into a frenzy of conversation. On *Blitz*'s bridge a signalman said something to the officer with the yellow beard, and the officer scowled and bit his nails; that close, they were.

The Duke gave them a smarmy smile, and raised his hand, every inch the Ambassador. The Duke made a noise like a seal blowing, and lit himself a cigarette. 'Last we'll see of them,' he said.

'Unless they decide to sink us,' says Sam.

'Why would they do that?' says the Duke. 'Their invasion's spoilt, I take it?'

Well, that was true. Tomorrow's tide was bigger than today's but not much. That might take them a week to float what had gone aground, all the while with no commanding officer, and the weather to worry about, and only a bit more than half the force, and all those mouths to feed . . .

'If they decide to have another try, they'll send a destroyer after us,' said the Duke. 'But they won't. They know they're rumbled, and now they're stopped, and they'll stay stopped. We've stopped 'em.'

As he spoke, the officer with the yellow beard shouted something down a voice pipe. The *Blitz* spun slowly, and pointed her silly low nose back at the islands. On the *Fata Morgana* bells rang, and she began to glide towards the horizon. The Duke puffed his cigarette smug as you like. 'We,' he had said. That was not the way that appeared to me.

The Duke knew what I was thinking, but he did not care. 'I've been out here since the tides started getting bigger,' he said. 'Just in case you thought you were . . . in charge.' His tone of voice made that quite clear we were back in a world where opinions were the prerogative of the ruling class. He pitched his cigarette

271

into the sea. 'Now, Gräfin. You'd like a bath, I expect. Webb, crew's quarters forward.'

Katya took my hand. 'I am happier with the Captain close by,' she said.

The Duke laughed then, at the stupidity of life, not because he loved that. 'Well,' he said. 'There's an empty stateroom on deck. Be a good fellow and take your boots off before you turn in, though. We use sheets up here.'

But I paid him no heed. I just stood there with Katya, and watched the *Blitz* run back, and fast launches tow white chevrons among the islands, and those barges that had come out onto the sea falter and anchor. From what I later heard, they were towed back into the *siels* on that night's tide. The whole mighty shambles took a week to undo, by which time the Home Fleet was conducting maneoevres off the Wash. And I did hear that for years afterward, the commerce on the rivers and waterways of Germany was conducted in a new type of barge, twenty foot wide and 120 foot long, with a sheer to the hull and a flare to the bow, as if that had been built for the sea.

And of course there were a lot of silly rumours about where and for what purpose they had been built. But the rumours faded as rumours do, shredded by time and blown into the great furnace of History.

Meanwhile, we sailed back to England.

EPILOGUE

Not long after we got back, I heard that the book Wilson had told me about in the bull pen at the Carolinenhof, the one written by Carruthers – Childers, we might as well call him – was out. The country was buzzing with it, though as with most things in the news, I paid that very little heed, certainly not having time to read that. For I was in charge of *Doria* again, and spending a lot of time on board, because of the number of people who spared no opportunity to tell me about the wickedness of Katya and myself.

Then one day we were anchored off Queenstown, in Ireland that is, and a dinghy pops out from the land and in this dinghy is a dirty beggar rowing and on the stern thwart Childers, whitish and tired looking, but his eyes glittering behind his pince-nez. Peter Bracket brought us tea, and we sat at the saloon table. 'Look here,' he said. 'I heard how you found Wilson. It's marvellous to have the old chap back. We're all very grateful.'

I had already been thanked for picking up Mr Wilson by a lot of people; though of course that had had very little to do with me, and a lot to do with Katya. A most popular gentleman, Mr Wilson, very highly thought of. So I changed the subject and congratulated Mr Childers on the way his book had caught on, though I confessed I had not read that my own self.

'No reason you should,' he said. 'It's all about messing about in boats, really.' Well I suspected he was not doing himself justice, but all the same I had heard that was about the joys of yachting, a subject about which I was not what you would call curious. He did not seem to want to talk about his story. I think that was something he had moved on from, not his property

273

any more, but the property of people who read it, launched like a boatbuilder might launch a boat. Then he looked at me with those very sharp eyes. 'You should write down your part of it,' he said.

Well I had to smile at that, and told him I was not the story-writing type, and he said nor was he, but that was a warning he had had to give, and I said, well, the warning was given now, and he said, yes that was, but the more warnings the merrier. He kept on at me for a while, saying he expected I kept a log, which of course was true. But even if I put that together, nobody would ever believe it. And even if they did, the public would not see much glory and splendour in our sneaking around on secret service; not cricket, as I now said, they would probably think. Amateur yachtsmen might be popular. But you could not expect nobody to care much about paid hands. After that he gave up, and started talking about the way the Germans were widening the Kiel Canal, and about Ireland, where he seemed to think the government was not being conducted all that well, and after an hour or so he got back in his dirty dinghy and left.

I must say that he had set me thinking. But I came to the conclusion I could never write a story myself, though perhaps I could dictate that to Katya and she could write that down. But not now. Later, if ever. You must remember I was young then, a racer, and thanks to the Duke's fee in business on my own account. Like everyone else of twenty-odd, what I was interested in was the future, not the past.

So there we were, first week in August, coming up to the Medina with *Doria* heeled over on her ear, tearing a long clean slice out of the Solent, tower of Egyptian cotton going up to the gates of Heaven, and David Davies the secret weapon up there in the jaws of the gaff. Sam was aft with Sir Alonso the owner. The crew were lying out along the weather deck very smug, for that day we had beat the King of England and the Kaiser of Germany, which as Sam said under his breath made three times running for the Kaiser. Beside me in a suit of navy-blue with brass buttons was my wife Katya, talking to her friend Clara Wilson née Dollmann, flushed with breeze and victory. At the helm was Wilson, looking like a boy with a new toy. Childers was there, too, in perfect flannels and hot, restless eyes. That was a reunion, all right.

And down we slid upon the boats anchored off the Squadron.

The *Hohenzollern* was there, and the *Victoria and Albert* with the Royal Standard at the mastheads and a Marine band on deck. And off towards Gurnard, smart as paint, black hull and buff funnels, the Duke of Leominster's *Fata Morgana*. Just for a moment I thought of poor Dacre. Just for a moment.

For as I trained my glasses over the *Doria*'s weather rail, they settled on a little party on *Fata Morgana*'s promenade deck. That damned Duke was there, and Admiral Fisher, and Sir Alfred Harmsworth, owner of the *Daily Mail*, and Mrs Keppel—

And another woman in a cream dress with a parasol. A woman with red hair and eyes that matched the emeralds high on her throat.

Hetty.

Not a Hetty who was a lady's maid, or a companion, or a governess. A Hetty who was talking to the company on its own terms. A lady – not that she had ever been anything but.

'What is it?' said Katya. Katya could always tell.

'Someone I haven't seen for a bit,' said I, with a feeling about the weskit as if I had been shot. Shot unawares. But not shot in the heart. That was the property of my wife Katya, and was not open for target practice.

Goodness knows how I got *Doria* head to wind and sails down and onto her anchor. All I know was that I told Katya I should be back in a minute and that she should go back to *Delphin*, that we had had brought over, and I should see her there late, for she had a dinner on with some Dutch chaps I was in the way of doing some business with in the shipping line – I should say here that I was on *Doria* as a Corinthian skipper now, having handed over command to Sam before the wedding.

But all this is by the by, and used up no space in my head as I pulled myself in *Doria*'s dinghy under the high black sides of *Fata Morgana*. I paused there a moment, hearing the screams of gulls, the rattle of flags from the ships dressed overall. Then I looked up.

A pair of pop eyes was looking back down at me. That

damned Duke. He made a signal, and a couple of bosun's mates piped me aboard.

I went up the gangway steps two at a time. Hetty met me halfway down, terrible unladylike. 'Charlie!' she said, in a voice like cut diamond, and I carried her back up the rest of the way, not at all gentry. Then we hung onto each other for a bit. After a while I came up from my earful of lace and powder. I believe her hat fell off, but we had better things to do than think about hats. We seemed to go and sit on a slatted bench one deck down from the promenade deck and out of sight of that.

She had changed, all right. She was a full-scale full-sized lady now, like a galleon under sail. We sat there and perhaps we had a bit of trouble finding something to say. So I had a stab at opening the conversation. 'What are you a-doing of here?' I said.

And she dropped the cut-glass voice and said, 'I sleep with that damned Duke,' broad Norfolk.

That was a stopper, as you can imagine. I asked her what she meant.

'What I say.' She was grinning at me from over her emeralds, damn-your-eyes, same old thing. 'Joe sold me to him.'

'*Sold* you?'

'He was desperate. So was Dad. So he told me to go and sleep with the Duke. He didn't like that, of course.'

'Nor did you.'

'Well *actually*,' said Hetty, blushing a bit. 'I wasn't so averse to the idea.'

'*What?*'

'Ent no such thing as a Duke between the sheets,' said Hetty. 'And there is a lot to be said for Dukes anyway. He's not such a bad chap once you get to know him. Tell the truth I enjoyed that.'

I stared at her. I thought about the pump house after the funeral. She had run away then not because of Joe being dead, but because of that damned—

'Oh, I always liked you best,' she said. 'That made me proper sad in that pump house. And next time.' She coloured up. 'The time we went to Newmarket.'

'Hell,' I said. '*Hell.*'

'Since when are you a swearer?'

276

'Now. One and only time.'

'Anyway that wasn't Hell, that was Heaven,' she said. 'And I don't know what you're swearing about. You've found some gentry of your own, boy.'

She was right there, of course. I said, 'Why did you leave me at Newmarket and not get back in touch?'

'I knew you,' she said. 'I knew if you knew where I was and what I was doing you'd come after me, and you'd start a fight with Buffy, and you'd lose.'

'Who's Buffy?'

'The Duke.'

'Oh,' I said, and sat and watched my head spin.

'So that was goodbye,' said Hetty. 'Our goodbye treat, and you might like to know that nearly killed me to leave. He took me to Le Touquet. He was afraid of you, boy. He knew you liked me, and I liked you. A Duke, afraid of you.'

I remembered the Duke's house in London, that smell of flowers or perfume on the stairs that had reminded me of Hetty – reminded me because Hetty had been there. I wondered if the Duke had taken satisfaction as well as advantage from the Emma affair. Of course he had.

She stood up, not speaking, and I do not think she could have spoken even if she had wanted to. We had neither of us been perfect, that was for sure. She put out her hand in its white glove – Hetty in white gloves, I ask you – and said, 'Come you here.'

She took me to a window. The stateroom inside was fitted out as a nursery, with a cot, and a rocking horse, and a nursemaid, and a baby in the cot that looked too young for the rocking horse, as if that was the gift of a proud father. 'The Marquis of Blakeney,' she said.

'The who?'

'My son.' She looked me flat in the eye. 'The Duke's heir.'

I looked back at her, and I knew what she wanted me to know, but I did not believe her. That is not the sort of thing that you believe, after all.

'If I had told you then,' she said, 'that would have been you and him against the Duke. If I told the Duke now, that would be the same thing, and nobody would get nowhere.'

'You married him,' I said.

'Two days after Newmarket. Special license. In Le Touquet.'

The little baby sort of swam on the other side of my reflection in the glass; the reflection of a fisherman and yacht hand. The reflection of the father of a future Duke, and the husband of a Countess who in six months would bear his child.

'Well, well,' I said. 'Your Gracefulness. Let us go in and meet his Royal Highness or whatever we are supposed to call him.

The Duchess of Leominster nailed me with her eye. 'His name,' says she, 'is Charlie.'

And that is more or less that, except for one thing I should mention. Three months previous, Katya and me had taken the train to Eastbourne. From the station we had walked up to St Jude's. That was a church built fifty years ago from hard grey stone, and the kindest thing you could say was that that had a respectable look. That look extended to the graves in the churchyard, very tidy, with white headstones neatly arranged, as if dead or alive the inmates were determined to keep up appearances. The sexton pointed us down a neat gravel path. We stood in front of the headstone and read the words: IN LOVING MEMORY – ERICA DACRE 1872–1898.

I stooped down and took the black book in which Dacre had written his notes, and his unsent letters to his poor twin, poor twins both of them. I raised up a flap of turf, and dug a hole, and buried that, and put the turf back on again. Katya stuck a bunch of spring flowers into the vase, and took my hand. We walked away, out of the deadly order of that churchyard, into the flood of light that came pouring at us off of the great, flat, blue-grey sea.